FINAL FINESSE

FORGE BOOKS BY KARNA SMALL BODMAN

Checkmate
Gambit
Final Finesse

FINAL FINESSE

KARNA SMALL BODMAN

A TOM DOHERTY ASSOCIATES BOOK   NEW YORK

This is a work of fiction. All of the characters, organizations, and events portrayed in this novel are either products of the author's imagination or are used fictitiously.

FINAL FINESSE

Copyright © 2009 by Karna Small Bodman

A Forge Book
Published by Tom Doherty Associates, LLC
175 Fifth Avenue
New York, NY 10010

www.tor-forge.com

Forge® is a registered trademark of Tom Doherty Associates, LLC.

Library of Congress Cataloging-in-Publication Data

Bodman, Karna Small.
  Final finesse/ Karna Small Bodman.—1st ed.
    p. cm.
  "A Tom Doherty Associates book."
  ISBN-13: 978-0-7653-2252-4
  ISBN-10: 0-7653-2252-8
  1. Presidents—United States—Staff—Fiction. 2. Natural gas pipelines—Accidents—
Fiction. 3. Terrorism—Prevention—Fiction. I. Title.
  PS3602.O3257F56 2009
  813'.6—dc22

First Edition: May 2009

Printed in the United States of America

0 9 8 7 6 5 4 3 2 1

FOR PAT FOSS . . .
*Whose courage trumps that
of any heroine in a novel!*

ACKNOWLEDGMENTS

When I decided I wanted to write another political thriller that not only spans continents and analyzes public policy but also includes some of the lighter (some may say ridiculous) side of activities in and around the White House and Capitol Hill, I knew I could use a lot of help.

I'm very grateful to a number of senior officials at our Department of Homeland Security, including Chris Doyle, Jim Tuttle, Kevin Reilly, and Jim Caverly, for taking the time to clue me in on our most recent efforts to deal with threats to our national security. A big thank-you to Ambassador Otto Reich, former National Security Council colleague Jackie Tillman Harty, and energy experts Hal Burlingame, Jim Cosgrove, Kenny Dubose, and Don Chapoton.

Chuck Vance was a Special Agent and Supervisor in the United States Secret Service assigned to protect the President for many years. His ideas were invaluable. At the CIA, agent and fellow author Chase Brandon gave me terrific insights into the life of a clandestine officer, while another undercover agent, who had to ask for anonymity, provided details of illegal activities along our southern border.

For the latest on military technology, I'm thankful for the (sometimes wild) suggestions of Jim Shilling, Greg Blonder, and John Kubricky. I also was impressed with the writings of James M. Roberts at the Heritage Foundation, as well as columnists in the pages of *The Wall Street Journal* and *The Washington Post*. And for clever phrases, I'd like to thank Didi Cutler, John Carlson, and Glenn Beck.

Finally, readers might be amused to know that references to special interest groups, earmarks, and Congressional resolutions were all inspired by actual requests made over the last several years. Yes, this is a novel, but perhaps instead of "fiction," we could call it "faction." Now, I hope you like the story.

CHARACTERS

THE PRINCIPALS
Tripp Adams, Vice President, GeoGlobal Oil & Gas
Samantha Reid, Deputy Assistant to the President for Homeland
   Security

WHITE HOUSE STAFF
Gregory Barnes, Assistant to the President for Homeland Security
Ken Cosgrove, National Security Advisor
Angela Marconi, Special Assistant to the President for Public Liaison
Evan Ovich, Special Assistant to the President for International
   Communications
Joan Tillman, Administrative Assistant to Samantha Reid

OTHERS
Joe Campiello, Grayfield Company Operative
Cassidy Jenkins, Senator from Oregon

David Major, FBI Agent
Godfrey Nims, Lobbyist for GeoGlobal Oil & Gas
Will Raymond, CIA Agent
Dick Stockwell, Greyfield Computer Expert
Harvey Walker, Senator from Oklahoma

FOREIGN NATIONALS
Victor Aguilar, President, GeoGlobal, South America
El Presidente
Eyeshade, Gang Leader
Simon Gonzales, Field Worker
Juan Lopez, Field Worker
Carlos Mendoza, Field Worker
Diosdado Rossi (The Fixer), Assistant to El Presidente
Rafael Santiago, Gang Member

Finesse: v. "To handle with a deceptive or evasive strategy."

FINAL FINESSE

"All nonessential White House employees remain home due to ice storm. Update in four hours."

Samantha Reid stared at the e-mail and pushed a strand of her long brown hair back off her forehead. She knew that most everyone would try to show up for work today because nobody wanted to be thought of as "nonessential." At least she had a four-wheel-drive jeep she'd been driving for years. Not the most chic car that regularly parked on West Exec, the driveway separating the West Wing from the Eisenhower Executive Office Building—or EEOB, as they all called the big Empire place that housed most of the staff—but it was a car she'd bought near her parents' home in Texas, where everybody drives jeeps.

She glanced out the picture window of her tiny Georgetown apartment overlooking the Whitehurst Freeway. Just beyond was a narrow park lining the Potomac River, its trees weighted down with icicles. To the right, the Key Bridge was silhouetted in the dim predawn light where a lone taxi, trying to navigate the icy roadway, suddenly spun out and slammed into a guardrail.

Good Lord, she thought. *It may look like a scene out of* Swan Lake, *but it really is treacherous out there.* She had known a front was moving in, but an ice storm in early December didn't happen all that often and nobody had predicted it would be this bad.

She looked down at her computer again. She always checked her e-mail when she first woke up, as she often got urgent messages from her boss, the head of the White House Office of Homeland Security. They had been working practically round the clock on a whole list of issues and new safety measures, coordinating with the agencies, following up on tips and executing Presidential orders. She had stayed late last night summarizing the fallout from a threat to a big shopping center made the day after Thanksgiving. Thankfully, that one turned out to be a hoax.

Today she knew they would be focusing on other problems, including a new missile defense system they were trying to get deployed on a number of commercial airplanes. She checked her schedule and remembered that a group of airline executives were due for an 11:00 a.m. meeting in the Roosevelt Room. The mastermind of a new 360-degree laser defense, Dr. Cameron Talbot, was supposed to join the airline officers. But now, with the storm raging, she doubted if any of them would make it in.

She also had a meeting to follow up on an attack on the Metro. Transit cops had nailed a guy trying to leave a backpack filled with explosives on board a D.C. train headed for the Pentagon. When the Metro was built, some genius had designed a stop directly underneath the building. *What were they thinking?*

She shoved her computer aside and padded into the tiny galley kitchen. It looked like it could have fit into a train, with shallow cabinets on two walls, sparse counter space, and a stove that was a relic from the eighties. Her whole condo was less than four hundred square feet, but she had gladly exchanged size for the convenience of a Georgetown address that put her within minutes of the White House, though this morning, inching along the icy Washington streets, she'd be lucky if she'd make it in an hour's time.

She flicked on the small TV set that took up way too much space on the kitchen counter and heard a commercial advertising a new drug. There were pictures of a kindly-looking grandmother pushing a laughing child on a swing while the announcer said in the tone of an afterthought, "Side effects could include dizziness, nausea, muscle weakness, weight gain, and, in rare cases, temporary loss of vision, coma, or stroke." She shook her head at the absurdity of it all, but then heard the news anchor come back on with the weather report. His map showed a wide swath of storms, snow, and ice reaching from Oklahoma all the way up to Delaware, with D.C. on the leading edge.

She measured the coffee, stuck an English muffin into the toaster, and checked her watch. She'd have to skip her morning workout in the basement fitness center. With the added commute time, maybe they'd delay their usual early-morning staff meeting, but she couldn't take that chance. As she reached for a coffee mug, she made a mental note to remind her boss about his appearance on CNN at noon to discuss the Metro train arrest and the shopping center situation. She knew she'd have to write his talking points, but wondered what other potential disaster would have to be added at the last minute.

2

"Honey, wake up! Something's wrong."

Her husband rolled over and made a muffled groan.

"Really. Wake up. It's freezing in here. Furnace must have gone out or something."

"Uh-huh," he mumbled and burrowed down inside the covers.

"Please, honey. I mean it." She reached over and tried to turn on the bedside lamp. "Oh great. Just great. The power's out." The windows in the old farmhouse rattled as a strong gust of wind pushed sheets of ice and snow against the north wall. "It's gotta be thirty degrees in here. We have to get the furnace going or something." She yanked open the drawer in the table and fumbled until she felt the flashlight. She flicked it on and shoved the man until he finally opened his eyes.

"What the . . . What do ya mean it's thirty degrees?"

She pulled the heavy quilt to one side and he snatched it back. "See what I mean?" she asked. "The furnace. Do something."

He slowly turned the covers back and ambled to the bathroom, where his terry-cloth robe was hanging on the door. "Okay. Okay. I'll check it out."

"Do you want me to go with you?"

"Nah. Stay warm. Gimme the flashlight. With this wind, it's probably just the pilot light. I figure we should get a new heater one of these days."

"You know we can't swing that now, not with the bills and all."

"I know," he sighed. "Just wish I didn't have to keep fixing the damn thing all the time."

The stairs creaked as he made his way down to the basement and headed to the back. He peered at the furnace and checked the pilot light. Sure enough. Out again. He held the flashlight with his teeth and tried to light it, but it wouldn't come on. He turned the gas valve on and off and tried again. Nothing. He grabbed the flashlight and muttered, "Damnation. Gas ain't gettin' through. Must be a clog or somethin' in the line. Better check the fireplace."

He climbed the stairs, went into the living room and knelt down in front of the weathered brick hearth. He tried the switch that turned on the gas logs. Nothing. He shivered and pulled the belt on his robe tighter. "Never shoulda put in the damn gas logs," he whispered to himself, "regular ones burned fine. But no, she says they're too messy to clean up, so we get the gas logs. Fine mess we're in now."

"What's happening down there?" she called over the banister. "There's still no heat coming on."

"I know, damn it. There's no gas gettin' into the house. No furnace, no fireplace. Nothin' works. Call your sister and see if we can come stay in town till we can get someone to fix the line."

"I can't call her now. It's five thirty in the morning."

He got to his feet and started up the stairs to the bedroom. "So we wait an hour. Get back in bed. There's nothing we can do now but wait."

Several miles to the south, an underground bunker is covered by a golf course. Built in the sixties, it has an elevator taking workers down to a ten-thousand-square-foot facility complete with living quarters, a kitchen, bathrooms, and storage areas, all to support a massive control room where employees of GeoGlobal Oil & Gas monitor their maze of pipelines. The supervisor pointed to a large board covering an entire wall showing a map with red, yellow, and green flashing lights that indicate the status of the lines stretching over a multistate area. Five computer screens have the capability of zooming in on a section of pipeline, checking diagnostics and analyzing their operation.

"Pressure drop on number twelve," he shouted. "What the hell!"

His assistant rushed over and stared at the map. "What the devil is that?"

"Gotta shut her down," he called as he hit a series of computer keys.

"Must be a break of some kind. Helluva storm out there, you know."

"Storms don't knock out our lines. Where the hell were you during Katrina, huh?"

"Yeah, I know, but . . . I just wondered . . ."

"Stop wondering and start acting," he ordered.

Suddenly several phone lines began ringing at once. The supervisor grabbed the one closest to his console. "Control room here."

"Hey Joe, that you? This is Sheriff Chapoton. Big fire west of town. My deputy just called it in and now our phones won't stop. He says it looks like some gas line exploded. That's gotta be one of yours."

"Exploded? How the hell could that happen?"

"You're the gas guy. You tell me. I've got the fire chief on his way out there with his boys."

"We saw a pressure drop and so we closed down that line. Fire should burn off pretty quick."

"Fine. But what's going on out there?"

"Right now I can't say. But we'll get our crews out there pronto to check it out. We're on it."

The head nurse on the third floor of the small country hospital raced down the hall. "Blankets. We need more blankets," she called out, almost colliding with a doctor coming out of the neonatal unit.

"It's way too cold in there," he exclaimed as he ran out the door.

"With that storm getting worse, we'll probably lose power now, too."

"If that happens we're in deep trouble. No gas coming in and the generator is being repaired."

"We've been begging for a new one for ages."

"Fat chance," he said. "Generator, MRI, CT scan, you name it, we don't have it. Not in this town."

"Could you try to get some portable generators from Don over at the hardware?"

"I'll try, but they won't open for a while."

She looked distraught as she headed into the unit where five tiny souls were wrapped in pink and blue blankets. "He's got to help us," she called over her shoulder as she picked up one of the babies and held her close. The newborn was whimpering. "Whatever happens in this storm, we've *got* to save the babies!"

Samantha pulled up to the Southwest Gate of the White House and waved at the agent inside the guardhouse. He saw the sticker on the back of her rearview mirror, and waved back when he also saw the badge she fished from inside her coat. The massive black wrought-iron gate opened to the driveway on West Exec. She headed toward her assigned parking space, giving a mental thank-you to her boss for securing parking spaces for the six heads of his directorates. Gregory Barnes might have an inflated opinion of himself, but she had to admit he looked after his employees, especially the ones who made him look good to the powers that be.

After she had graduated from Princeton with majors in English lit and geology, Samantha had quickly figured out she couldn't make a living with the English part, but geology opened a whole raft of job offers. Her dad was in the oil and gas business, she had been raised near the Texas oil fields, and it was only natural that she would feel quite at home with a subject where she already knew the history as well as the lingo.

She had accepted a position with a consulting firm specializing in energy issues, and when one of her op-ed pieces on energy independence was printed in the *Wall Street Journal*, Greg Barnes called to ask if she'd accept a position at the Department of Energy, where he was Assistant Secretary. She had called her dad to ask his advice on whether to take a pay cut and go into government. She always remembered his reply: "You can either serve yourself or serve your country!" She took the job.

Secretary Barnes came to rely on her to do his research, write his speeches and statements when he had to testify before Congress, and pull everything together when he appeared on television news shows. The man could speak in great sound bites, and while others in the agency ridiculed his ego behind his back, the talk show hosts loved his act.

When the President asked Greg to be his White House Chief of Homeland Security, figuring he would be a great mouthpiece for the administration, he took Samantha with him. Now every time there was even the hint of a new threat to the country's national security, the television stations clamored for Greg Barnes's take on the situation, which meant Samantha often felt like an adjunct to the White House speechwriters' office, except she wasn't writing for the President, which would have been a total head trip. No. She was writing sound bites for the biggest egomaniac on the staff. And she was sure that today would be no exception.

As she pulled into her spot, she saw the snow swirling against the windshield. Suddenly, she was five years old and her dad had just brought home the little glass globe with a tiny house and the snow inside that swirled when she shook it. She thought about her father down in Houston and wondered if he had been affected by the storm. She'd have to remember to give him a call a bit later.

Grabbing her purse and a black leather folder with some notes for the CNN interview she had drafted last night, she hurried to the door of the West Wing basement and pushed inside. A blast of warm air greeted her in the vestibule. "Good morning, sir," she said to the Secret Service agent as she again waved her White House pass hanging on a silver chain around her neck.

"Morning, ma'am. You made it."

"Took forever, but I'm glad to be here." She quickly walked across the blue carpet, past the door to the Situation Room, and headed up the narrow stairway to her office on the second floor. As Deputy Assistant to the President for Homeland Security, she was one of the lucky few who had an office in the West Wing. Greg had seen to that, too. Hers was a tiny cubicle next to his, but she was grateful for desk space in this building. Most of the staff had expansive offices in the EEOB with sixteen-foot ceilings and tall windows. Some even had fireplaces and conference tables in their offices, complete with leather chairs and bookshelves. Her office didn't even have a window. But that was all right. She knew that if anyone were asked if he would prefer a conference room in the EEOB or a closet in the West Wing, the answer would be obvious. Proximity to power was the name of the game. At least that's what it was in Washington, D.C.

Tossing her folder on the desk and stashing her purse in the bottom drawer, she powered up her computer to double-check the headlines. She scrolled through updates on the nationalization of more American companies in Venezuela; trouble with the new virtual fence on the Texas border; the resignation of Congressman Davis Metcher, who had been sued for additional child support by a former congressional page; the extent of the ice storm, which now had knocked power out in a number of areas; and a gas line explosion in Oklahoma, which killed one and left thousands of people in freezing conditions.

She clicked on the last headline and read the details. A local officer, Sheriff Chapoton, was quoted as saying, "There was a huge gas fire that sent flames sky high. One firefighter has died and another one is in the hospital. GeoGlobal Oil & Gas sent their team to investigate but they told me that so far they haven't figured out how it could have happened. We're in a real state of emergency around here. No gas, no electricity, no telling when the line can be repaired." The article went on to say that hospitals and nursing homes were scrambling to move their patients to other locations. Calls to GeoGlobal had not been returned.

That's odd, she thought. *Gas lines don't just explode. And that poor fireman. This is awful.* She remembered that a terrorist group in Mexico had sabotaged a number of gas lines some time ago and it had caused huge problems, but she couldn't fathom that a group like that would have a reason to do the same thing here in Oklahoma. She added the story to her notes for the morning staff meeting.

"Okay, folks, a lot on our plate today." Gregory Barnes shuffled some papers as he glanced around the small conference table at the heads of his six directorates.

There was the man in charge of the Executive Secretariat, who managed all the paperwork coming in and going out to the various agencies they worked with on threat levels and the efforts to coordinate policy, especially through the Department of Homeland Security, with its some 200,000 employees.

The deputy in charge of Borders and Transportation had her hands full working on security for the railroads and illegal immigration, especially the Mexican paramilitary groups who were teaming up with drug lords to smuggle people as human decoys to divert border agents from the billions of dollars of cocaine shipments coming across at different locations. The Sinaloa Drug Cartel had consolidated most of the routes into Arizona, and its rival, the Gulf Cartel, was focusing on Texas. Problems with the virtual fence just added to the challenge. At least the International Narcotics Enforcement Office at State was being very cooperative on that one. She had been somewhat amused to learn that this particular office was known as "Drugs and Thugs."

Next to her sat the head of Chemical and Biological Defense, then came deputies for Preparedness, Response, and finally Samantha, whose portfolio included Nuclear Defense and Energy, as well as keeping up to speed on all of their issues so she could write Greg's speeches and interview notes.

As he often did, Greg turned to Samantha first. "Are we set on the talking points for the CNN interview today?"

She nodded and pushed a two-page summary across the table. "I know they'll be asking you about the Thanksgiving threat and the great save on the Metro Pentagon stop. The guy is still being questioned, but it should be a good opportunity to highlight coordination between the agencies on that one."

Greg perused the points. "Coordination? Right. Good idea. Most of the time we can't announce plots that we stop because we can't compromise sources and methods. The press keeps hitting us for surveillance techniques, saying we might be infringing on somebody's rights somewhere. But when those contacts pan out and we actually prevent an attack, we can't take any credit. I mean when does this White House get accolades for things that don't happen?"

The deputies nodded as their boss went on. "Drives me crazy. At least with the nutjob on the Metro, we got lucky. Can you imagine what could have happened if that backpack had been detonated right underneath the Pentagon?"

"There's an awful lot of concrete between the Metro and first floor of the building, so I'm not so sure . . ." one of the deputies remarked.

"Forget it. People *on* the train would have been killed and we just don't know what could have happened to the building. Anyway, put that one down in the win column. Don't have too many of those these days."

"Uh, Greg," Samantha interrupted, "I wanted to mention something I saw in the headlines this morning that you might be asked about."

"What's that?"

"The gas line explosion in Oklahoma early this morning."

"I saw a headline about it in the White House News Summary, but so what? It was probably some maintenance issue. That's the gas company's baby to fix, not ours."

"But there was a huge gas fire, one guy is dead, and it reminded me of the terrorist group in Mexico that blew up a whole series of lines down there. Remember?"

"Of course I remember. But that was EPR blowing up state-owned gas lines, Pemex lines, and because those zanies . . ."

"The People's Revolutionary Army," Samantha supplied the name.

"Yeah, that group wanted the government to release some of their guys they've got in prison. Look, I can't imagine Mexican rebels coming up here and blowing up a gas line in Oklahoma, for God's sake."

"But what if . . ."

"Forget it. We've got too many other issues right now. As I said, let the gas company handle their own problem. But now that you bring up Mexico, they announced in the Senior Staff meeting this morning that at least their government now has those Bell 412 transport helicopters and CASA CN-235 surveillance planes up and running, the ones we gave them. Mexican police should be using them to track the drug dealers not only at our border, but the speedboats that are bringing the stuff from South America to some of the remote Mexican drop-off points. Anyway, we all know it's a big goddamn problem."

"So they've got the planes, but what about tracking those submarines?" a deputy asked.

"That's another big problem," Greg said. "Ever since we found out they were building submarines in the jungles of Colombia, loading them up with as much as twelve tons of cocaine, and dropping it off on the west coast of Mexico, it's just one more huge headache." He turned to the deputy. "That reminds me. Get hold of that contact of yours over in the Pentagon and see what they're doing about those things, if anything. I heard they have a working group trying to figure out a strategy, so check on that. I don't want to elevate this to the SecDef's office at this point. But if they don't come up with some sort of solution, we may have to get some high-level attention for this one."

Greg then ticked off a number of other issues including the 11:00 a.m. meeting with the airline executives. "That meeting isn't going to come off today. Dr. Talbot said she could make it in, but with the ice storm grounding so many planes, the airline group can't get here. I doubt that we'll get any cooperation from the airlines anyway. They pretty much stiffed the Secretary of Transportation over the idea of installing Talbot's antimissile laser system on very many of their planes. They're too broke to take that one on. At least that's their excuse. The thing is, her system would cost about a million dollars a plane."

"But that's a hefty price when you consider most of the airlines are in deep shit right now," said one of the deputies.

"Get off it," Greg said. "A million bucks? That's about what their audio systems cost. And you tell me. Would you rather fly on a plane with a fancy music system or one you knew had protection from a possible attack?"

No one said anything.

"Point made," Greg said. He gathered up his papers and pushed back from the table.

Samantha closed her leather notebook but got up with a feeling of unease about the meeting. They went over national security issues every morning of every week, but something about the storm and the gas line explosion wasn't sitting right.

4
WASHINGTON, D.C.—MONDAY MORNING

"Any word yet from headquarters on that mess in Oklahoma?" Tripp Adams, Vice President of GeoGlobal Oil & Gas, asked his lobbyist as he hung up his overcoat in the closet of the spacious office overlooking K Street.

"They're really scrambling down there. A whole crew went out at dawn. They shut down the line and finally got the fire out, but you probably heard there was one fireman who died in the fire. And now they say it'll be a while before they can figure out what happened."

"We've had our share of maintenance issues, but nothing like this. I mean, a gas line doesn't just suddenly explode and burst into a big fireball."

"You got that one right. Our guys said it looked like something Red Adair would have handled in the old days."

"Jesus!" Tripp walked over to the bay window and stared out at the empty street. "Amazing sight out there. How'd you get in anyway? Does that Prius of yours make it on the ice?"

"More or less. I didn't really want to buy it, but I figured it might be a good image for an oil and gas lobbyist, you know?" Godfrey Nims said with a grin. "It's bad enough having to go up to the Hill all the time to meet with the Members. I mean, it's tough up there. Last week, when I was giving the Energy Committee a description of the small amount of land we'll be using if and when they finally give us permission to drill on that lease we want in Alaska, they hit me with so many counterpoints, I felt like a goddamn piñata."

"Welcome to Washington!" Tripp said. "Then again, it might have had something to do with the fact that you told them the size of the drilling area compared to the whole wildlife acreage was like the mark of a BB gun on the ass of a grizzly."

The lobbyist looked slightly chagrined. "Yeah, well."

"Anyway, I'm glad we both made it in today. I had my own problems getting across Key Bridge. There was a taxi smashed against the guardrail."

"Anybody hurt?"

"They had a police car there, but I couldn't tell. At least there weren't many other cars around, so I got by that one. Guess the admin staff isn't coming in, right?"

"Right. They've been calling. I didn't expect any of them. I picked up my coffee at Starbucks on the way in."

"Rats. I should have thought of that. Do you think there's any in the kitchen?"

"Sure. You'll just make your own."

Tripp sat down in his black leather chair and grabbed a copy of the *Washington Post* off the pile of newspapers on top of the desk. "At least the paperboys are working today."

"Right. I found our stack at the front door and brought it in. Take a look at that story on the front page of the *Post*."

Tripp glanced down. "You mean this one about the new hearings on oil and gas exploration?"

"Yep, that one," Godfrey said. "That's why I was up there last week, trying to forestall those hearings until we can get more of our ducks in order. Since Congress has been hassling over exploration and drilling for, what, decades now, a blip like this Oklahoma thing could really screw up what little chance we have with the latest bill, you know?"

Tripp furrowed his brow and paused. "Damn. You're right. And with the bitch from Oregon chairing the hearing, you're going to have your hands full, my friend."

"I know. Every time I have to deal with Cassidy Jenkins, I wonder how that woman ever got elected."

"Are you kidding? She's got the women's vote, and every eco-type in the Northwest thinks she's their hero."

"I doubt if she'll continue in hero status when the prices of all sorts of commodities go up again."

"Sure she will," Tripp said. "She'll just call for more wind power like she always does."

"That's what they've got at these hearings." Godfrey shrugged and added, "Well, let's just hope that we can get our gas flowing again."

"We can hope. But with this storm, the ice and the blackouts all over the place, we could have people freezing to death down there."

"Jesus, Tripp, don't talk like that. Nobody is going to freeze to death."

"How the hell do you know that? You know damn well that half the homes in this country are heated with natural gas. A lot of it is ours. And then there are the schools, the hospitals, and the factories that can't operate either."

"Let's not get all hot and bothered until we find out what's going on in Oklahoma. They should be calling us pretty soon with an update."

Tripp stood up, straightening his six-foot-one frame, and headed toward the door. "Okay. While you wait for the phone to ring, I gotta make some coffee. Can't get through a day like this without a caffeine fix."

5
OKLAHOMA—MONDAY MORNING

"Did you see the report about all the people who won't leave their homes? The sheriff was saying they could freeze to death," the supervisor in the control room said to his assistant.

"Heard it on the radio a little while ago. Trouble is, schools don't have heat. Big companies don't have heat. Where are the folks supposed to go?"

"I hear a lot of them are hunkered down over at the Grange Hall where they've got those big fireplaces. At least they have a lot of firewood there. Not sure what the hospitals are doing though."

"When are our crews going to get that line repaired?"

"I have no idea. They haven't reported back yet." He looked up at the map of intertwining lines and colors and studied the display. "Everything else seems to be running smoothly. Did you check on the maintenance reports on that number twelve line?"

"Sure did. They ran diagnostics on that one just two weeks ago. It was A-okay. I still can't figure out what happened."

The supervisor reached for the remote control and flicked on the TV set. "Gonna check the news. Maybe they have something on the evacuations or the hospitals or something."

They watched in grim silence as video of snowplows filled the screen. The announcer was explaining that the plows were trying to clear the roads so the hospitals could be evacuated. The staff could be seen bundled up in heavy coats and boots, loading stretchers into ambulances, trucks, and SUVs. A nurse, her white hat visible under a hooded jacket, was carrying what looked like two small bundles in pink blankets as she scurried toward a waiting car.

"Must be the babies out of that neonatal unit they have over there," said the supervisor. "At least the car heaters will keep them warm."

"For now, anyway. If this storm keeps up, the power is out for a long time, and we can't get our line repaired right away, this whole area is going to turn into a major disaster."

"Remember when those Mexican lines were blown up some time back?"

"Sure. But that was a bunch of crazy rebels."

"Shut down all the factories though. Nobody could go to work. Their economy took a real hit."

"Ours could, too."

The news anchor gave a weather forecast that called for more snow and ice for at least the next forty-eight hours. Then he launched into an appeal for portable generators, since the hardware stores and other suppliers were all sold out.

"No way anybody is going to give up a generator with this storm carrying on," the assistant said.

The phone began to ring and the supervisor grabbed it. "Control room here." He listened for a while, nodded twice, and then leaned forward as he practically shouted into the mouthpiece. "What in the world are you talking about?"

"What is it?" his assistant said.

The other man held up his hand for silence as he continued to listen to the call. "That long?" he bellowed. He listened for another few moments and finally banged the phone down.

"Good grief!"

"What?"

"The explosion, or whatever it was, really tore up the line. Now, with the storm, getting equipment in there, parts and all, they say it could take weeks to get that line operating again."

"Weeks? We haven't got weeks."

The supervisor shook his head, stared at the map of lines again, and turned to his assistant. "Listen. If we don't get that line up and running in a matter of days, maybe hours, what started out as a small disaster could turn into a big body count."

"Hey, Samantha, did you see this report from France on what's going on over at the Economic Summit Meeting?"

Samantha glanced over to see her administrative assistant, Joan Tillman, standing in the doorway, waving a copy of the *New York Times*. "Not yet, I've been swamped with Greg's priorities. As usual. Why? What's up?"

"This is hilarious. So the President is over there and they have one of those press briefings and word gets out that first, the President brought along his own drinking water."

"So? He always does that."

"But in France? The Evian people are royally pissed off."

"Evian?" Samantha said. "Did you ever notice that 'Evian' spelled backwards is 'naive'?"

Joan giggled and continued. "Anyway, then their French chefs practically went out on strike because our food tasters wanted to supervise their sauces. And finally, get this. Some French reporter is claiming that we've got Secret Service frogmen in the fountains at Versailles."

"Do we?" Samantha asked with a wry smile.

"Probably," Joan replied. "So are you going to watch Greg on CNN?"

"I guess I'll have to tune in. But I hope they put him at the top of the hour because I'm starved and I want to get down to the Mess. I'm having lunch with Angela today."

"Well, when you see her, tell her that I just heard from Scheduling that the Association of Alpaca Growers has requested an event in the Rose Garden where they want to present an animal to the President. She'll probably get a request to support the idea."

"There's an Association of Alpaca Growers?" Samantha asked.

"Yep. Turns out Congress passed some sort of Jobs and Tax Relief law a while back that lets small business owners write off one hundred percent of new assets the first year. So now you've got people buying an alpaca for something like twenty thousand dollars, writing that off, and then after a few years, they fatten them up and sell them for half a million. You can put about eight of those things on an acre of land so it's cheap to feed them and keep them around. Pretty sweet deal, huh?"

Samantha burst out laughing. "I thought we got through the llama craze and then the ostrich craze. Now you're telling me we have an alpaca craze?"

"Something like that. They use 'em for fleece, and some of the better ones even get stud fees."

"Sounds like the law of unintended consequences," Samantha said.

"Well, we do a lot of that around here. Anyway, I didn't mean to bother you. Is there anything you need me to follow up on from the staff meeting?"

"As a matter of fact, there is. Did you hear about that gas line explosion down in Oklahoma early this morning?"

"Sure. It was on the news. You think that's something for our office?"

"Well, Greg doesn't think so. Then again, he was pretty focused on his CNN show."

"He's always focused on the next TV show. What else is new?" Joan asked.

"Anyway, with the power being out and the gas off down there, this could be a huge problem."

"Sorry, but what do we have to do with that?"

"I'm not sure. It's just that I know a bit about that industry."

"I know. You grew up in it. So what's your take?"

"Something's strange. Something's missing from the reports. I don't see how one of those gas lines just explodes in the middle of a snowstorm. I mean, it's weird. Tell you what, find out who owns that line and see if they've got any people in town I could talk to. It's got to be one of the majors and they all have offices here. See what you can track down. Set up a meeting if you can swing it. The sooner the better."

"Got it. Will do."

7

Hustling down the narrow winding stairs to the basement of the West Wing, Samantha first walked by the desk of the agent sitting right outside the door to the Situation Room with its numbered keypad and went to the entrance of the White House Mess.

"Good afternoon, Miss Reid," the maître d' said. "Miss Marconi is already seated. Right this way."

Samantha followed as he left his walnut podium and walked past a four-foot-long display case holding a model of the USS *Constitution* in Plexiglas sitting right outside the door to the dining room. Members of the White House staff who had the rank of Special Assistant to the President or above were granted the privilege of eating in this most prestigious of all Washington restaurants. Other staff members could get takeout from a window on the other side, but this room with its paneled walls and ship paintings was reserved for senior staff and their guests. Some staff brought business or political contacts to lunch on occasion, but it was verboten to bring in a member of the press who might overhear conversations at nearby tables about unannounced administration plans.

She walked past a large round table with seating for twelve. That was known as the staff table, and anyone who was eating alone could sit there and pick up all kinds of in-house gossip over the salad or chowder. She spied her friend Angela Marconi sitting at a small table for two along the wall. As Special Assistant to the President for Public Liaison, Angela had to deal with all sorts of outside groups vying for the President's attention. At five foot nine, she was just an inch taller than Samantha, but Angela was a size twelve to Samantha's size eight. Then again, Samantha often wondered how Angela, who came from an Italian family in the restaurant business, stayed in shape at all.

"Hi there. That pants suit matches your hair," Samantha remarked as she pulled out the wooden chair and sat down.

"Yes, I know. I'm all tan today. Sometimes I think I look like a bran muffin."

"You do not!" Samantha said with a smile. "Anyway, in this weather, we all need to wear slacks and jackets. Did you see the forecast? They're calling for another two days of this snow and ice."

"At least," Angela said. She picked up a navy blue menu with a gold Presidential seal on the front and a piece of gold braid down the center. A waiter walked up to the table, tablet in hand.

"For you, Miss Marconi?"

"On a day like this, how about some Manhattan chowder and half of a turkey sandwich?"

He jotted it down and turned to Samantha. "And for you, Miss Reid?"

"Soup sounds good to me, too. And then just a fruit salad. Thanks." She turned to her friend, "So what's happening in your bailiwick today? Everyone make it in okay?"

"Actually, most everyone on my staff got here. Some were kind of late, but you know how it is around here. We all try to get in. It's the out-of-town groupies that have problems."

"Like which ones?"

"Well, for starters, we had scheduled meetings today with East Europeans pushing for publicity to finish the Romanian bear sanctuary.

Then the Association of Cowgirls wants to get on the President's calendar because the House passed a resolution congratulating the Wyoming cowgirls on their victory in some tournament and the national group says all of them are just as important as the Wyoming girls."

Samantha shook her head as Angela went on. "Then there's that new Food Council that wants all the restaurants to list calories, fat, and sodium on their menu and call products by their correct names. They want support from the White House chef on their idea."

"Fat chance," Samantha laughed.

"Well, they do have a point. They sent me an analysis showing that at Outback Steakhouse, for example, they've got Aussie Cheese Fries that have twenty-nine hundred calories and a hundred and eighty-two grams of fat. And they're listed as a starter."

The waiter came to the table with two bowls of chowder.

"Oh, and did you know that what they call orange roughy is actually a slimehead?"

"Jeez, Angela, glad I didn't order the fish special. At least you can keep a sense of humor over in your shop. Can't say the same for mine."

"So what have you got today? Besides holding up a mirror for Mr. Telegenic to preen some more?" Angela asked.

Samantha tasted the soup and explained. "Greg just did CNN and they hit him with the Metro bombing. The almost bombing, I mean."

"I always wondered why they ever put a stop under the Pentagon," Angela said.

"Exactly. Anyway, he talked a little bit about the shopping mall threat because even though it wasn't an actual plot, we're trying to get all the big malls to beef up their security. Then he mentioned the problems with the airlines who can't afford a missile defense system."

"Of course not. They're all broke. I mean, who can blame them?"

"Right. But there's another idea that might get the ball rolling. If we could get a small appropriation in the defense budget, the Pentagon could put some of those laser systems on the commercial planes that transport our troops overseas and then, since the system is portable, if there were more threats of a missile strike against an airliner, they could quickly put the laser system on other planes."

"That sounds like a good idea."

"Yes, I added that talking point at the last minute so Greg could float the idea. Anyway, then there was the gas explosion in Oklahoma."

"I heard about that. But isn't that an industry problem? We don't get involved in that stuff. Not at this level, anyway."

"I know," Samantha said. "And Greg wouldn't even talk about it in our staff meeting, but I figured he should be prepared if they hit him with the question."

"Did they?"

"No. They ran out of time. Greg's good at running the clock so he uses up the time on issues *he* wants to talk about, not the host."

"You're right about that. Sometimes I wonder whether the President would keep that guy around if he weren't so articulate. I mean, if we didn't have television, we'd probably have an entirely different bunch of people in government, don't you think?"

"Probably," Samantha agreed. "Come to think of it, if we'd had TV back during the 1860s, Abraham Lincoln probably wouldn't have been elected, with that high-pitched voice and dour look."

"Right on. So, back to the gas line. What's your opinion on that? Do you think it's some kind of maintenance issue?"

"I have no idea, but I've asked Joan to set up a meeting with whoever owns that line."

The waiter cleared their soup bowls and brought Angela's sandwich and Samantha's fruit salad. Then he replenished their water glasses and quietly slipped away.

"Trouble is," Angela said, "the owner of the line probably can't even get to the White House in this storm. Guess you could just talk on the phone though."

"I'd rather have a face-to-face on this one. I just have a strange feeling that something weird is going on. I saw a report on CNN right after Greg's interview that showed people being evacuated to buildings in Oklahoma that had big fireplaces. But there are still tons of folks out in farm country that are pretty far away from any sort of help. And with the roads being so bad, what are they supposed to do with no heat and a power failure besides?"

"What about the hospitals?" Angela asked.

"That's the worst of it. They said that one of the preemies almost died."

"A baby? Oh my God," Angela exclaimed. "The've *got* to save the babies."

"That's exactly what a nurse said that they had on tape."

"Well, I for one am glad you're going to follow up on this one. What if it's some crazies or some bunch of terrorists or something?"

"I have to admit that's pretty far-fetched."

"What if it's an inside job?"

"What? You mean some gas company's employees would attack their own line? And in this weather?"

Angela sat back and thought for a moment. "No, I guess that doesn't make a lot of sense, even if they were offered a bunch of money. It just doesn't track. Especially in a place like Oklahoma. I mean, what's more *American* than the state of Oklahoma?"

"When I was a kid, that musical, *Oklahoma,* was the first show my parents took me to. I loved it."

"They don't make them like that anymore, it seems. Anyway, let me know how your meeting turns out. That is, if you get a meeting."

As they finished their lunch, Angela glanced over to a nearby table and whispered, "See that guy over there?"

Samantha looked over her shoulder. "You mean Hunt Daniels? He's on the NSC staff."

"I know. Do you think there would be a hunk on the White House staff that I haven't checked out?"

"So what about Hunt?"

"Well, he always seems to keep such a low profile, I wondered what he's up to."

"I know what you mean about the low profile," Samantha said. "When everybody around here looks like they're trying to leapfrog over everybody else, Hunt seems to be doing the limbo."

Angela snickered. "I know. So I just wondered if he was still seeing that scientist?"

"You mean Dr. Cameron Talbot?"

Angela nodded.

"Last I heard they were still an item. She was supposed to come to a meeting with the airline people today, but the planes can't land in the storm, so we called it off. She's totally brilliant, you know."

"I know the story. I mean, who doesn't know that she invents all of these missile defense systems? Hunt is probably smitten. Guess it follows since he's into defense issues here."

"Why do you ask?"

"Just hoping he might be available, that's all," Angela said, sneaking another look at the handsome man sitting at the staff table.

"Forget it, friend. He's taken. Besides, I thought you were still seeing that guy your mother fixed you up with. The guy who's buying a restaurant near DuPont Circle."

"I did go out with him a couple of times, but he's new to the city, all he talks about is food, and he has no clue what's going on around here. He thinks Rock Creek Park is the new Korean Ambassador."

Samantha burst out laughing and put down her fork. "So now you're back on the prowl, huh?"

"Until Mr. Right comes along, I guess I'm always on the prowl. But how about you? You haven't been out with anybody."

Samantha's shoulders suddenly sagged and she looked down at her plate. "I just don't feel like it. You know that."

Angela reached across the table and touched Samantha's arm. "Hey, I know how tough it's been since Dexter died. Sorry. I shouldn't have brought it up. But that was, what? Two years ago? I know he was a great guy, a good husband, and you sure had a great life together."

Samantha looked up, her eyes glistening. "He was the best. And the way it happened. I mean, his falling like that."

"I know. I know. It was a freak deal. You guys climbing the Tetons and all. You were both good climbers but then that storm came up with the wind and all. You told me how he fell and landed on a ledge and you couldn't get help for a long time."

Samantha faltered as she remembered the horrible scene. She and her husband had reached a ridge and were just starting their next climb when huge gusts of wind hit them and Dexter lost his footing.

When he fell, she cried out and slammed to the ground. Then, peering over the edge, she saw his twisted body as he lay on a narrow outcropping some thirty feet down. She had screamed his name over and over and then grabbed her cell phone to get help. But by the time the medics made their way up the mountain and airlifted him out, his internal injuries were too severe, and he had died on the way to the Jackson hospital.

Ever since that horrible day, Samantha couldn't bring herself to look down from any height. Whenever she even got on a glass elevator, she had to face the door for fear of bringing back the haunting vision of the man she loved fighting for his life way out of reach. She took a sip of water and faced her friend.

"I know it's been a long time. Maybe someday I'll feel like getting involved again. But right now with all of the threats, the late hours, the bureaucracy screwing everything up all the time, I don't know when I'd have time to concentrate on much of anything else anyway."

"Well, I'm still keeping my eyes open for you, kiddo," Angela said in a soothing tone. She checked her watch. "Now I've got to be back. I think we still may have a meeting this afternoon with some Indian tribe looking for restitution for their land."

"Why isn't the Bureau of Indian Affairs at Interior handling those folks?"

"Don't worry. After the groups try to get our attention, we're usually able to kick them over to the proper agency. Maybe we'll recommend another casino or something."

"I just hope they're not from Oklahoma," Samantha said, pushing back from the table.

"At least over in the EEOB, we've got heat in the meeting rooms. Now, be sure to let me know how this gas line thing turns out. You've always been pretty prescient about things."

"Well, I'm not sure how Delphic I feel today, but I'll keep you posted."

8

OKLAHOMA—MONDAY AFTERNOON

Simon Gonzales loaded duffel bags into the back of the rented SUV while his boss, Carlos Mendoza, paid their bill in cash at the motel desk. When he came out, he tossed his own bag in the back, slammed the hatch down, and slid into the front seat.

"Hey, Carlos, we got enough money left?" Simon asked as he got into the front seat on the passenger side.

"Of course we have money left. The Fixer set up a special account."

"What if they trace it somehow?"

Carlos put the car in gear, turned on the windshield wipers, and pulled out of the small parking lot. He headed toward the interstate. "Nobody's going to trace anything. We've got money for rooms, for food, for supplies, everything. That's my job and I do my job."

"I know," Simon said, "just checking. I have to say I'm glad to get out of that motel. They got no heat. We gotta get out of these parts fast."

"That's what we're doing," Carlos said. "We're heading east. We'll hole up at another place until we get the next assignment. You charge your cell phone back there?"

"Sure," Simon chimed in. "Like you said. I always follow your orders."

"Well, let's be sure we keep it that way."

"Can we get some lunch somewhere?" Simon asked, looking out the window at the snowdrifts.

The boss turned onto the highway and said, "Let's clear the state line first. You can hold out for another hour or two. Besides, we have to get someplace where they have heat, right?"

"Right. Why don't you turn on the radio? See if there are any more reports."

Carlos leaned over and turned the dial, but all they heard was a series of country songs. "I hate that music," Simon said. "Isn't there anything else around this stupid place?"

The boss hit the scan button several more times, and they finally heard an announcer giving a traffic and weather report. He was advising people to stay off the roads because the storm was going to intensify that night with temperatures dipping down to the twenties again. "Makes you wish we were back home, doesn't it?"

"Sure does," Simon said. "This weather is the pits. No heat. No good music. No good women."

"Forget the women," the boss intoned. "We don't need any complications on these jobs. Besides, when you think about it, having a little adventure up here beats working the oil and gas lines back home, don't you think?"

"I know. Just talking. I miss Maria, that's all."

"Maria will be glad to see you when you come home with a bag full of money, so cool it."

"I'm already cool. In fact, can you turn up the heater a bit?"

They drove along the road, recently cleared by massive snowplows, and listened to news updates on the time it would take to get the power back on in parts of Oklahoma and other areas hit by the storm, the continuing evacuations due to the pipeline explosion, and then the announcer gave a report on how the price of corn had tripled owing to its use in ethanol production.

"I wonder what they'll charge us for tacos and tamales now," Simon asked.

"Probably more than they're charging us for gas for this car, I'll tell you that," his boss said.

"You're the money man. You would know," Simon remarked.

"And, speaking of money, if we do our jobs right, the price of gas, the heating kind, will go through the roof."

"Trouble is, doing our jobs right means we'll need some help next time. We almost messed up back there."

"I know that. I told you we were getting help."

"But when?"

"The Fixer's last message said that Juan Lopez would be coming. He's been working our fields for years and knows more than most anybody. Don't you remember?"

"Sure. But when's he going to get here and how will he find us?"

"I've got that covered. That's why I'm the boss and you carry the bags."

"So I'm not boss material. Yet," Simon said. "But *when* is he coming? Did they tell you that?"

"The way I figure it, he should already be hooked up with the cartel and it's their job to get him across the border. They're working with the same paramilitary group we came in with. Relax. They've got their section of the border cleared."

"But what about the border patrol?"

"Since when are you worried about the border patrol? When they brought us across, it only cost ten thousand apiece and we came with a convoy."

"Us and the drugs. Least they could have done is give us some samples."

"They don't give out samples, you idiot."

"They didn't even give us water. You'd think we were prisoners or something," Simon complained.

"We made it, didn't we? We got across, just like they promised.

And they had this car waiting for us. I'd say that was pretty good service. We got treated better than the trafficking guys, so quit griping."

"I wasn't griping. I'm just worried that Juan may not make it. Not everybody makes it, you know."

"I'd say about ninety-five percent make it. The rest end up in jail or get sent back. But so what? They just wait a week and try again."

"So, when do you think we'll see Juan? He's great with the tools. We could have used him last time."

"I figure we'll get word in a day. Two at the most."

"That new Vice President of GeoGlobal should be here any minute," Joan said, looking at the wall clock. "Of course, that depends on whether he can navigate the ice on the sidewalks between here and K Street."

"What's his name?" Samantha asked, looking up from her computer.

"That's the funny part."

"Funny?"

"Well, I've cleared an awful lot of people into this building, but this one's got the most highfalutin name I've seen yet."

"Really? What is it?"

"Get this. Hamilton Bainbridge Adams the Third!" Joan replied.

"Tripp Adams?" Samantha exclaimed.

"You know this guy?" Joan asked in an astonished tone.

"There can't be two Hamilton Bainbridge Adams the Thirds, now, can there?"

"I'd hope not. So who is he? I mean, I know who he is. He's the new Vice President of that big oil and gas company. But how would you know him? You said to find out whose line exploded. You said you didn't know."

"I didn't know what company owned that one and I certainly didn't know that Tripp Adams was working for GeoGlobal. This is absolutely surreal."

"Surreal? What gives? How do you know him?"

Samantha leaned back in her dark green leather desk chair and folded her arms. "Tripp Adams." There was almost a reverence in her tone of voice as she repeated his name. "Tripp and I both went to Princeton."

"I know you went there. So he was there at the same time?"

"Sort of. I was a freshman and he was a senior. A gorgeous senior, I have to admit. You know how it is in school. All the freshmen look up to the seniors and get crushes on the neat ones, but they never even notice us."

"So you had a crush on this guy?"

"Absolutely. He was tall, had a great bod. He was on the crew team as I remember it. You know, the guys who rowed all the time. We all used to talk about him, but he always seemed so focused on studying and sports and graduation that I don't think he ever noticed any of us."

"This is amazing," Joan said. "Well, he's certainly going to notice you today. And he's going to have to answer to you, too."

"I don't know that I'd put it that way. I just want to hear what his company is doing with their gas lines and what really happened down there in Oklahoma. I want to be sure this wasn't some sort of sabotage, but just a maintenance issue. Then again, they should have better maintenance than this, if that's what it was. Anyway, let me know when he hits the complex." Samantha sat back and began to picture the senior she had pined for so many years ago. She didn't know much about him except that he was tall and athletic and reportedly was quite a brain. She had a vague recollection about hearing that his family wanted him to go into some business but he was hell bent on joining the Navy or the Air Force or something. Maybe it was the Navy.

She couldn't quite remember. But what she did remember was not only the attractive guy with the subtle grin, but the way he made her feel when he passed her in the hallway. She shook her head to try and clear away the old images. *Teenage hormones,* she said to herself. *Of course. That's all it was.*

"Samantha, Mr. Adams is here."

Samantha was reading a summary of the President's scheduled return from the Economic Summit in France. She raised her head, pushed her hair back, and started to get up from her desk. She saw a tall man standing in the doorway wearing a dark blue overcoat, its collar pushed up.

Joan said, "Sir, let me take your coat. We have a rack right out here."

He slipped out of the coat, handed it to her, and walked over to Samantha, extending his hand. "Hello. I'm Tripp Adams."

"Yes, I know," Samantha said, coming around to shake his hand. "Still pretty frigid out there, right?"

"Yes. Even with gloves, my hands are pretty cold."

"Come, sit down. Would you like some coffee?"

"Coffee? Sure would. Just black is fine. Thanks."

"Got it," Joan said from the doorway. "Some for you, too, Samantha? The usual?"

"Yes, please." She sat back down at her desk as Tripp pulled up a chair. She couldn't stop staring at the man. He hadn't changed much at all in the dozen years since she had seen him. His hair was still dark brown. Darker than hers, and cut fairly short. The shoulders were broad. She wondered if he still rowed on occasion. Then there were the eyes. Dark eyes. A deep brown that could melt a freshman's heart with one extended glance. But wait a minute. She wasn't a freshman anymore. She was Deputy Assistant to the President for Homeland Security and she had better remember why this dream of a man was sitting in a chair in front of her desk. It's just that she was suddenly feeling slightly off balance. Slightly breathless. Slightly weird. *Get a grip,* she thought.

She cleared her throat, reached for a lined tablet and a pen, and endeavored to adopt an all-business tone of voice. "So, Mr. Adams . . . uh . . . Tripp . . . thanks for coming over this afternoon. I realize you had to walk in this awful weather. I appreciate your taking the time."

"When the White House calls, we answer," he said with a smile.

That mouth. That subtle grin. She had to stop staring and start concentrating. "Yes, well, I wanted to talk to you about the gas line break in Oklahoma. We normally wouldn't get involved in a single issue of this kind, but in this particular circumstance, with this ice storm and the power outages, I was hoping you could fill me in on the cause and also how soon you think you can get it up and running again."

"Here you are," Joan said as she walked into the office and handed Tripp and Samantha mugs with the gold Presidential seal on the side of each one. "I'll hold your calls," she whispered to Samantha, who nodded her thanks.

Tripp took a sip of the steaming coffee, sat back, and studied the young woman with the long, wavy brown hair. She sure was a knockout. She had one of those little widow's peak things in the center of her forehead. And the hair, the masses of hair, seemed to billow out and down over her shoulders. He caught himself wondering how it would feel to run his fingers through all of that hair. He'd had plenty of women floating in and out of his life in the last decade or so. Some lasted longer than others, but he had moved around so much, he never found one he wanted to take with him from place to place.

This one almost seemed out of place sitting there in her office chair. The dark green leather sort of matched the color of her eyes. Here was this tall, attractive woman who looked like she could have been starring in some made-for-TV special, working in the White House, surrounded by a lot of political hacks and professorial types. Well, maybe the staff people weren't really hacks, but they certainly didn't look like the cast on *West Wing* reruns. And this lady. Well, she was something else again.

As he quickly scanned her features, something gnawed at his memory. "Excuse me. But have we met?"

"Met?" She sounded nonchalant. "We didn't exactly meet, but I did see you a lot on campus."

"On campus? Princeton? That's it. I *knew* I knew you. This is amazing. What year were you?"

"I was a freshman. You were a senior. Underclassmen usually knew the upperclassmen. It was rarely the other way around," Samantha said matter-of-factly.

"Of course. I do remember you."

"You do?"

"Yes. You were studying geology, right?"

"Right. And so were you. But we were never in the same class."

"No, but I do remember seeing you around that building. That was it. I remember the hair," he said, smiling.

She reached up and swept a strand behind her ear. "The hair?"

"Sure. It was long then, too."

"You remember hair?"

"Well, among other things."

"But you never talked to me."

"My loss," he said, shifting his weight and leaning forward. "Look, I'd like to talk to you some more about those days. Maybe we can do that sometime. But right now, I'm on kind of a tight schedule. I'm supposed to be on a conference call with headquarters in about an hour, but I will tell you what I know so far."

Samantha was momentarily disappointed as her mind's eye had once again focused back on days when she had seen Tripp taking long strides across the campus, walking through Blair Arch or sitting quietly in chapel. They were pleasant musings. The most pleasant she had felt in the last two years. She snapped back to attention and started to make some notes on her pad.

"So what caused the break?"

"We don't know for sure. Here's the thing. Our southern control room registered a sudden drop in pressure on this particular line. They shut it down immediately and then started getting calls that there was a huge fire outside of town. Our crews and the local firemen put it out pretty quickly, but they reported that there was an awful lot of damage and our engineers are out there right now assessing the situation. Last thing I heard is that maintenance had been done as recently as two weeks ago. So it doesn't make any sense at all that it was our fault. Now, I'm not saying for sure, because we just don't know . . . yet."

"How long before it's up and pumping again?"

"That's the thing. They're telling us it could be a couple of weeks."

"A couple of weeks?" Samantha asked, her voice rising slightly. "Why so long? I mean, those people are dependent on your gas supplies, and with the storm and the power outage, what are they supposed to do?"

"I'm with you on this. We're extremely concerned. It's just that the storm is exacerbating the situation. Where that particular line is located, well, it's hard to divert the supply right now. And getting the right parts, we've got that on a fast track, of course, but evidently the damage was quite extensive."

"I see," she said without looking up from her notepad.

"Look. I realize we've got a big-time problem on our hands, but I didn't think the White House would . . ."

"Get involved?"

"Well, yes. Is this something you're now monitoring?"

"Not exactly monitoring. In fact, we wouldn't normally contact you at all. It's just in this particular circumstance, I've studied the oil and gas industry and . . ."

"You have? I mean, well, yes, you're in this position."

"You see, this is my field. In my directorate, I cover nuclear and energy issues, and ever since those gas lines were blown up by rebel groups in Mexico, I've tried to keep close tabs on our own gas and oil pipelines, even though I know that the Departments of Transportation, Energy, and Homeland Security also have people on this issue."

"So you have a personal interest?" Tripp asked.

"I wouldn't exactly put it that way. It's just that when I saw the report on your gas line, something just didn't ring true to me. When does a gas line simply explode on its own?"

"It doesn't," Tripp admitted.

"So, I'd like to be kept in the loop on anything you find out on this one. Can you do that?"

"Sure. Be glad to." He looked at his watch and started to get up. "I'm sorry if I have to run, but I don't want to miss the conference call."

Samantha got up from her chair at the same time and walked toward the door. She put out her hand. When he took it, she felt a frisson of electricity pass between them. She looked down as he shook hands again. The grip was firm and smooth. She didn't want to let go. He looked down into her eyes and smiled.

"It's been great seeing you. Again. And yes, I will definitely keep you in the loop." He reached for his wallet and pulled out a card. "Here's my business card. My cell is on there."

She took his cue, reached over to a stack of cards on top of her desk, and handed him one. "And here's mine. But let me add my cell. They don't usually print those on the White House stock." She scribbled a number and handed him the white card with a gold eagle embossed in the top center of it.

He shoved it in his pocket and headed to the door. "Thanks so much for coming by," she said. "And if there's anything new on that conference call, I'll be here until late tonight. I'm usually here kind of late."

"I'll let you know." And with that, he took his coat from Joan's outstretched arm and headed down the hall, with Joan leading the way back to the West Wing lobby.

Samantha stood at the doorjamb and stared at the tall man in the blue overcoat as he turned a corner. Suddenly, she felt lonely. Here she was surrounded by staffers, clicking computer keyboards, and ringing telephones, and yet she felt a sense of loss because he was no longer in her sight. She hadn't felt this way since Dexter had left her life. She had told herself that she would be self-sufficient, and she'd buried herself in her work, her research, her passion to play a small part in the defense of her country. All lofty goals. But what about her personal goals? Up to now, they had all been pushed aside. Now, in the space of a short meeting, a meeting that brought back old memories, old dreams, old feelings, she felt uneasy, slightly adrift. Could a few minutes with one man rekindle all of that?

She turned back to her desk and picked up a classified report on nuclear materials that might have been shipped out of North Korea. Now, *that* was an issue that really needed her attention.

The Secret Service agent saw National Security Advisor Ken Cosgrove hurrying down the hall. He turned and punched a series of numbers into the keypad next to the door to the Situation Room complex and held the door open for the senior official. Ken nodded and briskly walked inside. He passed through a reception area featuring a lead-lined cabinet where visitors had to deposit their BlackBerries and cell phones and noticed one of his NSC staff, Evan Ovich, making a secure phone call in one of the glass-encased booths. He figured Evan was getting an update from one of his contacts in South America. Evan caught his eye, gave the thumbs-up sign, and then held up one finger, indicating he'd only be another minute.

Ken went into the conference room, where two other members of the National Security Planning Group were waiting. They were seated in black leather chairs around a long conference table. Behind them, six large screens with split-screen technology showed a series of news programs, now on mute. They wouldn't be needing to use the screens today, or the cameras or microphones hidden in the ceiling. This was going to be a private NSPG meeting, as they were called, focusing on covert actions to deal with pressing problems developing in Venezuela and neighboring countries. Problems that Ken worried could escalate and cause major headaches for the United States and her allies.

Evan rushed into the room, notebook in hand, and quickly sat down to join the meeting. "Sorry if I've held you up, Ken, but I just got off a call with our Station Chief in Caracas. Looks like El Presidente may finally be calling snap elections soon after Christmas. Guess he figures that his opponents will be too tied up with the holidays to get much of a rally going and he'll be able to slide through once more."

"Sounds like a crafty plan," Ken said, and then addressed the others in the room. "Even though they voted down his new constitution and that whole 'elect me for life' amendment he tried to foist on those poor people, he still maintains a helluva grip on the economy. And now he's starting to have an impact on ours." He turned back to Evan, Special Assistant to the President for International Communications. The title was a cover for the job Evan was really doing.

Growing up in a family that had escaped from Yugoslavia in the fifties, when the Soviets were in charge, Evan knew from firsthand family lore all about the heavy hand of dictators, the destruction of property rights and individual liberties, and how totalitarian governments completely sap individual initiative and yet enhance the thirst for freedom. Now Evan worked with several opposition groups in countries around the world to undermine other dictators. Right now his focus was on hot spots in South America.

Though certain U.S. laws precluded a whole list of activities aimed at sitting governments, there were still myriad ways to help groups seeking free speech and fair elections, and Evan had become an expert on methods to secretly support their efforts.

Ken said, "Evan, give us a quick recap on the situation in Caracas."

Evan scanned his notepad. "We all know about the takeover of the radio and TV stations, the crackdown on student protesters, the price controls that have dried up supplies of simple things like bread and milk. They're now saying that an egg is a delicacy and they can't even buy toilet paper." He referred to his notes again. "And, then there's the inflation, highest in all of South America. Latest estimate is something around thirty-eight percent. The corruption is rampant and their President is running out of things to nationalize. He's already taken over the telecommunications companies, the farms, the utilities, the oil and gas companies . . . well, most of them anyway . . . oh, and did you see where he even redesigned the country's coat of arms? He's got this white horse pointing left now. Guess that's supposed to track with his whole agenda.

"Of course, the only way he's managed to keep this circus going is with his oil and gas revenue, and we're contributing to all of that. They're number four on our import list and now El Presidente is talking about trying to put together some sort of South American gas OPEC. So we're dependent on this guy even though he hates us and is doing everything in his power to undermine our influence in South America. Just when Castro shuts up, we've got this guy taking over the bullhorn."

"Yes," Ken said, "but even worse, he's been supporting what's left of the FARC terrorist group even though he keeps denying it, and we all saw reports of FARC trying to get hold of some nuclear supplies for the production of dirty bombs."

"And he's been cozy with North Korea, Iran, Libya, and Algeria for years. Did you hear that they've inaugurated direct flights between Caracas and Tehran?" The others nodded as Evan continued. "We all know that Russia is getting more involved. He had them all down for a fancy powwow, inviting them to help develop the Orinoco River basin."

"Right," said another staffer. "That's the biggest known oil deposit, at least that we know of. I think they've got something over a trillion barrels of extra-heavy crude."

"And now he wants the Russians to develop it because he calls our oil companies 'vampires,'" Evan said. "Then there are the kidnappings for ransom. Even after that big rescue in Colombia, the whole routine is spilling over into Venezuela, too. We've got a lot of our own people still down there. I don't like the looks of any of this."

"Your point about our importing their oil is a big one," Ken said.

"The last number I saw was forty-two billion dollars in Venezuelan imports, including the oil. So while he rants about our economy, he benefits from us, and this has got to stop."

"Agreed," Evan said. "So here's the latest on the opposition group efforts. If snap elections are called, there are three main student groups determined to stage rallies and field alternative candidates. The biggest one is Frente Renovadora par la Libertad, the FRL."

"What does that mean?" another staffer asked.

"It means Renewal Front for Freedom," Evan answered. "Pretty good title. Trouble is, they know if they get too vocal, they'll be arrested and their candidates will be disqualified. On the other hand, if we can get crowds that are large enough, really big, thousands to jam the streets, they can't jail all of them."

"Shades of the work we did with Lech Walesa's Solidarity group in Poland during the Reagan days," Ken observed.

"You got it. So we'll get our contacts in place down there, supply them with the printing presses, the cell phones, the computers, the radios to distribute in the countryside, and then we'll call for international observers to validate the whole election process. We can get alternative newspapers on the streets, clandestine radio broadcasts beamed in from offshore ships. We've got a whole list of priorities."

"The funding won't be a problem," Ken said. "I know you're working with the CIA on all of this. I've got a meeting lined up with the National Intelligence Director and I'll brief him on the plans. Get me a summary and some talking points," he said to Evan. "The meeting is early tomorrow."

Evan made some notes and nodded. "Do you think we need to get State to put out a travel advisory?"

"Not yet," Ken said. "With all the trade going on and a number of our people still going back and forth as private contractors, we can't do that yet. Besides, their President knows he needs expertise, not only from us but from European business, so he's likely to leave our people alone. For now anyway."

"I still don't like the FARC connection."

"Neither do I," Ken admitted. He turned to the others in the room. "I want all of you to keep close tabs on this situation. We've got tough winter months ahead. We're importing more oil and gas all the time, and if Venezuela becomes more of an economic disaster, they could take parts of our economy down with them. And remember, Evan's work is classified. I shouldn't have to tell you that. But in this case we have to make a special effort to keep this whole thing under wraps."

"Everything we do is classified," another staffer remarked. "So we never get bragging rights." He turned to Evan. "Talk about hiding your light under a basket."

"Yes, but this is a national security basket," Evan said, "and I'm just praying it doesn't leak."

"So how did it go at the White House?" Godfrey asked as Tripp breezed through the door, shaking snow from his overcoat and stamping his feet.

"A big small-world-ism." Tripp replied. "Got any coffee left? I had some over there, but I still can't get warm. Bloody blizzard out there."

"Yeah. I made some fresh a while ago. So tell me what they wanted."

"Well, first, it wasn't *they*, it was *she*."

"She? Who?"

"Samantha Reid. She's the Deputy over in the White House Homeland Security shop and it turns out I knew her. Well, I sorta knew her."

"How? Where?"

"At Princeton. Can you believe that?"

"Did you remember her?"

"I do remember her seeing her around, although I never had anything to do with her on campus. She was a freshman and I was trying to graduate and head into the Navy, so I didn't pay much attention. Should have though."

"Why? What's she like."

Tripp sat down at his desk, leaned back, and put his hands behind his head. "I gotta say she's really impressive."

Godfrey pulled up a chair and said, "In what way? You mean beautiful, or what?"

"Oh yeah! Smart, too. She studied geology when I did, so we ended up in the same building for classes some of the time. But the thing is, she's got all this brown hair."

"Hair? You get summoned to the White House and you talk about a staffer's hair?"

"Sure. If you'd seen it, you'd know what I mean. And then there were the dark green eyes and the high cheekbones."

The lobbyist shook his head and laughed. "So when did you ever see a woman with low cheekbones?"

"I guess I haven't. Anyway, she wanted to know all about the gas line problem."

"What did you tell her? I mean, what can you tell her? We don't have a clue what's going on down there."

"I know. I had to vamp. I gave her what we had and said we'd keep in touch."

"Looks like you'd like to keep in touch, huh?" Godfrey asked with a slow grin.

"I wouldn't mind. And boy, that hair."

"At least it sounds like she's not another one of those fancies you usually take out."

"Fancies?" Tripp asked with a quizzical glance.

"Yeah. FNCs. Fox News Clones. Those newscasters with the straight blond hair and great legs who all look alike. I can't tell one from the other. There must be a journalism school someplace that only takes blondes and teaches them to laugh out loud in English."

Tripp chuckled. "Guess you have a point there. I don't seem to have anything fancy around right now." He turned to a pile of papers on his desk. "But I do have a ton of work to keep me occupied." He glanced at the clock. "Anything new on the gas line?"

"Nope. Nothing on that. But we did just get a memo about the situation in Caracas."

"Again? It's bad enough they've been nationalizing everything that's nailed down. What are they up to now?" Tripp asked.

"More of the same, I'm afraid. Turns out our last drilling division is on their radar scope again and they're talking about confiscating the last of our property for a song."

Tripp jumped up from his chair and started pacing his office. "Damn it! We invest billions in that country. We produce oil and gas. They reap record profits and they just want to take it all. And for what? More of their crazy schemes? You'd think they'd sit up and notice that their guys have no clue how to run those fields. Stuff breaks down. They don't have the engineers, the expertise. They need us and they keep trying to throw us out."

"We still have a bunch of patents though."

"A lot of good those will do us if we're out of the country." Tripp ran a hand through his hair in frustration. "So what is headquarters going to do?"

Godfrey motioned to the papers on Tripp's desk. "It's all right there in a memo. Take a look. They're talking about sending someone down there to negotiate. And you know who our top negotiator is."

"Oh Christ!" Tripp said, reaching for the memo.

"You got it, buddy. That would be you."

Tripp quickly read the memo and blew out his breath. "So now they're saying they might send me to Venezuela? We're coming up on the Christmas season, for cripe's sake."

"Then again, it would get you out of this weather. I mean, who wants to hang around D.C. in December anyway?" Godfrey said.

Tripp looked out the window again and saw the wind-driven snow sticking to the outside. "Guess you have a point there. I guess it'll be warm in Caracas. But that could hardly make up for the idea of flying nine hours to meet with a bunch of corrupt bureaucrats who are on the payroll of that sleazebag of a dictator." He pointed to a paragraph in the memo. "At least it's not a done deal yet. They say that Victor still has more meetings coming up. I mean, Victor Aguilar is the President of our operations for all of South America. You'd think he could handle this."

"You'd think. But he wasn't able to handle the last round of confiscations, now, was he?"

Tripp sighed. "You're right. But let's just hope he can stave this off for a while. We've got too many other things on our plate right now."

"I know. The new energy exploration bill, the gas line explosion, the White House situation. Then again, sounds like you might want to spend a little more time on that particular situation."

Tripp looked up and cocked his head. "Yeah. I just might."

The Mexican farmer trembled as he faced the Zeta member holding a submachine gun. "Silver or lead, amigo?" the man demanded. The farmer stared down at his torn jeans and nervously twisted the bandanna in his hands.

"I said silver or lead," the imposing man repeated. Then he softened his tone and lowered his weapon. "Come now, you know the rules here. Work for me and you get silver."

"And if I don't?" the farmer whispered in a halting voice.

"Then we kill your family. That's the lead, my friend. And you do want to be my friend, don't you?"

The farmer wiped some dust off his forehead with the back of his hand and asked, "What do I have to do?"

"You know what goes down here. We need pitazos like you to help the polleros get our people across the border."

"But it's not just people," the farmer said.

"Of course not. We are businessmen. Now you will be a business-
man as well. I'm here to tell you that we have a convoy coming through
here soon. Probably tomorrow night. You will go ahead and be a look-
out. We will give you a gun and ammunition."

"But the border patrol. We all know they are there. We know they
have people from their government, from their FBI and ICE and all
the others. You cannot get through."

The agent laughed. "Don't believe those stories. We have secured
the Falcon Reservoir south of Laredo. It's turning out to be one of
our best crossings."

"But that's where the firefight was. People were killed."

The agent shrugged. "That was a fight between two of our paramilitary groups."

"Our groups?" the farmer asked, wide-eyed.

"The Mexican Army fought with the Mexican Navy over control of
the northeast shoreline. So it got a little bit out of control. We worked
that out. Believe me, the Americanos were not even there."

"Who is coming here tomorrow?"

"Now that you are with us . . . and you are with us, right?"

The farmer nodded.

"Then I will tell you. MS-13 from El Salvador is working with us.
We have a special cargo and some special people. This will be the last
leg for the cargo. We brought it up on a submarine from Colombia."

"Colombia? So far away?" the farmer said.

"Our operations extend a long way, my friend. We have an endless
supply but we need more people. People like you." He tossed the
farmer a small wallet and retrieved a pistol from his knapsack. Handing it over he said, "Here is money for your family. Head toward the
border and by tomorrow night, if you see any of the patrol, you fire
two warning shots."

"But then they will know I am there."

"Just stay on this side of the border. They won't follow you. Don't
worry. We have many more pitazos all along the way."

"But my cousin at the next farm. They recruited him, too, and he
was killed last week. He left a family. Many babies. I have babies, too."

"There are lots of risks in life, but like I said, you want silver or lead?"

The farmer opened the wallet, counted the pesos and murmured, "*Sí.*"

13

"Excuse me, Samantha. Call for you on line two," Joan said. "It's Mr. Princeton."

Samantha took a deep breath before she picked up the phone. So he was calling. But why? Maybe he had an update from his company on the pipeline situation. She hoped it would turn out to be some sort of maintenance screwup. With all the other problems they were facing now, to say nothing about trying to implement the latest HSPD, as the new Homeland Security Presidential Directives were called, she had enough to worry about without adding an energy issue to their list. The tips seemed to be proliferating like kudzu and they dealt with possible threats to dams, transportation, mass transit, the energy grid, emergency services, and pipelines. This new HSPD was number twenty-four. She pushed it aside and took the call.

"Samantha Reid."

"Good morning. Tripp Adams. Thought I'd check in with you."

"Nice to hear from you. Anything new on the pipeline in Okla-homa?"

"Well, that's what I wanted to talk to you about, among other things."

"Other things?" she asked.

"Yes. Seems that there's a lot going on and now that the snow has stopped and the roads are being cleared, I wonder if you might be able to break away so we could get together?"

"Again?"

"I didn't mean another White House meeting. I was thinking, well, I've got a chock-a-block day going here and I'm sure you're busy too . . ."

"Always," she replied. "So what did you have in mind?"

"Any chance we could grab a bite later?" he asked.

"You mean lunch?"

"No. I was thinking dinner somewhere. I mean, if you can get away. It could be a late supper if you're tied up."

"Uh, dinner? To talk about the pipeline?" she asked cautiously.

"Sure. That and a few other things we've got going here. I'll fill you in later. Then again I thought maybe we could catch up a bit on the old days."

"Catch up? Oh, you mean about Princeton?"

"Sure. Do you think you can get away? I could meet you some-place. Or I could pick you up? Where do you live?"

This was rather sudden, she thought. Here she had just met the guy and he was already asking her for dinner. Was it a business meet-ing or was it a dinner date? Then again, they had some sort of history from college days. She had to give him that much. She hesitated. It had been so long since she'd accepted a dinner date with anyone. Sev-eral friends had arranged group dinners, trying to introduce her to various guys from the Hill who all looked like they were poster boys for the Hair Club for Men. And then there was the guy whose only ambition was to be on the Olympic luge team. Since she wasn't really into toboggans, that didn't go too well. She hadn't been out alone with anyone since Dexter. It had always just been too hard to airbrush him out of her memory. But Tripp? Talk about issues? Princeton? Why not?

She twirled the telephone cord around her finger and answered. "I live in Georgetown, near Key Bridge, but I could meet you somewhere."

"Hey, that's handy. I'm just across the bridge in Arlington. So, let me think. How about Chadwick's around eight? Would that work for you?"

"Uh, sure. I guess so. That's right down the street, I can walk from my place."

"Oh, there's my other line. Gotta run. See you at eight."

Tripp pushed through the wooden doors with beveled glass panels leading to Chadwick's, a restaurant at the foot of K Street that had been popular with the Georgetown set for the last forty years. The Rolling Stones' "Jumpin' Jack Flash" was playing on the jukebox. When he heard the line "It's a gas," he thought about his own gas line problem. *Can't seem to escape that one.*

He found a stool at the long bar, crowded with a horde of thirty-somethings, and glanced over at the action on the TV screens next to the mirrors on the back wall. He waved to the bartender and ordered a Sam Adams.

Tripp looked at his watch. Not quite eight o'clock. He figured Samantha might be late. Most women he knew were late. Then again, most women he knew weren't much like Samantha Reid. He thought about their short meeting the day before and realized that he'd been thinking about her off and on for the last twenty-four hours. And that was weird. He couldn't remember the last time a woman had so captured his imagination that he had to conjure up an excuse to see her. Other women usually called him, and he often made excuses that he had to work late, just to avoid the pushier ones. But this one was different. At least she seemed different. He couldn't be sure. Their meeting had been awfully short. Yet, there was something about her. Some combination of smarts and curiosity. All-business yet all-woman. He liked that. And besides, it wouldn't hurt to have an ally in the White House, if that's what she turned out to be. He was new to this job, though he wasn't new to the city.

He had grown up in Potomac, Maryland, and gone to St. Albans prep school in the District, the elite school that shared the highest point in the city with the National Cathedral. It was the place where Senators and diplomats, businessmen and lobbyists sent their sons, if they could get in. He had played football with kids from Jordan and studied Spanish with boys from Argentina.

His parents still had a place in the area, but spent most of their time in Naples, Florida. He thought about the beaches down there and imagined lying on the warm sand with Samantha next to him. But there was no chance he was going to get away to Florida any time soon, unless it was on the way back from a trip to Venezuela. And even if he pulled that off, he knew he wouldn't have a busy lady like Samantha with him. Somehow the thought made him wistful.

He felt a cold blast of air and swiveled around to see the woman in his imagination ducking through the doors, pushing strands of wind-blown hair out of her eyes. There was that hair again. *Damn she looks good. If she looked any better, she'd need a bodyguard.* He jumped up and went over to her.

"Glad you could make it. You're right on time."

"I try to be," she said demurely, shedding her coat and hanging it on a rack by the door. "Do we have a table?"

"I made a reservation just in case. We're upstairs." He reached into his pocket for his wallet and pulled out a dollar bill. "But first, I think I'll feed the jukebox. Any favorites?"

She smiled and said, "That's one of the great things about this place. They've got all kinds of music."

"So what do you like?" he asked, walking over to the jukebox.

"Country." She glanced down at the list and pointed. "How about 'Boot Scootin' Boogie'? I love that old one."

He shoved the dollar into the machine, punched some numbers, and took her arm. "You got it. Twice."

They climbed the open staircase to the left of the bar and took their place at a small table with blue-and-white checkered table-cloths. He pulled out her chair and noticed the lithographs on the wall, colored scenes of old Washington homes along the canal and ancient schooners on the Potomac. They looked a little bit like some of the prints his father had in his study.

A waiter handed out menus and offered to take their drink orders. "A glass of pinot noir, please," Samantha said.

"I'll have another Sam Adams, thanks," Tripp added, and opened the menu. "So, since this is your neighborhood, what do you suggest?"

"They're kind of famous for their ribs, if you don't mind getting rather messy when you eat them," she said with a smile.

That smile, he thought. *I always like a woman with a great smile.* "Ribs? Maybe. Let's see. Instead, I think I'll go for the New York strip."

"I'll try the shrimp pesto tonight." She laid her menu aside, leaned her elbows on the table, and laced her fingers together. "So, tell me the latest from the world of GeoGlobal. Most of the papers had stories about the trouble caused by the ice storm, the power outages, and how it was all made a lot worse by the gas line break. The *New York Times* had pictures of tiny babies being carried out of hospitals and people crowding into some grange hall with a big fireplace. In fact, now that I think about it, there were major stories in all the papers, although I only saw a couple of lines in *USA Today.*"

"*USA Today?* Summarizing seems to be their specialty. Maybe there should be a Pulitzer Prize for best investigative paragraph."

Samantha smiled again. "You've got that one pegged. But really, the whole thing is causing major headaches down there. Is there anything new on how it all happened?"

The voices of Brooks and Dunn began to drift up from the bar as Tripp leaned forward to answer the lady.

He told her everything he knew about the gas line problem, which wasn't much. He then talked about the situation in Venezuela, the nationalizations, and the possibility of a trip to Caracas to negotiate with their government's energy officials. Samantha seemed to know a lot about Venezuela. She mentioned the Orinoco fields and how the Russians were moving in to take a lead on their development.

The waiter brought their drinks and took their dinner order. Samantha continued to listen to Tripp talk about his company. She couldn't take her eyes off of him and she liked the way he made eye contact with her. He obviously wasn't one of those guys who talks with one person while trying to scan the room at the same time for somebody more important or more attractive. No. She had Tripp's full attention and for the first time in a long time, she wanted to revel in it.

But he said that he might be going out of town soon. "You mean, you might have to go to Caracas? Christmas is coming. You don't want to be traveling down there now, do you?" she said in a more lamentable tone than she'd meant to reveal.

He shrugged. "We've got the President of our South American operations making another stab at this whole issue. So I won't know for a while. But hey, let's talk about something more pleasant than a damn dictator. I'd like to hear something about Samantha Reid. How did you go from a Princeton geology class to the White House staff?"

"It's kind of a long story," she said, taking a sip of her wine.

"Okay, so who's in a hurry? After I left Princeton, you graduated three years later, right?"

"Not exactly."

"Not exactly? You sound like an old Hertz commercial," he quipped.

"Well, I went back to Houston for a while."

"Houston? That's where you're from?"

"Uh-huh. My dad's in the oil and gas business."

"Like father like daughter."

"Yes. But, as I said, I had to take some time off."

"Why?"

Raising her eyes, her expression turned somber. "My mom got sick. Cancer."

"Oh Lord! What happened?"

"I went home to be with her and take care of my younger brother, who was still in high school back then."

"So you went home. For how long?"

"I stayed a year, until she died."

He reached over and touched her hand. "Samantha, I'm so sorry."

"It was a pretty rough time for all of us." She took another sip of her wine and settled back in her chair. "Then again, that was a long time ago. We pulled together, my dad, my brother, and I. You know how it is. Family sticks together and all of that."

He nodded and continued to stare into her eyes.

"And, well, after that year, my brother graduated from high school and went off to Purdue to study engineering and I went back to Princeton to finish up. I hated to leave my dad, but he insisted I get my degree."

"How's he doing now?"

"He's fine. Still living in Houston. Still working too hard. I keep hoping he'll meet somebody nice."

Tripp took her hand and squeezed it. "Sometimes it happens, you know."

Samantha gazed up at him and pulled her hand away. *What's really going on here?* she wondered. A picture of Dexter invaded her mind's eye. It happened from time to time, though the instances were getting farther and farther apart. She struggled with the image for a moment and tried to refocus on the conversation. "So anyway, after I left Princeton, I got a job with a consulting firm working on energy issues. Then Greg Barnes hired me to come into government."

"When he was Assistant Secretary of Energy?"

"Right. And then when he got the White House appointment, he asked me to come along. So there I am. Chief cook and bottle washer for Mr. Barnes."

"I'd hardly classify your position that way."

"Maybe not, but I do feel like we're in hot water all the time."

The waiter hurried up to their table, put Tripp's steak and Samantha's shrimp at their places and asked if they'd like another drink.

"Another pinot?" Tripp asked.

"Sure."

"And I'll switch to a glass of cabernet, thanks." Tripp turned back to Samantha. "Now then, where were we?"

"Well, I was talking about taking the job at the White House, but I can't really talk about what goes on in our shop."

"Everything's classified, right?"

"More or less. So let me turn the tables and ask how you got from Princeton to GeoGlobal? Come to think of it, I thought I remember hearing that you were heading out to join the Navy or the Air Force."

"You've got a good memory. Yeah. I was hell-bent to get on board a ship and get out of town. I went through a lot of training."

"What kind of training?"

"Nuclear power, submarines, explosives."

"That's pretty heavy stuff."

"I loved it."

"Then what?"

"I was recruited by Greyfield."

"The government contractor?"

"Well, we did get a lot of government contracts as well as commercial work for all sorts of companies around the world. I found myself on an oil rig at one point, checking their security, possible explosives, that sort of thing, and that's when I got to know the GeoGlobal people. They made a pretty good offer so I took it and did a bunch of assignments for them. Then one day, when they had a big labor dispute, I ended up defusing it. To use a term. I was able to negotiate an agreement. Guess they figured I was a better negotiator than troubleshooter. So here I am, Vice President of the company."

"And that's why they may send you down to Caracas to negotiate with those socialists?" Samantha said.

"You get the picture."

"But back on the Greyfield job. I've heard that many of those contractors end up in pretty dangerous situations. Were you in war zones?"

"Sure. I remember Joe and I, uh, Joe Campiello was one of my buddies at Greyfield. Joe and I got into all sorts of scrapes. He saved my ass a couple of times."

"And you saved his as well?" she asked.

"Yeah. I guess you could say that."

The waiter came up to clear their dinner plates. "Would you folks like some coffee or dessert?"

Tripp looked at Samantha and raised his eyebrows. "Anything?"

She shook her head. "I'm fine. Dinner was great."

"Just the check, please."

Tripp paid the bill. They headed toward the stairway and heard a heavy metal song blaring from the jukebox. "Listen to that one," Samantha said, making her way down the stairs. "Isn't that awful?"

"Yeah."

"It makes 'Ninety-nine bottles of beer on the wall' sound positively lyrical."

Tripp burst out laughing and took her arm as they walked toward the coatrack. He helped her on with her coat and resisted the urge to touch her hair as she pushed it out of the way of her coat collar. He grabbed his overcoat and opened the door, and they were met with a blast of frigid air. "Now, where is this place of yours? I'll walk you back."

"It's just two blocks down. Are you sure? I could just . . ."

"I'm not leaving you alone on a Washington street at night. And you shouldn't be walking around alone either, my lady," Tripp said.

Samantha liked the way he took her arm and led her down K Street toward her condo. No other man had tried to take care of her since Dexter. She hadn't told Tripp about him. She'd told him enough tonight. That part of her life could wait until the next time. If there was a next time.

"I suppose you're right about Washington streets," she said. "I read in the *Post* that there were nineteen robberies on Capitol Hill last week, but police have been spending their time enforcing dog leash laws at Logan Circle."

"Figures," Tripp said.

"Here's my place. It's one of the smaller condos in this building. But I love the location." She hesitated and then thought, *Why not?* As he walked her into the lobby, she turned and said, "We didn't have coffee at the restaurant. Would you like a cup before you drive home?"

"Thought you'd never ask," he said with his subtle grin.

Up in her apartment, she quickly made a pot of decaf while he stared out her living room window. It was almost an entire wall of glass, which helped to make the tiny condo less confining. Even in the small space, she had a beige couch with dark green throw pillows. The green fabric was repeated in a pair of simple side chairs flanking a wooden butler's table. There was a photo on the table. A picture of Samantha with a guy. Tripp leaned down and scrutinized the scene.

They were somewhere out West. There were mountains in the background and the two of them had their arms around each other. *Who's that guy?* he wondered. *Maybe I don't want to know.*

Samantha came into the room carrying a tray with two mugs of steaming coffee. "Cream or sugar? No, wait. I remember you had it black at my office."

"Good memory," Tripp said. He pointed out the window. "I can see my place from here."

"Where?"

"Turnberry Tower. It's one of the buildings across Key Bridge. Over to the right. Not quite as close to downtown as you are, but almost."

They chatted about Washington real estate and exchanged a few more stories about previous jobs, and Tripp realized he didn't want to leave this woman. But when he looked at his watch, he was surprised to see that it was already after eleven. He got up from the couch and caught a glimpse of the photo again but decided not to bring it up. At this point, he just wanted to get to know her. He didn't want to screw it up by delving into her past. "Guess I'd better head out."

As she stood up, he reached for her, drew her close, tipped her chin up and gazed into her eyes. "It's been a nice night, Samantha Reid." Then he pulled her to him and lowered his mouth to hers.

The kiss was deep. Intense. She opened to him. Leaned into him. He tightened one arm, and with the other, he cradled her head and prolonged the kiss. Heat shot through her. She felt tense and weak at the same time as he molded his body to hers. She heard a slight moan and didn't know if it came from her or from him. She couldn't think. Didn't want to think. His mouth was demanding, hungry, probing. His hand was fisted in her hair, pulling her ever closer. She didn't want to break away. Didn't want it to end. Then the jarring sound of his cell phone broke the spell.

He lifted his head and muttered an oath. "What the . . . sorry." He fished the phone out of his pocket and with one arm still holding Samantha, he put it to his ear. He listened for a moment and suddenly pulled away. Samantha took a step back as she watched his face. It had turned somber, angry. She held up both hands as if to say, "What?"

He slammed the phone shut and turned to her. "There's been another explosion."

"What the hell?" an FBI agent said, staring at the e-mail. "There's been another one of those gas line blow ups. Can you believe that?"

"Where? Not here in Texas, I hope," Agent Dotson said.

"Nope. This one looks to be in Kansas. But Jesus! Storm is still raging up there and now they've got people with no gas and probably no power in two states."

"Damn! With two now, I figure they're going to call in a bunch of our folks and all sorts of local law enforcement on that one, wouldn't you think?"

"Sure. At least it's not on our local radar right now." He hit another key and exclaimed, "Hey, Lee, we sure have something big on our scope tonight. We finally got some strategic intelligence on that new sub landing. Look at this. What do you think?" The agent printed out the report and handed it to his colleague.

"They finally figured out where the narco boys are landing those things." Lee said, perusing the report. "Problem is, they off-load the cocaine onto cigarette boats and we have no idea where *they're* going to land."

"Among other things," the other agent admitted. "What we need now is tactical intelligence. We need to know when and where their convoys are crossing."

"At least we got those new cameras and seismic sensors installed at that last sendero."

"Yeah, the opening. But as soon as the coyotes figure out we've got it covered, they move to another track. This whole virtual fence thing just isn't working. We need more guys down here."

Lee's cell phone rang and he grabbed it from the pocket of his jacket. "Agent Dotson here." He listened for a few moments, raised his hand, and made a circle sign with his thumb and forefinger. "Great . . . you sure? What about DEA and ICE? We got any Rangers in the area? They could help us, too. Okay. Thanks for the tip. We'll spread the word."

"What's up?"

"Convoy heading toward the Laredo crossing. This looks like a big one. A sheriff's posse heard shots."

"Warning shots, do you think?"

"Who knows? They could be fighting with each other again, but we've got our guys on the way this time."

Juan Lopez sat hunkered down in the Humvee and tried to check his watch. It was so dark he could barely make out the hour. 2:15 a.m. They had planned this run when they saw that clouds and a light drizzle would blank out any light from the moon. He was cold, shivering, and scared. He was wearing the same light parka he had on when he left Venezuela, the same blue jeans, the same sweatshirt. They told him not to bring any big luggage because of space constraints. But he had to bring one large duffel bag, which he kept on his lap the whole time. It contained some special things, things that Diosdado Rossi had procured. He didn't know what they were. The Fixer had told him they were a type of canister—two of them in metal cases of some sort. He had instructions not to open the cases under any circumstances. He was to bring them to Simon and Carlos and then keep them safe until they all received orders to use them.

Juan hadn't thought much about them; he had carefully packed them in the bag along with his cell phone, some money, a handgun, bullets, a few bottles of water, and some sandwiches. The food and water were gone now, and he still had a long way to go.

He peered ahead at the battered army trucks making their way across the rough terrain. They told him the recruits had left their army posts to join the paramilitary group and brought the stolen trucks and Humvees with them. The guys from MS-13 were better dressed. They all had fancy weapons and belts of ammo over their shoulders. They looked confident, cocky, as they guarded their precious cargo.

Suddenly there was a burst of gunfire. The Zetas were firing. But where? Was anybody firing back?

"Out. Get out and run," the driver commanded.

"Where?" Juan said as he jumped out of the vehicle, hauling the bag with him.

"Over there. Fan out. Through those trees. The convoy will head left. You go right. Keep going. Don't stop."

Juan lifted the heavy duffel bag, threw it over his shoulder, and stumbled as the Humvee headed west. More gunfire. More commands. The voices were getting dimmer as the entire convoy veered away. Juan tried to run but it was hard, carrying the bag. He jumped over clumps of cactus, caught his sneaker on the edge of a prickly plant, and went down. His face hit the dirt. He heard voices off to the left and more gunshots. He scrambled to his feet, picked up the duffel, and scurried toward the stand of trees. He kept running through the underbrush.

Where was the border? Where were the agents? He kept running. A mile, maybe two miles. He had no idea where he was. All he knew was that he had to get away. Away from the guns. Away from the drugs. Away from the coyotes, the Zetas, and MS-13. The agents would go after those guys, not him. He was pretty sure of that. But what if there was a fence? What if there was a camera? What if he ran right into a policeman of some sort?

He stopped to catch his breath and check the time again. 2:47

a.m. They had told him they'd be across by 3:00. But across where? His shoulder was aching now. The light rain had soaked through his jacket and into his sweatshirt as well as his pants. He had dirt on his hands and face and he was out of water. But he didn't care as long as he could get across. He listened. Nothing. The guns had stopped. He could no longer hear the rumble of the trucks or the Humvees or the shouts of the commanders and the coyotes. He was alone. He wondered if there were any real coyotes in these parts. And what about snakes and lizards?

He tried to shake away the fears. After all, he was on a mission. He had volunteered for this. He would make a lot of money if they could pull off their assignments. Assignments that were important for his country and bad for the American country. That's what they had told him. And that was fine with him. They all hated the Coloso del Norte, didn't they? The North America that lorded over everybody in the hemisphere with their White House bullies and their Monroe Doctrine and all the other ways they tried to maintain control over everybody. He had learned about that in school and he didn't like it one bit.

Now he had a chance to right some wrongs. Sure, he was just one cog in the wheel. Simon and Carlos were part of the plan, too, and once they were all together again, it was going to be great to watch the Americanos squirm and wonder how it all happened.

He picked up his duffel bag and once again ran for the border.

15

"Did El Presidente get his books and DVDs?" Diosdado Rossi asked the attractive secretary sitting outside the suite at the Palacio de Miraflores, otherwise known as the Presidential Palace.

She glanced up at the short, slim man with the carefully groomed black hair and replied, "Don't I always follow your wishes?"

"That's what I like about you. You are very good at keeping me and the big man happy." He appraised her full figure and flashing eyes and added, "In more ways than one."

"I don't know why he keeps reading those books on English and French history though," she remarked.

"It's all part of his fascination with the way the old kings and queens ruled their countries."

"But he's *acomplejado*," she said in an undertone. "I know I shouldn't say that, but you know what I mean."

The Fixer, as he was called by everyone in the palace, gave her a knowing look. "We both know that. He grew up in a poor family and says he hates the ruling class."

"He can study all he wants, but he'll never turn his barrio beginnings into a Renaissance village. And yet he reads about them. It doesn't make a lot of sense."

"Sure it does. Just because you hate somebody doesn't mean you can't learn how they got to be successful. And in the case of those books, he pores through them looking at the way those kings issued decrees and dealt with people they thought were traitors."

"That's what worries me. He put some more students in jail yesterday. They weren't doing much of anything. They were just having a meeting, talking about the election. I'm afraid that they could really rebel and get a big rally going. And then where would we be?"

"Don't worry, my dear. We may have a lot of problems around here, but we know how to handle dissidents. We've learned from the pros."

Rossi thought about his predecessors. Vladimiro Montesinos in Peru was the powerful enforcer for Alberto Fujimori back in the nineties. He knew how to be a combination Chief of Staff, handler of dirty tricks, briber of members of Congress, and head of the intelligence service, all at the same time. A rather impressive list of credentials. His downfall came when he videotaped it all so he could blackmail his contacts later if need be. And he got caught. Rossi wasn't about to be that stupid.

Then there was López Rega, the brains behind Argentina's Isabel Perón in the seventies. A great case study on how to amass power and influence. Rossi had learned from them all. A man has to learn from mistakes. Hopefully, the mistakes of others.

His mother had not made any mistakes, though. He thought about the elderly woman who rose early to pray every morning in the little chapel in the village where he was raised. He had been told many times about the years that his mother had wanted a son, prayed for a son. And when he was finally born, she had named him Diosdado, which meant *Gift of God*. He still went back to see her as often as he could, but now he had more pressing things on his mind. As El Presidente had accumulated more power, Rossi's portfolio had increased as well. It was all happening just as he had planned it.

He had figured out, early on, that his boss would rise to the number-one job. Rossi had joined the team years ago and structured the President's plan so that the people would see him as a reincarnation of Simón Bolívar. That is, if they didn't have too strong a grasp of history. The legacy was a popular one, especially with the peasants, since Bolívar was revered as a champion for the oppressed of South America over two hundred years ago. Of course, Rossi knew that Bolívar would probably turn over in his grave if he saw the same kind of Latin American *caudillo,* or strongman, in charge today that he had fought against so many years back. But that didn't matter. Rossi and his boss had appealed to the poor, the oppressed, the underdogs with many programs for land redistribution, handouts, and promises of education and health care. The fact that price controls, mismanagement, and corruption had thwarted some of those plans didn't bother Rossi. They still had a firm grip on the economy, and he also was building up a nice offshore account in the Caymans while he was at it.

He strolled into the President's office, a memo in hand. "Here is the plan to take over the last piece of that American company's oil and gas division," he said to the imposing man clad in his signature red shirt.

The President grabbed the paper and quickly read the summary. "I see you want to change the name from GeoGlobal to Petroleos Nacionales, S.A. That sounds good. We'll call it PeNaSa for short. Has a nice ring to it, don't you think?"

"But of course," the Fixer said.

"What about their people? Will any of them stay on to supervise the rigs?"

"No. I'm sure they will pull all of their people out, just like the others did. But our workmen are manning the rigs. They have learned how to handle the fields. And we're training some of them to move up to be supervisors."

"If we have more trouble, maybe we can get some of the Russians or the people from Iran or Belarus to fill in the gap."

"Good idea. I'll pass that along to the Energy Chief. He's been negotiating an exit for GeoGlobal, offering them their initial cost as a payment to leave the country."

"How's it going?"

"Just what you'd expect. They're balking. They say that if you buy a stock for ten dollars and then invest in the company and build it up so the stock is then worth fifty dollars, you should get fifty dollars for it. But we're only offering them ten."

"They know the rules here. It's take-it-or-leave-it. Take the ten or leave all of their equipment and get nothing."

"We do have problems with that sector though," the Fixer said.

"Don't you think I know that? Our production is down fifty percent."

"And the skimming of the profits has depleted our funds from the health program you promised." Rossi knew that he was one of the few people in the palace who could point out trouble to the President and not get sacked for it. He knew because he not only pointed out problems, he brought solutions. "We may have to replace the head of Petroleos de Venezuela. He's getting a bit too greedy for my taste."

The President swiveled in his chair and put his hands behind his head. "You may be right. PdVSA may be the best state-owned asset we have, but the profits are sinking. We have to bring it under control."

"Of course, we too have been using their funds for our programs," the Fixer observed cautiously.

"That's where we get the majority of our money for the poor. We all know that. But we need more. There were some riots in the food lines yesterday. We can't have that. And yes, your idea of replacing those people may help." He got up from his chair and started pacing his lavish office. "There's another thing we have to handle."

"What is that, sir?"

"The gangs. The kidnappers seem to think they can roam around and impersonate FARC. I don't care what FARC does in Colombia, but we can't have their copycats operating here in Caracas. We still need foreign expertise to run some of the companies and we still need the tourists." He gazed out his window at blue skies with a few wispy clouds off in the distance. "Look at it out there. Is this not the most beautiful city? Is this not the very best weather? Is this not paradise?"

The Fixer joined him at the window and quickly agreed. "Yes it is. And the tourists will be coming for the holidays. They are having big storms, snow and ice up north while we bask in sunshine. It is a glorious country, Mr. President. You should be proud."

The President beamed and said, "Yes. We may have our problems, but we also have our plans. And speaking of plans, how did you like my speech the other day at Santa Ana's Chapel?"

"It was brilliant. I got the message. It was carried out perfectly."

"I'm pulling together a Crisis Action Team," Samantha announced as she stood in front of her boss's desk.

"Aren't you being a little jumpy about this? It sounds like GeoGlobal just has a bad maintenance issue on their hands and you want to call in the cavalry."

"Sorry, Greg. I've got a very bad sense about this one. I've already set it up. We're meeting in half an hour over in the Cordell Hull."

"In the SCIF?"

"Yes, the SCIF," Samantha repeated, referring to Room 208, the Sensitive Compartmentalized Information Facility in the EEOB across West Exec. It was one of many completely secure rooms where communication lines were scrambled, computer systems were hardened, and the walls and floors were shielded from prying eyes and ears.

"Well, I need you here."

"I can't be here. I'm going to be there," she said defiantly. "I be-lieve we may have a major problem with sabotage on those gas lines. We've got people freezing in three states and if you don't think there's a problem, well . . . I'll be glad to brief you after the meeting."

"Samantha. Listen to me. I know you're all hell-bent to watch out for our oil and gas supplies. Okay, fine. That's in your bailiwick. But I've got the whole damn directorate to worry about. You heard what happened near Charleston."

Samantha crossed her arms and stood her ground. "Yes, I know. They confiscated possible components of a dirty bomb off the coast there."

"Now, *that's* what I call a Homeland Security issue, not a gas line fizzling out."

"They didn't fizzle out. They exploded!"

"So they exploded. Let Transportation or Energy worry about that one. They've got a division that's supposed to be overseeing the pipelines in this country. They've probably got a GS-15 down there right now investigating the whole thing."

"We've got what could be a major disruption of an energy supply in this country and you think a GS-15 in Oklahoma should handle it?" she asked in an exasperated tone.

"Yes, I do. If you must go play mother hen on this one, go ahead. But remember, I need talking points on the Charleston situation. I'm on MSNBC at three."

Samantha rolled her eyes and stepped out of the room.

Shoving her notes into her black leather folder, Samantha hurried down the first flight of stairs leading to the West Wing basement and then stood aside as Vice President Jayson Keller, accompanied by his retinue of Secret Service agents, walked up the other way.

"Afternoon, Samantha," the charismatic man said as she nodded a greeting. "More trouble in your shop today? I heard about Charleston and now with another gas line going up in flames, you've got your hands full."

"Yes, sir," she said, holding up her leather folder filled with papers.

"I'd appreciate it if you'd keep my people in the loop on both of those."

"Of course, sir. We always try to do that."

"Thanks, appreciate it." With a slight wave, he and the agents were gone.

At least he gets it, she thought as she continued down the stairs and out the door to the EEOB. She shivered as she raced across the driveway. She never bothered to put a coat on to run between the two buildings. No one ever did. They just ran, especially in the winter months. She was wearing a black pin-striped pants suit, so temperatures in the thirties didn't bother her too much. She headed inside and walked along the black-and-white tiled corridor to the elevator that took her up to the second floor.

Inside the SCIF, she took her seat at the head of a small conference table. Staffers from the Departments of Energy, Transportation, and Homeland Security were already there. As she greeted them, two others breezed into the room. Dave Major was a smart-mouthed FBI agent who seemed to run afoul of the bureaucracy quite frequently. She had worked with him some months back when there were attacks on some American airliners. It seemed as though every agent, operative, and intelligence source had been working on that one, but she particularly liked dealing with Dave, even if he was the most irreverent of the bunch.

She had also invited a CIA agent, Will Raymond, another source who had proved invaluable in the airline attacks. He obviously had a huge Rolodex of contacts all over the world, and she wanted him on her team for this investigation, though she figured he probably had a lot of other pressing issues at the moment.

"Thanks for coming over on short notice," she said, opening her folder. "You all know what happened in Oklahoma and then again in Kansas last night on the GeoGlobal lines. There are some who may just want to blame the company for faulty maintenance, but I'm afraid we may have a situation of sabotage on our hands and we're going to need a thorough investigation."

"If it's criminal, FBI takes the lead," Dave said.

"Wait a minute, if this looks like a terrorism issue, and it very well could be, then obviously, DHS is the lead agency. Our intelligence people are already looking at this one," the DHS deputy said.

"With two hundred thousand employees, how can they even *find* their intelligence people?" Dave whispered to Samantha.

"What was that, Dave?" the deputy asked.

"Just wondering how we're going to figure out who's in charge of this thing, that's all," Dave replied.

"Look, folks," Samantha said, taking control of the meeting, "let's review what we've got so far and also take a look at a similar situation in Mexico. Trying to sabotage energy supplies is nothing new. We all know that EPR took credit for a series of attacks on natural gas and propane lines in Celaya and Coroneo, near Mexico City. Those pipelines fed the area where a whole host of companies, including some of ours like Kellogg, Hershey, and several auto plants, were operating. They all had to shut down. It was a mess and the Mexican economy took a nosedive."

"Those rebels were just trying to get some of their guys released from prison," Will said.

"I realize that. But the interesting thing is that we all figured EPR was made up of a bunch of peasants, but those attacks showed that they've reached a new level of sophistication, if we can put it that way," Samantha said.

The deputy from the Department of Energy chimed in. "That's true. They targeted valves, sections that were aboveground, and also some of the transfer terminals. But are you trying to say that the same group has come up here to mess with our pipelines? That seems like quite a stretch. I mean, what's their motive?"

"I didn't say it was EPR," Samantha said. "I'm just saying that blowing up pipelines is nothing new and we need to get on this problem and figure out exactly what happened here."

The Transportation Department official commented, "Our guy in Oklahoma was out there inspecting the damage. He reported back that the section that was damaged in Oklahoma was just above ground, but our field office that covers Kansas just called in and said that the particular break there occurred just underground, and so they can't figure out how it happened. I mean, you couldn't get a visual on that particular stretch of pipeline to set an explosive."

Samantha stared at the man. "Strange. Very strange."

"On the other hand," Will said, "more to your point about attacks on energy supplies gaining momentum, remember the arrest of almost two hundred Islamic militants who were evidently plotting to attack oil installations in Saudi Arabia? If they had pulled off even half of their plans, the price of oil would have gone through the roof."

"Again," Dave murmured.

"And with the Saudis pumping out ten percent of global supply, you can imagine what would have happened," Will said.

"To say nothing of the hit that their own economy would have taken," Samantha added. "Okay, so we know that we've got a huge vulnerability here and we don't know, yet, what really happened in Oklahoma and Kansas. Dave, see what you can dig up from your sources in those states. Suspicious activity around the pipelines. Local law enforcement. Anything." The agent nodded and made some notes.

"Will. Let's see if our station chief in Mexico City has heard anything new about groups down there. I know it's far-fetched, but we have to check out every possibility."

"Look, Samantha, with all due respect, I think we've got this one covered," the deputy from DHS said. "Our people are the experts at fusion function, combining our intelligence with what we get from the private sector. We collect the dots and then we string them together."

"Fine. We know that," Samantha said. "You collect your dots, but we all know it sometimes takes a lot of time to work all those dots through the bureaucracy. I'm trying to short-circuit the process here, folks. I think we all need to work together on this one. Anyone picks up anything, and I mean anything, you let me know and you copy the others. Do we have that straight?"

David looked at Will and shook his head. "This'll be a first."

"Then let it be a first," Samantha said. "And while I wait for any intel you get on those explosions, or whatever they were, I'll be coordinating with GeoGlobal."

"You got a pipeline into that company? Uh, so to speak?" Dave asked.

Samantha hesitated for just a moment, closed her notebook and simply said, "Yes."

17

Tripp punched the power button on the Technogym treadmill and started his warm-up. The Turnberry Fitness Center was bustling with a half-dozen others going through their early-morning routines, but Tripp ignored them all as he shoved a pair of earphones over his head in an effort to be left alone.

The television set in front of his machine had been tuned to the SciFi channel, where they were playing a show called "Countdown to Doomsday." *Well, that's apropos,* he thought, grabbing the remote and switching to CNN. He heard the news anchor list the 6:00 a.m. head-lines. The President was due back from the Economic Summit Meet-ing in France, another small submarine had been spotted off the west coast of Mexico, and nineteen Haitians had swum ashore in Naples, Florida. Tripp jerked his head up and watched as pictures of wet, bedraggled men, three women, and two young boys trudging down Gulf Shore Boulevard filled the screen. *I'll have to call Dad and find out if he saw them,* Tripp thought.

Then the announcer said, "This word just in. An elderly couple who had refused evacuation from their farmhouse in Oklahoma was found dead early this morning. They had died from hypothermia. Meanwhile, in Washington, senators from Kansas and Oklahoma have called for congressional hearings on the gas line explosions in their states. The hearing may be combined with another hearing on energy issues and could be scheduled as early as the day after tomorrow as investigations proceed on the cause of the disruptions."

Dead? A couple has died? Frozen to death? My God! Those poor people. This is a total disaster. And now, instead of getting generators and actual help to their constituents, Congress wants hearings? Jesus!

He hit the Quick Start button. He was running now, running from the frustration of not knowing why or how their lines were being sabotaged. Running from the frantic phone calls from the control rooms down south. Running from the pressure of a possible trip to Venezuela that was certain to be a total waste of time. He pulled the small white towel from around his neck and wiped the sweat from his forehead. The only thing he didn't want to run from was Samantha.

He had seen her again last night. He had called her on his way home. He said he had wanted to give her an update on the Kansas situation, but the truth was he just needed an excuse to see her again. She had sounded harried, saying she was working late again, but she finally agreed to a late-night glass of wine at her place.

He had driven to Georgetown, not certain what he could tell her because they were still getting reports in from the field. He figured he could finesse that one. All he really wanted to do was see her again, hear her voice, hold her, touch her. He hadn't done much of that last night, although he did manage to kiss her good night. *Better not rush that one. Don't want to screw it up.* After all the other women he had known over the years, Samantha was suddenly the one thing in his life that seemed to make sense. Everything else made no sense at all.

He finished his run and went over to lift some weights. He saw a familiar face, a rather attractive redhead lifting a pair of small barbells. He had seen her in the hallway a few times, and before he had met Samantha he had toyed with the idea of getting to know her. But not now. She was wearing a T-shirt that read, "Cancel my subscription. I don't want your issues." He shook his head and thought, *I don't want my issues either, but there's no way I can cancel myself out of my job.*

"Take a look at this," Godfrey said, careering into Tripp's office at the end of the day. "We've got problems."

"What else is new?" Tripp asked. "I've been on conference calls all day, we've had complaints from the Hill, the negotiations in Caracas are breaking down, I can't get hold of Samantha . . . uh . . . the White House . . ."

Godfrey gave him a knowing glance and said, "No, I mean bigger problems."

"What's bigger than our lines going up in smoke and congressional hearings in two days? I'm getting to feel like a traffic cop in a straitjacket," Tripp said.

Godfrey handed Tripp a memo marked URGENT.

"What's this?"

"Just read it and tell me what the hell it means," the lobbyist said.

Tripp quickly glanced at the document, ran his fingers through his hair, and exclaimed, "Holy hell!"

"Right."

Waving the piece of paper, Tripp almost shouted, "But how could that be?"

18

"Samantha, thanks for coming," Angela said. "I know you're swamped and I didn't want to impose, but Mom really wanted to include you tonight."

Samantha took off her coat, hung it in the hall closet of the modest two-story colonial, and handed her friend a bottle of Chianti Classico with a ribbon tied around it. "New outfit?" she asked, staring at Angela's white skirt and puffy red blouse.

"Hey, thanks for the wine. We'll serve it for dinner." She glanced down at her blouse. "This outfit? Mom gave it to me to wear tonight." She lowered her voice. "I wouldn't wear it anywhere else. Trouble is, I look like a strawberry shortcake."

Samantha scrutinized the outfit, grinned, and said, "Um. You may have a point." She glanced at her watch. "I'm afraid I can't stay long. I've got more work to do at home tonight."

"Still working on those gas line problems?"

"Absolutely. We're trying to figure out the who, how, and why of it all. I mean, why would anybody want to blow up a gas line in the middle of winter?"

"Beats me. But whoever is doing it is causing real havoc down South. I mean, people have been killed!"

"Believe me, I know!" She followed Angela into a dining room with red flocked wallpaper, brass sconces, and a large table with two leaves in the middle set for ten. "Can I help you with anything?"

Angela handed Samantha a can of Pam spray and reached for a votive candle on the table.

"What do I do with this?"

"Just spray a little bit in the bottom of each holder. Then I'll put the candles in. Makes it easy to pop them out when they burn down."

"Oh, clever," Samantha said, squirting a bit of the oily spray into the small glass containers.

"Here I'm working on votives and you're working on motives," Angela said. "Guess that's why they pay you the big bucks."

Samantha smiled. "Not really. I'm only one rank up from your job."

"Yes, but you get to work on national security issues. I get to meet with the Tile Council of America. Well, at least you can take a break and have dinner with us. My parents are really pleased you would drive all the way out here tonight."

"Wouldn't miss my friend's thirtieth, now, would I?" Samantha said, finishing her task.

"C'mon, say hello to my mom." Angela led the way. They pushed their way through swinging doors into a warm kitchen filled with the pungent aroma of bay leaves, melting butter, and yeast rolls. A wrought-iron rack held an odd assortment of pots and pans hanging over a large island where white china platters, vegetable dishes, and a gravy boat waited to be filled with the evening's entrees. A refrigerator stood in the corner covered with snapshots of Angela and her brothers and sisters at various ages beginning with kindergarten.

"Look who's here," Angela said.

Mrs. Marconi, a plump woman, her dark hair swept back in a bun, dried her hands on her apron and held out her arms. "Samantha. You smart girl. You come to my baby's birthday dinner. This is wonderful." She gave Samantha a hug. "I'm so proud of my Angela. First girl in our family to get a college degree. First girl in our whole church to get a job in the government. And it's the White House. It's always so exciting, you girls working there on all those important things."

Angela's violet eyes twinkled as she murmured, "Little does she know what important things I actually work on."

"Stop whispering and get your friend something to drink. Dinner will be ready in a little while. Your dad will be home soon. We have other guests coming in a few minutes. Go relax in the living room." They walked back through the swinging kitchen door.

"We never use the living room except on Christmas," Angela said.

"Nobody ever does, but guess we should go along with her plan tonight."

Angela opened the Chianti and poured two glasses, and they me- andered into a room with yellow walls, a floral sofa, and a skinny Christmas tree in the corner decorated with colored lights, a series of miniature churches, and crosses with tinsel strewn on every branch.

"Oh, your folks have their tree up already."

"Always," Angela said. "They put it up the day after Thanksgiving and don't take it down until twelve days after Christmas."

"This is the first one I've seen. Guess I should try to start getting in the mood, but there's been so much going on, I can't even find time to do any shopping." Samantha sat on the couch while Angela perched on a brown leather Barcalounger.

"Okay, now tell me what's going on in your shop. Two gas line ex- plosions? Was it sabotage? I mean, do we have some new terrorist group operating in Kansas?"

Samantha leaned forward. "Sounds pretty far-fetched, doesn't it? I've been in meetings all day and that's not our only problem, you know."

"Of course I know. Well, I don't always know what's going on. Seems that everything over there in the West Wing is classified while I'm working with groups that either want to export more ceramics or save red-cockaded woodpeckers. Life's not fair."

Samantha chuckled. "There are times I wish we could trade places, believe me."

"Don't be too sure. It's not only my White House life but my private life that you wouldn't want."

"What do you mean?"

"Well, Mom fixed me up with a doctor last night. He was in town for this big meeting going on at the convention center. You know, the new one downtown."

"You mean the building that looks like it was designed by a communist?"

"Yes, that one. It does kinda look like the Kremlin. Well, anyway, so I go out with this Italian doctor who's the son of some old friend of Mom's. He asks if I can take time off and come to some of the breakout sessions at the conference."

"What's the conference about?"

"It's 'Digestive Disease Week,'" Angela said.

Samantha almost choked on her wine. "You're kidding."

"No, really. So here's this guy and he wants me to come listen to a presentation he's making on 'Unusual Perspectives on Peptic Ulcers.'"

Samantha started laughing. "Sorry, but that's the first time I've laughed all day. So what did you tell him?"

"I explained that my White House job is really important and I couldn't possibly take time off." She took a sip of her wine and added, "He didn't need to know that in addition to the woodpeckers, the same group I met with today wants protection for the white-tailed prairie dog, the Preble's meadow jumping mouse, and twelve species of Hawaiian picture-winged flies."

"Send them over to Interior. You need a transfer."

"Tell me about it," Angela said.

"So, you don't like nature?" Samantha asked with a slight smile.

"I like nature. But for me, it's more of a screen saver." She took a sip of her wine and continued, "But let's get back to real issues."

Samantha's cell phone rang. She got up to retrieve her purse from the hall table and murmured, "Sorry."

"No problem. We're all on call. All the time."

She picked up her cell. "Samantha Reid."

"Hi, it's Tripp. Sorry to bother you. I know you said you had a party of some sort."

"Yes, I'm out in Silver Spring. Why? What's going on? You sound upset."

"It's more than that. Look, I don't want to talk on the phone but I'd sure like to see you as soon as you can break free. We have a new development about what happened to the lines and we may need some help. There's more but I can't go into it all right now. I need to brief you. Any chance you can get away?"

Samantha checked her watch and replied, "Hold on a minute." She put her hand over the cell and went back into the living room. "Angela, it's Tripp. You know. The man from GeoGlobal I've told you about."

Angela raised her eyebrows. "What's up? Other than his obvious interest in you."

"He says it's something important. About the gas lines. He says we need to meet."

"Only the gas lines?" Angela said with a grin. "You sure this isn't a booty call?"

Samantha shook her head and responded, "No way! This sounds important or he wouldn't be calling. I mean, he wouldn't have bothered me. Not here. I really think I need to get back."

"Mom's made a pot roast, but she can put some on a plate and you can take it with you. She knows how White House jobs are. You go see Tripp. I can handle the other people tonight. We have a whole gang coming anyway. We'll get you back for dinner another time."

"I'm really sorry, but I think I should check this out." Samantha got back to Tripp. "Okay, I'm going to leave here shortly. I could meet you at my place in thirty minutes or so."

"I'll be there. But take care of yourself. There are still patches of ice out there."

The gray stucco motel stood just off I-44 next to Denny's Restaurant. Simon Gonzales was stretched out on one of the twin beds, watching the Univision channel while Carlos checked for text messages on his cell phone. "Here's one from the Fixer," he said.

Simon glanced over and asked, "Another assignment?"

"Looks like it."

"Where did the signal come from this time?"

The boss read the message again. "It came from a speech at Jane's Diocese."

"A woman's name. Sounds like this will be ours again. Any special instructions this time?"

"No. He's leaving it to us to pick the spot." Carlos pulled a set of maps from his travel bag and studied a printout of intersecting lines superimposed on a map of Missouri. "I think we're pretty close to a good site. We'll drive over and scope it out after we get some dinner. Better to do that in the dark anyway."

Both men jumped up when they heard a banging on the door. Carlos grabbed a pistol and moved to one side. "Go see who it is."

Simon went to the door. Leaving the chain in place, he opened it a few inches and peered outside. He broke into a smile, pulled the chain away, and pushed open the door. He threw his arms around a young man standing there, clad in filthy blue jeans, a dirty sweatshirt, and a torn jacket, dragging a heavy duffel bag.

"You made it," Simon said. "Get in here before anybody sees you. Have any trouble at the border?"

Juan Lopez gingerly placed his bag on the floor and slumped down in the one overstuffed chair in the room. "Oh yeah. Big fight. Rain. Agents. I think they were agents. I don't know. Coulda been their own guys fighting with each other over control of that piece of the border. Not sure. But when they started shooting, the convoy driver told me to get out of there. So they went one way, I went the other. I just ran for my life."

"But you made it. And the car?" Carlos asked.

"I did what you said. As soon as I got across, I checked the map and found the rental car you had stashed in that border town. But it was okay. It all worked out okay. Sorry it took a while to get here."

"You look like you could use some cleanin' up. There's a shower in there and we've got some extra clothes. We'll find a Laundromat somewhere later. Go get yourself ready because we just got our orders."

"From the Fixer?" Juan asked.

"Yep."

"What about the tools, the stuff we need to pull it off?" Juan asked.

"We've got it all," Carlos said. "The first two jobs went like clockwork. The parts we need now are stashed in the trunk of our car. We'll make a dry run first."

"Good idea," Juan said. "The Fixer told me that as soon as the signal comes, we'll have just a day or two to make things happen. You know how he is, always looking for fast action on his ideas." He pointed down at his bag. "And he got some special equipment, canisters or something from a special place. Iran, I think. He told me to be very careful and to bring them here. We're not supposed to use them until he gives us the word."

"What's in them?" Simon asked.

"I'm not sure. But they're inside some heavy cases. I almost didn't make it across the border because I had to carry these things. Rossi said to guard them with my life and to store them in a safe place until he gives us instructions. So, where should I put them?"

"We'll keep them in the trunk of my car with the other equipment, the new explosives we picked up and everything else we need. I think we can fit it all in," Carlos said. "Tomorrow we'll turn in your car. We should all stay together in one car anyway."

Juan shrugged. He was tired, hungry, and his arms still ached. All he wanted right now was a hot shower, some decent food, and a good bed. He wasn't sure if he had made the right decision to come up here and take on this assignment. Then again, when the powerful Diosdado Rossi recruited him and the others for this job, he knew it was a chance of a lifetime to make so much money he could quit his job on the oil rigs. He hated the grueling work in the fields, but it was the best-paying job he could find back home. Now this job could make him a small fortune and he'd be able to live anywhere he wanted.

He got up and headed toward the bathroom. "Just before I left, Rossi told me to tell you that you're doing a good job and if we keep going like we are, the price of gas, and probably oil, too, will hit the moon. That means more money for them, and so there'll be more money for us, too, at the end of the line."

"But when's the end?" Simon asked.

"Quit asking questions," Carlos said. "We'll know when the time comes." He shoved the pistol in his pocket and reminded his helpers, "Right now, we've got work to do."

"Missed you, Samantha," Tripp murmured as he took her into his arms.

"Missed me?" she replied. "It's only been one day."

"I know. You're getting to be a habit with me."

"There's an old song with those lyrics."

"See? Somebody else felt the same way."

She hesitated, enjoying the warmth of his arms, but then pulled away and led him to the kitchen of her condo. "Have you had anything to eat?"

"Eat? No. I've been so swamped, I haven't thought about it. Living on caffeine fixes these days."

"That'll never do," she said. "Here. I've got dinner." She took the tinfoil off a plate she had warming in the oven.

"What's this? Did you make it?"

"Nope. I don't have any time either. My friend's mom in Silver Spring gave it to me to take home."

"Sorry if you had to miss their dinner. It's just that I . . ."

"Let's sit down. You can tell me all about it." She motioned to the sideboard, where a bottle of wine sat opened on a coaster. "Bring the merlot and a couple of glasses."

They sat down at her small table by the window. "Now then," she said. "Talk to me."

Tripp looked into her deep green eyes. He felt a tether whenever he stared at her and their eyes met. A kind of string drawing them together. It was strange. Strange for him. He was used to being in total control, but now he often found himself waiting for her cues, taking her pulse, her mood, and going with the flow. He began to outline the situation.

"First of all, we just got a report in from our crews in the field. Both teams, the one in Oklahoma and the one in Kansas, came up with the same conclusion."

"Conclusion? You mean how the lines exploded."

"Uh-huh. You're not going to believe this. But in both cases, the explosions happened *inside* the lines."

"Inside?" she questioned, raising her voice. "But how is that possible? I figured it had to be some gang setting some dynamite or something aboveground. How in the world could they have exploded from the inside?"

"Beats the hell out of me."

"What are your engineers saying?"

"They're still analyzing the pipes. Or what's left of them. The explosions and fires really tore up a huge segment of the lines. People saw the fires from miles away. Well, we talked about that before. We've never had anything like this happen. Not in the history of GeoGlobal."

"They did sabotage gas lines in Mexico," Samantha volunteered.

"Yeah, but I heard that was an aboveground operation. It was pretty crafty, I'll give them that. But this. Jesus, Samantha, I'm racking my brain trying to figure it out. Then again, I'm not an engineer. I don't design pipelines. That's for the experts."

Samantha took a bite of the pot roast and thought for a moment. "I wonder."

"You've got some faraway look in your eyes. You wonder what?"

"I was just thinking." She shook her head. "No, that would mean an inside job. I mean inside the company."

"Inside job? What inside job? What are you talking about?"

"Pigs!"

"Pigs? You mean the little robots that crawl through the lines checking operations and cleaning up?"

"Sure. Pigs. You use them. Everybody uses them. They flow through the line along with the gas, kind of like bowling balls rolling down an alley, and they send signals back about how everything's working."

"I know we use them. I always wondered why they call them pigs, though."

"My dad used to talk about them. He says that when they go through the line, it sounds like a pig squealing."

"And you think that somebody put an explosive in one of our pigs and somehow got it inside the line?"

"Why not?" she asked. She paused as she took another bite. Then, waving her fork, she said, "Okay, now stay with me on this. Let's say that some guy, or a bunch of guys who know something about gas lines, somehow get hold of some pigs and they figure out a way to put an explosive device along with a timer or something inside. They stick them in the pipe at one of your pig-launching stations, which you've probably got all along the lines. So they launch them and then run away. Somewhere down the line, the pig explodes and causes a huge fireball and you're . . ."

"Screwed!" he said. "Jesus! Do you really think something like that could happen?"

"Give me a better explanation," she challenged.

He took a gulp of wine, sat back, and crossed his arms. "I don't know. It all sounds so far-fetched. I mean, first you've got to have people who know what the hell they're doing. Then they've got to get the pigs. I mean, you don't just buy them at Wal-Mart or something."

"No, but you've got them in your warehouses, right?" she said. "For starters, how about a company-wide inspection of all your properties, especially in Oklahoma and Kansas? Well, make that nationwide. I mean, if these people were smart enough to get inside your facilities, get maps of your lines and steal some pigs, wire them up and get them inside your lines, the question is, how many *more* have they got?"

"Christ! You're right." He ran his fingers through his hair and swore again. He shoved his chair back so hard, it almost toppled over. He reached back and caught it before it hit the floor. "Sorry. But I've gotta make a call." He fished his cell phone out of his pocket and dialed a number. "Calling our control center. This is far out, but we've gotta check it out."

Tripp talked to their chief engineer and explained Samantha's theory. The engineer said he had thought about the pigs, but dismissed the idea, calculating that they were way too sophisticated for a bunch of terrorists to figure out. Then again, if Tripp wanted an inspection done, he'd get on it immediately and report back as soon as possible. Tripp shoved the phone back in his pocket.

Samantha had cleared their plates and was loading the dishwasher when Tripp came into the kitchen. "Inspection's under way. Trouble is, if they find out some of the pigs are missing, there'll be hell to pay with our security and we still won't have any idea who took them and where they might strike next. That is, if there is a next time."

"Looks like you'll have more to do than just an inspection," Samantha said, carefully lining up the wineglasses in the dishwasher.

"What do you mean?"

"How about an inspection, or surveillance if you will, of *all* your employees? E-mail? Phone calls?"

"You think it could have been some of *our* people? You can't mean that."

She turned to face him. "Look, I have no idea who's doing this, but I think we're agreed that it wasn't just faulty maintenance. It's sabotage. And sabotage means a threat to the country. At least parts of the country. And sabotage could mean threats to a lot more people, their jobs, their lives if we don't figure out what's happening here."

"I know you're right. It's just that I can't fathom why anyone who works for us would blow up his own livelihood. I mean, what are the chances that we have terrorists on the payroll of GeoGlobal, for God's sake?"

"Probably slim, I admit. But we've got to check out every possible lead here. You know that."

"So I get the company to review e-mail and phone records. That'll probably end in lawsuits over privacy and all that crap."

"What choice do you have? The company has a right to check e-mail of its own employees, you know. It's not like you're the phone companies we asked to help us after 9/11."

"Thank God for small favors."

"I know. But we've simply got to get to the bottom of this before any more lines get blown up. And before any more firemen die or other people freeze to death."

"Look, Samantha. Come sit down. I've got more to tell you."

"More?"

"Yes." He took her hand and led her back into the living room. He pulled her down next to him on the couch and put his arm around her. "Come here. I miss you already."

"What do you mean? I'm right here," she said, snuggling in closer.

"I have to take a trip."

"A trip? Where?"

"To Venezuela."

"Venezuela? You mentioned that once before. But why now? It's the Christmas season. I was going to invite you to . . ."

"To what?" he asked.

"The Senior Staff Christmas party in the East Room."

"At the White House?"

"Sure. The President and First Lady will be there. It's a nice affair. And well, I thought you might like to come with me. It's next week."

"Damn. There is nothing I would rather do than stay here and be with you. Party sounds great, but I don't think I'll be here that long. It's not like I want to go. But we talked about how their crazy president is threatening to take over our last oil and gas division down there."

"Yes, I know. They've nationalized just about everything already."

"Just about. I think they still need some people in the fields who actually know what the hell they're doing though. The head of our South American operations has been talking to them, trying to stave this off, but they keep making puny offers for our facilities and it's getting dicey. We have a hell of an investment in that country. We don't want to have to write it all off. Besides, we need the oil. And if they take it over, they'll screw it up for sure."

"When would you have to leave?"

"Not sure. I'm waiting to hear back. Oh, and that's not all."

"There's more?" she said, raising her troubled eyes to his.

"The hearings."

"You mean the congressional hearings on the gas lines?"

"They're trying to schedule them."

"Will you have to testify?"

"I'll get the testimony in order, but if I have to head south, we've got Godfrey Nims. He's our chief lobbyist and a very bright guy. Then again, they may demand that our CEO, somebody higher up on the food chain, come before the committee so they can have a really high-profile officer to beat up. They usually do."

"I heard that they might have a hearing pretty soon, but now you're saying you might have leave before that?"

"As I said, I'm just not sure yet." He stood up, pulling her up with him. "So what say we don't waste what little time we have now."

She leaned into him, raising her mouth for the kiss she knew was coming. It was long, deep. She loved his mouth, his tongue, the way he held her in an almost viselike grip. With all the tensions in her life, being in his arms was turning out to be the one place she felt safe. Protected. Almost cherished. But now that she'd found him, he was about to leave her.

Suddenly, he picked her up and started to walk back to her bedroom. Nobody had picked her up since she was about four years old. Now this man who had so captured her imagination over a decade ago was carrying her through her condo. It was obvious where they would end up. She didn't object. Why would she? Maybe she'd only really known him a short while. And yet, she felt she had known him for years, starting back at Princeton when she had fantasized about a moment just like this. She leaned her head against his neck as he gently deposited her on top of her green and white comforter. She lay against the shams and throw pillows that were arranged in front of a carved walnut headboard.

He lay down next to her and took her in his arms once more. "I want you, Samantha. I've wanted you since the first day I laid eyes on you."

"Not at Princeton," she teased.

"Maybe I wasn't smart enough then to know what I wanted. But I know now."

He kissed her gently and then began to lift her sweater up. She raised her arms in subtle submission as he swept the garment over her head and tossed it to the side of the bed.

It had been a long time, such a long time since a man had treated her this way. A long time since a man, any man, had gotten this close to her. There had been no one. Not since Dexter. She had a fleeting thought about the framed photograph on the coffee table. Tripp had never asked. She had never volunteered. She knew she'd tell him sometime. But not now. Now she wanted to feel again. Revel again in the sensations building up where he was touching her.

Their clothes were off, the comforter was pulled back. They were lying together on cool white sheets. He kissed her again, and then his mouth left hers and trailed down to savor her entire body. Wherever he touched her, her skin tingled and itched at the same time. Wherever he teased or taunted her, she felt a mosaic of emotions. Wanting, wishing, craving, almost crying. His moves were slow, tender, tantalizing, and driving her crazy.

She reached for him, pulled his mouth up to hers, and whispered, "Now. Please."

That was all he needed. He levered himself over her, staring down at the beautiful green eyes, clouded with desire, the outstretched arms beckoning him. He fisted his hand in her hair and covered her body with his. They moved together, slowly at first, then gaining momentum until he felt her muscles contract and heard her call out his name.

They lay together, entwined on tangled sheets, damp, spent, but breathing evenly. He had shifted his weight to one side but his arms still held her close. She felt his heart beating slower now and while he slept, she lay there wondering. What would happen next? When would he leave her? When would she see him again? As she turned and gently kissed his shoulder, she realized that she had absolutely no idea.

"Did you see this report from the American Drug Czar?" the Fixer asked, holding open the door to the Presidential limousine.

"Of course, I saw it. Drug Czar. The Americanos give their people fancy titles, but in truth, they are powerless to do their jobs."

"How right you are. It says here that this man, who carries out something called their National Drug Control Policy, told the press that the drug cartels are using our ports to ship cocaine to Europe."

El Presidente climbed into the backseat and mumbled, "So?"

The Fixer followed him, put his briefcase on the floor, and quoted from the article, "And the number of flights from Venezuela suspected of ferrying Colombian cocaine to Haiti, the Dominican Republic, and other transfer points have increased by a hundred and sixty-seven percent in the last year."

El Presidente chuckled. "And what does it say they're going to do about it?"

"Nothing. They do complain a lot though."

The driver pulled away from the palace and headed through the teeming city, surrounded by security teams in front and behind the limo.

"Let them complain," the President continued. "As long as we get our cut, why should we be bothered because their people are so stupid they buy every drug that hits their streets? Of course the flights are increasing. It's big business."

"Speaking of flights, I have a meeting this afternoon when we get back. It's with the Iranian ambassador about the Caracas-Tehran route."

"What about it?"

"It's going well. Our Conviasa Airlines and Iran Air have a new code-sharing agreement. We are going to be talking about increasing the number of direct flights between our cities."

"Good news, wouldn't you say?"

"Indeed. And in my meeting, I have a few more ideas about increased trade with Iran. I won't bore you with the details. Just trust me on this one."

"I always trust you, my friend," El Presidente said.

"And speaking of trust, since our little project to raise gas prices and create a bit of havoc up in the States is going so well, I've decided that next week, I will use our field office for a while. We have worked out our signals. I will be monitoring the location of all of your speeches. I'll know when to contact our agents. I think it's probably wise for me to handle all of these details and stay out of sight for a while. After all, we want you to have, how do they call it? Oh yes. Plausible deniability."

The President's mouth curved into a half smile. "Yes. That would be wise. I am watching the price fluctuations and seeing all of the reactions on CNN. The stupid Americanos have no idea what is happening in their country. Their Congress will hold hearings but they'll never figure it out. We are too clever with our scheme." He turned to the Fixer. "Your scheme, which is brilliant. They think they are so superior. We will teach them who is superior, who has the natural resources, who will benefit when the price goes through the roof. They can afford to pay. Our people will reap the benefits. Yes, it is a brilliant plan."

"And I have a few more ideas about how to make this even more effective," the Fixer said. "But, as we are agreed, you don't need to be bothered with the details. You can just leave it to me."

"By the way," the President asked, "is there anything new on the negotiations with GeoGlobal? Are they finally seeing the light?"

"Their President for South America, Victor Aguilar, may know his business but he doesn't know ours. He keeps refusing our offer for their operations."

"What's the next step?"

"I hear they may be sending down some negotiator from the States."

"Good. Let him come. We still won't change our position. Even if they ask for arbitration like ExxonMobil did, that will take years to settle. I am not concerned. It will cost them money. Meanwhile, we take their oil and gas and get even higher prices for it all, thanks to all of your plans."

The Fixer pulled on his pristine white cuffs and wiped a speck of lint from his navy blue suit. As their motorcade moved to the out-skirts of the city, El Presidente glanced over and said, "You may be a bit overdressed for this stop."

"We won't be there long and, as I said, I have a meeting later this afternoon."

After several more minutes, the series of cars pulled up at a con-struction site down the road from the La Planta jail where hundreds of prisoners were crowded into small cells.

"We can't stop at La Planta," the Fixer remarked as they pulled up to the new site. "We'd cause another riot. We had enough of those last month."

"Why would we want to? We don't need to spend time with that scum. Nothing but gangs and common criminals over there." The Pres-ident's bodyguards swarmed around the car and opened his door to the jarring sounds of hammers, shouts, and the incessant beeping of trucks backing up to the side of the building. "I just want to see some progress on this new jail. I figure if they know their president is watching, they will finish up on schedule in the next few weeks. We may need this place if those students decide to protest the elections."

"Yes, sir. It's a good strategy."

As soon as they emerged from the limo, workers began to wave and cheer. A dozen men scurried down a scaffolding, others raced outside still holding their tools. They all started to crowd around and shout his name. The bodyguards formed a line in front of the President and tried to hold them back. The President smiled and waved back. "These are my people. See how they love me?" he said.

The Fixer surveyed the chaotic scene and then stepped back to allow the President to be the sole center of attention. The foreman pushed forward to shake hands. The President slapped him on the back, chatted about the progress on the building, and waved for the workers to quiet down. "I come here to see your fine work. You are making good progress. You are all part of my plan. My plan to lock up the people who would do you harm." The men nodded and began to cheer. The President shouted over the din. "I want no harm to come to you. You work hard. I work hard for you. Today. Every day. You are with me?" They shouted and chanted his name as the midday sun beat down, reflecting waves of heat radiating off the bright concrete.

"I must go now. Keep up the good work and tell your families that I came to you today to tell you how much I appreciate your labor. Your labor for your country." He turned, waved once more, and headed back toward his limo.

The Fixer moved in lockstep with him and murmured, "Your decision to nationalize the cement industry last year meant that we could advance the schedule here and add another story." He pointed to the top floor of the four-story building.

"Yes, and if we do have protests, there will be plenty of space to lock up the students until well after the elections."

One of the bodyguards opened the back door to the limo, and the two men ducked inside. Looking out the window, the Fixer said, "And with this new facility, nobody can accuse us of inhumane conditions."

The President leaned back against the soft leather seat and laughed. "Hardly. This is no El Dorado prison."

"And there is no Henri Charrière to write another *Papillon*."

"Ah, the movie."

"Yes, from the biography. You know that *'papillon'* means butterfly."

"I assure you, my friend, that no one, and I mean no one, will fly away from my prisons. Not while I am in charge."

"So, Greg, here's what I think we should do." Samantha was briefing the White House Homeland Security team on the gas line situation at their regular morning staff meeting. "After two explosions, caused by something *inside* the lines, GeoGlobal will be inspecting every one of their warehouses to see if any of their equipment is missing, things that might have been used inside the lines."

"Wait a minute," Greg said, "you're saying that something inside the line exploded and that caused the lines to flare? Again, it sounds to me like GeoGlobal has a big problem on their hands. It's not on our hands."

"But Greg, GeoGlobal didn't do anything to blow up their own lines. That's absurd. This has never happened before."

"There's a first time for everything," Greg said.

"No. I believe it was deliberate sabotage, and if somebody or some group is sabotaging a major energy source in our country, I believe this *is* a concern of ours. Or at least it should be. So, while the company is checking their own operations on the ground, I have an idea of how we can help to prevent another attack, if, God forbid, there's another one in the works."

"And what would that be, Miss Sherlock?" Greg said derisively.

"I believe we should utilize our domestic satellites to focus on their entire network of lines throughout the South and Midwest. We could get MASINT from the satellites. We could overlay suspicious activity against a map of pipeline locations."

"Now, wait just a damn minute," Greg said, raising his voice. "You think they're going to let us get measurement and signature intelligence from our domestic satellite program? I told you before that you were overreacting to this whole situation. We've got real threats to the country that we should be working on. As for your idea of using our satellites, do you even have a clue the kind of firestorm you will create?" He looked around the table and shook his head. "Pardon the pun, but I'm serious here. Do you have any idea how hard certain members of Congress will come down on us if we even suggest using our domestic satellites? They'll call it domestic spying and say that we don't have enough legal safeguards. They'll ask for detailed plans and programs of how we intend to coordinate with local law enforcement. We'd have to create working groups, a top-down nightmare, and assure them that the satellites wouldn't be used to intercept communications, but only to watch simple things like gas lines."

"But," Samantha tried to interrupt.

"No buts, Samantha. You've never had to deal with the National Applications Office. That's the place that gives access to satellite imagery, but it's designed for domestic emergency response, security, things like that. Not to babysit some company's property. Get real and follow the rules for once!" he bellowed. He glanced around the room again. The other deputies looked somewhat taken aback by his outburst. He immediately lowered his voice and added, "Samantha works hard, but sometimes she needs to contain her enthusiasm."

Yes, and when I was a kid, I never colored within the lines either, she thought. She felt her temper rising. She looked at her colleagues and didn't see any potential allies among the other deputies, only faces shifting back and forth between her and Greg. It felt like some surreal tennis game and she had just lost match point.

After her discussion with Tripp last night, she knew his company was all over this problem. They would be sweeping through their buildings, warehouses, offices, checking e-mails and phone logs, trying to find any possible connection between their employees or their equipment, or loss of equipment, and the disastrous blowups that now had left thousands of their customers in freezing conditions as the winter storms continued to rage in several states. She wondered how many more people would try to stay in their homes. How many more hospitals, nursing homes, hospices, schools, factories would have to stay closed and for how long before they got the lines repaired and flowing again.

Worst of all, she wondered how many more explosions it would take before bureaucrats like Gregory Barnes woke up and realized that they had a real crisis on their hands and it could get real ugly if they sat on their hands right now.

She sat there in complete frustration as Greg moved on to his next issue. Some nuclear components had been confiscated from a ship off the West Coast. Since her portfolio included nuclear as well as energy issues, Samantha was forced to pay attention, take notes, and put aside her plea for help.

"Those staff meetings are like drawing on Etch-a-Sketch," Samantha said, skirting around Joan's desk to get back to her own office.

Her assistant looked up from her computer. "What do you mean?"

"Just when I think I've got a good idea and a good design, Greg comes along and shakes the box."

"Oh jeez. Again? What was it this time?"

"I want to use our domestic satellites to watch for any kind of strange activity around GeoGlobal's gas lines."

"Sounds like a good idea to me," Joan said.

"Not to Greg. He's afraid of objections from Congress, lawsuits, bureaucratic hassles and all of that."

"So how are we going to preempt another attack, if there is one, I mean?"

"Exactly!" Samantha let out an exasperated breath. "He treats me like the Energizer bunny or Robocop or something."

"Sorry, I don't follow that one," Joan said.

"I mean, I stand up there and Greg just knocks me down."

"But hey, the whole point is that you always bounce back."

"It seems like it's getting harder and harder." Samantha glanced down at Joan's desk. "So what's this?"

"Oh, it's a memo from the East Wing. They're planning a welcoming ceremony for the Moroccan President and they can never find enough Moroccans to round up to make it a decent photo op, so they've invited the support staff to be in the audience."

"In this weather?" Samantha asked.

"Well, it's tomorrow, so maybe it'll warm up a little bit."

"I wouldn't count on it. But if you want to go out on the South Lawn and watch another motorcade arrive, just be sure to take your heavy coat."

"Will do. Come to think of it, didn't we have issues with Morocco a while back?"

Samantha paused. "Well, I remember the story about the King of Morocco signing a pact with Libya, way back when Libya was a huge problem for us. Our ambassador to Morocco evidently wasn't paying attention or something and didn't know about the pact."

"But isn't that what ambassadors are supposed to know about?" Joan asked.

"You would think," Samantha replied. "Anyway, it was kind of a mess. But that was a long time ago. Now with Libya coming over to our side, more or less, and Morocco trying to help out on the whole terrorism front, well, I guess it's time to play nice. But not too nice."

"Makes sense. The memo said it wasn't a full state visit, so there's no big dinner, no joint press conference, just a lunch or something, so I kinda wondered."

"Yes, I heard it would be a lower-profile visit," Samantha said. "And speaking of lower profiles, guess that's what I'm supposed to maintain right now. But darn it all. I just can't." She turned, went into her office and quietly closed the door.

She was poring over papers and memos trying to figure out whether she should call another meeting of her Crisis Action Team when Joan buzzed her. "Mr. Princeton on line one."

Samantha grabbed the phone. "Tripp?"

"Hi Samantha. I've been waiting to get hold of you. Figured your staff meeting would be over by now. Look, there's a helluva lot going on right now. But first, I wanted to say . . . about last night . . ."

She held her breath. What would he say? Would he hint that it was some kind of mistake? Something too much, too soon? Would he figure out a way to back off for a while now that he won the race, so to speak? She tried to push her doubts away, wondering why women seemed to have second thoughts after a night of incredible sex with a great guy, especially after a first night like last night. "Yes?" she asked tentatively.

"You were terrific, and I just want you to know that."

She let out a breath. She hadn't even realized she was holding her breath. "Thanks. I could say the same for you. It's been a while, and I . . ."

"Let's not try to analyze it. Just wanted to call and tell you that. Well, that and a lot of other things. Another crisis, I'm afraid."

"What?"

"Just had a call from Operations and there's been another huge pressure drop on our southern Missouri line."

"Oh no. Was it another attack?"

"Looks like it might be. I'm on hold right now. I just dialed your number from my cell while they're checking it out. Can you hang on for a minute?"

"Sure." She pressed the phone tightly to her ear, straining to hear what was going on in Tripp's office. She heard his voice and then suddenly she heard him shout, "Jesus! Are you sure? My God! Our people are on the way? Okay. Get back to me.

"Samantha. It's another explosion," Tripp blurted into the phone. "It's bad. Really bad. I don't have all the details, but I should have more pretty soon. Can you believe this? Three in three states?"

"Have your people figured out anything about the pigs or any reports from the inspections? Anything at all?"

"They're working on that. But it takes time. They're doing a complete inventory and our security people are all over the e-mails, logs, maintenance reports, everything. They say the home office looks like another Hurricane Ike hit it."

"I've got to get our people more involved," Samantha said. "I've got a Crisis Action Team monitoring things, but we've got to kick this into high gear around here."

"I wish you would. We could use any help you can give us. Oh, and now with this, well, can you imagine what the hearings are going to be like next week?"

"They're set? For sure?" she asked.

"That's the word. With this latest attack, I'm sure our CEO will try to get another delay so we can gather more evidence. But you know the Hill."

"Absolutely. If there's a headline to be had, they want their names in it."

"You got that one right. And there's one more thing."

"More?" she asked.

"And this is really a bummer. I've got to leave for Venezuela."

She felt her entire mood heading farther south. He was leaving her. And right in the middle of a huge crisis. A crisis on her watch and in her department. "When?"

"Tonight. Well, late tonight out of Dulles. Look, with all that's going on, I'll be in pretty bad shape by the end of the day. But I still want to see you before I go. I'll have to pack and all, but still . . ."

She thought for a moment and made a suggestion. "I could pick up something for dinner and bring it to your place and we could talk while you pack. I mean, maybe that would help your schedule. What do you think?"

"I'd think you were an angel," he said. "Are you sure? Your staff must be going crazy too, right?"

She thought about Greg and his constant objections to her constant warnings. "Well, they will now. I'm sure of that. But about tonight, what say I drive over there around 7:30 or so. I know where Turnberry Tower is. I can see it from my place, remember?"

"I remember everything I've seen at your place," he said in a soft tone. "Oh, wait. Quick. Do you have a TV set in your office?"

"Yes. Why?"

"Turn it on. CNN. Right now."

She reached for the remote and flicked on the small set perched on a bookcase along the wall. The CNN news anchor was saying, "And this just in to our newsroom. A massive explosion in southwest Missouri set off a giant fireball that ignited a series of buildings and tank cars in the vicinity. Our correspondent Keneesha Jackson is on the scene and has details."

Samantha stared at the screen and sat upright when she saw flames shooting several stories high, engulfing a series of factories and what looked like boxcars on a nearby siding. "This massive fire near Interstate 44 in southwest Missouri is believed to have been started when a gas line feeding into this industrial complex exploded a short while ago. Three maintenance workers who had been on the overnight shift were just pronounced dead at the scene, while several others have been taken to a nearby hospital. Local firemen continue to battle the blaze, but their efforts are being hampered by high winds and freezing temperatures. The names of those killed and injured in the fire are being withheld pending notification of next of kin. This is Keneesha Jackson reporting for CNN."

"Three killed?" Samantha practically shouted into the phone.

"This is the biggest goddamn nightmare I could imagine," Tripp said. "Look, I gotta go. Phones are going wacko. See what you can do. And hopefully, we'll hook up tonight. Call me from your cell when you're on your way over, okay?"

"Will do." Samantha shoved the phone down, bolted up from her chair, and raced into Greg's office.

Harvey Walker scurried down the stone hallway of the Senate Hart Office Building. The halls usually emptied out on Thursday nights as members headed back to their states for weekend politicking. Now with the gas line attacks, the stock market dive, and the press demands to "do something," everyone was staying at the Capitol trying to appear relevant.

He passed a series of offices, all with walls of glass overlooking a ninety-foot-high atrium lined with trees planted in black pots that matched the gigantic black iron sculpture in the center. The contraption was called "Mountains and Clouds" and featured a bunch of jagged pieces of steel over fifty feet high topped with floating pieces of aluminum that were supposed to be clouds. He had heard that the cloud apparatus weighed over two tons, and he always worried that the darn thing would come crashing down one day. The whole thing was painted jet black, and instead of it looking anything like real mountains or real clouds, Harvey thought it kind of looked as if a bunch of medieval monks had hacked up the starship *Enterprise.*

He continued down the hall until he came to the office of Cassidy Jenkins, the Senator from Oregon. As Chairman of the Energy and Natural Resources Committee, she had turned out to be his nemesis on a whole host of issues. He felt she was beholden to her environmentalists, who kept pushing for more bans on oil and gas drilling and an increase in support for most anything else. As the senior senator from the state of Oklahoma, Harvey didn't feel beholden to anybody, but he was sure he knew more about the oil and gas business than she did, and right now he was fuming about her plans for the hearing. He figured a little personal diplomacy might stave off the worst. He barged inside.

"Good afternoon, Senator Walker," the receptionist chirped. "Senator Jenkins is expecting you. Please go right in." Of course he would go right in. What else did he ever do? He opened the door to an office with a navy blue and gold rug on the floor, a blue and gold couch along the back wall, and two gold wingback chairs in front of a massive mahogany desk. Behind the desk were two flags, an American flag on the left and the flag of the state of Oregon on the right.

"Hello, Harvey. Glad you stopped by. Guess we should go over plans for the big hearing," Cassidy Jenkins said as she swiveled her dark brown leather chair around to face him. Wearing a black-and-white striped blouse, the petite woman with mouse-brown hair looked sort of pert. Petite and pert. Kind of like an overage cheerleader. But Harvey always thought she was cheering for the wrong team.

He sat down in one of the gold chairs. *Figure she's just got left-wing chairs in here,* he mused to himself. "Right you are, Cas. I think we need a slight postponement. And as I look at your lineup of witnesses, I'm concerned."

"Concerned about what?" she asked, and added "this time," under her breath.

"It looks to me like you might try to use this dog and pony show to rake our boys over the coals instead of trying to figure out how to stop obvious acts of sabotage to our energy supplies."

"Rake our boys over the coals? Is that how you see my efforts to rein in the profits that *your* boys are making these days? We may have someone trying to sabotage those lines, but all that's doing is driving up the price of natural gas, which means higher profits for *your boys.*"

"All it's doing? People have been killed, Cas. People are freezing and dying in my state. More have died in neighboring states and all you think about is the price of natural gas?"

"Look, Harvey, I'll consider somewhat of a delay, but the hearing will give us all a chance to quiz the head of GeoGlobal along with two other companies. They can tell us what happened to their lines. And if it really is sabotage, well, that's a job for the FBI and local law enforcement. Our job is to ensure an adequate energy supply for the entire country, and it doesn't look to me like your gas buddies are able to provide it, now, does it?"

"Wait a minute, Cas. Our boys have been breaking their backs trying to drill for oil and gas all over the place to meet the demand. Drilling where you let them, that is."

"Breaking their backs? I'd call it breaking the banks. The piggy banks of their customers. In fact, I'm recommending legislation that would repeal eighteen billion in tax incentives and use that money for solar, wind, and ethanol production."

"Ethanol?" he snorted. "Give me a break. We've had this discussion before. You know full well that it takes almost as much energy to produce a gallon of ethanol as the energy that comes out the other end. It's been driving up the price of food for years now. And, by the way, when *your people* talk about global warming, well, this whole ethanol fiasco is adding to the problem with farmers taking down forests and planting corn. But if you really wanted more ethanol in this country, you'd vote to get rid of all of the tariffs. We could buy ethanol cheaper from Brazil than we can produce it here. But no, too many members in the Senate are more concerned about the farm vote, so you keep out the imports. You *know* this, Cas. Why in the world are you still pushing this nonsense?"

"It's not nonsense. It works. Besides, we've been talking for years about how we're sending billions to the Saudis for their oil. Now, wouldn't you like to cut that bill with conservation and other alternatives? Lord knows what terrorist groups they support with all that oil revenue." She sat back and folded her arms across her chest.

"Okay. I agree we pay too much to too many bad guys, including Mexico and Venezuela, too. But we wouldn't have to if we'd just let our guys drill where the oil and gas happen to be. And that doesn't just mean those leases from years back. At least some people are finally dealing with this particular issue, but it isn't enough."

Senator Jenkins glanced at her watch. "Look, I've got some constituents coming in here in a few minutes. Let me just say that I've taken note of your position. You'll have ample opportunities to question the CEOs."

Harvey started to get up. "Fine. But I want to say that what we ought to be doing now is figuring out how to help our own producers, especially when it looks like we may have a new bunch of ecoterrorists on our hands."

"Who said anything about *eco*terrorists?" she demanded.

"So we don't know for sure. But let's try to find out who's blowing up our lines before they blow up any more of our people." He headed for the door and added in a softer tone, "Let's just try to work together for once." And with that, he turned and headed out.

Gregory Barnes strode through the West Wing reception area and down the short hallway to the office of the National Security Advisor. Ken Cosgrove had summoned him to a meeting and he wasn't sure why. He slicked his hair back and walked up to the secretary's desk. "I've got a meeting with Ken," he said, though he was sure that Wilma, the ever-efficient assistant, knew all about it.

"Yes, Mr. Barnes. Let me see if he's free." She picked up her phone and buzzed the NSC Advisor. "Mr. Barnes to see you, sir." She nodded and replaced the handset. "You may go in now."

Greg opened the tall mahogany door and walked into the large corner office with windows on two sides, a wall of bookshelves to the left, a desk in front of the back wall, and a small round conference table with four chairs in the right-hand corner.

Ken came around his desk and motioned for Greg to sit down at the table. The usually unflappable NSC Advisor looked somewhat distracted today as he pulled up a chair and tossed a series of memos on the table. "I wanted to talk to you about these three pipeline explosions. The President is extremely concerned. We're being besieged by members of Congress from all over the country, not only Oklahoma, Kansas, and Missouri. Now it seems that every member of the House and Senate Energy Committees, Homeland Security Committee, and even the Foreign Relations Committee thinks he might know who's attacking our energy supplies. It ranges from Al Qaeda, of course, to Mexican rebels to Islamic groups from Trinidad, Tobago, and Guyana."

"You mean the guys we arrested for that plot to blow up the fuel lines going into Kennedy Airport a few years ago?" Greg asked.

"Well, some people think they may be trying to do something like that again. Only this time, hitting the Heartland. And then there are others who think it's some type of environmental freakos. What we want to know is what *you* know so far about this crisis? And believe me, it *is* a crisis."

Greg shifted in his chair and adopted his most serious gaze. "You are absolutely right. I've been concerned from the beginning. My deputy in charge of energy and nuclear threats has convened a Crisis Action Team. Actually, I had her set it up after the very first explosion. Never hurts to be on top of the situation."

"Good thinking," Ken said.

"And she has people from Energy, Transportation, CIA, FBI, and a few others on board. They've all been on it since day one, checking sources, working with local law enforcement. I don't believe she asked a member of your staff to sit in on those initial meetings. We know you have a full plate of international issues you're dealing with now, with the Moroccans in town and all."

"Forget the Moroccans. We're talking about Americans here. The very first job of the President is to protect the country. That's the turkey on the platter. All the rest of it is parsley as far as I'm concerned."

"Yes. Of course, you're right."

"So, as head of our Homeland Security operation, I want to know what specific steps you're taking. The Crisis Action Team is a good first effort, but obviously, we've got to get on top of this, find out who's attacking our lines and causing death and destruction in our heartland."

"Right. Absolutely right," Ken said, leaning forward in an earnest pose. "As you know, we've been working on a whole host of issues. The mall threat, the Metro bomber, the possible dirty bomb off Charleston, the nuclear components on the West Coast. Our people are working with all the agencies on all of these problems."

"Yes, we know. And we have to keep working to preempt future threats. But the gas lines are being blown up *now*. People are dying *now*. The elderly are freezing *now*. And since nobody in the entire government seems to have a line on who is responsible, we've got to ratchet this up to the highest levels."

"Of course. Of course," Greg said. "Actually, I do have an idea of something we could do in terms of our investigations and surveillance."

"What is it?" Ken asked.

"I was just thinking that we could request MASINT from our domestic satellites. What I mean is, we could get measurement signature intelligence, and if we pick up any suspicious activity, we overlay that on a map of the country's pipeline locations. With that type of intel, we might be able to identify the perpetrators. It may not forestall another attack, but it would certainly give us a leg up."

"Excellent idea!" Ken said. "I'll put through that request immediately. Meanwhile, as for your deputy's action team, that would be Samantha Reid, right?"

"Yes. Samantha."

"Bright lady, that one."

"She certainly is. I brought her here from my staff at Energy."

"Yes. I seem to remember that. Have her include my deputy in her next meeting. I want to be kept totally up to speed on this issue."

"Will do."

"Oh, and send me a summary of Samantha's efforts to date. I'll be briefing the President first thing tomorrow." He pushed his chair back, effectively ending the meeting. As Greg walked to the door, Ken added, "Let's just pray there are no more explosions."

25

Samantha drove her jeep out of the garage and headed down K Street. She was going to pick up some dinner items at the deli, take them to Tripp's place, see where he lived, and then discuss the disastrous developments of the last few days. After three explosions, she was scared that some new breed of terrorist was roaming around the country. She was frustrated with the bureaucracy and worried sick that more Americans could be killed. She had worked on national security issues for quite some time now, but they had always seemed somewhat removed, more general, almost amorphous. This time the threats and the deaths were very real and the whole issue was right there in her own White House directorate. She felt a personal responsibility to the President, to her colleagues, to the people they were all trying to protect. It was a huge weight. One that kept her up at night analyzing data, searching for answers, reviewing strategies. She hadn't slept well in days. Not since the first attack, when she saw the video of a nurse carrying tiny babies out of that hospital in Okla-homa. She had prayed they all had survived.

She had talked to her dad about the situation and told him how she felt. He had reminded her that she had a real opportunity to make a difference here, that most people never had that chance, and he also told her to hang tough when dealing with the various levels of gov-ernment. "You can do this, Samantha. I know you can," he had said. But could she? Tripp had been a great help, a sounding board, a kind of partner in this race to find the bad guys, but now he was leaving and she'd be very much alone . . . again.

She drove down the street and noticed the marquee at the movie theater across from Washington Harbor. They were showing a new movie, *Mutant Zombie Vampires from the Hood.* She shook her head and wondered who in the world went to movies like that. She cer-tainly wouldn't be going to movies anytime soon. No, she had a crisis to deal with. She wondered if she also had a crisis of confidence. At least Tripp didn't think so. He had been terrific. In fact, their bud-ding relationship was the one thing that had kept her on a more or less even keel the last several days.

She thought about her last night with Tripp. How he had held her, kissed her, stroked her cheek, and run his fingers through her hair. She glanced at her watch. Seven o'clock. She'd better get a move on if she was going to get the food, drive across Key Bridge, find his apart-ment building, and spend much time at all before Tripp had to leave for Dulles Airport.

She was lucky to find a parking place near the deli. She jumped out of the car, locked the doors, and rushed in to pick up her order. The store specialized in Italian takeout and she thought some veal parme-san with a side of pasta might be a good bet. She gave the clerk her name, reached for a bottle of valpolicella from a shelf, and fished out her personal credit card. For this dinner, she decided she shouldn't use her government credit card, even though she might have argued that it was a business dinner. No chance. She remembered all the scan-dals about government employees being caught using their govern-ment cards for things like Internet dating, lingerie, and vacations, and knew she had to be purer than Caesar's wife in this job.

Back in the jeep, she slowly maneuvered through the Georgetown traffic, crossed Key Bridge, drove through two stoplights, and turned right on North Nash Street. There on the right side was Turnberry Tower with its sleek steel and blue glass façade and balconies off every one of the floors. Craning her neck, she guessed it had at least two dozen stories. Quite a contrast to buildings in Washington, where the legal height limit originally dictated that no building be higher than the Capitol. Then it was amended slightly, but still. There was nothing in D.C. higher than the Old Post Office, except for the Washington Monument, which didn't count as a building. There were lots of tall buildings in Virginia, but, *My God, this is huge,* she thought as she drove up to the porte cochere and saw a uniformed valet. *A valet and doorman? This is better than the Ritz-Carlton.*

She grabbed her purse and the takeout bag and slipped out of the car, with the valet taking her arm. "Welcome to Turnberry Tower," he said in a slightly British accent. *Where do they find these people? The manager of my building barely speaks English.*

She walked through the two-story lobby, past the concierge, and gave her name to the desk attendant, who pointed to a bank of elevators. She rode up in a private elevator to the eighteenth floor. As soon as the doors opened, she saw Tripp, standing there in gray slacks and a black sweater. His hair was slightly damp. *Must have just gotten out of the shower,* she thought. He swept her into his arms and she almost dropped the bag.

The kiss was hot, deep and urgent. "Could hardly wait to see you again, Sam," he said, gently touching her cheek. He looked down at the bag. "Here, let me take that. And give me your coat."

She followed him down the hall and into a European-style kitchen with modern cabinets, Miele stainless steel ovens, cooktop, microwave, and Sub-Zero refrigerator. It even had a stainless steel sink. "Wow. You could be a professional chef in this place," she said, running her hand over the gleaming white granite countertops.

"I guess. Except that I'm a lousy cook. All the units have this stuff. I only use the fridge and microwave, it seems." He opened the bag. "So what have we got here?"

"I was thinking about trussing a squab," she said, trying to sound lighthearted in spite of her mood, "but I brought veal parmesan and pasta instead. Is this okay?"

"Okay? It's perfect. I'll just warm it up a bit." He shoved the container into the microwave, opened a cabinet, and pulled out two plates.

She stared at the microwave. "This morning I was so rattled about the explosions that when I went to heat up my coffee, I punched my security code into my microwave. Sometimes I think I'm really losing it."

He chuckled. "Believe me, I know what you mean." He pulled a bottle out of the bag. "Oh, great, you brought wine, too. Lady after my own heart," he said. When the microwave dinged, he scooped the veal and pasta onto the plates and took some silverware from a top drawer. "Let's eat in the living room. I don't have a dining room table yet. Why don't you bring the wine? I've got glasses in there by the bar."

They walked into a cavernous space with ten-foot-high ceilings, black leather couches, a collection of Eames chairs, and sliding glass doors out to a massive terrace with expansive views over to Georgetown, downtown D.C., and the Capitol. "This place is incredible," Samantha said, scanning the room.

"They just finished the building a few months ago. I don't have enough stuff yet. I mean, the walls are pretty bare and with all the space in here, I'm not sure how to fill it up. Any ideas?"

She did a three-sixty and looked up at the ceiling. "Guess you could hang a mobile."

"C'mon, let's sit down. I don't really want to waste time with you talking about decorating." He put the plates on a glass coffee table in front of the couch.

"I know," Samantha said. "I hate to spoil the mood here, but we've got a real disaster on our hands. The White House is going nuts over this last attack. Well, they're going nuts over all of them now, and so am I."

"You should see our headquarters. We've got every conceivable engineer, security force, control room, supervisor, everyone down to the janitors working on this thing. This latest blowup was like the *Hindenburg* effect."

"What about the inventory?"

"You want the good news or the bad news?"

"Both, I guess," she said as she took a bite of her veal.

"They scoured every warehouse and facility in the country and figured out that there *are* some pigs missing, along with a bunch of maps showing our lines and pig insertion points."

"My God! They really used the pigs?" she exclaimed.

"Looks like your theory was right on the money."

"Is that the good news or the bad news?"

"Well, at least it tells us the how. We still don't know the who or the why."

"What about the number?"

"That's the bad news. There are seven missing."

"Seven! Oh no!" She dropped her fork and faced him. "You've had three attacks, so that means . . ."

"Four more? Maybe. Who the hell knows?" He opened the wine and poured several ounces into her goblet. "This is the biggest nightmare we've faced since I've been with the company. I mean, sure, I saw a lot of action in the Navy and then at Greyfield. Guys got killed. Countries got invaded. What I mean is that companies like Geo-Global haven't had actual sabotage on their facilities. Not in *this* country. We've got problems around the world. But here? Attacks on our own lines? Killing innocent people?" He ran his fingers through his hair. "And the worst of it is that we still don't have a clue how to protect ourselves. Our lines run all over the country. Those insertion points are all over the place, too. We can't police them all. We can't even police one. Not the whole line, I mean."

She put her hand on his arm and felt the tension in his muscles. "I know. Believe me, I know. When the first one exploded, I tried to get Greg to focus on it. He said it was probably just some maintenance issue."

"I thought he was in charge of threats to the country. Well, not him alone, but isn't that his job? To worry about things like this, get agency support and all of that?"

"Supposedly. Trouble is, Greg is usually just thinking about his next TV interview. I mean, even after the second attack, I kept talking about it, but I ended up feeling like the canary in the coal mine, except that Greg was topside and nobody was listening."

"What a jerk," Tripp said.

"I do have one thing to report though. Just between you and me."

He nodded and she went on. "We're going to be focusing some of our domestic satellites on areas closest to the most recent attacks along with places in nearby states. I've been screaming about using every surveillance tool we've got, and suddenly this afternoon Greg comes waltzing in and says that *he* got it all okayed." She rolled her eyes.

"Can you do that? I mean with privacy lawsuits and all that crap?" he asked, twirling some of the pasta onto his fork.

"Sure we can. Better to apologize later than ask permission, as they say," she responded.

"Right on! But even if they can photograph things going on out in the middle of nowhere on one of our lines, how will that help us to prevent the next attack? Doesn't it take time to analyze that stuff? Can it really help?"

"I don't know if it will, unless whoever is doing this makes a dry run or something. Then again, if there is another explosion, the satellites will obviously pick that up along with activity in the area. So hopefully they can track vehicles, bad guys, whatever. It may take a while to get it all set up, but at least we're on it."

"That's the first good news I've had all day."

"Right. There's been so much going on at the White House today, I'm amazed he even got that ball rolling."

"Yeah, I caught the news when I got home and saw that arrival ceremony for the Moroccan crowd. Kind of funny-looking outfits though."

"You mean all those fezzes?"

"Yeah. The South Lawn sort of looked like a Masons parade."

"Either that or a scene out of Dan Brown's long-promised new novel," she quipped.

"Sometimes I think that what we're going through right now could be in a novel." He reached for the wine bottle. "Here, have some more. Maybe it'll settle our nerves."

Settle her nerves? She was beginning to feel a bit of a buzz. Was it just the wine? Or was it the proximity of this man sitting so close to her that she could smell the soap he must have just used? It made her want to grab his shoulders with both hands and pull him to her so she could taste his mouth on hers, feel his arms around her, and make her forget about pipelines, explosions, satellites, and surveillance. But no, she knew she needed to put her emotions on cruise control. They had too many other things to talk about.

She picked up her wineglass and asked, "So tell me about this trip to Venezuela tonight."

He leaned back against the soft leather and sighed. "I feel like I'm heading into the People's Republic of Caracas. That damn dictator has put more qualifications on this deal, if you could even call it a deal. They're taking our property right when we've been exploring and gearing up to drill in what we think will be the most productive area in South America."

"The Orinoco Basin?"

"Yep. That one. So now they want to take our assets, our equipment, our transportation facilities and pay us pennies on the dollar for our investment. And I hear they'd rather bring in the Russians to drill it. Not us."

"But if it's a done deal, so to speak, why do you have to go?" she asked in a plaintive tone.

He set down his glass, took both of her hands in his, and gazed into her eyes. "The last thing I want to do is go down there. No, what I mean is, the last thing I want to do is to leave you. But the powers that be seem to think I might be able to eke out a few more concessions, especially if we offer to keep some of our experts down there as special contractors. The thing is, every time they nationalize an industry, production falls through the floor. They don't have a clue how to run our businesses. They just put some of their political hacks in charge and sure, production continues for a while, but then they just skim off any profits and El Presidente either uses them to buy off the peasants or stashes it in some offshore account for future reference."

"I wish our government had more sway with that guy."

"So do I. We can protest all we want to the international courts, ask for arbitration and all that bullshit, but it just costs all of us a bundle of legal fees while his people move in and take over anyway."

She thought for a moment. "So you've got meetings set up?"

"The head of our South American operations, Victor Aguilar, is a good guy, but headquarters thinks he doesn't have enough heft to really make a difference. So I drew the short straw for a meeting with Diosdado Rossi."

"Who's that?"

"The power behind the President. Everybody calls him the Enabler or Fixer or something like that. He's the kind of guy who seems to pull a lot of strings. Think Machiavelli with a Spanish accent."

"I don't exactly see their President as some sort of puppet."

"No, I don't mean that. I think the President gives orders and Rossi carries them out. But he's probably responsible for putting a lot of that garbage in the President's head in the first place. He's smart. He's calculating and he's gonna be a tough son of a bitch to deal with."

"With the travel and all, did you ever have a chance to get things ready for the hearings?"

"I tried. I put together a bunch of stats for our CEO. Then we got word late today that Senator Walker is trying to delay the hearing again until later next week to give us a chance to finish our investigations and get our act together. I hope to hell he can pull it off."

"Thank God for small favors," she said. "But now, when do you have to leave?"

"Flight leaves at eleven thirty. Guess I should be out of here by nine." He glanced at her and added, "Or maybe a bit later. It'll only take about a half an hour to get to Dulles from here. But since it's an international flight, well, you know how they want you there way in advance and all that nonsense."

"Have you packed yet?"

"Oh yeah. Did that as soon as I got home. I wanted to clear the evening to be with you," he said, pulling her close to him and lowering his mouth to hers.

He lingered. She felt languid. The tension from the day's events seemed to ebb a bit. But it was replaced by a different kind of restlessness. She knew the feeling well even though she had only experienced it recently. It happened every time she was near this man. She wanted him. She needed him, and yet he was leaving her. She stole a glance at her watch. Not much time.

As if he were reading her mind, he pulled her up from the couch, took her hand and led her down the hall to his bedroom. She made a mild protest.

"Come with me, Samantha. I know I have to leave, but . . ." He suddenly turned and yanked her to him, kissing her with such force, she could hardly breathe. He pushed her against the wall and pressed his body to hers. She could feel his rigidity, his strength, his weight as she leaned into him and he deepened the kiss. "Got to have you, Sam. Please."

He grabbed her arm and drew her into a room with a king-size bed, a couple of bedside tables, and windows looking out at the same cityscape, with the lampposts lining Key Bridge in the foreground and twinkling lights of Georgetown just beyond.

They had to hurry now. He yanked off his sweater, tossed his trousers toward the foot of the bed and watched as she shed her black slacks and green turtleneck. They tumbled onto the covers together, arms entwined, legs wrapped together, mouths connecting like urgent magnets. It was powerful, almost feverish in its intensity. As he kissed and stroked her, she arched to meet his touch. Her whole body ached for more, like an itch that only he could stop. But she didn't want him to stop. They moved together, faster, harder until he whispered, "Come with me, Sam." She arched once more and felt her soul shatter into sparks and spasms. She cried out and once again he pressed his mouth to hers.

"Shhh," he whispered, shifting his weight and stroking her cheek. Her hair was splayed out across the pillows, tousled and tangled. He gently ran his fingers through it and murmured, "God, you're beautiful. I'm really going to miss you."

She felt herself drifting out of a fog. She opened her eyes and saw him staring down at her. He was going to miss her. But for how long? When would he come back? What would happen when he did come back? Would they see each other every day again? Could she get through the days without seeing him? Suddenly she felt lonely again. Lonely in his arms. She brushed aside the strange thought and met his gaze.

"When will you be back?"

"I'll try to make it in a few days. A week at most."

"Christmas is coming."

"I know. What would you like from South America?"

What would she like? Him. Just him. "Uh, I don't know. Just come back safely. That would be the best Christmas present of all."

"That's the easy part. You sure you don't want to send me off on some shopping spree?" he asked with a slow grin.

"How can you think about shopping at a time like this?" she murmured.

"Well, don't worry. I'll think of something. Tell you what. When I get back, if things have quieted down a bit . . ."

"That's a pretty big if," she said.

"I know, but let's say they do. So I'll get back and then maybe you can take a few days off for Christmas and we'll head down to Naples."

"Naples?"

"Sure. That's where my folks live. Well, they live there in the winter. In a place called Port Royal. It's on the water. Nice beaches, palm trees, great weather. Trust me, it beats the heck out of what we're going through up here. What do you think?"

He wants to take me to meet his parents? She was stunned. Or was she? Yes, this whole affair had happened awfully fast. Then again, how much time did you need to figure out you absolutely *fit* together? A week? A month? A year? It had taken her much longer to get used to the idea of spending her time, her life, with Dexter. That had turned out to be a good time in her life. Until . . . She pushed thoughts of her former husband aside and thought about Tripp's invitation. She wasn't very keen on flying. The whole fear-of-heights thing still haunted her. But as she analyzed her reaction, she realized that going to Naples with this man would be the best Christmas vacation she could imagine. She had no idea if she could get away. Nobody on the White House staff had set vacations. You simply served *at the pleasure of the*

President and that meant you were on call 24/7. But, as Tripp said, if things calmed just a little bit, she certainly deserved a few days off.

"I'd love to go with you," she said, reaching up and gently touching his face. He took her fingers, kissed them, and replied, "That's my girl. We'll try to make it happen."

He looked over at the alarm clock on the bedside table and rolled away. "And now I've got to make something else happen. Like get my act in gear." He got up from the bed, leaving the sheets in a rumpled mess. "C'mon in here. Time for another quick shower."

She followed his lead into the marble bathroom. She saw two shiny sinks but thought they looked like two gigantic cereal bowls stacked on top of a slab of gray marble. Not quite her style, she mused, but she could hardly fault this man for his taste in fixtures. No, come to think of it, she couldn't really fault him for anything.

Tripp turned on the water and tossed a pair of white towels onto a hook just inside the glass door. She stepped inside and let the warm water sluice over her as he moved in behind her. He took the bar of soap and began to lather her body. As his hands roamed down to her legs, he turned her around and moaned, "Once more with feeling?"

26

Tripp stretched his legs as far as he could in the first-class cabin, finished his coffee, and handed his tray to the flight attendant. "We'll be landing in a few minutes, Mr. Adams. Hope you got some sleep."

"I tried," he said. "Never do sleep much on these international flights. At least I hope we'll have some decent weather here."

"Oh, for sure," the attractive woman said. "This time of year, it's pretty dry and warm. Probably in the eighties, I'd say. Well, I'd better get back to the galley. If you need anything else, you just hit your call button."

As she headed down the aisle, Tripp noticed a nice pair of legs. *At another time, in another life, I might have gone after that one. But not now.* He thought about Samantha and checked his watch. When they landed she'd be in her morning staff meeting and some other meetings she had told him about. He wanted to talk to her, but figured that could wait until he got to his hotel. Maybe he'd just send a quick e-mail from the car.

He knew that even on a Saturday he'd have some sort of welcoming committee from GeoGlobal's Caracas office. It might be Victor Aguilar himself. They had planned it so Tripp could spend two days getting ready for his meetings with Rossi and other energy officials. The entire GeoGlobal team would be working all weekend to try and stave off the latest onslaught on the company. Tripp glanced down at his briefcase, stuffed under the seat in front of him. It was jammed with briefing papers on the planned nationalization, the points that Victor had made, the counterpoints made by the Venezuelan energy officials, and a list of extensive talking points and positions Tripp could pursue with the Venezuelans.

"We will be landing in Caracas shortly, where the temperature is eighty-six degrees Fahrenheit. Please fasten your seat belts. We'll be on the ground soon. Thank you for flying with us. It's been a pleasure to have you on board." The announcement was then repeated in Spanish, giving the temperature in centigrade. Tripp understood those phrases as well. He had studied Spanish at St. Albans and again at Princeton. That was one of the reasons GeoGlobal had sent him on this mission. *Maybe if I had studied French or German I wouldn't have had to leave D.C. . . . and Samantha,* he thought.

After a smooth landing, Tripp cleared customs, and moved out of the baggage claim area. "Tripp, welcome to Caracas." It was Victor Aguilar himself rushing up to greet him, hand outstretched. "Good to see you. How was your flight?"

"Good food, decent wine, didn't sleep much, but that's par for the course. Nice of you to come get me," Tripp said, shaking hands and following Victor out into the bright sunshine of a Venezuelan morning.

"We have your security detail in those cars over there," Victor said, pointing to a pair of shiny black limousines.

"Kinda obvious, isn't it?" Tripp asked. "I mean, driving around town in limos?"

"Actually, they help get us through some of the worst traffic, get parking spaces, get respect, if you know what I mean."

"I guess," Tripp said, climbing into the backseat of the first car.

Victor pointed to the driver. "This is Manuel. Manny for short. He's been driving for us for years now. And next to him, that's Steve. He's one of your bodyguards."

Tripp leaned forward to greet the two men. "Manny? Steve? Good to meet you."

"They're good people. Manny's quite the guy. Has a big family. Six kids. And Steve? He's American. From Oklahoma. Former military. He's been pretty worried about that first gas line explosion. He's got family up there and he calls them all the time. Been working for us for about two years now. Does a good job." Victor turned and motioned to the car behind them. "And there's more security in the backup car."

"Do we really need all of this?" Tripp asked. "You'd think one guy would be enough. I mean, who knows I'm even here?"

"That's just it. We don't announce where our people are going, but Rossi evidently put out a press release about how an executive of Geo-Global was coming down to try to renegotiate the whole nationalization contract and how the strong Venezuelan government was going to stand firm for the sake of the people and all that nonsense. So all of this," he motioned to the bodyguard in the front seat and the car behind them, "this is company orders. You can't be too careful around here. The government has enough problems on their hands. They never seem able to control the street crime."

"That bad, huh?"

"Worst murder rate in all of South America, sorry to say," Victor said.

"I guess I didn't realize that. Who are the bad guys? Druggies, or what?"

"Just about everybody. Prices are up, wages are down. You've even got local policemen who take bribes to *protect* certain neighborhoods or switch sides."

"Protection money? Like Chicago in the twenties?" Tripp asked.

"More like Moscow right now," Victor said. "So you've got corrupt policemen, gang leaders, drug cartels. It's bad in Rio. There, they steal your gold watch. But here? Here it's a lot worse. So I've got my orders. You don't go anywhere, and I mean anywhere, without Steve in the front seat and the backup car trailing you."

"Got it," Tripp said.

. . .

They drove through heavy traffic, never noticing the dark Subaru that shadowed the two limos all the way through the city. They didn't see the driver talking on his cell phone, giving descriptions of the limos, the people inside, and the precise route they were taking.

Tripp dug into his pocket, pulled out his BlackBerry, and turned to Victor. "Excuse me a minute. Just want to send a quick note to someone." He put in Samantha's e-mail address. "Arrived in Caracas. Nice and warm here, just like Naples will be. Meetings later . . ." He looked up and saw a sign that read POLICE DETOUR.

"Here we go again," Victor said, glancing out the window at a barricade ahead manned by two men in police uniforms. One of the officers waved Tripp's car through. Manny turned right, as directed, and drove around a bend in the road. Victor looked through the back window. "Backup car's not there. Must have been detained for some reason. Maybe we should wait." Manny started to slow down just as a large truck pulled up behind them, effectively cutting off the backup car. Another truck came from a side road and slammed to a halt just in front of the limo. Manny jammed on his brakes and barely avoided a collision with the truck. "What the hell?" he shouted. They were completely hemmed in. There was nowhere to go. Tripp shoved the BlackBerry back in his pocket and tensed as four men jumped out of the first truck armed with MP5 submachine guns. They rushed to the front of the limo, and, shouting in Spanish, opened fire. The windshield shattered in a hail of glass shards, the bullets just missing the men in the front seat. Steve ducked down and drew his gun. He then raised it above the dashboard, aimed, and fired through the open windshield, killing one man, but the other three had moved to the side.

"Down, get down," Steve shouted. Victor and Tripp hit the floorboards of the backseat.

"Christ! Got any weapons back here?" Tripp yelled to Victor.

"Not back here."

"Shit," Tripp exclaimed. "Where's the backup car?"

"Truck cut them off. These must be pros."

Steve fired again and they heard one of the attackers scream in pain. One of the others rose up from his crouched position just outside the car, aimed, and opened fire on Steve. Tripp looked up to see Steve's head slam back against the front seat. Blood and flesh were splattered across the console as Manny made a futile effort to turn the wheel and steer the limo off the road around the truck. But there wasn't enough space. They were trapped. The two remaining men converged on the front door, yanked it open, and shot Manny in the chest.

"My God in heaven," Victor screamed.

Tripp jumped up and tried to reach into the front seat for Steve's gun, but it had fallen to the floor. He heard more gunfire coming from way behind them. The backup car. They must be attacking the backup car. The two men outside shot at the door lock and pulled the back door open. They shoved Victor aside and grabbed Tripp. He struggled, kicked, and tried to get a grip on one of them. If only he could wrest the MP5 away, he'd have a chance. Maybe he could save Victor.

One of the men hit Tripp with the butt of his gun. "What are you doing, you fool?" the other man shouted in Spanish. "We need him alive."

"I just knocked him out so he wouldn't fight us. Now we can get him into the truck."

"What are you doing with him?" Victor shouted.

"Shut up or you'll end up like the others." Then, with one man aiming his gun at Victor, he said, "Stay there or we take you, too."

The first man then hauled Tripp out of the backseat and dragged him over to the truck. The second man waved his gun at Victor. "Don't move."

Victor didn't have a weapon. He had no choice but to cower in the corner of the backseat. He watched in horror as the men lifted Tripp into the back of the truck and threw a tarp over his inert body. One man got into the back while the other raced to the driver's seat, got in, and sped away.

This is so weird, Samantha thought as she read the abbreviated message on her BlackBerry for the umpteenth time that day. "Arrived in Caracas. Nice and warm here, just like Naples will be. Meetings later . . ." and then, nothing. *Must have either run out his battery or been in a bad zone,* she thought as she clicked it off and shoved it into her black evening bag. She had sent several messages back to him, but so far hadn't received a response. She'd keep checking it whenever she had a discreet moment during the evening.

She was waiting to get into the Vice President's residence at One Observatory Circle for his annual Christmas reception. She wasn't in much of a party mood, but figured this was a must-show-up deal and she was glad to have been included on the guest list. She was behind at least a dozen other cars, all lined up like toy soldiers in Tchaikovsky's ballet. As she inched her jeep forward, she speculated on who else might be on the guest list.

Jayson Keller was becoming quite the talk of the town. After his wife had died some years ago, the handsome politician stayed out of the social scene for quite a while, but now was getting back into the swing of things. She had heard that he even tried to put a move on the brainy scientist Dr. Cameron Talbot a while back. But evidently Hunt Daniels won that competition. Interesting that Dr. Talbot had chosen the quiet, intense NSC staffer over the dynamic Vice President. After all, he was the odds-on favorite to win the next election, and she could have become First Lady of the land. On the other hand, as Samantha thought about it, if she had a choice like that, between someone like Jayson Keller and someone like Tripp Adams, she had no doubt she'd grab Tripp. In a heartbeat. Whenever she thought about him, her heart seemed to skip a beat.

She had thought about Tripp all day while she was working at the White House. Everyone in her directorate worked on Saturdays and sometimes on Sundays. Especially when they had a crisis on their hands. She had convened her interagency group and pressed Dave Major about his FBI field staff and what they were doing on the pipeline investigation. She had also quizzed Will Raymond about any CIA intel on the attacks, but both had come up empty. The same held for contacts at Transportation, Energy, and DHS. At least they had a lot of people in Oklahoma and Kansas searching for clues, interviewing residents, and going over the GeoGlobal investigations. Everyone was exercised about the theft of the pigs and maps, and the company was trying to figure out ways to divert enough gas to keep their customers from freezing to death. Power was slowly coming back to some areas, but thousands were still scouting for warm places to sleep.

In the midst of it all, the price of natural gas had skyrocketed, and it was followed by a similar spike in the price of oil, with every news organization speculating that if the gas pipelines were vulnerable, so were the oil pipelines. And to add to the misery, the Dow had taken a huge hit the day before, along with the auto companies, airlines, FedEx, UPS, and any other company dependent on gas and oil supplies.

Samantha put the jeep in gear and moved up the driveway closer to the white nineteenth-century house overlooking Massachusetts Avenue. She knew that it had been the official residence of Vice Presidents for decades now. But it wasn't always that way. It was originally built way back in the 1890s for the head of the United States Naval Observatory. But the house was so nice that higher officials kept shooing out various lower-level types so they could live there themselves. It wasn't until President Ford's day that Congress decided to turn it into the Vice President's home. Ford never got to live there because he became President before it was ready. Nelson Rockefeller only used it for parties, but after that, every Vice President had called it home, at least for four years at a time.

A Secret Service agent motioned her to move forward. She rolled down her window, flashed her White House ID badge as well as her invitation. He nodded and pointed to where she should park.

As she walked up to the front door, she noted a series of lanterns lighting up the walkway. Once inside, she saw that the entry hall was lined with large red poinsettias, and she could see a huge Christmas tree in the main living room with twinkling white lights and ornaments that looked like they might represent industries in different states.

A series of lovely oil paintings ringed the walls. They all had small brass plates at the bottom identifying the artist and which museum had loaned the original for display in this historic house. She gave her coat and scarf to an attendant in a gray uniform and joined the crowd in the main room. A pianist was playing "Jingle Bell Rock" on a Steinway in the corner, and waiters in black tie were passing sterling silver trays of champagne, white and red wine, and Perrier. She grabbed a glass of chardonnay and scanned the room.

She saw a friend who headed up the Mideast Section of the State Department and went over to say hello. "How did the meeting with the Moroccans turn out?"

"Let's just say we had to figure out whether to call it a frank discussion or a candid discussion," the Assistant Secretary said in a serious tone.

"Okay. So that's diplo-speak meaning the meetings produced either a difference of opinion or a hostile disagreement, right?" Samantha asked with a grin.

"Well, yeah," he admitted. "Trouble is, we need those folks on the terrorism front, the energy front. All sorts of fronts."

"Considering all the other visits we have coming up, I'm sure you're swamped with all of this."

"You can say that again. We've got Madagascar, the Maldives, Monrovia, and Malawi on our list for the next three months."

"Flag guys must be going nuts," Samantha remarked, taking a sip of her wine.

"Yeah. I wouldn't want that job of keeping flags from every country in the world and hauling them out every time some new dude comes to town. I mean, get a letter or two out of order and you've pissed off an entire country."

"I know. They've got hundreds of those flags stored in the basement of the EEOB. Then again, you've got your own supply."

"Speaking of supply, our supply of oil and gas is getting pretty tight. Aren't you working on all of those pipeline problems?"

"Sure am."

"I hate to ruin a nice party by bringing it up," he said, looking around the room. "Then again, what else do we talk about at these shindigs? Oh, excuse me, but there's Senator Jenkins over there. I'm going to see if I can bend her ear a little bit on a couple of energy issues."

"No problem," Samantha said. "Go ahead and work the room." Another waiter came by with a platter of crab cakes with a remoulade sauce. Samantha was glad to have one. She had missed lunch and was starved. She started to move toward the dining room, where she hoped there would be some sort of buffet.

"Excuse me, it's Miss Reid, right?"

"Oh, Senator Walker. Nice to see you this evening. Lovely party," she said.

"Yes. Yes. So many Christmas things going on, it's hard to keep up," he said, taking a swig from his cocktail. "There's a full bar over there in case you want something stronger than wine."

"Oh, this is just fine. By the way, I hear you're planning some congressional hearings on energy issues pretty soon, right?"

"I've been trying to get Cassidy Jenkins to delay them. Too much going on right now. Can't expect the CEOs to fly in here and be at our beck and call just when we've got pipelines exploding right and left, prices going sky-high, and all the rest, now, can we?"

"I would hope not. On the other hand, isn't that what Congress usually does?"

"Oh, you mean, Congress likes to get in on the news cycle? Of course we do, my dear. Name of the game. Keep the name in the forefront. But right now I'm damn worried about all of this sabotage. Started in my state. Well, you know that. Aren't you the one working that issue at the White House?"

"Yes, sir, I certainly am. And I'm worried sick about all of it, too."

"Is there anything new?"

"I guess you've been briefed on the fact that the explosions happened *inside* the lines and that equipment and maps have been stolen from GeoGlobal's facilities."

"Yes. Yes. We know all about that. Damn mess, I'd say. Costing that company a ton of money for repairs, to say nothing about trying to get heat to their customers, the factories, and hospitals. In some places, they've had to bring in stocks of firewood, for God's sake. Shades of 1930!"

"In terms of an economic hit," Samantha said, "I figure they have insurance for the pipelines."

"Maybe they had it, but with all of these attacks, I doubt if Geico would write them a policy now." Senator Walker took her arm and led her into the dining room. "Might as well enjoy some of those vittles over there while we're discussing national security."

She grabbed a white plate rimmed in gold with the Vice President's seal in the center and got into the buffet line. "Senator, we've been trying to figure out other ways we can police the pipelines and try to catch these guys. Whoever they are."

"Yes. I got a briefing by Ken Cosgrove on using our domestic satellites. Even though there are some on the intelligence committees who are screaming about that, I say let's go for it. Trouble is, it'll probably take a while to get all the necessary permits. Too many rules in place, if you ask me. Wish we could use the Army, too, but I know we can't," he said as he moved forward to spike a large slice of ham and add a few chunks of pineapple to his plate.

"I know. The Posse Comitatus Act," Samantha said. "But at times like this, I wonder what else . . ."

"Good evening, Samantha. Welcome to my home."

Jayson Keller smiled at her and held out his hand to Senator Walker. "Good to see you too, Harvey. I see you found the bar."

"Wouldn't miss a chance to try your Hiram Walker, you know," Harvey said with a smile. "Almost my namesake."

"Well, good to have you both here tonight."

"Didn't you just get back into town from that funeral in Macedonia?" she asked.

"Got in just a few hours ago. You know the motto of the Vice President when some head of state passes. 'You die, we fly.'"

Samantha had to laugh. "Yes, I've heard that a few times. Well, we're glad you're back safely, sir."

"Have to get around and see everyone, but you folks enjoy the buffet. Oh, and Merry Christmas."

Merry Christmas? Would it be a merry Christmas season without Tripp? Samantha thought about that. Would he be home in time for the Senior Staff party in the East Room next week? She doubted it. But hopefully he'd make it before Christmas Eve. And then after Christmas, maybe they really could take a couple of days and head down to Naples. The idea that he would want to take her there, introduce her to his folks, be with her over the entire holiday was the one thing that was keeping her sane while everything around her seemed to be falling apart. Or blowing apart.

She saw her boss coming into the dining room with his wife. *That woman has quite an overbite,* Samantha thought. *And she could use some serious highlights.* "Hi Greg, Mrs. Barnes. Christmas greetings," Samantha said.

"Hello again," Greg said. "Long day of meetings. Glad we could take a break." He turned to his wife. "See if you can fill up a plate for me, I'm heading to the bar for a refill." The woman nodded meekly and got into line.

I'm not surprised he's heading to the bar. That man drinks more than Harvey Walker, Samantha thought as she filled her plate, held on to her wineglass, and looked around for someplace to sit down. No such luck. In a crowd like this, you had to be a juggler and try to balance the wineglass on your plate while you picked at the food, or else find a coffee table or breakfront on which to set down your glass while you tried to eat something. Then a waiter would invariably come and whisk the glass away when you weren't looking. She could see why her father used to complain about going to big cocktail parties, calling them "just another stand-around."

She meandered through the crowd and into the study. She finally found a ledge where she could put down her glass. She knew she shouldn't be looking at her BlackBerry, but she was back in a corner and was able to put the plate down next to the glass, fish in her purse, and steal a glance at her cell. She discreetly turned it on and waited to check for any new e-mails. There were several from members of her staff, two from her interagency team. She'd read them as soon as she left the party. She scanned down the list, wishing, hoping for some word from Tripp. In the dim light of the corner, she stared at the tiny screen and realized that there was . . . nothing.

28

At least they had taken the blindfold off. Tripp looked around his spartan surroundings. A cabin of some sort, or rather a little casita, with adobe walls, a small fireplace in the corner filled with cold ashes, a rusted wrought-iron lamp sitting on top of a scratched wooden table next to the single bed where his leg was chained to the footboard. At least it was a long chain. It looked like it would allow him to hobble to a nearby bathroom, but that was about it. There were two windows where he could see a bit of the evening sky through a tangle of trees and bushes. Two black spiders were crawling across one windowsill. *Sorry guys, we're all trapped in this hellhole.*

He lay on the hard mattress, rubbing his head where one of the kidnappers had whacked him. He remembered coming to on the floor of some sort of vehicle. Must have been a truck. They had thrown a tarp over him and had tied his hands behind him and put a blindfold over his eyes while he was knocked out. When he woke up he had trouble breathing. But he had managed to inch over and nose up a corner of the tarp to get some air without provoking his captor, who was sitting on the other side of the truck bed.

His first thought was about the driver, Manny, and Steve the body-guard, who had been killed by these maniacs. They had spared Victor. At least, he thought Victor was still alive when they had hit him and dragged him from the limo. Maybe they had wanted Victor to live. Maybe they had it all planned so that Victor would get back to GeoGlobal and tell everyone about the kidnapping so they would know these guys were serious. Serious enough to commit murder in cold blood. And what about the security team in the backup car? Had they been shot, too? Had they all been killed because of him? Because he had come to Caracas to negotiate with the government?

These guys, whoever they were, might be operating on their own. He figured the government wasn't directly involved in kidnapping businessmen, although with all of the recent harassment, he couldn't be sure of anything. And those goons did have police uniforms on. The government's human rights record, as the politicians dubbed it, had headed way south with the arrests and indefinite jailing of oppo-sition leaders, rebellious students, and anybody else who happened to disagree with their policies. It was hard to tell who was on what side of anything down here. Tripp thought about all of this during the ride in the truck. Then he had tried to concentrate on where the hell they were taking him.

They had been driving on a smooth road at first, but then they had made a number of sharp turns and the road got rough. At one point, he almost rolled over as the truck began a rather steep climb. The road got even steeper as they made their way up some sort of hill or mountain. Tripp had tried to pay attention to his surroundings, listening for any clue as to where he was or where they were going. At first, he had heard city noises, horns honking, brakes squealing, peo-ple talking and shouting off in the distance. Then it got quieter as the road got bumpy. He started to hear birds. He knew they had left the city and were somewhere up in the hills. The steep climb was strange. Back and forth over terrain that didn't even feel like a road, but more like a gnarled path of some sort.

They had finally come to a stop. The driver had opened the back of the truck and when they pulled the tarp off, the two men hauled him out and carried him into the casita. Tripp had feigned unconsciousness as he heard them arguing in Spanish. "We take him into the bedroom. We chain him to the bed."

Tripp thought about ways he might be able to take on the two of them at some point, but he was in no position to fight back. Not yet anyway. He still felt weak from the blow to his head, he had no weapon, and his hands were tied. He hated the feeling of helplessness as they started to drag him out of the truck. He'd have to wait awhile. Wait and watch for his chance.

"No, Eyeshade. Maybe we should chain him to the chair here by the kitchen. Then we can watch him."

"We don't need to watch him if he's chained. He can't get away. Come on, Rafael. Help me. He's a heavy bastard."

They had finally dumped him on the bed and started going through his pockets.

"Look, Eyeshade," Rafael said as he held up the BlackBerry. "We can use this, no?"

"Let me see that." Eyeshade grabbed the BlackBerry and pushed a few buttons. "This could be even better than our original plan."

"You mean we could use it to send our messages? You think?"

"Why not? He's got a list of company contacts in here and a lot of other stuff. We'll figure it out. It'll be a lot better and safer than sending a courier."

"But can't they trace where messages come from and find us here?"

"Not if I go somewhere else to send them."

"Good thinking. Besides, we have plenty of time to figure out what contacts to use. Let them sit for a day or two and wonder what happened to their important man. Let them get upset and worry that he may be dead like the others. If they worry, they will be willing to pay. Well, you're the money man, you know."

"That's right." Eyeshade grabbed hold of the chain and opened the lock. "Here. Fasten this chain and untie his hands. When he comes to, he can use the bathroom and get water. We can feed him later. We've got to keep him alive or he's no good to us."

They had shuffled off into another room, leaving the bedroom door open. Tripp ripped off the blindfold and glanced toward the door. He could hear them turn on a television set and switch through several channels until they got to a soccer tournament. But it was being interrupted by a news broadcast. He then heard the man called Eyeshade complaining about how the government announcers always interrupted their games.

The man called Rafael came into the bedroom sometime during the afternoon and said in broken English, "I see you awake. You get water in there. We get food. No try to escape." He pointed to the chain around Tripp's ankle. "Because you can't." And then he burst out laughing and walked back to the TV.

Tripp tried to sit up. His head was killing him. He pulled himself up and dragged the chain to the bathroom. He splashed some rust-colored water on his face, found a ragged towel on a hook, put it under the cold water faucet and then held it against the back of his head where a large bruise was swelling up. *Okay, so you've been in worse shape than this a bunch of times. Tough it out. Just think about all the times you were in deep shit with Joe Campiello at Greyfield. You got out of it okay, didn't you? Then again, you and Joe were more or less in charge. This time, you've got no control at all. These idiots are in charge. They'll probably ask for some sort of ransom. The company will try to get the State Department involved. But they'll be clueless. The company will then call in their negotiator and he'll screw it up and they'll end up paying some enormous amount of money to save your sorry ass.*

Tripp knew the drill. He had heard about other businessmen being taken off the streets in Colombia by the FARC crowd, and then it happened a few times in Venezuela. But the more he thought about it, he remembered that two other GeoGlobal employees had been held hostage in Nigeria some time ago. The trouble was, Nigeria was a tougher act than Venezuela and those two never made it out. When the company had tried to negotiate, those kidnappers had first cut off a few fingers of their captives and sent them to the company, but then they lost patience and simply killed the guys. Tripp shuddered at the memory. At least these guys seemed focused on contacting his company and getting money. He could understand their conversations, although he wouldn't let on that he could speak their language. He knew he'd learn more that way.

He soaked the towel again. The cold water was helping a little bit. He just hoped he could hold down the swelling. He finally went back to the bed, lay down, and listened to the TV blaring the sports scores. He thought about Samantha and how the last time he had been on a bed, it had been with her. He thought about how he had held her and run his fingers through all that glorious hair. He thought about how he had touched her and how she had cried out his name. *Damn. Not the time to be thinking about her,* he told himself. He wished he could get his hands on his BlackBerry. He knew they had it in the other room, but he couldn't get that far, couldn't send a message to Samantha or Victor or Godfrey or anybody. He lay there and listened.

There was a commercial and then another newscast. This time the announcer said they had pictures of El Presidente giving an important speech. He was returning to Santa Ana's Chapel to announce a new program of food coupons for the poor. There was some sort of religious festival going on in connection with the Christmas season, and the President was expecting a big crowd.

Tripp looked down at his hands and counted his fingers. Then he listened to the President's speech. What else could he do?

"What do you mean your people have no idea who these thugs are?" Godfrey bellowed into the phone. "You've got a driver and bodyguard murdered, two backup security guards wounded, and Tripp Adams kidnapped, for God's sake. And you have no clue who took him? What kind of an operation are you running down there anyway?"

Victor Aguilar was answering on a secure line from GeoGlobal's office in Caracas. "I know this is the worst possible thing, but I was almost killed myself. The men in the trucks, they all had machine guns. There were two trucks and after the first one took Tripp away, the men in the other truck held me hostage all day. They must have wanted to be sure that the others got away safely before I had a chance to talk to anybody."

Godfrey took a deep breath and softened his tone. "All right, Victor. I realize you went through hell. But didn't you get a good look at the guys or at their truck? Have you called in the police or gotten in touch with the authorities down there?"

Victor hesitated. "That's just it. We're having a conference here. Everyone is in today, even on a Sunday, trying to figure out how to handle this. When I first met Tripp at the airport and we were driving back, there was a sign that said POLICE DETOUR and there were men in police uniforms and that was the trap. Don't you see? You can't trust anybody in this city. We all know that. There have been a few other kidnappings down here. Not as many as FARC has pulled off in Colombia, but still there have been some. And, as you know, this happens all the time in Mexico. At last count there were maybe two dozen people, Americans, who have disappeared in Mexico and are presumably held for ransom."

"I know that, and look what happens. Some are never heard from again. As for Venezuela, what's happened most recently?" Godfrey pressed.

"Companies paid a ransom and most of the people were returned. At least in this country. That's not the case in Colombia, I'm afraid. And if FARC is involved here, we have a much bigger problem than finding money for a ransom. They've been known to keep people for years. Well, until the government pulled off that rescue some time ago. But, you know that."

"Has anybody heard anything? Any contact? Any messages? Phone calls? Anything?"

"No, of course not or I would have told you right away. We are here in our conference room analyzing our best contacts. We've even brought in our negotiator."

"Tripp's the best negotiator GeoGlobal's got. That's why he flew down there."

"I mean the insurance negotiator for our K and R."

"You've got one of our top Vice Presidents being held by a bunch of crazy thugs who want we don't know what, and you're thinking about Kidnap and Ransom insurance? I don't believe this."

"Down here it's company policy. We have the insurance. They have a negotiator who deals with the gangs. They pay the ransom, or at least they try to negotiate a fair price and we get people back. Hopefully in one piece."

"So now you're telling me you're going to send some goddamned negotiator to deal with narcoterrorists or whoever they are to try and *lower* the asking price for Tripp's life?" Godfrey almost yelled into the phone.

"Look, Godfrey, we're with you. We know how you feel."

"Do you?"

"Yes, we do. We've seen this happening down here. This country is full of lawlessness, payoffs, bribes, corruption. We've got the highest murder rate in South America. It wasn't always this way, but now it is. So we're here figuring out who our best contacts in the underground might be, who we might be able to deal with, how we might learn something. Believe me, we've got our entire security team working on this."

Godfrey leaned forward into the mouthpiece. "Okay, you do that. But I'm going to the State Department. I can't just sit here while my boss, and I might add, my good friend, is being held by some gang of terrorists or hoodlums or drug dealers or . . ."

"Maybe State can help, but I doubt it. We've already contacted our embassy here. They're scouring their sources as well. All I can say is that I will keep you completely informed of every development. Oh, and right now, we think it's best to keep this under wraps. No publicity. We have to wait and see what they want. So, no press right now."

Godfrey heaved a sigh and sat back in his desk chair, still holding the receiver to his ear. "Okay. Fine. You stay on it with your people. It's just that this is such a horrible crime. This, in addition to everything else we're dealing with up here."

"We know. The gas line attacks. Is there anything new on that front?" Victor asked.

"No. I'm afraid not. Congress is up in arms, prices have gone crazy and the Dow is in the tank. There'll be hearings this week. That's all we need right now."

"I can imagine. Let us know every development. And in the meanwhile, we want you to know that we have staffed a war room down here with all of our best people. We'll find him, Godfrey."

"Yeah. Thanks." He hung up the phone and wished he had that kind of confidence in their South American operation. The fact was, he had no confidence at all. He checked a number on his computer and dialed the Watch Officer at the Department of State.

Samantha pulled into her parking place on West Exec, took her purse and leather folder from the seat, and headed to her office. She barely noticed the agent at the door, the two staffers huddled in the West Wing basement reception area studying a new set of Presidential photos being hung on the walls, and almost bumped into Ken Cosgrove as he was coming down the stairs.

"Oh, excuse me, Ken," she said absentmindedly, pushing a strand of hair behind her ear.

"No problem, Samantha. Busy day today," and he hurried on by. She hadn't slept much last night. Just like the night before. She kept thinking about Tripp and wondering why he hadn't been in touch with her. Even if his BlackBerry didn't work in Caracas, he could at least have found a telephone. As she had analyzed the entire previous week, a week of dinners, phone calls, and passionate nights, she wondered, *Was it all just too fast for him? Out of sight, out of mind and all of that?* She was upset, depressed, and was beginning to question her own judgment. But wait. She had always been a good judge of people. People, bosses, coworkers. And that kind of talent didn't suddenly evaporate when Tripp Adams waltzed into her life. No. Something was wrong. Something was definitely wrong.

She walked past Joan Tillman's desk and could barely manage a polite "Good morning."

"Hey, what's up, Samantha? You look like you just lost your best friend or something."

"Funny you should mention," Samantha said. "Maybe I have."

"What do you mean? Say, want some coffee. We've got fresh."

"Maybe. I mean, yes, that would be nice. Thanks." She tossed her coat on the rack and went into her cubicle of an office. She slumped down in her chair, pulled out her BlackBerry, and stared at it again. How many times had she done that in the last forty-eight hours hoping for some sort of an e-mail from Tripp? Ten times? Twenty? She had lost count long ago. Surely he could have it charged by now. Okay, so he was in meetings and yes, this was an important mission for GeoGlobal. But how long did it take to send an e-mail? Or . . . was something really wrong? Maybe he was sick. Maybe he got food poisoning on the flight. Maybe . . .

"Here's your coffee," Joan said, handing Samantha a mug. "Now, want to talk about it?"

Samantha took a sip of the steaming brew. "Something's wrong. I haven't heard from Tripp since he arrived in Venezuela Saturday morning."

Joan leaned against the doorjamb and cocked her head. "He's probably in meetings. Didn't you say he went down there because they were nationalizing GeoGlobal's facilities down there? I mean, that's pretty heavy stuff, you know. And it was a weekend. They probably had all kinds of things planned. You know, dinners, meetings with all the top people. Stuff like that."

"No. It's more than that. It has to be. I'm going to call his office."

"You're going to call GeoGlobal on a personal matter?" Joan asked, raising her eyebrows.

"I know what you're thinking. But no, this isn't *just* personal. I've got a feeling, and it's not a very good feeling right now." She glanced at her watch. "It's only seven thirty. I wonder what time those people get in?"

Joan shrugged. "Probably nine. I don't think I've seen a K Street office open at dawn or burn the midnight oil like we do in this place."

"Well, I'll call in a little while. Then I'll keep trying until I get somebody who can tell me what's going on."

Samantha felt like a zombie as she sat through their usual morning staff meeting. Greg was now more focused on the pipeline issue. *Well, thank God for small favors,* she thought. They were sending more DHS people out to coordinate with local law enforcement in various states. The President was scheduled for a major press conference and he wanted answers, wanted to be able to tell the American people that his administration was all over this issue and was taking steps to halt the steep rise in gas and oil prices. *Nothing new here. Whatever he comes up with, Congress won't let him do it anyway. Drill even more in Alaska? Who knows? Clean coal technology? Only the guys from West Virginia ever vote for that one. Nuclear power? Everybody takes a hike whenever that subject comes up even though we've been running nuclear-powered submarines safely for decades. Maybe somebody will invent a really small reactor to power our cars. Yeah, right. Build more refineries? Where? It's like "déjà vu all over again,"* she thought.

Greg was droning on about wanting her shop to provide talking points on this issue because Greg would be going on Fox News right after the press conference to bolster whatever points the President was able to make. She knew he'd be asked about conservation. But with the economy and the population expanding, that never worked very well. Other reporters would likely bring up hydroelectric and wind power. But she knew that all the good dam sites were already taken and still it only gave us about ten percent of our energy supply. As for wind, well, that was completely unpredictable and last she heard, there was a shortage of turbines. She made some notes but couldn't concentrate.

She checked her watch. She wanted this meeting to end. She wanted to call GeoGlobal.

"Joan, can you get GeoGlobal for me now? Get anybody in charge over there, would you please?"

"Sure thing."

Samantha waited, tapping her fingers on the top of her desk. She had a stack of memos in front of her along with the President's schedule and a summary of their interagency efforts on the pipelines, but at this very moment it had to take a backseat to her first concern. Tripp Adams. Where was he?

"I've got Godfrey Nims on line two," Joan announced.

Samantha picked up. "Good morning, Mr. Nims. Samantha Reid here."

"Yes, I've heard a lot about you, Ms. Reid."

"Please, it's Samantha. I wanted to give you a call because I haven't heard from Tripp Adams." She hesitated. She didn't know how much this man knew about her relationship with Tripp. "I mean, you might have heard that we've been meeting about the pipeline explosions and all . . ."

"I know. Tripp told me. Look, Ms. . . . uh . . . Samantha . . . I don't know how to tell you this, but we have a situation down in Caracas . . ."

"A situation?" Samantha started to feel uneasy as she heard the tension in Godfrey's voice.

"Yes. I don't want to say too much on this line."

"What is it?"

"Let's just hope that it's okay to communicate by phone here."

"What are you talking about?"

"Tripp has been taken."

"Taken?" Samantha bolted upright in her chair. "What do you mean, taken? Do you mean he's been kidnapped? In Venezuela?" She felt her mouth go dry.

"That's exactly what I mean. A gang of some sort ambushed his car on the way back from the airport, killed the driver and the security guard, took Tripp off in a truck somewhere, and our president, Victor Aguilar, was held hostage until yesterday. They finally let him go and he made his way back to our headquarters in Caracas. They've got a war room set up and are working with our embassy down there."

"But . . ."

"And I've already been in touch with our State Department. I'm not sure how much they can do except to contact the Venezuelan government, and we all know that they're not likely to give us much cooperation."

Samantha was stunned. She was speechless and realized she was also terrified. She hesitated as Godfrey went on.

"I'm sorry to be telling you this. We don't want any publicity on this situation, which is why I'm reluctant to go into any more details over the phone. But considering your position over there, any help you could give us would be greatly appreciated. As I said, State is on it, but there's only so much they can do."

Samantha took a deep breath and asked, "Have you heard anything from the kidnappers? Any demands? Anything?"

"Nope. Not a word. But we've been through this drill before with some of our people in other countries. It usually takes a while until they figure out a way to contact us. But believe me, we've got our entire security force in Venezuela working on this."

"My God! Let me think." She reached over for her coffee mug and took a sip, trying to quiet her nerves. The coffee was cold, but she drank some anyway. "I'm going to talk to our people here. Let me see what I can do on my end and let me give you my home number and my cell in case you hear anything. Anything at all." She rattled off the numbers and wrote down his personal contact numbers as well.

"Thanks, Samantha. As you can imagine, with all that's going on here in the States, to have this happen to one of our own vice presidents . . . to Tripp . . . he's a good friend, you know . . . let me just say that all hell is breaking loose . . . all over the place."

Samantha hung up the phone and put her head in her hands. *Tripp. Why Tripp? What are they doing to him? Is he hurt? Where did they take him? What do they want? And who are these guys anyway? Is it just some petty street gang out for a few bucks? Or could they be part of some larger movement? I've got to find out. Got to get help.* She reached for the phone again and dialed a number.

The club came down with such force that the student screamed out and blood began to soak his T-shirt. Five other students ran to help, but were held back by an entire phalanx of police armed with clubs and shields. The massive protest in the streets outside the Palacio de Miraflores was rapidly getting out of hand. Groups of students locked arms and chanted, "Elections, yes, El Presidente, no." A dozen were quickly surrounded and herded into waiting police vans, where a pair of officers waving their guns at another group advancing from the left slammed the back door shut, got in the front, and roared off to the new prison at the outskirts of town.

Despite the arrests, the clubs, and the guns, more and more students poured into the streets, singing and chanting. "They can't take us all," one shouted. "We want him out," another yelled, waving his fist at the palace guards standing at attention at the entry. Police sirens wailed as three more vans crowded toward the front of the building, almost running over a young woman waving a sign that read FRENTE RENO-

VADORA PAR LA LIBERTAD on one side and RENEWAL FRONT FOR FREEDOM on the other. More FR signs appeared and a trio of cameramen recorded the scene, rushing for a close-up of blood running down the side of the face of another student who had been clubbed and was now being dragged away.

"Get the cameras out of there," bellowed El Presidente as he watched the chaos from his second-floor window. His secretary raised troubled eyes and made a dash for the phone. "More police," he yelled after her. "I want more police, more troops. I want all of this shut down. Now!"

The woman relayed his orders into the phone and rushed back to his side. "They say they already have the entire force that's available either out there now or on its way."

The President stared as he saw another hundred or so students crowding in from a side street. "Where do they all come from?"

"There is no school today, sir. A teacher's holiday. You ordered time off for the teachers, remember?"

"Well, cancel it," he barked. "And start organizing a counter-rally of peasants who will show their support of all I am doing for them." She once again went to her desk and made a call.

"And get me Rossi," he yelled over his shoulder.

"I called him already. He was at his satellite office, but when word of the demonstration got out, he said he would come in. He should be here shortly. That is, if he can get through the crowd."

"He knows the back way," the President muttered. "I don't care if we fill up the entire new jailhouse. I want those students stopped. They say they want an election. Well, I have already announced an election. Right after Christmas. Are they satisfied? No. After this display, if we keep them locked up, they won't even be able to vote. So there goes their precious election. Our people will vote and they'll see. I will be elected once more for a proper term. And I will carry out the people's business."

"Yes, sir. I'm sure you will, sir," she said.

The door flew open and Diosdado Rossi careened into the room. "Mr. President, I came as soon as I heard."

"Yes, well. Do something. The police are more than useless out there. I've called for more troops."

"Troops? Are you sure you want to use our troops on civilians? And with the cameras out there?"

"I've already given the order to get rid of the cameras. They will all be confiscated, arrested. They are not our people. There are probably some CNN or BBC cameras out there. We will simply ship them home. We don't need their kind around here anymore."

"I'm not sure that is wise, Mr. President," Rossi said, joining his leader at the window.

"And why is that?"

"With the election coming, we need to show the world that we have free and open voting here. Besides, they will want to send election observers. They always do."

"That is for the election day. The roundup is for *this* day and I want those cameras and those students stopped. Do you hear me?"

"Yes. Of course, Mr. President. Come. Let's sit down for a few minutes. Let the police do their jobs. I have other problems to discuss with you."

"What's more important than this?" the President said, pointing and staring at the crowd below.

"If you'll give me a minute, I'll explain."

El Presidente finally turned and slowly walked to his massive desk and sat down. "All right. Talk."

"Remember I was to have a meeting with the people from Geo-Global today?"

"Yes, I remember something about that. You said you and the Energy Director had it all under control."

"We did until . . ."

"Until what?" the leader demanded impatiently.

"Until their man from the States was kidnapped over the weekend."

"Kidnapped?" the President asked incredulously. "How? Who took him?"

"We don't know yet. I got a call from the American Embassy. They have lodged an official protest and are asking our help in locating this man. His name is Adams and his car was ambushed on the way in from the airport."

"Do they have any idea who took him?"

"They say it was men in police uniforms who put up a detour sign and sent them into a trap. Two of their men were killed. Two others wounded. They took Adams and left Victor Aguilar alive to make his way back to his office. They are holding our government responsible for the murders and for Adams's life."

"Us? I had nothing to do with it."

"I know that. I told them that. They maintain that since the men were wearing official uniforms and since you are in charge, it is up to you and your government to get Adams back. Unharmed."

"And exactly how am I supposed to do that when I have no idea who these people are who kidnap businessmen? I assume it's for ransom. Have they made any demands?"

"Not yet. Shall I put our police on alert?"

"It all depends on which ones we think we can trust. We know that many of them take on other jobs, as they say. Call in the chiefs. The ones we know best. Get them on it to search the city, the other areas where these gangs have been operating. Get on it right away."

"I knew you would say that. I have already made a few calls. I'll arrange a meeting."

"We can't have foreigners kidnapped on our streets. That would kill our tourist trade, to say nothing about the Europeans and Russians who do business here. They might be worried that their people are at risk, too. See that there is no publicity on this. And I mean none. Is that clear?"

"Yes, of course. But that isn't all I came to talk about," Rossi said, pulling out a sheet of paper from his jacket pocket.

"There's more?" the President said in an irritated tone.

"I just wanted to give you some good news for a change."

"Then give it."

"After our first three exercises in the States, the price of gas and oil is up twenty percent, their stock exchange is down by almost that much, and we still have more plans," he said with a glint in his eye.

"Good. At least that is good news. I have seen the numbers and you heard my speech over the weekend."

"Yes. It was noted and passed to our agents."

"So now, I'm going to wait to visit those other sites on our list."

"Why wait when things are going our way?" Rossi asked.

"Because I want to see how the prices will fluctuate all this week and then make some new calculations. Also, I want to see if we can find this Mr. Adams. I have no love for GeoGlobal but we want their people to keep working in the fields and not be too distracted. At least for a few days. Just keep watching the schedule. You will know when to make another move."

"Samantha Reid to see Mr. Cosgrove," she said, standing nervously at Wilma's desk outside the NSC Advisor's office.

"Yes, Miss Reid. He's expecting you. Glad we could fit you in today." Wilma motioned for Samantha to head into the corner office to the left and then turned back to her computer and resumed typing.

Samantha walked through the open door as Ken was getting up from his desk.

"Come sit at the conference table, Samantha. I'm very concerned about Mr. Adams. I've asked Evan Ovich of my staff to join us. He's our Special Assistant for South American Affairs and is working on a whole host of issues in Venezuela right now."

"Evan? Yes, I know who he is. Any help we can get would be great right now."

"I did get a call from an Assistant Secretary over at State this morning, so when your call came in, I thought it best to meet and see what we can coordinate from here."

"Good morning, sir," Evan said, coming through the door.

"Why don't you close the door and we can get started," Ken suggested. "Now then, we have word that this man, this Mr. Adams of GeoGlobal was kidnapped over the weekend."

"Yes, I just got it too and evidently Diplomatic Security is looking into it," Evan said. "But to be honest, I don't know how much clout they've got in Caracas. I mean, sure, they protect our Embassy people down there, but I'm concerned they may not know the street types or common criminals who might have pulled this off."

"And there are plenty of those gangs around," Ken said. "What about CIA connections? I'm sure our Station Chief at the Embassy has contacts. Have you been in touch with him yet?"

"Yeah. He's got a few contacts with people who deal with the narcos. They're better organized. And he also tries to keep track of the police and politicians who are on the take. But the gangs? Not sure about that," Evan said.

Ken turned to Samantha who was watching the exchange with mounting fear. "You said you know this man."

"Yes, sir. I do. We've been meeting about their gas pipeline attacks." She didn't think a paragraph on her very personal connection was in order right now.

"What about his background? Is it your opinion that he can take care of himself? I mean, can he withstand some rough treatment? If that's what's going on here?"

Samantha tensed up. "Rough treatment? You think they . . . ?"

"We wouldn't know," Ken said. "We have had a number of kidnap cases, especially in Colombia, Mexico, and South Africa, that didn't end too well."

Samantha shuddered, folded her arms around her chest and took a deep breath as he added, "But we have no reason to believe they want him for anything other than ransom money. I doubt if whoever has him is trying to make any sort of political statement. After all, the report is that some local police were in on the abduction. So it's probably just for money."

Just for money. His life is in danger and it's just for money, she thought as she looked from Ken to Evan for reassurance. "Uh, you asked about his background. I do know that he was in the Navy and later worked for Greyfield."

"Bingo!" Evan said. "They must not have known that or they wouldn't have taken him. Navy? Greyfield? This guy can absolutely take care of himself."

"But for how long?" Samantha asked.

"Who knows?" Ken said. "First, I'm sure the company will get some sort of demand for a ransom. Once that contact is made, we'll have something to go on. If it's a courier, we're in luck, because we can often trace him back."

"And if it's just mailed in or something?" Samantha said.

"We'll have to wait and see about that," Evan said. "As you well know, our government doesn't deal with terrorist organizations or kidnappers of any stripe right now. That's our policy. If you give in to one group, you've suddenly put every traveling American in danger."

"So are you telling me that our government is powerless to find him and rescue him?" Samantha asked, her voice faltering.

"Our embassy has already contacted the Venezuelan government. They say they know nothing about it, and in this particular case, we're inclined to believe them. State has its people going over the details . . ."

"And GeoGlobal says they've set up a war room down there," Samantha interjected, "but what can they do?"

"Look," Ken said, "the situation in Venezuela is pretty dicey right now. Since you're involved in this issue, let me bring you up to speed on some other developments."

"Other developments?" she asked, arching her eyebrows.

"Yes. Well, Evan, do you want to fill her in on your project? She's got all the clearances."

"Sure. You see, their President has called for snap elections right after Christmas. Guess he thinks the people won't have much time to rally the opposition. This guy is very cagey. I've been studying him for a long time. He's part populist and part dictator. He says he wants to help the peasants, but he reads books about the old French and English kings. My sources say he loves to find out how they held on to power. That sort of thing. But this is the twenty-first century and the students are fighting back. They have a whole slate of candidates, including a pretty strong guy who's running against the President. Now they're organizing rallies."

Evan looked over at Ken. "Did you hear about the big march this morning? They arrested dozens of kids and hauled them off to some new prison they just built. I got an e-mail from a contact in FR. He said it almost turned into a bloody riot." He turned back to Samantha. "And it's not just students who are protesting the government. Reporters Without Borders, Human Rights Watch, even Amnesty International are all weighing in on this schmuck. So there's a lot riding on these elections. As for the rest of our efforts, I won't bore you with the details, but with all that's going on, I'm pretty sure their President wouldn't be out there kidnapping American businessmen. He's got enough to worry about just trying to stay in office, even if he does control most of the election machinery."

"I see," Samantha said. "What do you think the chances are that he'll be ousted?"

"Not very good right now. Sure, the students are organizing, passing out cell phones, sending text messages, handing out radios. We're beaming in newscasts from a ship offshore and they haven't been able to jam that signal yet. We keep changing the frequency and our contacts let the people know how to tune in. But still, it's a tough row. As you know, we can only do so much, and it's mainly in the area of communications. That's it right now."

"I realize he's a terrible dictator," Samantha said, "especially when he keeps nationalizing all of our industries. That's why Tripp, I mean Mr. Adams, went to Caracas on Friday. He was supposed to have a series of meetings with their energy people to try and stop this last takeover of their operations down there."

"Taking our assets, that's not the half of it," Ken said. "We're also focused on his contacts with Iran, China, Russia, as well as the Hezbollah militia that's taken root in South America, especially in the tri-border area. He cooperates with those terrorists in smuggling operations, training camps, and all the rest. Just the way he's cooperated with, or at least turned a blind eye to, FARC's activities in Colombia."

"In fact," Evan added, "we've decided that the tri-border area, where Paraguay, Brazil, and Argentina come together, is probably the most important base for Hezbollah outside of Lebanon. They're using it for training and recruitment, and with easy access up through Brazil and then Venezuela, they can work their way north to our border. It's not a happy thought."

"And there are even more extremists harbored in the Trinidad and Tobago area right off the coast of Venezuela," Ken said. "And right now, we get two-thirds of our LNG from Trinidad, and we don't know how long that source is going to last."

"Liquid natural gas. Yes, I know," Samantha said.

"That government is run by a bunch of Islamic militants who are cozy with El Presidente. They all hate our guts," Evan said. "So as you can see, his continuation in office poses huge problems for us in more ways than one."

"You say we're dependent on Trinidad for LNG, but we're also dependent on Venezuela for a huge percentage of our oil supplies. They're fourth on our list of importers. But their production has been falling, so our supply there could be in jeopardy, too," Samantha said.

"You're getting the picture," Ken said. "They're cutting more and more deals with China, Russia, and other countries. Pretty soon, they could decide to sidestep our market altogether. Oil and gas are fungible commodities. No matter who he sells it to, the price goes up—as it has with these pipeline explosions—and he makes money, which not only hurts our entire economy, but further entrenches him and his ilk."

"So if there were any way to dislodge this guy and get more of a democratic government installed, more of an ally instead of a Castro type, it would be better for us and for all of South America. Europe, too. That's for sure," Evan said.

Samantha sat back and looked from one man to the other. "So you're saying there's a lot on the line right now and the kidnapping of Tripp, uh, Mr. Adams, is just one more problem we don't need."

"I wouldn't put it quite that harshly," Ken said. "We're always concerned when an American citizen is in trouble."

"But isn't there anything we can do to try and find him?" Samantha pleaded.

Evan met her gaze and answered, "I'm going to go back to our student contacts. See if they've gotten any gossip from the streets. See if any of their people might have heard about these gangs or where they might be holed up."

"Well, at least that's something," Samantha said. "Oh, but Geo-Global is saying that there shouldn't be any publicity on this. Not yet. They want to wait and see if they get some sort of ransom message first."

The two men nodded. Ken checked his watch and got up from the small table. "I've got another appointment, but we'll all keep working this issue. Evan, you be our point man here. Coordinate with State, especially their Diplomatic Security people at our embassy there. Meanwhile," he turned to Samantha, "if you hear anything from Geo-Global, about Mr. Adams or anything new on the pipelines, I'm sure you'll let me know."

She stood up, pushed her hair back off of her forehead and muttered, "Sure."

As she walked out of the NSC suite of offices and headed toward the stairs, all she could think about was the fact that she had come to the NSC Advisor hoping he would have some brilliant idea about a way to find Tripp and rescue him. She had hoped that with all of the government's contacts, undercover agents, and all the rest, she would be given some idea of a plan that was already in place or at least one they were working on. She had visions of special forces pinpointing his location using some newfangled surveillance equipment and rushing in to free Tripp from a bunch of bad guys holed up in a cave somewhere. But she finally had to admit to herself that it only happened in movies and some of the more far-out thriller novels.

She felt upset, frustrated, scared. She knew that Tripp must be frustrated and scared, too. *That is, if he's still alive.* She shook her head, trying to dispel the macabre thoughts. She wondered if he had been hurt during the attack and the abduction. After all, two other men in the car had been shot. What if Tripp had been wounded? Would they take care of him? She figured they wouldn't take a chance on getting medical care for a captive. Her mind was racing as she pictured him in some shabby place, tied up, hungry and mistreated.

Walking dejectedly back to her office, she reflected on the meeting. Even with Ken's and Evan's assurances that they would check with all of their contacts, they didn't sound very encouraging. They had no solid leads. No one on the ground who had a clue who these marauding gangs were or who controlled them. She racked her brain, trying to think of where to go next.

33

Lightning streaked through the windows of the small casita, casting jagged white streaks across the adobe walls. Rain pounded down on the thinly tiled roof and was punctuated by rumbles of thunder.

"I said no more partners!" Eyeshade shouted. "Rafael and I are in charge of this operation. We don't need you here. We don't want you here."

"I don't care what you want or who you think is in charge. I was in the backup truck. My brother was killed by those security guards. I could have died, too, except that I got shots off that hit those bastards. I didn't kill them. I left them there. The police recruits could handle them after I left."

"So you were part of the original plan," Eyeshade said. "Fine. You will be paid. Just like the others. I told you that at the beginning. Your fee will come as soon as we get the money. It is a set fee. You knew that right from the start when you agreed to drive the other truck."

"For the life of my brother, I want a percentage of the money."

"Sorry," Eyeshade said. "It's not going to happen. We had a deal. We all knew the risks. There are risks in every operation. You will be paid. Now, get out of here."

Another rumble of thunder drowned out his next words, but Tripp then heard the other man say, ". . . on the cable car."

"You took El Teleférico up here? People would see you. El Avila is crowded with tourists this time of year. How could you be so stupid?"

"In this storm, there are not many people up here now. Besides, it was the only way I could get up here. My truck was damaged in the shoot-out. I barely got out of there. But I knew you were bringing him here. There were only a few people on the cable car. A cleaning crew for the hotel, I think. Nobody was paying attention. Now I am here and I want in."

"Who else knows you are here?" Eyeshade said in a menacing tone.

"Nobody. I swear. I heard you and Rafael talking before about how you would keep him up here. I know this place."

"Who else *knows this place*?" Eyeshade asked, mimicking the other man's voice.

"No one. My brother and I were the only ones besides you and Rafael."

"So, no one knows you are here?"

"I told you that."

Eyeshade glanced over to Rafael, who nodded imperceptibly and quietly pulled his pistol out of his pants pocket. "Bad move," Rafael said as the other man turned and stared, horrified, at the weapon.

"Wait! I was part of the plan. I helped you. I stopped the security men. I followed all of your orders. All I'm asking . . ."

The bullets ripped through the man's head and throat and he fell against the TV set, almost knocking it to the floor. Eyeshade rushed over to steady the console as the man's body slumped down and blood began to pool on the dusty tile floor.

"Do you think anybody heard that?" Rafael asked, shoving the gun back into his pocket.

"I don't think so. If there are any tourists left at this time of night, they are probably way over by the Hotel Humboldt or maybe, before it started to rain, they hiked to San Isidro for pork sandwiches and strawberry juice."

Rafael stared at the blood on the floor. "Looks like strawberry juice around here," he chortled. "Come to think of it, I could use a sandwich. Should I go for some more food?"

"You should go dump this body somewhere first," Eyeshade said, resuming his seat in front of the TV. "Get him out of here. Let me know if you need help."

Rafael grabbed the other man under his shoulders and started to drag him out of the casita. "Where should I take him?"

"Too bad we're not near the Kanoche ruins," Eyeshade said with a disdainful laugh.

"Oh, you mean that place where that German doctor did all those strange things?"

"He made people into mummies," Eyeshade said over his shoulder. "You think you can turn that guy into a mummy?"

"No way," Rafael said, inching out the door. "I'll find some gulley and drop him in. Back in a while."

So Rafael is the trigger-happy one, Tripp thought, as he analyzed the scene he had heard in the next room. The other man had come up here on some sort of cable car called El Teleférico. They were in an area called El Avila, that would be the mountains between Caracas and the ocean. And there was a hotel with the name of Humboldt somewhere nearby. Now he was getting somewhere. If only he could get his hands on the BlackBerry. He glanced through the door but all he could see were the outstretched legs of the leader, the obvious money man, Eyeshade, as he lounged once again in front of the TV.

Tripp had heard the scores of so many games he had more or less tuned them out. But when the news anchor came on, he paid attention. They always began a newscast by recapping the schedule of El Presidente, talking about where their great leader had been, what peasant groups he had visited, what plans he had in place to raise their standard of living. *What a load of crap,* Tripp thought.

That day the President had given a speech to a rally of farmers. There was a short reference to it being a counter-rally. Tripp figured that meant there was a real march of some sort, probably by the opposition, and the President's people had to organize something to counter those effects. The announcer also talked about the upcoming elections and said that a small group of students had been arrested and interrogated regarding unlawful activities in front of the Palacio de Miraflores. *Of course, the poor kids were probably protesting in front of the President's home in the heart of Caracas.* He thought about the students. They were undoubtedly shoved into some sort of prison outside of town and they'd be kept there until after the election. That's how these people usually handled *free* elections.

He doubted if they were chained though. He glanced down at the chain at the end of the bed and then around the room. He had already scoured the place, the drawer in the rickety bedside table, the bathroom, even the lock on the window, trying to figure out some way to pry the lock open. No such luck. They had taken everything out of his pockets, even his keys and comb. He had his clothes, but against a heavy chain and sturdy lock, he had nothing. Nothing at all. Except his hands.

Rafael was gone. Eyeshade was alone. Tripp started coughing. He tried to make as much noise as possible, tried to sound like he was choking. Eyeshade came to the door and peered inside. Tripp was holding his throat as if he couldn't breathe.

"What's the matter with you?" Eyeshade said in halting English.

Tripp coughed some more and beckoned him over to help. Eyeshade drew his gun and walked cautiously toward the bed. Tripp kept coughing. As Eyeshade leaned closer, Tripp suddenly bolted upright and punched the man in the face. His gun went off, the bullet ripping into the mattress next to Tripp's leg. Tripp pounded Eyeshade again and grabbed for the gun. It skittered onto the floor and Eyeshade fought back. Tripp grabbed the other man's shirt to pull him in for another punch. If only he could knock him out, he could reach the gun, shoot the chain off, and get out of this place. But while Tripp was strong, Eyeshade was nimble. The little guy wrenched away.

"You bastard!" Eyeshade shouted as he hit Tripp in the chest, knocking the wind out of him. Tripp tried to swing his legs to the floor, but the chain caught in the footboard and he couldn't kick it free. He grabbed for Eyeshade's throat, but the other man twisted away, fell down, and rolled across the floor, out of reach. He reached for his gun and aimed it at Tripp. "You will pay for this."

"What's going on?" Rafael shouted as he tore through the door. "I heard a shot."

"He tried to attack me," Eyeshade said, wiping blood from his nose with the back of his hand. "Make sure that chain is fastened tight. And keep an eye on him. He's not going to get away from us. Not now. Maybe not ever."

"The hearing before the Senate Committee on Energy and Natural Resources is now in session." Senator Cassidy Jenkins rapped her gavel and began to outline the day's proceedings. Room SD-366 was jammed. A bank of cameras lined the walls, while reporters juggled notebooks and jockeyed for key positions and the best camera angles. Godfrey Nims was seated at the witness table next to the Executive Vice President of GeoGlobal, Roy Foss, who was reviewing his prepared testimony.

Scanning the room, Godfrey saw representatives of at least a half-dozen associations crammed on the left side of the room, including the American Petroleum Institute, the Nuclear Energy Institute, the Association for Wind Power, the Liquid Coal Producers Association, and the Renewable Resource Council. On the other side a passel of constituents, consumer advocates, and other assorted spectators were mumbling among themselves. Most all of them were wearing the latest rage around town—large buttons reading A–B–G. Some even wore T-shirts emblazoned with ANYTHING BUT GAS. Godfrey nudged Roy, pointed to the buttons and whispered, "Maybe those guys could do commercials for Beano." Roy chuckled under his breath and raised his head as Senator Jenkins called on him.

"I see on this witness list that Mr. Roy Foss, the Executive Vice President, is with us today representing GeoGlobal Oil and Gas. Mr. Foss, before you begin your testimony, may I ask why your Chairman and Chief Executive Officer is *not* with us? We had requested his presence, as I'm sure you well know," the Senator asked in an imperious tone.

Roy cleared his throat. "Madam Chairman, I'm afraid that our CEO is engaged in a very difficult situation today, one that I would be glad to explain to the committee in a closed session." Godfrey knew that Roy wasn't about to explain that their CEO and the rest of the Executive Committee were working all day on a strategy to deal with Tripp's kidnapping while trying to keep it all under wraps. At least for now.

"Closed session?" Cassidy said, her voice rising. She motioned to the bank of cameras. "As you can see, we announced this hearing, we have invited the public and members of the press so we can pursue an explanation into the disastrous explosions occurring on your pipelines. That subject, plus an examination of the soaring price of natural gas as well as oil that we have seen in just the last few days, is our focus today. These issues are of paramount importance not only to the Senators from the states where the lines have blown up," she nodded toward Senator Harvey Walker, who was sitting to her left, "but to all Americans, as we've seen many of our fellow citizens killed by these explosions and others driven from their homes due to lack of heat. The entire economy is taking a hit from this as the Dow has plummeted. Thousands are currently out of work because factories have had to shut down, and we live in fear of yet more *unexplained* explosions of your unprotected pipelines. And yet, you suggest that your CEO cannot make time to address this body?"

Roy tried again. "As I said before, Madam Chairman, there is a matter of urgency that our CEO is dealing with. I assure you that I have his testimony before me and am prepared to answer any and all questions about these acts of sabotage."

Senator Jenkins leaned toward her microphone. "Oh, very well. You may proceed."

Roy began to read his testimony about the extent of the damage, their efforts to repair the lines, divert the gas, and investigate the missing maps and equipment. Godfrey followed along, reading his copy. When Roy was finished, Senator Jenkins again took center stage.

"And so you are basically saying that GeoGlobal is powerless to police their own pipelines, secure their own warehouses and facilities, or have any impact whatsoever on keeping the price of natural gas at any sort of reasonable level."

"As you know, Senator, the price for our natural gas is set at Henry Hub in Louisiana, where most of the pipelines come together. It's a free market. As for control of the price, now with acts of pure sabotage, it's a question of supply and demand, especially future demand. However, working closely with local law enforcement as well as teams from the FBI, we are very hopeful that we will be able to catch the perpetrators before any more damage is done to the lines."

"Meanwhile, Americans are paying dearly for both natural gas as well as oil, which also flows through unprotected pipelines," the Chairman countered. "As we have been saying for years now, it is perfectly obvious that what we need in this country is less reliance on oil and gas and more reliance on alternative sources of energy, even more than we outlined in our last energy bill. Well, we'll get to that subject in a moment." She turned to her left. "I now recognize the Senator from Oklahoma for his questions of the witness."

Harvey Walker leaned forward in his black leather chair, pulled his microphone closer, and nodded to Roy. "Now then, Mr. Foss, thank you for coming today. First, let me ask you, it's not only these acts of sabotage, there are *many* reasons for the wide swings in the price of oil and gas today, wouldn't you say?"

"Of course, Senator. It's hard to know where to begin."

"Take your time. This is an important issue."

"Yes sir. Well, first of all, even in a slowing economy our oil imports alone have increased to over sixty percent of our consumption in the last few decades as our population has expanded, and even with recent legislation, we're still being prevented from developing many of our own resources. It wouldn't be so difficult and it wouldn't also have turned into such a national security issue if all the products we need came from safe places. But they don't. As you know, we are dependent on countries in the Mideast, Venezuela, Nigeria, Trinidad, among others—all places where oil and gas are controlled by state-run monopolies subject to the whim of socialist or Islamic regimes not necessarily friendly to our interests."

"Well, Mr. Foss, we all know that we import oil and gas from those places, but you said you were still prevented from developing some of our own resources. We've been having these debates for months now. Yes, we have environmental rules in place. Protecting the environment is very precious. Would you care to expand on your charge?"

Walker is obviously throwing us a softball with that one, Godfrey thought. And with that opening, he knew Roy could score a bit here.

"Sir, with all due respect," Roy began, "as we all know from debates we've had for years now, our country has simply not taken advantage of many of our own resources. There is plenty of oil and gas, especially when we've developed new methods for secondary and tertiary recovery. I realize we are developing some projects on the Continental Shelf, but there are still vast areas that remain off limits by our own Congress and various government edicts, sir. And others that are tied up in lawsuits Now, as I said, I recognize that there's been some expansion of our options there. Yet it's interesting that drilling can be done off the coasts of Denmark, the Netherlands, Norway and England, but not off parts of America. Yet, we get word that Russia and China are planning to drill in waters off Florida.

"And while we're talking about American oil reserves, a whole bevy of lawsuits are preventing us from drilling in Alaska in the Beaufort Sea area. I guess the migration of bowhead whales is more important than energy security in this country."

Titters came from the left side of the room, groans from the right as Senator Walker nodded and asked, "And the price hikes? My constituents are really hurting right now. More than ever. Care to expand on the prices you and the other big oil companies are currently charging?"

"I'd be glad to," Roy said. "First, our major companies have control of only about twenty-three percent of reserves. The rest is owned and controlled by these government monopolies I referred to a moment ago. Finding oil and drilling for it is getting more and more expensive. The easy oil has already been drilled. What we drill in the future will be much more expensive. Now I ask you, when you have a certain supply of an item, are you going to charge your customers what you paid last week for that item? Or will you charge what it will cost you to get a new supply of it next week?"

Senator Jenkins interrupted. "Your time is up, Senator Walker. Now, before I move on to the next Senator, I want to go back to my original question and that involves our use of alternative fuels. We have been putting policies in place for many years now to encourage the use of alternative sources of energy. Surely, you support those measures, do you not, Mr. Foss?"

"Of course we do. In fact our major producers are the biggest investors in alternative energy sources. We know we need it all. But here again, there are roadblocks. Nuclear energy is clean. It doesn't add to your concerns about global warming and while there's been more discussion about building nuclear plants, we've been stuck at producing less than twenty percent of our electricity from nuclear for decades. As for refineries, we haven't built a new once since 1976. We're working on biofuels but we had to backtrack when the price of corn hit the roof. I doubt if there's enough switchgrass to make up the difference, although some outfits are experimenting with pig fat."

Laughter erupted in the back of the room and Senator Jenkins banged her gavel. Roy went on with his extemporaneous list. "Then there's solar. Great idea but it gives us less than one-tenth of one percent of the country's electricity supply. And as for windmills—well, now there's a shortage of turbines, and besides, nobody on your committee wants to put wind farms near Nantucket or Rehoboth Beach, right?"

Now he's getting testy, Godfrey thought. *All good points, but we can't afford to piss 'em off any more than we usually do.* He nudged Roy, who seemed to take the hint.

"Madam Chairman, I mean no disrespect to the members of Congress. It's just that when we are called up here, as we are on a pretty regular basis, to explain our industry and our pricing, it does seem to fall on deaf ears. Yes, the price of oil has fluctuated a great deal in the past several months, and we know it is up thirty-five percent now with these pipeline attacks, but during the same time frame, the price of eggs also went up thirty-five percent, and I don't see any hearings being called for 'Big Egg.'" Godfrey kicked him under the table.

Senator Jenkins glowered down at the witness table. "Thank you, Mr. Foss, for your illuminating statistics today. We are all well aware of the difficult situations we face when it comes to energy production and yet we are here to serve the American people, to protect the American environment, and do our best to provide for America's security. We are all under a great deal of pressure right now, especially with the attacks on *your* gas pipelines. I'm sorry to hear that you have evidently made no progress in securing the remaining pipelines from further acts of sabotage."

Godfrey's BlackBerry began to vibrate. He knew he had no business even glancing at it in the middle of a congressional hearing, but he had told his assistant to only contact him if it involved an absolute emergency. He slunk down in his chair and reached in his pocket for his cell.

35

Samantha crossed Chain Bridge into Virginia and drove up Route 123 past the entrance to the George Washington Parkway and kept going until she saw the large green sign on the right, GEORGE BUSH CENTER FOR INTELLIGENCE NEXT RIGHT. She turned at the corner and drove past another sign, which read RESTRICTED FACILITY. She didn't turn right toward the VISITOR CENTER. She figured that was kind of a misnomer anyway. They didn't have many visitors to this facility. No public tours, at least. She kept going to the main gate, showed her ID, waited while the guard checked his log book, and then continued to drive, down a tree-lined road. She knew that in the spring and summer, this place looked like it could be a lovely gated community of posh homes where you'd almost expect to see a golf course off to one side or a swimming pool and tennis courts through the trees.

As she slowly navigated the roadway, she knew there were no posh homes here and no posh country club. She reflected on the word *posh* and remembered that one theory of its origin was that it had been coined over a century ago by the British who were ruling India at the time. When their officers traveled back and forth between the two countries, the highest-ranking men were allowed to sit on the shady side of the boat so they wouldn't be bothered by the heat of the sun. So it was *Port Out, Starboard Home.*

There were no boats here either, just a couple of very modern-looking buildings. And while it was called "the Campus," it housed more Ph.D.s than any university in the country. The original head-quarters building went up the day the Berlin Wall went up. Then, in a unique twist of fate, the new headquarters building went up the day after the Berlin Wall came down.

The grounds were quite lovely. Three hundred and fifty acres in all, and while the whole complex was technically located in McLean, Virginia, it was called Langley because it sat on the land that origi-nally made up the Langley estates, home to Camp Griffith and Camp Pierpont during the Civil War. In those days they had a rather differ-ent way of spying or keeping track of things. They launched air bal-loons to keep watch over the Capitol. So they ended up taking the name Langley to refer to this headquarters of the CIA. To add con-fusion for the Post Office, its mailing address was Washington, D.C. Then again, so was the Pentagon's, and it actually was in Virginia, too.

Samantha mused about government bureaucracies as she parked in the VIP lot and walked up the steps and through one of the ten glass doors into the bright lobby of the Central Intelligence Agency. It was because of government bureaucracy that she had taken a break and driven over here today to meet with her contact, Will Raymond. She was totally frustrated with the State Department, the NSC, the embassy in Caracas, the Diplomatic Protection Service, and Geo-Global's Security Team. She couldn't get answers from any of them.

There had been another gas pipeline explosion that day. She had been watching the congressional hearings and saw Godfrey Nims and the Executive Vice President jump up from the witness table, rush over to the Chairman, and ask for a recess. It was then announced that there had been another attack. She knew that GeoGlobal would be focused on that. She should be focused on it, too, but she had al-ready set up this meeting with Will, and she told Joan that she had an off-site meeting and asked her to make excuses in case anybody asked. She said she'd be back in two hours.

She walked past the eight white pillars in the lobby, stepped around the huge circular design in the center of the gray and white terrazzo floor with the outline of an eagle and a star embedded in the center. The star was known as the Compass Rose, meaning that it covered all points on the globe. She glanced at the left wall, where the statue of William Donovan stood sentry. She checked her watch and saw that she was a few minutes early, so she walked over to the wall on the right to read the names of CIA agents who had given their lives in the line of duty. Each name had a star next to it, but there were a number of stars with no names. She knew that it often took years for a name to be posted next to the star because they had to protect identities and families in the process.

She checked in with an agent and left her cell phone at the desk. No cell phones were allowed in the building, since outside forces might be able to pick up conversations. She wished that restaurants and Amtrak trains had the same rules.

At the back of the lobby, she looked through a wall of windows into a courtyard with a big tree that she thought was a magnolia. She once asked how they tended the garden, since there was no obvious way for big machinery to get in there. Will had told her that at one point they had solar-powered computer robots who rooted around and dealt with the plants. They developed a lot of technology in this place. Obviously duel-use technology, even mammography that they gave to medical science along with a lot of other inventions. The directorate that handled those things was called the DS&T—the Directorate for Science and Technology. She figured it was like the guy called "Q" in the James Bond movies.

There were four directorates in all. One dealing with support, payroll, and training. Another for the collection of intelligence. Those folks monitored TV programs, video, newspapers, photos from all over the world. They could analyze them, enhance them, figure out what was important and deliver the PDB, or President's Daily Brief, and NIE, National Intelligence Estimates, to the White House. She read a lot of those reports and marveled at how they figured out all that intel.

Today, she'd be meeting with Will, who was in the Directorate of Operations, known as the clandestine service. They established networks of operatives, recruited agents, spies, and assets all over the world. Oddly enough, it was the smallest directorate, with the fewest number of people.

As she was mulling all of this over in her mind, Will came across the lobby to meet her. "Hey, glad you could make it over to my shop for a change. Want some coffee or anything? We've got McDonald's and Starbucks in the Food Court."

"Coffee would be good. It's still freezing out there."

They headed to the counter and ordered a couple of double lattes and Will said, "Would you believe that this little Starbucks stand has the third-highest gross sales on the whole East Coast?"

Samantha looked around at the employees scurrying down the corridor. "Must be the stress level in this place."

"Gotta be. Come on. I'll take you up to the third floor." They headed down another hallway, past the museum sporting "The Clandestine Collection." "Did you ever see this stuff?" Will asked.

"I never really went through it." She glanced at the trophy cases and saw tiny cigarette lighters, small umbrellas, and pen-and-pencil desk sets. "What's all this?"

"Stuff we got from the KGB in the old days. They were masters at hiding cameras and listening devices in every conceivable place, even in pen sets they gave our ambassadors when they were welcomed to Spasso House."

"I'd love to check it all out, but I'm on a rather tight time schedule. There was another attack on the lines today."

"Yep. Saw that one. But you said you had something else you wanted to talk about and didn't want to do it inside the White House." They took the elevator up to the third floor and walked into a secure conference room with a mahogany table with sixteen chairs around it.

"We don't need a big meeting today. I just need to talk to you. Privately," she said as she looked around the room.

"I know. It's just handy to meet in here when nobody else is using it." He sat down. She took a seat next to him and tossed her coat and purse on another chair.

"Okay," Samantha began. "Here's the deal. I need your help!"

"We're already doing everything we can on the pipelines, but that's not it, is it?"

"No. I'm here about the kidnapping. Tripp Adams. I'm sure you know about it."

"Yeah. We know. Bummer. I haven't been involved myself but I hear that our people down in Caracas are working it. Why?"

Samantha leaned forward, an earnest expression on her face. "That's what everyone says, Will. State says they're working it. Geo-Global has set up a war room of some sort. I had a meeting with Ken Cosgrove and Evan Ovich yesterday."

"But?" he interrupted.

"But I don't think anybody is really doing anything. They say they are waiting for a ransom note, checking their contacts and all of that. But there's no action plan here." She pushed a strand of hair out of her eyes and pleaded with him, "Can you do something? I mean, can you and your people get involved in this case? Please?"

"Wait a minute," Will said. "We have an official policy of not dealing with kidnappers. You know that."

"I'm not talking about *dealing* with them. I'm talking about rescuing Tripp."

He studied her features, hesitated a moment and asked, "Why, Samantha?"

"Because . . ."

"Is this personal?"

This time she hesitated. She drew a breath and admitted the obvious. "Yes."

"In what way?"

"We've been meeting about the pipelines. Then we met some more, after hours, and then. Well, he's . . . he's a friend and I can't bear the thought of him being held by a bunch of maniacs, or whoever they are." She felt tears coming. She brushed her eyes with the back of her hand. She didn't usually get emotional in meetings. But this meeting was different. She needed help. Desperately.

Will leaned over and put his hand on her arm. "I think he's more than a friend, right?"

"Yes," she said quietly. "Oh God, can you imagine what it's like picturing someone close to you being taken at gunpoint and held somewhere by someone but you have no idea who they are or what they really want? And you have no idea if he's still alive, if he's been hurt or shot or wounded or any of that, or if he has any food or any water or . . ."

"Yes, I do know what that's like. You forget who you're talking to. I served overseas in a number of shitholes. I've seen friends, fellow agents taken, interrogated, killed in our line of work. So yes, I do know."

"So what can we do? Anything?" she asked, staring at him with tear-filled eyes.

Will stared back and finally said, "Samantha, this is new for me. I mean, seeing you personally involved in a case. Whenever I've seen you, you've been in total control. Control of a meeting, control of a staff. I always thought of you as . . ."

"A control freak?" she asked with a wan look.

"Not exactly."

"Not exactly? Tripp once said that expression sounds like an old Hertz commercial."

He stared at her. "Now you're sounding like the old Samantha. Look, let me see what I can do. We have assets in Venezuela. We have more in Colombia because of FARC and all of their shenanigans."

"You don't think FARC is involved in this, do you?"

"Not from what I've heard. It really seems more like a street gang of some sort. Those guys are strictly out for money."

She brightened a bit. "So if that's the case, they'd need to keep him alive, right?"

"You'd think so. At least you'd hope so."

"Merry Christmas, Mr. President. Lovely party," Samantha said, plastering on what she hoped was a sincere-looking smile. She certainly didn't feel like partying, but the White House Senior Staff Christmas party was an absolute must-show. When you receive an invitation from the President of the United States, you never, ever decline unless you're on your deathbed, and even then, you ask for a transfusion and a driver. She knew that.

"Good to see you this evening, Samantha," the President said. "Here, stand between us for the photo."

Samantha moved between the President and the First Lady as one of the White House photographers focused the camera. Samantha couldn't help but admire the blue silk Versace gown the First Lady was wearing. When you put that next to Samantha's red lace Filene's Basement model, at least it would turn out to be a patriotic scene. Samantha had found the dress on sale last week, when she had hoped Tripp would be her escort. She had raced into the store on

Connecticut Avenue after work in an effort to pick up a few Christmas gifts for her family and happened to see the dress on the markdown rack. It had a scoop neck and long sleeves and hugged her slim figure. She figured it would be just right for this command performance, not too dowdy, not too much décolletage. She tried to stop thinking about Tripp for a few moments and smile for the camera. She wished she could say something to the President about the kidnapping. Maybe he would take an interest and get some action from the agencies. But this was not the time or the place to ever push an issue with the First Family.

They were standing in front of a massive Christmas tree decorated with ornaments made by schoolchildren from every state in the country. And as she moved away to give another staffer their moment with the President, she realized that the First Lady's dress matched the decor. After all, this was the Blue Room. It was also oval in shape, like the Oval Office, so it was the perfect setting for the gigantic White House Christmas tree. She wondered how many florists it took, in addition to the four they had on the regular staff, to decorate the tree and the rest of 132-room mansion. Since it was the only home of a President in the world that was also a museum with thousands of visitors each year, it took an army of folks to spruce it up and keep it in shape, especially for the holidays. There were decorations everywhere, including a large gingerbread house complete with candies on the roof and sugarcanes lining a walkway. One of the five White House chefs always made one of those for the dozens of Christmas parties the First Family hosted each year. She had no idea how they ever got through such a grueling schedule in addition to the usual daily grind.

She meandered next door to the Green Room and saw Angela standing in front of the Duncan Phyfe bookcase, chatting with Evan Ovich. A portrait of Benjamin Franklin, the ultimate Ambassador, was hung over the nearby mantel. She decided to ask Evan if he or his staff had heard anything from our Ambassador in Caracas.

"Hey, Samantha, neat dress," Angela said. "Must have made a great picture."

Samantha looked down at the red lace and shrugged, "Uh, maybe.

Listen, you two, can I bring up a piece of business for just a minute here?"

"Sure," Angela said. "What's up?"

Samantha focused on Evan and almost whispered, "I've been waiting all day to hear some news from the NSC on the kidnapping case."

"I know. Isn't it just awful?" Angela said, leaning into the trio.

"I wish I had something concrete to report, Samantha, but I still haven't heard back from the FR leaders or anybody else. You know that as soon as anything comes in, we'll let you know," Evan said. "And I assume you haven't got anything new on that latest pipeline attack?"

"Not a thing," Samantha replied. "I can't keep bugging Geo-Global. They're up to here with disasters. We do have DHS all over it as well as folks from Transportation. They've got staffers in all the states that have been affected. And the FBI . . . well . . . the FBI is doing whatever the FBI does in these cases. Trouble is, it's hard to get everyone to coordinate, share reports. Well, you know how it goes better than anyone."

"Copy that," Evan said. "It's supposed to be our job to coordinate policy within the agencies and present it to the President. Talk about a bureaucratic nightmare."

"Hey, guys, since we don't have any good news to report tonight, how about we check out the buffet in the State Dining Room?" Angela said. "At least we should be able to enjoy ourselves for a few minutes, in contrast to our usual days around this place."

"So you've having a rough time of it, too?" Evan asked as they ambled to the Cross Hall, where the Marine Band, clad in red jackets with brass buttons and epaulets, was playing "Rudolph the Red-Nosed Reindeer."

"Everyone is having a rough time these days, trying to wrap up things before the end of the year," Angela said. "I was just talking to Pam Turner over in Legislative Affairs, and before Congress adjourns for the holidays, they're trying to get some agreement on a clean bill the President wants for a new missile defense system, but even though Congress says they're going to stop the practice of adding earmarks, they're still trying to load up the defense bill with nonsense. I mean, talk about a Christmas tree."

"What do they want this time?" Samantha asked.

"Let's see. Pam says that the top three are the New York goose control program, a North Carolina Teapot Museum, and a Seattle sculpture garden."

"Jeez!" Samantha said, trying to capture a lighter mood. "Oh look, there's Greg over there by the bar. And it looks like he's alone tonight. I wonder where his wife is?"

"Wouldn't surprise me if he just worked late, changed at the office, came straight over here, and left her at home. A lot of people have to do that, you know," Angela said. "Not many of us have the luxury of living as close to the White House as you do, my friend. You can go home and change. The rest of us always schlep our stuff in and change in the ladies' room."

"Guess you have a point there," Samantha said.

Evan walked over to join the crowd at the buffet table, where mounds of fresh shrimp, crab claws, and miniature lamb chops were piled on shiny silver platters. "Now that Evan's gone," Angela said in a low tone, "do you want to tell me more about Tripp? I just feel so awful about this. I know how you feel about the guy."

"Do you?" Samantha said, glancing up with troubled eyes.

"Are you kidding? As soon as you had that first dinner with him, you changed pronouns."

"I changed pronouns?" Samantha asked, furrowing her brow. "What in the world are you talking about?"

"You use to say 'I' or 'me' but then it was 'we' or 'us.'"

Samantha thought about that for a while. The image of Tripp Adams reaching across a dinner table to take her hand or stroke her cheek came flooding into her mind's eye. "Okay, Miss Perceptive. You win. I'm mad about him. But I'm also mad at the whole frigging government. I can't find anybody who can give me a glimmer of hope that we can find him, rescue him, get him out of there. Wherever *there* is."

"Good evening, Samantha . . . Angela . . . nice party tonight, but I need to talk to you for a moment," Greg said, waving his cocktail glass at Samantha.

Is he drunk, or what? Samantha wondered as Greg sidled up to the two of them. She knew he liked his martinis, but after all, this was the White House. You didn't put on a display in this place. Maybe he and his wife had a fight. Maybe that was why she wasn't here tonight. Or maybe he was just drowning his sorrows because everyone was coming down on their directorate over the latest sabotage on the pipelines, in addition to reports of new drug shipments being off-loaded in the Thousand Islands off southwest Florida, among other things. He certainly looked like he was teetering on his Gucci loafers.

"Uh, sure."

"Merry Christmas, Greg," Angela said. "I'll leave you two. Talk to me later, Samantha, I may have an idea for you." And with that, she sashayed across the room to grab some shrimp.

"So, what do you need?" Samantha asked her boss. Whenever he cornered her, it was usually because he wanted to give her another assignment. Couldn't he do that in the office?

"I just had a call. They want me on *Good Morning America* tomorrow. First segment as usual. So can you whip up a few talking points and e-mail them to me tonight? Just give me a few good quotes on the drug shipments and, of course, on the pipelines, the efforts we're all making, how the agencies are working together. You know the drill. Now, I've got to go chat with the Chief of Staff. Excuse me."

Samantha stood there, wondering what in God's name she could say about the agencies working together. There wasn't cooperation. It was more like a civil war. As she moved toward the bar to get a glass of wine, she saw the portrait of a brooding Abraham Lincoln staring down from the wall.

37

Gregory Barnes took the stairs down from the State Dining Room to the first floor and headed out to the colonnade along the Rose Garden. He was going back to the West Wing to grab his coat and a few papers from his office before driving home. He didn't feel like going home to face his wife. She would want to know why she couldn't go to the Senior Staff Christmas party. She had gone last year, but this time he had made an excuse that he had to work late and was just going to stop in for a few minutes. It was almost the truth. He did work late and then he did change in the office and head to the party. The fact was he just didn't feel like driving home to pick her up and dealing with her usual litany of complaints about his workload and late hours. He got enough grief at the office. He didn't need it at home. Besides, he had some other ideas about how to top off the evening.

He nodded to the agent standing by the door, collected his things, and went back down to the West Wing basement and out to West Exec, where his Lexus LS 430 was parked. He stumbled on the pavement, caught the door handle, and eased inside. *Guess I should have skipped that last martini,* he thought as he started the car and cranked the heater up to full blast. *Or maybe I should have had a few more lamb chops or coffee or something. Well, what the hell.* He put the car in gear and slowly drove out the Southwest Gate and up to E Street.

He turned toward the Whitehurst Freeway and thought about Samantha. He knew she lived around here someplace, and with this nice relaxed feeling, he wished he could just drop by her place, wherever it was, and talk her into a little private time. She sure had the looks and the body. Then again, he never messed with women around the White House. He had tried to make a bit of time with one of the analysts over at Energy, but she had wanted a lot more than an occasional hookup, so he dropped her after their first fling. No, he decided to stop by his latest conquest, the legislative aide who worked on the Hill. After all, she was young and impressionable and probably figured she could weasel her way into a White House job of some sort. He wasn't about to play that game, but he did enjoy her company once in a while.

The Lexus swerved and almost hit the guardrail along the freeway as Greg reached into his pocket for his cell. *Better give her a call and be sure she's alone tonight,* he thought as he tried to dial her number while negotiating a turn toward Georgetown. But he dropped the phone and had to lean down to pick it up. The car swerved again, but he turned the steering wheel just in time.

He knew it was against the law to talk on cell phones in the District, but it was pretty late and also pretty dark tonight. And he didn't see any cops around. He turned right on M Street and left onto Thirty-third. *Might as well aim for her place, just in case. Damn frigid out here tonight. Sure hope she's home and in the mood. I could stand a bit of warming up.*

He started to dial again but his right front tire hit a patch of ice and the car skidded toward the curb. He was looking down at his cell, checking the number when the car hit something. Jerking his head up, he slammed on his brakes and came to stop. *Jesus! What was that?* He couldn't see anything out of the windshield. He reached for the door handle and scrambled out onto the pavement. He raced around to the front of the car, and there in the gutter was the body of a man. *Oh Christ! I don't believe this,* he thought as he went over to see if the guy was hurt. He wasn't moving. Greg knelt down, and in the light from a streetlamp half a block down, he saw that the man was wearing a threadbare jacket, black pants with holes in them, and a pair of old tennis shoes caked with mud, and he had a stubbly beard. *Looks like some homeless guy who ought to be in a shelter on a night like this.* Greg tried to turn him over and that's when he saw the blood. Blood coming from his mouth. *Oh my God! I hit him and he's not breathing.*

He felt in the man's pockets for any kind of wallet or ID. Nothing. Only a few quarters and a coupon from the local Safeway. *I think he's dead. Did I kill him or was he already pretty wasted?* Greg could smell liquor on the man's clothes. He didn't know what to do. He thought about calling the police, but he had been drinking, too. He'd never pass a sobriety test. He worked at the White House as one of the President's top advisors. He'd be pilloried in the press. They'd be after him, his wife, his family.

It would never end. He'd never get another job.

He felt a sense of panic rising in his chest. What the hell was he supposed to do? This guy was a nobody. No ID, a drunk, a homeless nobody. Who would care? The city didn't take care of these guys anyway. Greg looked at the man's body again, crouched down, and pushed him back against the curb, next to a parked car. *When they find him, maybe they'll think that he was just so drunk he fell and hit his head or something. Yes, that's what they'll think. Gotta get out of here.* He looked around furtively. It was late. There weren't any lights on in the small carriage-type houses along this block. And there were cars parked all along the street that obstructed a view of the body.

He quickly walked back to his car, closed the door as quietly as he could, and slowly drove away. His cell was on the floor. He'd pick it up later. *Just as well that I didn't put that call through. I sure as hell don't want to see her now. I don't want to see anybody.*

He turned the corner without ever realizing that somebody else just happened to be watching.

"Hey Roy, it's them!" Godfrey shouted as he rushed into Tripp's old office. Roy Foss had decided to stay in town a few days after the hearing to pick up the slack in Tripp's absence. He had papers spread out all over the desk. A half-empty coffee mug and the remains of a cinnamon bun were sitting on top of a scrunched-up Dunkin' Donuts paper bag.

Roy jumped up from the desk. "What? Who's them?"

Godfrey waved his BlackBerry. "It's right here. A ransom demand. Can you believe this?"

Roy grabbed the cell and read the message. "Ten million U.S. dollars will be put in following bank account in Caymans or you will never see your man again." He then read off a series of numbers and wiring instructions. "Jesus Christ! How the hell did they know how to contact you?"

"They must have gotten Tripp's BlackBerry and checked his contacts. Pretty clever, I'd say."

"Can we trace it? Their location, I mean?" Roy asked.

"Don't know what kind of equipment they have in Caracas, or wherever the hell they are now. But I'll get to Victor right away."

Roy was reaching for the telephone. "Okay, you get to Aguilar, I'm calling headquarters. I'll also call State."

Godfrey headed back toward his office. "And I'll get to the White House."

"Oh good. Samantha Reid is your contact there, right?"

"Right. She's not going to want to hear this."

"Then again, she might. It means we've got a contact. It means Tripp must still be alive."

"How can you be so sure? They didn't say anything about his being alive or proving to us that he is. Just send the money. That's all it says. How are we supposed to know that he's okay and how are we supposed to get him back?"

"Beats the hell out of me," Roy said. "Let me get to our CEO and see how they want us to answer that message."

"Samantha Reid, please. Godfrey Nims of GeoGlobal is calling."

"Yes, Mr. Nims," Joan said. "I'll put her right on."

"Godfrey? Thank heavens you called. I haven't wanted to bother you, with the latest attack happening and all, but have you heard anything about Tripp?" she asked anxiously.

"That's what I'm calling about. I just got an e-mail on my Black-Berry from the kidnappers."

"Oh no! What did they say? Is Tripp all right? Where is he? Did they ask for money?"

"Slow down. Let me tell you." He read off the cursory message. "So now our Executive Vice President, Roy Foss, is here in the office calling our CEO and I'm about to call our head man in Caracas."

"Yes, I saw Roy giving that testimony. But wait, you say he's talking to your CEO. What are they going to do? Are they going to pay the ransom?"

"I don't know. We have K and R insurance, of course."

"Kidnap and Ransom insurance?" she asked.

"Of course. We all do."

"So will they pay it right away? We've got to get him back. He might be injured or sick or something."

"At this point, I don't know what they're going to do. They'll have to get the insurance negotiator in. They always do that."

"Insurance negotiator? You've got to be kidding. They're going to bring in some guy to *negotiate*? Kidnappers don't negotiate. They either get what they want or kill whoever they have," she practically cried into the phone.

"I hear you. Believe me, I hear you. We want to get him back as much as you do."

"Do you?" she asked.

"Of course we do. Good God! Look, I've got to get on the horn to our Caracas office. We'll be having conference calls on this. Meanwhile, have you been able to find anything out on your end about who these guys might be?"

"Not yet. I've got some contacts working on it."

"Well let me know what you hear. We need to work together. And as soon as Roy talks to headquarters and I coordinate with Caracas, we'll get you back in the loop, okay?"

"Sure. Sure." She hesitated and added, "I know you're working on it. I didn't mean . . ."

"It's okay, really. We're all feeling the stress of this whole thing. Tripp, the lines, the whole goddamn ball of wax. Now I gotta go. Take care."

"I'll try."

39

"They must not care about you, amigo, we hear nothing yet."

Tripp didn't answer Eyeshade. He sat up on the bed and rubbed his eyes. At least these guys spoke some English, and this Eyeshade person was obviously the brains behind the whole exercise. He appeared to have brushed off Tripp's feeble attack. At least he hadn't talked about it recently. Then again, when you've got the guns, you feel like you've got the power, and Eyeshade was going about his usual authoritative act.

"Coffee and bread. You eat," Eyeshade said, putting a chipped plate and a mug on the bedside table.

"Can I shave?" Tripp said, scratching his beard.

"What? You think if I had a razor I would give it to you?" Eyeshade threw his head back and laughed. "You're a stupid Americano." With that, the man drifted back into the living room and flipped on the TV again.

Tripp dragged the chain into the bathroom. There was a small round mirror hanging on the wall. He stared at his face, covered with a week's growth of beard. *I look like some Muslim,* he thought. *I just hope I can get out of here in one piece. I don't really care to meet up with seventy-two virgins in heaven. Then again, these guys don't appear to be worshipping Mecca or praying. Just common street thugs for sure. Seventy-two virgins?* The only woman he wanted to think about was Samantha. He wondered how she was, how she was reacting to this whole mess, what she was doing about it. If she really knew about the kidnapping, he figured she was bugging the agencies on an hourly basis asking for information. He doubted if they had any, though. What would their embassy or their ambassador know about a bunch of lowlifes who pluck people off the street for money? Probably not much. Even their Station Chief wouldn't have these kinds of contacts. Their CIA man embedded in the embassy would be working on bigger fish, the narcoterrorist crowd, big-time plots against the U.S. Things like that.

No, he doubted if anybody would be looking for him in the right place. Of course, GeoGlobal would be having a fit and would be trying to figure it out. He knew that Eyeshade had sent a message to Godfrey. He had heard them talking about the numbers. They were asking for ten million bucks to be put in some offshore account. These guys were more sophisticated than he first thought. They had their ducks in order, even a fancy bank account all lined up just waiting for a big fat deposit.

He wondered if GeoGlobal would deposit the money or if they'd do what they usually did and call in an insurance guy. The insurance companies never wanted to pay off on these big policies. And if they did get involved, that meant more communications and more delays. He pulled off his shirt and tried to take a short sponge bath without a sponge. He used part of the only towel in the bathroom and used the rest to try and dry himself off.

Suddenly he heard Eyeshade shouting for Rafael. He dragged the chain back into the bedroom and listened.

"Hey, Rafael, get in here. We've got an answer," Eyeshade said in

Spanish. "It comes not from the first guy, the guy I e-mailed. This is from another guy. He says he represents the company and wants to get more information."

"What kind of information? Will they pay? What does he say?" Rafael asked, rushing in from the outside, carrying a six-pack of beer. He shoved it into the small refrigerator behind the kitchen counter and pulled up a chair.

Eyeshade scrutinized the small device and read the message again. "Says here that he is negotiating for the company and he wants to know how we intend to release Mr. Adams."

"Release him?" Rafael said with a laugh. "We don't need to release him at all. We just want the money. Once we have it, who cares what happens to that jerk?"

Eyeshade looked over at Rafael. "How long have you been in this business? They always want to know that they're going to get their people back or else they're not going to pay. What kind of idiot are you anyway?"

Rafael looked slightly chagrined. "So we give him back. No big deal. He'd never be able to ID us anyway. We'd leave this place and take off. So I guess we can wait and decide what to do with him later."

"That's right. That's what we're going to do. But now I'm going to send back another message."

"What are you going to say this time?" Rafael asked.

"I'm going to tell them they have a deadline to get that money to the Caymans, and since they want to negotiate, we'll negotiate. We'll negotiate a higher price. Now it's fifteen million, and we want it in three days."

"But it's the weekend coming up and then there's Christmas. Do you think they can get it together with the weekend and a holiday? You know how Americans are with their time off."

Eyeshade swore and turned to face Rafael. "I don't care if it's Christmas or Easter or any other time. I want my money and I want it fast." He thought for a moment and added, "Three days or maybe we have to get rid of him just the way we got rid of the brother." He turned his back and started punching in another e-mail.

Samantha sat on a bench in Lafayette Park, across Pennsylvania Avenue from the White House. She had taken a lunch break, had to make a phone call and didn't want to do it from her office. She shivered as she pulled her coat tighter around her. The sun was out but it was one of those clear, cold days where the slightest breeze made you want to put on a pair of woolies. Well, she didn't have any woolies. At least she was wearing a pair of black slacks and a sweater under her coat. She had left her blazer in the office. It felt too bulky to wear under the coat anyway. Besides, she didn't think she'd be out here that long.

She pulled a small pad of paper out of her purse and read the notes she had made last night when she had researched Greyfield on her computer. The contractor had offices all over the world and she wasn't sure where to start looking for Joe Campiello but she was determined to make as many cell phone calls as it took to track him down. She was pretty sure that was the name of the guy Tripp had talked about so much, his buddy with this private contractor, the one who had "saved his ass" and vice versa many times.

She dialed a number at their home office and was referred to Human Resources and then to a field office in Virginia, near Norfolk. *Maybe they have contracts with the Navy*, she thought as she dialed another number. *If he's in the States, I'm really in luck.* After three more tries with three different offices and administrative assistants, she finally got through to what she hoped was the right office.

"Yes, Samantha Reid. That's right. I'm trying to reach Mr. Campiello. Could you simply tell him that I'm a friend of Tripp Adams. . . . Yes, Mr. Adams used to work for your company a few years ago . . . Yes, I'll hold." She glanced at her watch and held her breath. Finally, she heard a click.

"Campiello here."

"Joe? Joe Campiello?" she asked breathlessly.

"You got him. Who's this? They said Samantha Reid. Do I know you?"

"No, you don't, but I'm a friend of Tripp Adams."

"Tripp? God damn! How do you know my buddy Tripp?" Joe said in a more jovial tone.

"I work here in Washington, D.C., and Tripp was recently transferred here to head up the GeoGlobal office."

"Yeah, I knew he was with that company. Haven't heard from him in a while. How's he doing?"

Samantha took a deep breath and told him the story. She explained how she had been pressing every agency she could to get some help but had come up empty-handed. She told him she worked at the White House, but with their policy of never negotiating with kidnappers, her colleagues couldn't be any help. She also confided that she had a friend at the agency, but hadn't heard anything from him either. "So, I got to thinking about you and Greyfield and I wanted to contact you to see if there might be something you could do. What do you think?"

"Wait a minute," Joe said. "Tripp's been kidnapped by some bunch down in Venezuela that's now asking for a hefty ransom. And you want Greyfield to get involved? I would do anything to get him back.

Don't get me wrong. I'm just trying to get a line on exactly what you have in mind here. Is this something the White House is going to contract for? I can't quite see it. Now, if you were calling from the Agency or the Pentagon or even from GeoGlobal, I could see that, but not the White House."

"Well, no, I don't mean that the White House would be behind any sort of operation. But I have other options." Her mind was racing. Other options, what in the world was she saying? She didn't have any other options. Not yet anyway. Maybe she could figure out a few, though. "What I mean is—well, first, before we get to details, just tell me this. Do you think you and some of your people could try to mount a rescue operation? I mean, would you have any way to look for Tripp? Find him? Rescue him?"

Joe thought for a long moment. "So let me get this straight. You're saying that you, or somebody, wants us to put together a rescue operation down in Venezuela. Is that right?"

"Well, yes. Do you think you could do it?"

"I'd do it myself on my own if I could and if I had a clue where he is. But I know I couldn't pull off an operation by myself. And besides, nobody knows where he is, do they?"

"Not yet. No. But GeoGlobal has been exchanging e-mails as I explained . . . about the ransom money. They even have this insurance negotiator trying to send messages. But I just heard from GeoGlobal that the last time he did that, they got so mad they upped the ransom and put a deadline on it for three days. That's Monday," she said, her voice cracking.

"Let me think about this," Joe said. "GeoGlobal is balking at paying what? Fifteen million? That's a bunch of horseshit. They spill more than that every morning."

"I know. You're right."

"And I work for an outfit that could probably mount some sort of operation . . . we do have teams in South America. We've done a lot work down there."

"You have?" Samantha's tone brightened. "Then you think you might be able to do something?"

"Trouble is, I work for a private contractor. If I had to put a team together, and I would need a whole team for an operation like this, the company would want to be paid and I doubt if you have that kind of dough. Right?"

Samantha leaned back against the cold bench and thought of a scheme. "Tell you what. I do have an idea of how we might be able to put something together. What if I got GeoGlobal to pay your fee? It wouldn't be as high as fifteen million, would it?"

"Nope. Probably closer to a million or two, depending on the time involved, the number of guys I'd use, the expenses and all."

"I'm going to work on this. We don't have much time and the only way we know how to communicate is through the BlackBerry. We know they have Tripp's and so we can send e-mails to those guys, too. That's one in our favor."

"And if we put this deal together I already know how it could go down."

"You do?"

"Yeah. Let me put some ideas together, talk to some people. You talk to GeoGlobal. See what you can pull off."

"Could you go to Caracas yourself and head this up?"

"I think so. I'm finishing up a project here in Norfolk, but if we get a contract, I could be on the next plane."

And so could I.

41

"Why do all the stations have to show speeches by El Presidente all the time?" Rafael asked, switching channels on the TV. "They all have the same speech from some stupid church."

"So? It's Sunday and he's probably trying to get votes from the religious types with the election coming up in a few weeks." Eyeshade peered at the screen. "Hey, I know that place. My mother used to make me go there when I was a kid. It's that Church of Santa Catarina just outside the city. I wonder why he went way over there?"

"Beats me," Rafael said. "All he does is talk about how he's going to get more food for everybody. How can he do that when the price of bread is so high now? I had to pay twice as much for the sandwiches than I had to pay last time we were up here."

"Yeah. That's why we need the ransom money. To start over somewhere else."

"Maybe we'll go to Trinidad and Tobago. They've got good beaches, no?"

"Let's just get the money before we spend it," Eyeshade said as he reached for the BlackBerry. "Here we go again."

"Another message?"

"Yeah."

"What do they want now?"

"It's from that same guy who says he's representing the company."

"Why can't the company people contact us directly? They're the ones who have all the money," Rafael asked.

"Maybe. Maybe not. This guy says something about insurance, and he says that he's working on arranging the ransom."

"That's good."

"Yeah, but he now says that because of the Christmas holiday, he needs a few more days to get it all together, get it transferred to the bank."

"A few more days," Rafael said, pacing across the tile floor. He reached inside the small icebox for a beer, popped the top, and took a swig. "I don't like it. They're just stalling. Maybe we should give them a little incentive."

"Incentive?" Eyeshade asked. "What incentive?"

"I already planned something that would get their attention. And now, we might need it."

Tripp listened intently to the exchange in the other room as the TV droned in the background. So the company was vying for time. At least they were working some angle, some way to get him out of this hellhole. Sitting on the bed, he wiped his brow. The temperature had soared, and now with the sun beating down on what he figured was some sort of tin roof, the dusty casita was stifling. He regularly plodded over to the bathroom for water, but even that was warm and usually some kind of a rust color. His stomach was rumbling. They did give him some bread and coffee in the mornings; then it was a plate of beans at night. Much more of this routine and his guts were going to flame out.

Between rants by Rafael, he heard the speech by El Presidente about the food supply. That just made him all the more hungry for a piece of fruit, a vegetable maybe. Anything but bread and beans.

Then he noticed that the replay of a game came on after the President's speech. The commentators were talking about how one of the players had racked up his leg. Tripp looked down at the chain wrapped around his own leg. It had begun to chafe from all of the times he had dragged it to the bathroom. The skin was blistered and broken in several places. He had taken off his undershirt and tried to wedge it in between his ankle and the chain, but it wasn't working very well.

So tough it out. You've seen worse. He kept telling himself that he'd been in much worse physical shape during some of his exploits with Joe Campiello at Greyfield. But back then, they'd always had an exit strategy. Now, glancing around the dingy room, he wondered how he would ever get rid of this one.

Rafael and Eyeshade were out there drinking beer. At least they weren't shouting at each other. He heard the TV announcer come back on with a bulletin. "And now we see that El Presidente has returned to the Church of Santa Catarina. He appears ready to address the second service of the day." *Oh great. Now we get to hear about his grandiose plans for this socialist paradise all over again.* Tripp lay back down on the bed, put his arms behind his head, and did the only thing that had kept him sane for the past week. He dreamed about Samantha.

"Are you insane?" Angela said as she huddled with Samantha in the small den off the living room of her parents' home.

"You have to promise me you won't tell a soul," Samantha said, almost in a whisper.

"Don't you know that Greg will find out, you could be fired, or worse yet, you could be kidnapped yourself? This is positively the craziest thing I've ever heard you say."

"Maybe. Maybe not. It's just that I feel I have to do *something* to get him back. Nobody else is doing anything."

"What do you mean? You said yourself that the company has some negotiator working it, contacting the kidnappers, dealing with deadlines and all of that. And you think you're going to go and get into the middle of it all? I'm sorry, my friend, but this time I really think you've lost it."

Samantha sighed and leaned in closer. "But I have to get involved. You know our government isn't in a position to rescue our people.

Well, not usually unless they're military or something. And yes, okay, GeoGlobal is working on it. But whoever this negotiator guy is, he seems to be screwing everything up. He contacts them and all they do is raise the price of the ransom. They sound like they're getting edgy. At least, that's what Godfrey told me the last time we talked."

"So you went and found this Campiello guy and you think he's going to mount some James-Bond-to-the-rescue kind of operation? You think Greyfield is going to stick their necks out and figure out a way to find Tripp somewhere in an entire country in South America and bring him out? Alive? And you're going to go down there and arrange their rescue fee?" She shook her head. "I know I'm repeating myself, but this is the most unheard-of thing I ever heard of."

Samantha stared at her friend. "So, what would *you* do if you were in my place?"

"I don't know. Wait. You've only known this guy for . . . what? . . . couple of weeks? And you're going to risk your life and your job and everything else to go traipsing off to a foreign country and try to pull off something our own CIA can't pull off?"

"So I've only known him a short time. But during that time we . . . well . . ."

"You're in love with him, aren't you?" Angela said, softening her tone.

Samantha sighed and admitted the obvious. "Yes."

"Oh boy. Now let's recap how this thing is supposed to play out," Angela said. "You found this Campiello guy at Greyfield and he's agreed to put some sort of team together and head down to Caracas, right?"

"Right. And I'm flying down tomorrow night to coordinate every-thing."

"I don't get why you think *you* have to go to Caracas. If you're try-ing to act on your own and keep all of this from the White House, which, as I just said, is absolutely nutty, why would you leave the coun-try? How are you going to keep this secret? First of all, you know darn well that top White House staffers are watched all the time. By foreign agents, I mean. The Russians. The Israelis. The French. They all have teams that keep an eye on us. Well, maybe not me. I'm not that critical.

But people like you. People with your rank and other people on the NSC. They keep track of everybody. And then, the minute you land and you use your passport to get entry into Venezuela, they'll report it to our embassy. They always do, you know."

"I don't care about the Russians or the others. And I doubt if the Venezuelans have as sophisticated an operation in Washington right now. As for the passport situation, I've got that covered."

"How?"

"I'm using my old passport with my married name on it. We all have two passports. Our White House diplomatic passport and our old one. We didn't have to turn that one in, remember?"

"Guess you're right. Nobody has ever sent me overseas for anything, so I never thought about it. But still, what are you going to tell Greg? You know he can't operate without you."

"Well, he's going to have to, but just for a few days. Besides, tomorrow's Christmas and we all should be able to take a few days off anyway. Greg is going to some family reunion for a couple of days. So he won't miss me."

"Not until he comes back and gets asked to go on MSNBC or some other station and he can't figure out how to put two sentences together without your talking points," Angela said derisively. "By the way, I saw him the other morning on *Today,* and he looked kinda rattled. Rather unusual for Mr. Photogenic, I thought. Did you see that?"

"No. I see so much of him at the office, I don't feel like I need to tune in to all of his performances. Anyway, if he contacts me before I can get back, well, I've got some excuses I think I can use. For now, I've got things all lined up."

"Okay. So what's lined up?"

"I've got my ticket to Caracas on the overnight flight tomorrow. It's the same fight that Tripp took before. It leaves at eleven thirty p.m. Then once I get there, I have a meeting with Victor Aguilar at GeoGlobal."

"Wait a minute. I'm not following this. You said you were going to meet Joe Campiello."

"I am. But first I have to finalize the fee with Victor. Here's the deal. I told GeoGlobal that I've got Greyfield lined up to try and mount a rescue operation, and since it will cost a lot less than paying a fifteen-million-dollar ransom, they're willing to back the idea."

Angela eyed her friend suspiciously. "So they're playing with Tripp's life for the difference of a few million dollars?"

"No, that's not the whole deal. When I explained who Joe is and how Greyfield operates, they decided that Joe's team would probably have a better chance of getting Tripp out alive than relying on the goodwill of the kidnappers after the money is deposited in the Caymans."

"Did you tell GeoGlobal that you were acting on behalf of the White House?"

"Uh, not precisely,"

"But you left that impression? That's why they're cooperating, right?"

"Well, I sort of had to finesse that one."

"Oh, man. You've really done it this time, kiddo. And what, precisely, are you going to tell Greg when he comes looking for you?"

"I can always send him an e-mail saying I had to take a few days off because of a family emergency."

"Speaking about family, what about your own family? I thought they wanted you to come to Houston for Christmas."

"They did. Well, my dad did. He's been calling saying that my brother, his wife, and the kids are going to be there and they'd like me to come if I can get away. I wanted to be with them. Of course I did. But when this whole thing came together, I told them I just couldn't leave. I blamed it on the pipeline attacks. And Dad understood that."

"What about the pipelines? Shouldn't you be working on that right now?"

"I've got my interagency group on it. All the agencies are on it. We're also trying to get satellites on it. There's been a delay getting the right permissions, if you can believe that. More bureaucracy. But I hope they can get it through sometime this week. There's not much more I can do right now. Besides, when I think about Tripp being held by these . . . these . . . thugs or whoever they are . . . I just panic sometimes. But now I think I've really got a plan."

"And you think nobody at the White House will wonder where you are or what you're doing? Not your interagency team? Not your friend over at the agency? By the way, does he know what you're up to?"

"No, not yet. I want to see if we can make this work just using a private contractor. If the government gets involved, they could mess it up. I figure we just need one person in charge right now."

"And that would be you?"

"Well, not me exactly. I mean Joe Campiello would be in charge of the operation. I'm just . . . well . . . a facilitator."

"That's a new title," Angela said, getting up from her father's leather chair. "Okay, before you go jetting off like Robert Redford in *Spy Game* . . . I loved that movie, by the way . . . let's get a glass of wine. Mom's thrilled that you could come for Christmas Eve dinner. This is big in our house. We always celebrate on Christmas Eve. Aunt Evelyn is going to be playing Christmas carols after dinner if you can stay awhile."

Samantha got up and headed for the door as Angela called over her shoulder, "Besides, it might be your last meal."

"God rest ye merry, gentlemen, let nothing you dismay."

Samantha was dismayed, all right. Dismayed because she was getting so little help from all of her government contacts. While surrounded every single day by the supposedly best and brightest, she often wondered how anything really important ever got done by a government agency.

"Remember Christ our Savior was born on Christmas Day . . . To save us all from Satan's power when we were gone astray."

Things had gone astray, that's for sure. And poor Tripp must be under some sort of Satan's power. Just thinking of him rotting in some South American jungle killed any sort of Christmas spirit she was supposed to be feeling right now.

Aunt Evelyn finished the song, and everyone clapped and asked for another one. Samantha stole a glance at her watch. The Marconis had been so nice to her, inviting her to their Christmas Eve dinner, which was quite a feast. The turkey and dressing, mashed potatoes and gravy, had all been delicious, but she couldn't eat much. She was feeling so nervous, so distracted, even distraught every time she thought about Tripp and the kind of Christmas Eve he was enduring that she had only picked at her food. She hoped Mrs. Marconi hadn't noticed.

"We three kings of Orient are . . . Bearing gifts we travel afar."

She wasn't a king, but she'd sure be traveling afar. She did a mental checklist of things she should pack tomorrow—passport, comfortable shoes, casual clothes. She wanted to look like a simple tourist, not a White House aide or even a business type. She wouldn't take any jewelry. She just remembered that there was a twenty-four-hour CVS pharmacy on her way home. She could stop in there and buy a cheap Timex watch and leave her good one at home.

"Field and fountain, moor and mountain . . . Following yonder star."

Was he being held in a field or on a mountain? How in the world would the Greyfield team ever find him? Joe had said they had more tools than Black & Decker. But did they really? She'd have to wait another forty-eight hours to find out.

"Mommy, Mommy, Santa came. He really did!" the four-year-old girl shouted, pointing to her stocking filled with candy and a Barbie doll in a wedding dress peeking over the top. "And look, he ate all the cookies and the milk we put out last night."

"And look at all the Yu-Gi-Oh! cards," her brother exclaimed. "And the LEGO Speed Racer. This is so cool."

"I bet my stuff is cooler than your stuff."

"No it isn't," he replied.

"Now, children, children. Merry Christmas," the widow said, smiling from the stairway, clad in a flimsy blue terry-cloth bathrobe. "Let's see what else we have here."

The three of them gathered around the Christmas tree. The little girl reached way under it, pulled out a small box wrapped in tinfoil, and handed it to her mother.

"Why, what's this, honey?"

"Open it and you'll see," the girl said, her eyes wide in anticipation. The widow pulled the foil away and opened the box. Inside she saw a necklace made of plastic multicolored beads. "I made it in kindergarten, just for you, Mommy. Do you like it?"

"Oh, honey. It's the most beautiful necklace I've ever seen," her mother said, putting it around her neck. "It's got every color in the rainbow and it'll match anything I decide to wear." She pulled the child onto her lap and hugged her. "Thank you, sweetie. I love it. Love you, too."

The boy was about to hand his mother his own gift when the house was suddenly rocked by an explosion. The windows rattled, several china plates that had been displayed on a rack on the dining room wall crashed to the floor and the cocker spaniel let out a huge yelp. The woman grabbed the children and cried out, "What was that?"

The boy wriggled free and ran to the window. "Mom. Come look. There's a big fire out there. It's big, Mom . . . really really huge. There's flames and they're going higher and higher."

She rushed to the window and put her hand over her heart. "Lord in heaven, that's the gasworks over there. I have to call the police." She raced to the phone and dialed a number. Busy. She tried the fire department. It was busy, too. "People must be callin' it in from all over town."

The boy's gaze was fixated on the fire as his little sister craned her neck to see how high the flames were going. "Mommy, do you think it could come over here?"

"I don't know. But you children run upstairs and get your clothes on. We're not going to stay in this house another minute." The children. She had to get out of there and protect the children.

The boy ran up the stairs to his room while the little girl stopped to survey the scene by the Christmas tree. "Will our house be okay, Mommy?"

"I hope so, honey. Come on now. We've got to hurry."

"Okay," the girl said. "Just let me take Barbie."

As the widow dashed up the stairs to get some clothes, she grabbed a framed photo from the mantel. It was picture of a young Army recruit, smiling from beneath his helmet. Her husband had been killed in Afghanistan and now all she had left were the children. She pulled on a running suit and some sneakers, hustled the kids down the stairs and out the doorway. As they raced to the car, another explosion rocked the countryside.

Samantha pulled her carry-on over to the Arrivals and Departures board and checked her gate. The cavernous airport wasn't very crowded. Why would it be? Nobody in their right mind would want to travel on Christmas night. *Nobody except somebody desperately in love with a man being held captive by a bunch of crazies in a foreign country,* she thought. She pulled out her boarding pass and old passport and got into the security line. As it snaked toward the TSA employees, she figured that these Transportation Security folks probably weren't too happy to be on duty tonight either.

She reached into her shoulder bag and took out the plastic bag containing her moisturizer, small tube of toothpaste, travel-size hair spray, and lip gloss and put it on top of her purse in the bin. She wasn't planning on wearing much makeup on this trip, just enough to look decent for her meeting at GeoGlobal. After all, she was merely posing as a simple tourist, a lowly working girl with a few days off to see some exotic sites. At least, that's what she would tell the passport control people in Caracas. She then added her carry-on, took off her loafers, and walked through security without setting off any alarms. She was wearing a pair of lightweight khaki slacks and a green sweater. She had a trench coat with her, though she doubted she would need it in the warm summer climate in Venezuela right now. She had another, more businesslike outfit she planned to wear to her meeting, but the rest of the clothes jammed into her carry-on were things she used to wear when she went hiking out West, slacks, shorts, T-shirts, and comfortable walking shoes.

She had not brought her computer. The BlackBerry in her shoulder bag would have to do.

She stopped in the ladies' room and saw that all of the handicap stalls were occupied. It was practically impossible to drag a carry-on into a regular stall, turn around, and lock the door. *A man who only checks his luggage must have designed these cubicles.*

She meandered over to the People Movers, which were actually special shuttle buses that took passengers out to another terminal. When she got there, she found her gate and sat down to wait. She glanced up at the TV hanging from the ceiling and saw video of flames reaching skyward. The volume was low and she could barely hear the voice-over, but she recognized the report as one she'd seen earlier that evening. It was all about the two attacks on pipelines in Alabama. One had been set very close to a commercial gasworks building, and the whole thing had gone up in flames. Some men who had been on holiday duty had been killed. She couldn't imagine the heartbreak of families learning that their husbands or fathers had died. And on Christmas morning. Hundreds of people from the surrounding area had fled the scene, causing a traffic jam on the single road out of town.

She was amazed that there were two attacks in the same general area almost at the same time. Whoever was sabotaging the lines really knew what they were doing. They must have located two different pig insertion stations and timed their explosives to go off on two different but nearby lines. There were so many gas lines that converged in Alabama and Louisiana, it would be pretty easy to find some to hit.

She wondered how many terrorists were working together. It had to be at least two, probably more. She speculated about their motives. Everyone in the whole government had been trying to figure out that one. There had been no demands. No contacts. No claims of credit for all the chaos. It certainly wasn't the modus operandi of Al Qaeda or even EPR or any of the other groups they had been trying to track. But the effects were similar to what had happened in previous attacks. People are killed, the economy takes a dive, panic spreads, and in this case, the price of gas and oil was especially vulnerable and had gone sky-high. Just like those flames she was watching. *Who in the world would plan such attacks? What would be the point? Who would benefit? Unless . . .*

Her train of thought was interrupted when her flight was called. She had bought a tourist-class ticket, since she paid for it out of her own pocket. She saw that she was to be seated toward the back. Figured. When she finally got on board, she could barely stuff her carry-on into the overhead compartment. She had to roll up her trench coat and put it under the seat in front of her along with her shoulder bag. *Not much legroom here. How in the world are we supposed to sleep tonight?* She had been assigned a window seat. She had been so busy she hadn't checked that. She wished she had an aisle seat, because she still couldn't bear to look down from most any type of height. Not from a window. Not from a hotel. Not from anywhere. Her visions of Dexter's fall out in the Tetons had faded a bit, but she still got nervous whenever she was higher than the third or fourth floor of anything.

It was dark outside, but she pulled the window shade down and decided to leave it that way for the duration of the flight. She tried to fasten her seat belt but had to extend it. She hated having to do that. Some really skinny type must have been on the previous flight. Samantha had a paperback book in her bag, but she fished in the seat pocket in front of her to see what magazines might have been left there. In addition to the usual airline propaganda, the only other one she could find was *Skateboarding.* She leaned back and tried to relax.

A large man who looked like he once played linebacker for the Patriots and was still chowing down at the training table wedged himself into the seat next to her. She immediately jammed down the armrest between them, trying to secure what little space she could manage. He was talking on his cell phone, and even though she knew he'd have to turn it off eventually, she wished she had one of those electronic gizmos she had heard about. It was a pretty clever device. You just pressed a button and any cell phones nearby would automatically be cut off. She made a mental note to try and buy one when she got back home. She wondered when that would be. She hadn't bought a return ticket because she had no clue when or if this crazy mission would be successful.

Was it crazy? Was Angela right to say that she was insane? Probably. Would Greg come looking for her as soon as he got back and had to face the fact that there had been two more explosions that morning? Most definitely. When he tried to call her cell or e-mail her, would he blithely accept her excuse of a family emergency of some kind? No way. He'd order her to come back ASAP, citing all sorts of national security concerns. Concerns that she just couldn't deal with right now. She had the security of just one man on her mind. Tripp Adams. And it was going to stay that way for the next few days. She had to stay focused, had to convince GeoGlobal's South American President that hiring Greyfield was the smart thing to do and get them to process the funds so Joe Campiello could try and pull off a miracle.

Did miracles happen? And on Christmas? Only in *It's a Wonderful Life,* which happened to be one of the movies being offered on the video list that night. She had seen it several times and decided she wasn't in the mood for that one, although she could certainly use her own guardian angel right about now. After takeoff, the flight attendants came around taking drink orders. Samantha didn't order a drink. Not even a glass of wine. Just a bottle of water. She wanted to try and get some sleep and then be absolutely clearheaded when she arrived in Caracas. She was going to check in to her hotel first and then head to a meeting at GeoGlobal.

She had made a reservation at a small local hotel she had found online. It appeared to be fairly close to the GeoGlobal office. It was on the same street, Francisco de Miranda, so that meant it was downtown. She was somewhat amused that it was named Hotel del Valle. Hotel of the Valley. *Maybe it's buried in a valley of concrete between skyscrapers or something,* she mused. It looked like it catered to international tourists. It certainly wasn't fancy and it was pretty cheap. She had wanted to stay away from the big hotels like the Four Seasons or the Hilton, and she particularly wanted to stay away from the American Embassy. She knew that the embassy was located in a different part of the city. It had been moved to Valle Arriba. She'd avoid that section. The last thing she needed was some bureaucrat gumming up the works. No, what she wanted was a completely independent operation. One run solely by Joe Campiello.

When she had talked to him again to iron out the details of her trip, she tried to understand why Tripp had put so much trust in the man some years back. Joe certainly had ideas. He seemed organized, ready to move, anxious to get on with the operation. She wondered if he was too anxious, a bit too gung-ho, and maybe too trigger-happy. After only a few telephone conversations, she couldn't be sure. She'd have to take the measure of the man when she finally met him. As the airplane engines droned on and she tried to fall asleep, she wondered if she had made the right choice after all.

"Where the hell is she?" Gregory Barnes bellowed to Joan.

"Uh, I'm not sure, sir."

"You're her AA. An administrative assistant is supposed to know where her boss is. So what do you mean, you're not sure?" he said, leaning over her desk, skewering her with a piercing stare.

"All I know is that she had some sort of family emergency and said she had to take a couple of days off. After all, it *is* Christmas week."

Greg narrowed his eyes. "National security doesn't take a holiday, Ms. Tillman, or have you forgotten where you are working?"

"Uh, no sir. Not at all. It's just that I don't have a number where she could be located at the moment."

"Haven't you heard about cell phones and e-mail?"

"Well, sure. I'll try to reach her if you need her right away. It's just that she's out of town. At least, that was my impression."

"Your impression? You're supposed to have more than an impression when it comes to your boss's whereabouts."

"I guess I could issue an Amber Alert," Joan said under her breath as she reached for the phone.

"What was that?" Greg said.

"Nothing." Joan dialed Samantha's cell number. She listened for a few moments and finally just got her voice mail. She left a short message asking Samantha to please call the office. Then she hung up and turned to face Greg again. "Okay, I left word for her to call in. Is there something special you want me to tell her? Something that you need right now?"

"I need her in here. That's what I need. With those two attacks yesterday, the networks are all over us. They want me on Fox this afternoon, and the President and NSC Advisor both need updates. The President is going to go to the funerals of the people killed in the twin attacks and I need more information for him ASAP. Get me the list of people on Samantha's Crisis Action Team . . . the interagency people . . . and check with each of them on what they've learned about all of this. The press is going nuts. Did you see that headline in the *Post* this morning? 'Christmas Carnage'! Jesus! And Samantha picks this time to be out of town."

"She said it was a family emergency, remember?"

"It *was* a family emergency? So how long is this emergency supposed to last?"

"I guess it's a question of what the meaning of the word *was* is," Joan said, trying to deflect Greg's anger.

"Don't get cute with me, Tillman. Just find her."

Joan's phone rang. "Maybe that's her." She picked up the handset and listened for a moment. "May I tell him who's calling?" She raised her eyebrows and said, "Can you hold a moment please?"

"Is it Samantha?" Greg asked.

"No. Since your secretary is away from her desk, she forwarded her calls to me. This one's for you."

"Who is it?"

"I don't know. He wouldn't give his name. He just said that he had seen you last week in Georgetown. Do you want to take the call?"

46
CARACAS—WEDNESDAY MORNING

"Please fasten your seat belts. We will be landing in a few minutes at Caracas Maiquetía International Airport." The pilot repeated the message in Spanish.

Samantha rubbed her eyes and tried to stretch in what little space she had. The linebacker next to her had his arm draped over the armrest, and she thought she could still smell the several scotch highballs he had been drinking half the night. The lights came on in the cabin and she realized it was morning because other passengers were raising their window shades. She still didn't want to raise hers. She just couldn't bring herself to look out . . . or down.

She hadn't been able to sleep much. After her hefty seatmate finished his last drink, he dozed off and started to snore so loudly it sounded like a truck stuck in a bog somewhere. As she reached for her bottle of water, the plane jolted and started to shake. It was like a tremor and felt as if the entire cabin were trembling in fear of some larger being. She was startled and scared.

The captain came on again. "Sorry for a bit of turbulence, folks. There are a few thunderstorms in the area. Please keep your seat belts tightly fastened." There was nothing she could do but hang on. Now if only Mr. Big and Tall would relinquish the armrest, she'd have something to hang on to. He started to stir and finally sat up.

Leaning over, he asked, "What's happening?"

"Few storms around," Samantha replied, trying not to get too close.

"Happens a lot this time of year," he said. "I fly down here all the time. Well, I used to. Have to shut things down now."

"What do you mean?"

"Got a business here, but this government has been confiscating a lot of our property, so we're gonna get the hell out while the getting's good," he said, shifting his weight and drawing his legs back in front of him. "Sorry if I bothered you there. I sleep pretty soundly on these flights."

"No problem," she lied. "So your business is being taken over? I know other people in the same fix."

"Really? Well, there's a lot of us. That's for sure."

The plane lurched again and Samantha grabbed the armrest.

"Don't worry little lady. Anything happens to this plane, I'll get you out. By the way, I'll be in town for a week or so. Will you have any free time? I could show you the sights, maybe grab some dinner, or . . . even breakfast," he said, leaning a bit closer. "I know all the best restaurants. There's a Basque place called Urrutia that's great for Sunday brunch or, if you like Italian, my favorite dinner hangout is Vizio. Then there's French . . ."

Oh great. That's just what I need right now. Some lech following me around. "Uh, no thanks," she interrupted. "I've got a pretty full schedule."

"So where are you staying?"

She wasn't about to tell him. "I'm staying with a friend," she said as the plane swayed slightly to the left. "I sure hope we land soon," Samantha added, trying to change the subject.

"Put up your shade. Let's see how close we are?"

She hesitated, finally pushed it up, but looked away. He glanced over and pointed to the mountains. "See, we're almost there. The airport is near the ocean. The city is in a valley on the other side of those mountains. Takes about forty-five minutes to get into town. That is, if the bridge is okay."

"What do you mean, if the bridge is okay?"

"It fell down a while back. And while they were fixing it, you had to use an old Spanish road and that took about four hours."

"Four hours? But I can't . . ."

"Last I heard they had some temporary fixes on it. We'll just have to wait and see." He peered out her window again. "At least we're almost on the ground." The plane lurched again and she finally felt the wheels slam into the runway. The plane bounced twice and finally settled down.

I've seen lunar modules make better landings, she thought. *But at least we're on the ground.* When the other passengers finally filed out, the guy hauled his huge frame out of the seat and she was able to squeeze into the aisle. He helped get her carry-on down from the overhead and let her stand in front of him. At least now she couldn't smell his breath.

After clearing immigration and customs, she found a taxi and headed into town. She checked her BlackBerry and saw that she had a message from Joan, but she wasn't about to call the White House. Not now. Not for a long time. Greg would just have to figure out a way to get through an entire day without her. She could always say she had been in a bad zone and didn't get the message.

During the long drive, she marveled at the lush green countryside. The rain had stopped and the clouds were beginning to give way to patches of blue sky. As they got closer to the city, she saw a rainbow arched over a mountain. "What's that?" she asked the driver in Spanish.

"Oh, that's El Avila. Very pretty mountain. You should go up there. There is the Teleférico, like a tram they have on ski mountains. It takes you up and you see the city."

"Thanks. I may have to try that," she said. She wanted everyone to believe she was on a tourist holiday, even a taxi driver. But she knew she'd be too busy to go around sightseeing.

The driver was getting chatty now as he started to point out the sights and tell her all sorts of other places to go. "You go to the Galería de Arte Nacional. They have everything from Egyptian pieces to modern art. Then there's the Palacio Municipal. Our City Hall also has a museum inside. Very special place. But best of all is Casa Natal. That's where our famous leader, Simón Bolívar, was born."

"Yes, that would be very interesting. Thank you."

The driver made a turn and announced, "There is another demonstration in the city today."

"I've heard there have been protests," she said. "Is it another student group?"

"Yes, I think so. I hear they're marching around the Tribunal Supremo de Justicia."

The Supreme Court, she thought. "So are you taking a detour or something?"

"Yes. But don't worry, we are almost to your hotel."

Samantha continued to stare out the window at dozens and dozens of skyscrapers. The city was incredible. All these huge buildings interspersed with historic churches and parks with a verdant backdrop of mountains reaching up thousands of feet. *How can such a beautiful place spawn so much trouble?* she asked herself. They finally pulled up to the rather simple but charming Hotel del Valle. She paid the driver and saw that he was happy to accept American dollars. She checked in and found that her room was so small it was almost monastic. There was a single bed in the corner with a night table and lamp, a small armoire with three wire hangers for her clothes, and a bathroom with no tub, just a single shower stall, sink, and toilet. All she could think of was the silly line about how a room was so small, you'd have to go outside to change your mind.

Oh well, at least it's cheap and right in the center of town. I can probably walk over to GeoGlobal later this morning. She had told Victor Aguilar that she would call him as soon as she was checked in. She quickly took a shower, brushed her hair, applied a bit of makeup, and put on a black skirt and white silk blouse. She had brought this one decent outfit with her for her meeting with GeoGlobal because she knew that here in Caracas people dressed up for business meetings, even more than they did in the States.

"Good morning, Ms. Reid," the receptionist said. "Please go right in. Mr. Aguilar is expecting you."

When she opened his office door, Victor strode over with an outstretched hand. 'I can't tell you how pleased we are, all of us, to have a representative of the White House flying all the way down here to assist with the rescue of our Vice President."

He sat down in a side chair and motioned for her to take a seat on the couch. *Oh boy. I've really got to play this one carefully.* "Uh yes, well, I'm glad to be of assistance. As I said in our earlier conversation, we need to keep this operation extremely confidential."

"Of course. Of course. But I figured you would want your ambassador . . ."

"No. No. I mean, let's not get the embassy involved at this point. They do have their Diplomatic Security people who have been working their contacts. But right now, for this special situation with Greyfield, I think it would be best to keep it quiet, if you know what I mean."

"Well, if you say so. I realize that there are often differences of opinion within the government about the use of private contractors, so that must be . . ."

"Exactly," she said quickly. "This is a very special situation in that Tripp, uh, Mr. Adams, once worked for Greyfield. They know him. They want to help. The man I've contacted, Joe Campiello, had personally worked with Tripp. In fact, just between you and me, I hear that Tripp once saved Joe's life," she said in a conspiratorial tone. She was desperate to keep the whole plan private and figured that if she could persuade GeoGlobal that Greyfield had a personal interest, she had a better chance of pulling it together.

"I see. Well, then, it makes perfect sense that they would rush to put this together."

"Right. But since they have to put a whole team together and fly people in, they do have certain expenses that we . . . I mean . . . that I was hoping you could take care of."

"Yes, you said that on the phone. You say they are estimating the mission to cost anywhere from one to two million U.S. dollars, is that correct?"

"That's what Joe Campiello gave me as his first estimate. It may vary a bit depending on what they find and how long it takes."

"The fee shouldn't be any problem. After all, the kidnappers are demanding fifteen million. At least we were able to get a slight extension."

"A slight extension? How long?" she asked in an anxious tone.

"Our negotiator has exchanged a series of e-mails with them and explained that with the weekend and holiday it would take several more days to get the money to their bank in the Caymans. Since you were coming down with this new plan, we had to try for more time."

"Good. That's good." Her mind was racing. A few more days? They only had a few days to locate him and put together a whole rescue effort?

"Excuse me, Mr. Aguilar, would you and Ms. Reid like some coffee?" the secretary said, poking her head inside the door.

"Certainly. Thank you," Victor said.

Samantha knew that South Americans always served espresso at meetings—at every meeting, in fact. Right now she could certainly use some.

Victor turned back to Samantha. "So how soon can we meet this Mr. Campiello?"

"Today. He's already in town putting his plans together. I told him that I was certain that you would be glad to have Greyfield on board, and I just wanted to check your schedule." *Okay, so I went out on a limb with that one, too.*

"Good. I've cleared my calendar. Let's get him in here right away and figure out the best place to start."

The best place to start looking for Tripp? How in Lord's name were they going to find him? At this point, she didn't have a clue.

47

"Hey Juan, I have to say that you were a genius to get those two pipelines to go up like that. How long you been working in the oil and gas fields, anyway?"

"About fourteen years now."

"Guess you have more experience with the rigs and pipes than Carlos or me," Simon said. "No wonder the Fixer sent you up here to work with us."

Juan turned and looked through the back window. "You sure you got my duffel bag and all my stuff packed safe in the trunk?"

"Sure we do," Carlos said, steering their car onto the interstate heading west. "Why are you always worried about that duffel bag?"

"'Cause it's a special cargo Rossi told me to guard with my life."

"What would he want you to guard with your life?" Simon asked from his perch in the front seat.

"It's something special that he got from Iran," Juan said.

"Iran? You got stuff from Iran and you brought it all the way up here? Why? What does it do that our tools can't do?"

"Don't ask. The Fixer said that I was supposed to use it only when he sent me a special signal."

"I thought we were just going to use our last pig for another explosion. You know, pick a good line and go out with a bang," Simon said with a guffaw.

"Oh shut up," Carlos said. "Juan knows what he's talking about. If we get word from Rossi to do something different, we're going to do it. That's why we're here. To follow orders. Not ask questions all day long." He craned his neck to see around a line of cars in front of them. "This place sure has a lot of traffic. Looks like everybody is heading out of town away from the fires. Can't say I blame them," Carlos said, speeding up to pass a gray sedan. He glanced over and saw that there were a woman, a young boy, and a little girl in the car next to them. The girl was holding a Barbie doll in a white dress.

He thought about his own family back in Venezuela. He had a boy and a girl, too. They lived in a crummy barrio. It was all he could afford. He had taken the job in the gas fields to try and earn enough money to get them a proper house, not some shack on the hillside with a flat tin roof. The money wasn't much, but when he showed the bosses that he could manage the rigs and handle a lot of odd jobs, they had recommended him when Diosdado Rossi had asked their advice about workers to hire for a special project.

Now, when they finished these jobs, he would have lots of money. Plenty of money to get out of the barrio, find a nice house, or maybe leave the country and go to a place like Trinidad and Tobago like Simon said. He could find work in their gas fields. They were major producers. Or he could forget about work altogether and just lie on the beach and drink rum.

Just one more job. Probably a big job. He'd wait to see what Rossi told Juan to do. It would probably involve those canisters or whatever they were that Juan was carrying around with him like precious jewels. What could be inside those things? They almost looked like scuba tanks. Why would he haul tanks up here? Why couldn't they buy whatever they needed here in the States and not carry those heavy things everywhere? And what were the other things in the small carrying case inside the duffel? He had gotten a glimpse of a couple of weird boxes, some wires, and what looked like clocks, but he couldn't be sure. Whatever they were, they were a whole lot different from the things they had used on their other six jobs. Way different.

A banana. Rafael had actually given Tripp a banana with his coffee and bread. His stomach rumbled as it had been doing for days now. He grabbed the fruit, peeled it, and wolfed it down. *God, nothing has ever tasted so good.* It was the best thing he had seen since the edge of the rainbow that appeared outside his dirty window the previous morning. *Okay, so there wasn't a pot of gold, but a banana was as good a prize as I could expect in this hellhole.*

Tripp was sitting on the edge of the bed staring at his watch. At least they had let him keep that on. Rafael had gone to some shop to get more food, and as soon as he got back and tossed him the fruit, he had gone back into the other room, where Eyeshade was shouting about another message on the BlackBerry. It was obvious that Eyeshade was the real moneyman in this crude operation. He was always talking about dividing up the loot, getting it out of their Cayman account, and investing it in some clever way. No wonder he had garnered his nickname.

"This is new," Eyeshade said. "It's from somebody we don't know. They must have brought in new people. I don't like this. We told them no publicity. No nothing. Just pay the money."

"What do they want now? We agreed to more time," Rafael said, unpacking the rest of the groceries.

"It says they want a meeting. Sounds like a trap."

"What kind of a meeting?"

"They say they just want to be sure that their guy is alive, and if we agree to meet someplace they will give us a down payment."

"How much?"

"I don't know."

"Why don't they just give us all the money and we'll give the guy back?" Rafael suggested.

"I don't know. Sounds like they're stalling for time or something."

"They're probably just trying to figure out where we are. They'll send people to follow us back. We can't do this."

"I know we can't," Eyeshade said. There was a long pause. Nobody said anything. Tripp strained to hear if they were whispering. But it had been their pattern to always speak in Spanish about the messages and the ransom and most anything else. He never let on that he understood anything they said unless they said it in their broken English. Now he waited, tense, to see if they would fall for the meeting ploy.

"I don't know," Rafael said. "Maybe we show the guy, and we tell them they can only have one person at the most at the meeting. Then one of us stays there, maybe you stay 'cause you're the boss, and I take the guy back up here. But you stay there and keep him covered until I get away. Hold him there a long time and then you make him leave, and then you get away and go somewhere else."

"It's too risky. They could have other people hiding out. They'd track you back here."

"But if you make the rules and say we won't meet unless they follow the rules . . ."

What is this? Good cop, bad cop? Tripp thought as he listened to the continuing arguments. A meeting would be fantastic. First, they'd have to take the damn chain off. He could walk around, try to get some strength back. Stop the chafing on his leg. Maybe it could heal a bit. If there was a meeting, maybe they'd bring him some decent food. Back when he had worked for Greyfield, he and Joe had put together a couple of rescue missions and they had always brought food, candy bars, whatever they could stuff in their pockets. He had been through this drill before, but always on the other side. Just thinking about some of their exploits gave him hope. Hope that they had stopped relying on that idiotic negotiator, whoever he was. Hope that GeoGlobal was finally getting help in this whole fiasco. Hope that this whole nightmare might come to an end. He had thought about other ways to escape. Other ways to try and attack Eyeshade and Rafael. But as soon as the messages came in, he figured he'd hold off and see if an exchange was really in the works. Besides, one of the things he'd had to learn, one of the toughest things when it came to negotiations and rescues, was simply patience.

He sat up straighter as he heard Eyeshade finally make another point. "I don't like it. I'm going down the hill to send another message. It's time to pay up or they'll never see their Vice President again."

"Wait a minute," Rafael said. "Remember, I said I had an idea about something else we could send along that would help them make up their minds?"

"Hi there, Hunt, how goes it?" Evan Ovich said, settling into one of the wooden chairs around the staff table in the White House Mess.

Hunt Daniels looked up from his newspaper and said, "Busier than ever. You'd think things might calm down a bit during Christmas week. No such luck."

"Yeah. Same in my shop. I've been so slammed, I've been eating every meal at my desk. Today, I just decided to take a quick break. First chance I've had to get away. So what are you reading?"

"It's about Afghanistan," Hunt said, pointing to a story in the *Wall Street Journal*. "Here's a strange phrase."

"What's that?"

"I've never seen the word *detonated* used as a verb for a person before."

"What do you mean?" Evan asked, taking a menu from one of the waiters standing quietly next to the table.

"Says here that an Afghan suicide bomber injured dozens when he detonated near a NATO patrol."

"With all that's going on in the world, guess we need a new vocabulary, huh? Right now I'm crashing on getting the words right on the new Internet news site we've got up in Venezuela. Well, that, among other crises."

"I heard about that. It's kind of like what the Pentagon has going in the Middle East, right?" Hunt asked.

Evan turned toward the waiter and said, "Could I have one of the hamburgers today? Medium rare. But hold the fries. Oh, and an iced tea, please."

"Very good sir," the blue-jacketed Filipino waiter said, jotting down the order on his pad.

Evan turned back to Hunt. "So we've got this new site up trying to get some real news to those folks down there. Ever since their President took over the radio and TV stations, the people don't have a clue what's going in the world, let alone in their own country. And now with elections coming up, well, we've got a bit of a campaign of our own going on," he explained.

"I'm glad somebody is working that issue. I saw that NIE on what's going on down there about all the crime, corruption, playing footsie with FARC, the narco crowd, Iran. I see that Iran's QUDS force is now training terrorists to operate in South America. I mean, it's a nasty situation down there and I'm not sure enough people are paying attention."

"That's what we're working on. Getting people to pay attention. At least with the election coming up, we've been talking to a lot of our allies and they're now demanding that they be allowed to send election observers."

"I gotta say you've got your hands full if you think you're ever going to oust that guy."

"You're right about everything that's in that National Intelligence Estimate. For once all the agencies seem to be on the same page with this one. As for the upcoming election, it's not us that'll oust that President," Evan said, "it's the people."

"Afraid you're smoking something, buddy. That guy has control of the military, the peasants, the companies, well, the oil and gas companies that he's taken over, along with all the other ones. And now with the price hikes, he's gotta be taking in a fortune every week to fund his programs and pay off his cronies. Of course, our problem with the pipelines is only making his treasury fatter. I know it's not your issue, but have you picked up anything new on who's been blowing them up?"

"We've got DHS, the FBI, Energy, Transportation folks all over it. I did hear from Ken that we finally got a bit of a breakthrough."

"What was that?" Hunt asked.

"We've been trying to get it squared away so we could use our domestic satellites to check on activity around the pipelines, and you know how it works. You've got to go through hoops to use our own technology, for God's sake."

"I hear you. But you got it through?"

"Yeah. They'll be getting the photos and comparing them to a map of the lines. Had to deal with Senator Jenkins on that one though."

"Hopalong Cassidy came along on that one?" Hunt asked with a grin.

"Not really. She bitched and moaned about spying on Americans and all that nonsense. I mean, here she's the one screaming the loudest about how the sabotage is jacking up gas prices and yet she tries to tie our hands when it comes to finding the bastards. Well, anyway, Ken was able to push it through, so we should start getting some action in the next few days."

"Well, that's something. But back to the Venezuelan elections, I can't see how anybody is going to overturn that machine."

"I never said it would be easy. Sure it's a long shot, but we've got a lot going on, a lot of groups that we're supporting on the side. Mainly with communications," Evan said.

"So do you think we have enough assets down there?"

"I hope so. We've got the students organizing groups on Facebook and posting videos on YouTube, although with their last protest at their Supreme Court building, my contacts told me that a bunch more of them were thrown in that new jail the President just built."

"So if they're in jail, how can they help you?"

"There are lot more where they came from, believe me. They've given out so many cell phones that the text messages are getting around pretty quickly."

"By the way, I heard about that guy from GeoGlobal being kidnapped. Any news about him?" Hunt asked.

"Nothing yet. State and CIA have people on it, and our embassy is trying to get a line on the groups that are grabbing people off the street for ransom, but it's a pretty slow process. You know our policies about not paying ransom and all of that."

The waiter brought Evan's order. Hunt asked for a cup of coffee and a few chocolate chip cookies.

"So what's on your docket these days?" Evan asked, reaching for the bottle of ketchup.

"Working a whole bunch of proliferation issues, nuclear threats, missile defense. The usual."

"Still seeing that knockout scientist who works on missile defense projects?"

"Cammy? Uh, sure."

"Saw her in here a while ago. Got any plans with that one?"

"It's kinda hard to find the time. They keep sending me from here to Timbuktu so often she said I had too much in common with Robert E. Lee's horse."

"What the hell does that mean?" Evan asked, taking a bite of his burger.

Hunt leaned back and shook his head. "Horse's name was Traveler."

Evan chuckled. "I see what she means. Well, hang in there. I think she's a keeper."

"I'm trying. Believe me, I'm trying." The waiter brought Hunt's coffee and cookies and slipped away. "By the way, did you see Greg Barnes on CNBC talking about the price of oil and gas and what we're supposedly doing about it?" Hunt asked.

"Yeah, I caught a bit of it. He didn't look as smooth as he usually does. I hear that his Deputy is out of town or something, so he's got to write his own talking points."

"Without her, maybe he'll be relegated to *Dancing with the Stars*," Evan joked.

"I wouldn't put it past him. I wonder why politicians are so anxious to go on dumb TV shows?"

"I think it all started when Nixon went on *Laugh-In*," Evan said.

Hunt took a sip of his coffee and grabbed a cookie. "These are great. I'll leave one for you. But back to the situation in Venezuela, it seems like you've got an awful lot on your plate right now."

"We all do," Evan said, wolfing down the last of his hamburger. "You've got to worry about the Russians, the Chinese, the North Koreans. And I've got to worry about all the crap going on down in Venezuela. With the kidnapping, the crackdowns, the Iranians moving in, the narcotics moving out, I sometimes feel like the skipper of a little boat seeing a perfect storm on the horizon."

"Okay, strategy time," Joe Campiello said, as a dozen people pulled up chairs. They were huddling at the end of a long, shiny conference table at GeoGlobal's Caracas headquarters. Victor had turned the room over to the Greyfield team to use for their planning sessions and said he'd be in his office if they needed him. A pitcher of ice water and six glasses sat on a silver tray in the middle of the table and a carafe of espresso along with a set of tall narrow cups had been placed on a side cabinet. There was a series of photos in matching frames circling the wall, scenes of men on drilling rigs in a wide plain, pipelines snaking along a valley, and platforms in the middle of oceans somewhere.

Samantha sat on one side of the table, while Joe was at the head. She had told him she wanted to be included in any planning meetings, and although Joe said he didn't usually want outsiders messing with his team, she had put together the payment schedule with GeoGlobal, so he figured he owed it to her to be here. She watched carefully as he introduced the other members of his group. Most of them had some sort of military background. Two had been in special forces, two were pilots, one of them flew helicopters, the other fixed-wing aircraft. The youngest, Dick Stockwell, was their resident computer expert—head of the Greyfield Geek Squad, as they called it. Then there was Joe, about five feet ten, she surmised, with broad shoulders and muscles that seemed to strain at the fabric of his cotton shirt. His nose looked slightly off-center, as if someone had moved it over a notch. *Probably trained as a boxer at some point.* His hair was almost black, cut short, and his gray eyes were guarded. They told no stories, just took in every element in the room. He looked tough, a bit weathered, and he obviously was in control of this group. Then again, he had selected these men and they now looked to him to lay out a plan.

"So here's what we've got. You all know Tripp."

Every man at the table nodded.

"That's why you're here. You know how he works, how he thinks, how he reacts. That's why you're on this drill. Samantha Reid, here, she knows him, too." He turned to Samantha. "She may not know him as well as we do, but still, she may have ideas to contribute along the way. And besides, she got us this assignment. So we keep her in the loop."

Samantha started to speak, but thought better of it. Joe continued. "Now then, the only way we have to communicate with these guys, whoever they are, is to send a message to Tripp's BlackBerry. Other messages were sent by the GeoGlobal people, their negotiator, but that didn't go too well. In fact, I think he really screwed things up." There were a few snickers around the table. "So, now it's up to us."

"What about the agency?" one man asked. "Will they be trying to put something together and getting in our way?"

"I hope to hell not," Joe said. "You don't have anything new from your contact at Langley, do you?" he asked Samantha.

"No. Last time I talked with him, he said they were checking their sources on the ground here. There was no discussion of a rescue attempt. At least not yet."

"Okay. Good. Let's proceed on the assumption that we're the only ones in the game right now," Joe said. "About contacts, I sent one

Thursday when you all were on the G-5 flying down here. I asked for a meeting. That's always our first step, to get a visual. Verify proof of life."

Samantha caught her breath. *They need to verify proof of life? Oh God. That means that they think there's a chance that Tripp may have already been killed.* She sat forward in her chair, hanging on every word.

"So we get their reaction to that. Should come pretty soon. They always answered other messages within a day or so. I'm guessing that wherever they're holed up, they go somewhere else to send messages. They're probably afraid we'll triangulate and figure out their location. Trouble is, it's not that easy to do since we're getting no help from the government here. But that's okay. We have our own ways to pinpoint their hideout."

"You do?" Samantha asked.

"That's our business," Joe said. "Now then, we'll get their answer and if they don't agree, we make another offer. They want money. They've got no use for Tripp. So we'll offer to send one guy in. That would be me. I'll take a chunk of money with me, make sure Tripp is in decent condition, and that's when we'll work a little Greyfield magic."

"Magic?" Samantha asked.

"Right," Joe said.

"Are we're gonna use the glasses this time?" Dick asked. "That was a great ploy when we did that deal in Nigeria."

"That's the plan," Joe said. Turning to Samantha, he added, "We've developed miniature tracking devices that we put in prescription or sun glasses with a GPS transmitter embedded in the frame."

"Yeah, it's our TLX 1000 Tracker," Dick added.

"While your government is tied up with bureaucratic haggling, we've got the tools and we can move much faster on cases like this," Joe said to Samantha.

A ray of hope spread through her, the first optimistic feeling she'd had since she learned that Tripp had been taken. "That sounds terrific," she said. "So you think you'll be able to follow him? And then what?"

"Then we analyze the location and figure out what we need . . ."

Suddenly, the door burst open and Victor Aguilar rushed into the room, his face ashen. He was carrying a small box. "We just got an answer from the kidnappers."

Joe looked up. "And?"

Victor was visibly shaken. "They don't want a meeting. They want their money and they sent something. A courier just dropped it off downstairs. And he left before anybody got his name or his company."

"What is it?" Joe asked, getting up from the table.

Victor was about to hand Joe the box, but he glanced over at Samantha. "You don't want to see this."

Samantha's eyes were wide. *What could be so wrong?*

Joe came around the table and grabbed the box. Samantha jumped up to take a look. As Joe lifted the lid, Samantha stared in horror and screamed.

51

Juan Lopez studied the message from the Fixer on his cell phone. El Presidente was making a major speech today at Casa Natal, the place where Simón Bolívar was born, where the man all of Venezuela saw as their founding king had begun his life. Juan thought this was a good choice. Rossi said that in this speech, their President would be listing all of his initiatives for the New Year. Rossi said that this would be the signal for their final project. It would be their biggest hit and one that Rossi had personally planned. This was when Juan, Simon, and Carlos would have to find the right spot to stage their final assault on the Americans. Rossi said it was a brilliant plan, one that would wreak much more damage than the individual attacks on the other lines. While those other six events had resulted in tremendous price hikes with a small amount of collateral damage, this final job would have a huge effect.

If they could pull it off, Rossi had said their payment would be doubled. Juan was excited about the prospect of all that money, but he wondered why the Fixer was so anxious about this one last job that he would pay double. He knew that the canisters were important, but he didn't know what was inside. He couldn't read the markings on the side, because they were in Farsi. Rossi said he got them from sources in Iran. What could be so special that he had to get it from Iran? Simon and Carlos kept asking him that question and he didn't want to sound like he didn't know something, so he just kept putting them off. They asked too many questions anyway. They were getting irritating. Carlos kept acting like the boss, but the Fixer had told Juan that once he got over the border and hooked up with the others, he, Juan, would be the boss. After all, he had much more experience, he knew what he was doing, he had been given instructions by Rossi himself and he wished that Carlos would just shut up and take orders for once.

They were driving across the state line into Louisiana. They had listened to news programs, and while each of them could speak a little bit of English, they had kept trying to find Spanish-language stations. They wanted to keep up with what was going on with the pipelines, the repairs, and the price of gas and oil. Every time they heard about another price hike, they all cheered. The more it went up, the more money they would have. At least that's what they thought.

As they drove through the rather dreary countryside, Juan wondered if he really needed both of these guys to pull off the last attack. He had the instructions. He knew what he had to do once they figured out the best location. They would have to get fairly close to their final target and they would have to time things perfectly in order to make their getaway. That's what Rossi had told him in his last message. But the more he thought about it, he wondered if he could pull this off just using Simon and somehow get rid of Carlos. If there were just two of them left, that would mean they could split the money two ways, not three. He would be a rich man. Maybe not as rich as Rossi, but rich enough.

And as for the stupid Americans, they still had no idea who was sabotaging the lines. With all of their FBI, CIA, ICE, sheriffs, police, and all the others they talked about on the news, they were clueless. That made Juan smile. *We have outsmarted all of them. We are so much better than these Americanos. I will be rich. And these fools will still be running around looking for us and they will never find us.* He stared at the back of Carlos's head as he drove the car, and he listened to Simon's incessant chatter. Maybe Simon was too much trouble, too. Maybe he could handle this whole thing alone. Maybe after they set the final charge in place, he'd figure out a way to get rid of them both. He sat back and pondered the situation. He had a bit of time to make his decision. The Fixer had told him that as far as he was concerned, the best time for their next act would be late on December 31st.

Yes, overnight on New Year's Eve would be perfect. A perfect time to begin his new life.

"Get her a glass of water," Joe ordered as he slid the box across the table, took Samantha's arm, and eased her down into a chair. "Bad shock, I know," he said in a more soothing tone.

Dick took the box and showed its contents to team members on the other side of the table. "Damn it!" one said. "Holy shit," another remarked. "You think it's really his?" Dick asked as he took his pen and probed the severed finger lying in the box.

"We'll have to check the print," Joe said. "That could take a while but it's the first order of business."

Samantha fished for a Kleenex in her purse, blew her nose, and looked up. "You mean you think there's a chance it's not Tripp's?" she asked.

"No way to know," Joe said. "I will say this. It sure shows these goons are serious." He started to make some notes on a pad in front of him. "I'm going to send a message right back demanding a meeting again. These things usually play out like a seesaw. They think they're one up on us now, but we still have what they want. The dough. So now it's our turn to set some rules."

Samantha sat back and watched as members of the team tossed out ideas about the message, the ground rules, the time and place. The kidnappers would have to name the place, which was good because they couldn't afford to take Tripp too far from their hideout. At least that would give them some idea of where Tripp was being held, if it was near the city at all. It could be in one of the valleys or up in the mountains surrounding the vast metropolitan area. Maybe they were way out of town in some jungle. She had visions of deadly snakes and scorpions circling Tripp, who would be tied up somewhere, powerless to fend them off. She shuddered at all the images crowding her mind. She shook her head, and strands of her long hair fell into her eyes. She pushed them back behind her ears and tried to pay attention to the conversation again.

"So we'll ask for a meeting to make sure that Tripp gets medical attention. After all, if they did hack off his finger, he could be in real trouble."

"Yeah, infection and all that," Dick said.

"Don't remind me," Joe answered. "So a meeting right away and they have to show him to me. I'll be going in alone this time."

"What are you talking about?" one of the special forces men asked. "You need backup, for God's sake."

"I don't think we can risk it. They could have guys combing the area. We have no idea how many they've got. Besides, I'll bring some money as a down payment and tell them that unless we know that Tripp is okay, they obviously won't get any more."

"How much will you take?"

"Victor says he'll get me about half a million in cash. That should do it."

"Half a million should get their attention, especially if it's in dollars."

"That's what he's putting together."

Samantha sat there, still stunned by what she had seen. She dealt with terrorism issues, threats to the country, bombers, nutcases, all of it in her White House job. But she had never dealt with anything so . . . so personal. A man's life was in danger. A man she loved, one she hadn't stopped thinking about, dreaming about since the day he had walked into her office during the big ice storm. She thought back to that first day when he had showed up in his overcoat with the collar turned up and she had realized he was the same guy she had fallen for so many years before. Then everything had happened to fast. The dinners, the phone calls, the love scenes. *Oh God, the love scenes. He was so gentle at times, so forceful at other times. The way he used to touch my cheek, run his fingers through my hair, put his arms around me and hold me even after we made love.* She had a fleeting thought about the old song "After the Lovin'" and realized that Tripp fit the lyrics perfectly.

It had all been so beautiful. So perfect. Even in the midst of the crises at the office, the pipelines exploding, the people being killed, the stock market crashing, and Congress screaming, the presence of Tripp in her life had made her feel almost like a Pollyanna, finding something good and optimistic in every single day. Now it had all come crashing down and she had turned into a Cassandra, seeing threats and doomsday scenarios everywhere. At least now people were believing her and finally, finally, some of them were taking action.

She thanked God that Tripp had told her about Joe Campiello, told her about some of their exploits and how Greyfield operated. If she had to wait for the government to try and rescue him, he could be there for . . . for . . . she just couldn't bear to think about it.

Joe was winding up the meeting. "I'm heading back to Victor's office to send the message. From now on, you know the drill. We check our equipment, we stay in touch, and we wait for an answer."

WHERE ARE YOU? HAVE YOU FOUND HIM? CROWN IS CRAZY
OVER TWIN XMAS ATTACKS . . . MORE REPORTS OF DEATHS,
INJURIES, SUPPLY DISRUPTIONS. ALERT LEVEL RAISED. JOAN
SAYS GREG GOING BALLISTIC OVER YOUR ABSENCE. SAYS
HE'LL FIRE YOU, ACTS LIKE THE TERMINATOR ON STEROIDS
(EXCEPT IN FRONT OF SR. STAFF OF COURSE). I WORRY
ABOUT YOU. PLEASE TELL ME YOU'RE OK . . . ANGELA.

Samantha read over the e-mail on her BlackBerry. So Crown, Secret
Service code name for the White House, was going crazy. Well, so was
she. She wondered if she should reply. She had not been in touch with
her office since she'd arrived in Caracas. She wanted to maintain the
impression that she was unreachable, in a bad zone or something,
though she knew that was pretty lame. She was stalling for time. Of
course she was. But she was simply praying that, working with Greyfield, they would get Tripp back. And once they accomplished that,

she figured Greg and everybody else back in Washington would forget about how she broke every rule in the book. At least every rule in the White House Staff Manual.

She appreciated Angela's concern but decided to wait a little while longer, at least until she had something concrete to report. Right now all she had were hopes. Hope that the kidnappers would actually show up at a meeting. Hope that Tripp was alive. Hope that Joe really could pull off some sort of rescue attempt and get them all out of the country and back home. Hope that while she was gone, the FBI and all the other agencies had gotten a clue on whoever was sabotaging the lines and then worked together to run them down, or at least prevent another attack.

She was back in her tiny hotel room after having spent the evening with Joe, Dick, and the others. They had all gone over to the Centro Lido Hotel, right there in the financial district, where the team was staying. It was also on Francisco de Miranda Avenue but was nothing like her cheap hotel. Their place had a sleek modern entrance with a fountain in front and was known as one of the best boutique hotels in the city.

Joe had told her that they were on a good expense account, so why not stay in decent digs? They had all gone up to Le Nouveau Restaurant, which had an incredible view of the city. "Good place to get our bearings," Joe had said. "Besides, when I checked in, I saw the menu and it's one place in town where we can get a T-bone steak with Texas BBQ sauce, can you believe that?"

Seated at a circular table with a white cloth and flower arrangement in the middle, Samantha sensed the incongruity of it all. Here they were on a mission to free a man who was probably being held in a cell of some sort, eating Lord knows what, and they were up in a penthouse restaurant dining on steak with special sauces. She began to review the entire scene in her mind.

As their entrees were served, Joe had said, "Okay folks, time to chow down. We've got a big day tomorrow. Meeting is all set."

"Wait a minute," Samantha asked, looking over at him expectantly. "Did you hear back already?"

"Just got a message. I've got the BlackBerry, and the goons now say that I can come and see Tripp."

"But that's terrific. When? Where?"

"Meeting's set for late tomorrow afternoon. Maybe they figure they can keep an eye on things, you know, make sure that I'm alone if it's still daylight. Then again, that means they've picked a spot where they don't expect anybody else to wander by."

"Well, where is it?" Samantha pressed.

Joe leaned over the table. He had specifically chosen a table way over in the corner so there were no other diners near by. Still, he lowered his voice and replied, "I've got it pinned down. They say it's a place on El Avila."

"The mountain?" she asked.

"Yep," Joe said, pointing to the landscape they could see out a far window. "That big one over there." He motioned to Dick. "See what kinds of maps you can take down of the entire area." Dick nodded as Joe continued. "They said to take the cable car up the mountain and then hike two miles due east. He gave some more instructions. I have it all in my room. So here's what we'll do. We recon the whole area first thing tomorrow morning. We'll take the first cable car up, scout the whole scene, figure out where the meet will be, and then come back down. That way I'll be sure to be on time and I'll also know the best way back. This also means that they must be holed up not too far from there. Who knows? But we'll know how long the ride up takes, how long the hike is, all of it. Then I'll go back up alone tomorrow afternoon."

"But I think we should go up with you and just stay some distance back," one of the pilots said.

"Not sure that's a good idea," Joe said. "But after we scope it all out in the morning, we'll make a final decision."

Snakes and scorpions crawled through the underbrush toward someone tied to a tree. As they got closer and closer, the man squirmed, straining at the ropes and chains. He heard rustling in the leaves nearby. He tried to stamp his feet to scare them away, but they kept coming. Always coming. The man was alone, hungry, tired, and un-kempt. There was no one to help him. No one to free him. He pulled at the restraints but the knots only grew tighter, chafing at the bare skin of his arms and ankles. And they kept coming. Closer and closer.

Then he was falling. Falling over a cliff, plummeting down, land-ing on a jagged ledge, screaming for help. His body was quivering at an odd angle, bent, broken. No one could come. No one could reach him. No one could stop the bleeding. A final breath seeped out of him because there was no one there to help.

Samantha bolted upright in the narrow bed, her forehead damp and glistening, her head pounding. The nightmares about Tripp and Dexter were morphing together now, becoming more terrifying with each replay, and she had no idea how to turn them off or hit Delete. She switched on the bedside light, pulled her knees up, and sat there, arms around her legs, head down. She was panting as if she had just run a very long race. But here she was in bed with nothing on but a horrified expression. When would the nightmares stop? When would she be able to sleep again? She thought the dreams about Dexter had faded. They had dwindled over the years and she hadn't dreamt about him after she first met Tripp. But now with the kidnapping, they were coming back, the scenes of his body falling over the cliff mingling with shadowy impressions of Tripp being held in a strange place by strange people with strange animals and insects crawling all over him.

She knew she wouldn't be able to get back to sleep for a while, so she switched on the small TV set perched on top of the dresser and scrolled through the channels. She could understand what she heard on most of the Spanish channels, some of the other channels even broadcast in English. There was a show about a twenty-foot-high storm drain in Kuala Lumpur that doubled as a toll road. She flicked past a few more stations and saw that they actually had a history channel here. But they weren't showing anything historic. In fact, the show was titled *Modern Marvels*. She kept clicking and finally came to a food channel that was praising "The History of Cheesecake." She remembered that she hadn't eaten much at the dinner with Joe and the team. Even though they were making plans, she still couldn't work up much of an appetite. She had barely tasted her dinner, fresh salmon with a teriyaki sauce, while the team went over their recon plans, their trackers, sensors, helicopters, night-vision goggles, and weapons, and the latest gadgets on Greyfield's Gulfstream 5, which they had flown down here. *Boys and their toys*, she had thought at the time. She just prayed that some of those toys would come in handy in the next crucial days.

She finally found a twenty-four-hour news station and saw a re-broadcast of a speech by El Presidente. It looked like he was in some sort of a museum, but she couldn't be sure. But what she did note was that his audience was wildly enthusiastic. They kept interrupting his remarks, clapping and shouting. *Bad as he is, the guy sure has a following*, she thought. She listened for a few more minutes as he ranted on about the devils up north and then described how his country was benefiting from the high price of oil and gas. And he explained that the income to his treasury meant he could subsidize the price they were paying for food and make it affordable for all of the peasants. More cheers. More applause. She didn't want to listen to someone making political points from the anguish of others.

She turned off the set and padded the few steps into the bathroom. She found a few Tylenol tablets in her makeup bag, gulped them down with a glass of water, and crept back into bed. She grabbed her paperback book and began to read. She heard a "ding" in the hallway, then a grinding noise. *Why do I always get a room between the elevator and the vending machine?*

She read several chapters and then put the book aside, flicked off the bedside light, and closed her eyes. But could she possibly get some sleep now without the intrusion of dire images of two men in dire trouble? The only two men, besides her father, that she had ever really loved?

"Get up! We go now," Rafael called from the doorway to Tripp's room.

"Go where?" Tripp asked, sitting up on the threadbare mattress. He knew from their discussions that there would be a meeting of some sort today, but didn't let on that he understood any of their discussions.

"Go clean up."

Tripp stood up and started to haul the chain to the bathroom. Instead, he turned and pointed to his ankle. "Take the chain off, okay?"

"When we leave," Rafael said, and sauntered back into the other room.

Tripp lifted the chain as he walked to keep it from chafing his leg any more than it already had. He splashed some of the brown-colored water on his face, ran his hand through his hair, which hadn't been combed in over a week, and stared at his rough beard. *Looks awful*, he thought. *Then again, I could probably fit right in with some of the terrorist groups that Samantha is chasing down.* There it was again. The thought about Samantha that kept popping into his mind at the oddest moments. He wondered where she was, whether she really knew about the kidnapping and what she might be going through right now if she did.

He thought about this meeting and tried to figure out if it would be with one of the GeoGlobal security guys. He had heard Rafael and Eyeshade bitching about a negotiator. Then they said they had a message from somebody new. Tripp had no idea who that would be, but he was cautiously optimistic because it meant there was some sort of deal in the works. Maybe the company had figured out a way to pay the ransom and ensure that he got out of there alive once the money made it to the Caymans. He didn't know how they'd pull that off, but at this point, he was glad just to get out of this stifling hole, even for a few hours. He had also heard them arguing about whether one should go to the meeting with Tripp and one should stay back. Eyeshade had said that he didn't trust the prisoner, that he might try to escape, and so both of them needed to go, and both had to keep their guns ready at all times.

He dragged the chain back into the bedroom and called for Rafael.

The young man came into the room along with Eyeshade. Both had their guns drawn. Tripp put his hands up. "You don't need those," he said.

Eyeshade kept his gun trained on Tripp as Rafael shoved his pistol back into his pocket and unlocked the chain. Tripp leaned down to rub his ankle and pointed to the blisters and cuts. "Any bandages around here?" he asked. For a fleeting moment, he thought he might be able to whip his head up, knock Rafael off balance, use him as a shield, and lunge toward Eyeshade before he had a chance to get off a shot. But just as he was about to raise his head, he saw that Eyeshade had taken several steps back toward the door, and he thought better of it. *Damn. Maybe later while we're on the way to wherever the hell we're going, I'll be able to nail these two bastards. Maybe I'll get a little help from the guy we're meeting. Whoever it is. I'm almost out of patience now.*

Rafael laughed. "You're lucky I took it off. Just for a walk though.

You come with us now." He shoved Tripp in front of him and the trio walked out the door. "Good thing you no fight back," Rafael said as they walked along a trail. "We get along fine. Need you to get the money. Then all is okay."

We all get along fine, huh? So what are we supposed to do now, hold hands and chant "Kumbaya"? His legs felt a bit wobbly. He hadn't had much exercise except for walking back and forth to the john and some push-ups he did from time to time. He wished he could jog, run somewhere, anywhere, just to get away from these idiots. But both of them had their weapons out and they were watching his every move.

They trudged along an ill-defined path through the jungle and dodged a big spiderweb with dozens of black flies caught in the center. *I know just how you feel,* he thought, staring at the insects embedded in the web. Eyeshade led the small parade, pushing branches out of the way. They were obviously staying off any sort of road. Tripp remembered they had driven on some sort of makeshift roadway to get up to the casita, but as he looked around, all he could see were trees, exotic plants, and tangles of vines wrapped around most everything in their path.

They came to a clearing, and Tripp saw an amazing sight. He could look out and see the entire city of Caracas, some six thousand feet down in a valley. From this vantage point, the city looked beautiful, its skyscrapers ringed with areas of rich forest. If only he could figure out a way to nail these guys, he knew there would be some way to get down this mountain and back to civilization. After all, hadn't Rafael gone for sandwiches and beer? There must be shops or tourist hangouts somewhere within walking distance.

"We stop here," Eyeshade said. Pointing to a stump, he ordered, "Go sit. We wait now."

Tripp checked his watch. Almost five o'clock. Whoever it was would be coming soon. Would he take a picture to get proof of life, as they used to say when he worked back at Greyfield and went out on a number of these rescue missions? Would he bring some food with him? *Now, there's a good thought. I could sure use a candy bar, a bottle of decent water. Anything.*

. . .

Joe studied the cable-car operator. Old guy, bored, not paying much attention to the gaggle of tourists crowded on board, except when he spied a particularly good-looking younger woman. Then he leered for quite a few minutes. Joe found a flier stuck in a side pocket that advertised the Humboldt Hotel, built half a century ago by some strongman, but now it had been turned into a museum. There were also ads for some little shops in a town called Galipán. Then, on the back side, he found what he was looking for. The schedule. He had checked it briefly that morning when he made his first trip up and noticed that they weren't too punctual about it. The operator had left when the car was full and that was about it. The trip up the mountain took about twenty minutes. Now he wanted to gauge when the last run would be. He made a mental note, folded the ad, and shoved it in his pocket.

When they got to the top, he jumped out and checked his compass. He started to walk due east again. This time it took a little less than a half hour, since he had already scoped out the place. The message said there would be a clearing with a series of tree stumps around the edge and a view of the city below. Now he was getting closer.

He peered ahead through the trees and slowly worked his way toward the clearing. He moved slowly, quietly. Even though he had no plans to try and rescue Tripp at this point and didn't even have a weapon with him, he had always valued the idea of stealth and surprise. He pushed some vines aside and there, on one of the stumps, he saw his old buddy, sitting quietly, but scanning the area, side to side. *Never saw him with a beard like that. And the clothes. Must be the same ones he was traveling in.* He looked gaunt, but still strong, still vitally aware of his surroundings.

Joe saw the two guys sitting across from him, holding guns in their laps. They never took their eyes off Tripp. They were dressed in jeans and T-shirts. They also had stubble on their chins and both wore ball caps. *So we have some sports fans to deal with here. They look like a couple of overgrown punks. Tripp and I could take them in a heartbeat, but this is not the time or the place. Besides, we're operating in a foreign country, and if I can pull this off without killing anybody . . . well, that's the plan.*

Joe moved around through the trees until he was facing Tripp and the goons had their backs to him. He made a circular motion.

Tripp saw it and was careful not to react too quickly. *What the hell? Joe Campiello? I can't believe this. How in the world did he get involved in this mess? Did GeoGlobal hire him? How could they have known to call Joe?* He couldn't believe his eyes. He decided to let Joe make his own entrance. He was a pro. He obviously knew the score here.

"*Buenos días,* gentlemen," Joe said, pushing his way into the clearing. Rafael and Eyeshade jumped up, whirled around, and trained their guns on Joe. Again, for a fleeting moment, Tripp toyed with the idea of jumping them, but quickly pushed it aside. He couldn't take a chance that Joe could be shot, and he probably didn't have a weapon on him. He looked around for a rock or branch, but didn't see anything nearby.

Joe came closer, held up his hands, and said, "You speak English, right?"

"*Sí.* Yes," Eyeshade said, and turned to Rafael. "Go make sure he doesn't have a gun."

Rafael sauntered over to Joe, ran his hands down the sides of his legs, and pointed to a bulge in his pocket.

"It's the money," Joe said. "That was our agreement. But first, I want to see your prisoner."

"You can see him there. He's right in front of your eyes," Eyeshade said, stepping aside and pointing his gun at Tripp. "You see he is okay. Now give us the money."

Joe moved toward Tripp and reached into his shirt pocket.

"No tricks," Rafael shouted.

"Not tricks," Joe said, extracting a pair of glasses. "I brought these. I figured that in all the . . . uh . . . chaos of taking this man prisoner, he may have lost his glasses."

"He said nothing about glasses. He sees okay," Eyeshade said.

"He's not the complaining kind," Joe said in a lighthearted voice.

He handed the glasses to Tripp, who put them on. Recognizing the signal, Tripp paid close attention.

Joe then said, "I want to check his hands. We got your last message and it was not a good one." Tripp wondered what he meant by that. He held his hands out.

Rafael gave a half laugh. "So take a look. So we sent somebody else's. So big deal." He turned to Eyeshade and muttered, "I thought I was pretty smart hacking off a finger of the brother before I dumped his body, don't you? It got us results."

Eyeshade grunted and kept his gun trained on Joe and Tripp. "As you see, he's all in one piece. Now give us the money."

Joe shook hands with Tripp and said, "Glad to see you're all right. Now be sure to stay hydrated. Gets pretty hot this time of year. And take care."

Tripp nodded and put his hands back in his pockets.

Joe turned and said, "Now that I see that this man is okay, we will work out plans to wire the money to your bank account as you asked."

"Good," Eyeshade said. "Fifteen million. And when?"

"Today is Sunday. Monday is New Year's Eve and Tuesday is a holiday. So fourteen and a half million will be sent to your account on Wednesday. As we agreed, I have the first half million with me. But first, I want to know your plans for turning this man over to us."

Rafael looked at Eyeshade and raised his bushy eyebrows. "What do you think?"

"I think we see that we have the money, then we have no need for him." Eyeshade looked at Joe. "We will bring him here again, and you can take him back. We will send a message as soon as we know the money is there."

"And you think we would trust you to bring him here again and just let him go? You believe you would expose yourself to me and my people again?"

Eyeshade hesitated and thought for a long moment. "We don't want him. We don't want to feed him or do anything else with him. We want to get rid of him. All we want is our money. Now where is the down payment you promised?" he asked, waving his gun at Joe.

Joe reached into his pants pocket and took out the package. "It's all right here. And we will arrange to have the rest wired to the Caymans as you said. We have figured out a way to do that, using a computer of course, and you will be able to watch us hit the Send button when you return this man to us. Do we have a deal?"

Eyeshade glanced over at Rafael, who nodded. "A deal. We will meet here again. Same time, on Wednesday when you say the money will be ready."

"Okay," Joe said. "Now, I also have something for our man." With his other hand, he took two power bars out of his side pocket and handed them to Tripp.

"I said no tricks," Rafael said, grabbing the bars and tearing off the wrappers. "This could be a trick."

Tripp shook his head and said, "Just a snack. Just a snack. I am pretty hungry, you know."

Rafael broke both of the bars in half, stared at them and said, "So you eat it all now."

"No problem," Tripp said, gobbling down all of the pieces. *They must have thought there was some sort of knife or maybe a tracking device or something in the candy bars. Dumb shits!*

"The money," Eyeshade bellowed.

"Here you are," Joe said, handing over the packet. "Half a million dollars."

Eyeshade tore open the packet and saw the bills tied tightly together. His eyes gleaming, he waved it at Rafael. "So we do business with this guy."

Rafael stared at the money and gave a wide grin. "Yes, but now we want the rest."

Joe nodded and turned back to Tripp. "I'll go now. Just remember, take care." And with that short phrase, he ambled back through the trees.

As soon as he was out of sight, Eyeshade walked up to Tripp, tore off the glasses, threw them on the ground and stomped on them. "I trust no one," he said as he left the broken glasses on the ground and led Tripp away. "No one at all."

55

"Take me with you," Samantha said as the team sat huddled in Joe's hotel room surrounded by maps and equipment.

"Are you insane?" Joe asked.

Angela asked me the same question when I told her I was coming down here. Does everybody think I'm nuts? They better not, because I put this whole operation together, and I want to see it through. Besides, I spent my life hiking around oil fields, traveling first with Dad, then later with Dexter. We climbed the Tetons. Well, we almost climbed the Tetons. Still, I know what I'm doing in tough places. I should go along now.

She pushed her hair back behind her ears and faced Joe. "Look, I know you all work as a team and you've done things like this before. And I know you think I'm just some White House aide who sits in an office all day long. Well, that's not entirely true. I've got lots of experience hiking and climbing, even rock climbing, and besides, you know I would not be here unless I had a strong personal interest in seeing that Tripp gets out of this alive."

"That's the whole point," Joe said. "Getting Tripp out alive. Now, I know you've got some sort of soft spot for him. Or, well, maybe it's more than that. Whatever. This is serious business. We've got a plan for our pilots to helo over that mountain tonight, try to pinpoint their location, get word back to the rest of us while we head up on the cable car and move in. Timing's going to be tight, but we figure that tonight is our best shot." He turned to Dick. "You double-checked the weather?"

"Sure did. And you're right about tonight. Should be clear, but early tomorrow there's a front moving in that could last another day or two. And it could get messy, so we've got to move tonight."

"With what I left him, we've got our best chance at tracking Tripp tonight as well."

"Okay, so we all go tonight," Samantha said.

"Look, Samantha, I told you, I'll have the pilots in the air, the rest of us go up in the cable car and go to the hideout. We'll have weapons, gear, all sorts of things with us and we'll have to move fast. We don't know how many guys they have up there. We could be walking into all kinds of trouble, and we just don't need one more person that we have to rescue. Get the picture?" Joe said.

"It's just that I've come all this way. I put the deal together with GeoGlobal. I got you the contract. I arranged the payment, and now I'd like to see it through. There must be something I can do to help," she said, almost pleading.

Joe scrutinized her face and looked around the room at the other members of the team. Their expressions were unreadable.

"There is one thing . . ." Dick ventured.

"Yeah, what?" Joe asked.

"You said that the cable car goes to the top all day long and on into the late hours." Dick grabbed the schedule lying on the bed next to the maps. "And it says here that they make their last run at midnight. Guess they give the tourists time to go up and have dinner or look at the city lights or whatever people do up there. There probably won't be many people though at that time of night, except maybe some cleaning crews that have to go up and do their thing and then maybe come down again."

"And your point is . . . ?" Joe asked.

"So, looking at our schedule, let's say the helo goes up as soon as it gets dark. They're able to get a line on the location and get word to us that he's somewhere on that mountain. By then it could be nine or even ten. So then let's say we've taken the cable car up and we get word on the location by, say, ten. That gives us two hours to find the place, work our way in, get Tripp out, and get back to the cable car. But, what if it takes us longer than that? What if there's a screwup? Well, we all know the what-ifs. Anyway, maybe we could use Samantha as a delaying tactic?"

"A delaying tactic? What the hell are you talking about?" Joe asked.

"Okay," Dick continued. "Say we all go up together and she takes some cleaning stuff with her and acts like a maid or something. We saw that cable car guy. If it's the same guy, he can't keep his eyes off anything that looks good in a skirt. Besides, she speaks Spanish."

"So you're saying she goes up and then if we get delayed, she tries to, what? Make nice with the cable car operator?" Joe asked. "You've gotta be kidding."

"No, wait," Samantha interrupted. "I could do this. We could all go up, just like Dick said. You do the whole rescue operation. I get off and head out of sight. You contact me when you're ready to head back. And I keep an eye on the cable car guy. And if it looks like he's going to head down and it's the last run, I can try to divert him. I can do this. I know I can." *But can I really do this? It means going up the side of a mountain in a little car suspended on a wire or something. It means looking down thousands of feet. It would be far worse than looking over a cliff in the Tetons. Oh God, can I really do this? I'll just have to.*

Joe shook his head and paused, "I don't know. Sounds risky to me."

"Joe, think about it," Samantha said. "If you do get Tripp out of there and the cable car has already left, what are you going to do? Hide out in the woods until it starts up again tomorrow morning? And with a storm coming in, it may not go up at all. And unless you've killed all the kidnappers, they're going to come looking for you, right?"

One of the special forces team members weighed in. "She's got a point. Our plan is to try and extricate without killing anybody, remember?"

"How are you going to do that?" Samantha asked.

"Leave it to us. We've got it all scoped out. But I guess there is a matter of time," Joe conceded. "And if she stays near the cable car and doesn't hike in with us, I suppose I can buy it."

"Good," Samantha said. "Then it's all settled. But let me be clear. I have no intention of getting in your way. I know how serious this is, and I truly appreciate what you're putting together here. I mean, I know you're risking your lives to try and save Tripp. I just want to be a part of it." *And I also want to see him as soon as I possibly can.*

"Okay. Okay. She comes along." Joe checked his watch. "Let's synchronize." He turned to the pilots. "Time for you to head out. We've all got our communication gear, cells and everything else we need." He motioned for the others to gather up the equipment and stuff it in their backpacks. He finally turned back to Samantha. "Go get your roughest clothes on, but something that the cable car guy still might appreciate. And see if you can find some rags or sponges or something just to have along." He tossed her an extra canvas bag. "You can use this. We don't need this one. Put your stuff in there and plan to meet us back here at eight o'clock sharp."

Samantha got up and headed to the door. She was excited. This was it. Her plan had finally come together, and tonight they would find Tripp. At least she prayed they would. She turned and said, "You know, I have no idea exactly *how* you're going to get him out."

"You don't have to worry about that," Joe said. "Let's just say we call it Shock and Draw!"

56

"What's that?" Rafael shouted as he ran to the window of the casita. "Sounds like a helicopter or something."

"So? A helicopter flies around. Planes fly around. I heard that they're bringing up all sorts of gear to set up fireworks on this mountain for New Year's Eve tomorrow night. They're probably airlifting the stuff up here," Eyeshade said, shuffling a deck of cards.

"You sure about that? Seems kind of noisy and close. Like maybe they're circling or something," Rafael said. "Maybe that guy we met with is trying to track us down. You think?"

"I don't see how he could. We smashed the glasses. That was a dumb trick. Probably had some sort of tracking thing in them," Eyeshade said. "And when he tried to give the guy that candy. Well, you saw it. Just candy, right?"

"Right. It was in the wrapper. I broke it apart. Nothing in there. Besides, we made him eat it."

"So, just wait a few minutes. They'll go away. Come on, we haven't finished the game."

Tripp perched on the edge of his bed listening intently to the sound of the rotors. Sure enough. A helo. Joe's helo? He prayed to God that a plan was in the works. For the past many days, he had thought about his own plans, ways he might be able to take on Rafael or Eyeshade. When one was out, he had tried to lure the other one into his room, to ask for something. He knew he could handle at least one at a time if he ever got close enough. But even when one brought him some food, the other had stood at the door with his gun drawn. It looked like they had been through this drill before, or at least tried to pull it off. They were both antsy, trigger-happy, and while he tried to remain vigilant every minute of every day, they had never let their guard down, and he had never seen an opening. It was frustrating as all hell. He had hoped that after several days, if he appeared docile, they would ease up a bit. But they never had. They didn't know he had a background in the military. They had no idea of the kinds of missions he had been on. Sure, he had taken on Eyeshade that one time, but anyone would try to get away at least once, so they had to be expecting that. Now all of his experience had done him no good in this situation, with his leg chained and no access to any tools, knives, wires, or anything else he could use to try and free himself. He lay back on the bed and figured this whole sorry scenario had to end soon. Maybe it would be tonight.

"Too damn many trees down there. I can't get an image," the team member said to the helo pilot. He continued to search the area. "Wait a minute. Over to the right, I think I see the clearing where Joe had the meeting. Head over there and then we'll circle the whole place again." He was scanning the hillside with his Night Optics TG-7 Thermal Goggles, looking for images, though he didn't know how many he was looking for. He just knew that he had to find images that were similar and then one image that would be differentiated from the others. That would be Tripp's. At least, he hoped Tripp's body heat would show up differently. Their whole plan depended on it.

．　．　．

Samantha crowded into the cable car with Joe, Dick, and the others and moved to a spot away from the windows. She didn't want to look down, didn't want to think about how high they were going. Her palms were moist and she realized she was holding her breath. Was it because she dreaded the cable car ride up the mountain? Or was it because she was scared she might screw up her role in the operation? Or was she terrified that the whole rescue plan would somehow come apart and the team and Tripp could be killed?

The Teleférico started to move. There was a sudden jerk and then a slight swaying as it ground its way up the cable. She remembered an old James Bond movie she had seen years ago where there was a fight on board one of these cable cars, where good guys and bad guys battled it out, hanging from open doors, crawling across the top of the moving car. She even thought she remembered a scene where the car came crashing down to the valley floor. She shuddered at the memory and tried to refocus on the people around her. The car wasn't jammed. There were perhaps a dozen on board in addition to the team. There was a young couple, their arms entwined as they gazed out the window. Must be newlyweds, she thought. *They're probably headed up for a look at the city lights. There must be places up here where lovers can find a romantic spot to spend a summer night.* Would she ever be able to spend a romantic summer night with Tripp? Would this be the night when she would see him again? Would he be okay? How would he look after all of this? She said a silent prayer that Joe and the rest of the team could pull off a miracle.

"There, over there, I think I've got 'em," the team member said.

"Where?" the pilot asked.

"Three o'clock. Head over. Let's circle once more and I'll mark the map. We don't want to spend too much time around here. They'll hear us and might try to move out."

"Got it," the pilot said. "Radio Joe and let's get out of here."

"See, I told you they'd leave, whoever they are," Eyeshade said and dealt another round of cards. "We got any beer left?"

Rafael walked over to the small icebox and pulled out two bottles. He popped the caps and held one out to his partner. "Not too much more time to go now. Just a couple of days and then we're rich men."

"We're rich already," Eyeshade said, glancing over at the table where the packet containing the half-million dollars was sitting.

"Shouldn't we put that away somewhere?" Rafael asked, following his partner's gaze.

"Where? There's nobody up here. Who's gonna find it? The guy in the back room?" Eyeshade grunted. "He's not going anywhere."

"Dead ahead," Joe whispered. He then motioned for the team to spread out and check the door and windows of the shabby casita. They pulled their guns and inched forward while Joe crept toward a side wall where there were no windows or openings. He carefully set down his canvas bag, opened the zipper, put on his headset, and took out his silent pneumatic drill. He looked over his shoulder, waiting for confirmation that he was in the right spot.

Dick pulled on his own TriPort tactical headset and adjusted the small black microphone. He knelt down next to a stand of trees. Focusing his thermal-imaging goggles, he analyzed the images inside the building. He could make out two forms on the right side and a brighter form way to the left. He whispered into his microphone, "Two to your right, sitting down. Move about a yard farther right. Should be okay. Tripp's way left. Probably in another room."

"Got it," Joe whispered into his own mike. He grabbed the bag and his tools and shifted right. He then took the drill, put it up against the adobe wall, and turned it on. It began to make a small hole the diameter of a pencil. He took his time, being careful to hold it steady and not make any noise. He could hear the men inside talking and arguing over something. He couldn't quite make out the words, but he thought they said something about money and bank accounts. *You've seen all the money you're ever going to see, you bastards,* he thought as he continued to hold the drill with a steady hand.

"Wait. Stop," Dick whispered. "You've got to move. One of them just got up and moved to your location. Looks like he's leaning back against the wall."

"Shit!" Joe whispered, turning off the drill. He tried to pull it out of the wall. "Can't move. It's jammed."

Samantha glanced at her watch. 11:15 p.m. She had walked away from the cable car and meandered along a road away from the tourists and lovers. She had partially unzipped the canvas bag so she could be sure to hear if one of the team tried to contact her on the small PRC-710 radio she had inside. It looked like a walkie-talkie. They had told her it was the lightest handheld radio they had. On the trip up, she had noticed the cable car operator leering at her. She hoped and prayed the team could get in and out quickly so she wouldn't have to spend time with the old lech. She wandered around and tried to avoid looking down at the city. She was still a bit queasy from the ride up and didn't want to add to the tension, so she sat down under a tree. Her fear of heights had come on full force during the ride. She had tried to take deep breaths and then close her eyes from time to time. But having them closed just made her dizzy, so she had concentrated on their mission and tried to control the fear. Once she got off and headed into the woods, she started to feel a bit better. Now she was getting nervous again. She checked her watch once more, stared down at the transmitter, and waited.

"What's the matter with you? You don't want to finish the game? Just because I won the last hand?" Eyeshade said in a mocking tone.

"I'd rather watch a game than play one with you," Rafael said. He had been sitting in a chair by the wall, leaning back and looking through an old magazine. He stretched his legs, got up, and turned on the TV set. He saw a news story about preparations for New Year's Eve celebrations. Workmen were stringing lights in a park and setting up a bandstand.

"See, I told you," Eyeshade said, "there's going to be all sorts of stuff going on tomorrow night. Probably fireworks up here, too. What better place to shoot off fireworks than the top of El Avila, huh?"

"I guess you're right. But we have to miss the parties. We're stuck with this jerk."

"I never said this would be easy. I said it might take a while. But think about it. We're getting results in less than two weeks. The guys in Colombia and Mexico have held their hostages for months, years sometimes. We got lucky with this one."

"Okay, he's moved. Try again," Dick whispered.

Joe turned on his drill. This time it kicked in and started silently grinding farther through the wall. He felt it break through. He stopped, listened, and heard a TV set blaring. *Good. This is helpful. They'll never notice a thing.* He pulled at the drill and after a bit of twisting and tugging, he was able to get it out of the hole. He then whispered into his headphone, "Filtration masks on."

He put the drill into the bag, put on his own mask, and retrieved a small green container that looked a bit like an oxygen bottle. It had a small tube screwed into the end. He fit the other end of the tube through the hole. Then he took a deep breath and turned a small nozzle where the tube was connected to the pressure bottle. He heard a hissing sound, and as he held the bottle and tube against the wall, he turned away and took another breath of fresh air. Then he waited while their new chloroform-based concoction, which they called chlorohydronate gas, seeped into the room.

Dick peered through his goggles and scanned right to left. Left to right. He watched as one of the images on the right appeared to bend over. Then the one on the left looked like he had his head back. Leaning back. He scanned way left and saw Tripp's body image lying flat. It hadn't moved. *Must be lying down on a bed or something.* He scanned right again. The other two images hadn't moved. He whispered into his microphone, "All down."

Joe pulled the tube out of the hole in the wall, shoved the bottle in the canvas bag, and crept around to the door, where two other team members were waiting. He dropped the bag and drew his gun. Dick had instructions to stay outside as a backup in case there was trouble.

The three men gently turned the doorknob and pushed. The door creaked on its rusty hinges. They stopped and listened. The TV was on but that was all they heard. Joe motioned them forward. They opened the door a crack and looked inside. They saw Eyeshade keeled over on top of the table, his arms splayed out on top of small stacks of playing cards. Farther to the right, Rafael was slumped down in his chair in front of the TV.

"They're out. C'mon. Gotta get Tripp and get out of here. We don't have much time." They moved into the other room and found Tripp lying on the bed. Joe slapped a mask over his face while one of the team members began to hack off the chain around his ankle. "Ankle's a bit of a mess," the guy said.

"We'll fix it later," Joe said. "Let's get him outside. He's under, but the gas may not have penetrated into this room as fast. He'll come around in a while."

They lifted him off the bed and two of them hauled him out into the fresh air. Joe walked through the other room, saw the packet of bills on the table, grabbed it, and, once outside, shoved it into his bag. Then he called to Dick. "Let's get the hell out of here. It'll take us longer than thirty minutes to get back to the tram, since we're carrying Tripp. But hurry up. We've gotta make that cable car."

"What about Samantha?" Dick said, as they gathered together and hurried away from the casita. He checked his watch. "It's eleven forty-five. We're never gonna make it if the guy really does take the last car down at midnight."

"I know," Joe said. "I didn't want to use her. But now we've got no choice." He reached into his bag for his radio and pushed the button to make contact.

"Hi there, big guy," Samantha said, plastering a big smile on her face as she approached the cable car.

"Hi to you, too," he said, eyeing her tight T-shirt and the long brown hair falling over part of her face. She had worn a bandanna on the trip up, but now she had pulled it off and shaken her hair out to let it hang loosely over her shoulders. She walked up to the cable car and checked her watch. 11:55. There were only two other people on board. She recognized the lovers from the ride up. They were totally engrossed in each other and weren't paying any attention.

"How much time do we have before you head down?" she asked sweetly.

"Was just about to leave," he said.

"Oh dear. There aren't many people here yet, and I have some friends who are on their way. We all really need to get back. This is the last trip down, isn't it?"

"Sure is, lady. About time I got some sleep, you know."

"I completely agree with you," Samantha said as she came closer to the tram. "Do you live far from the base? I mean, do you have a long way to drive home?"

"I live a ways out. Can't afford to live in town."

She sat down on a nearby ledge and hiked her skirt up over her knees. "So tell me about where you live."

He stared at her legs. She followed his look and started to swing one leg back and forth as she leaned back, thrusting out her chest. "So, uh, as I said, tell me about your home."

"My home?" he replied. "Not much to tell. Say, why don't you come on board? As I said, I better get moving here."

"Oh, just give it a little bit more time, would you? You look like a man that doesn't need to hurry things. Am I right?"

He grinned at her, showing dark stains on uneven teeth. "Not if I don't have to, I guess."

"It's such a beautiful night, don't you think? I mean, being up here, smelling the flowers and trees, being able to look down at all those twinkling lights. I just love coming up here. I was so glad to get this cleaning job because it means I can come up at night when it's cool like this and not have to work around too many people in the heat of the day. Do you know what I mean?" She was trying to make conversation, trying to keep him off-guard, trying to be sure he looked at her and not at his watch.

She didn't want to look at her watch either. She had no idea how soon the team could get here. All she knew was that they had found Tripp and got him out of there. Joe told her they had to carry him. She didn't know what that meant. She hoped it didn't mean he was sick or injured. She knew that they hadn't cut off one of his fingers.

Joe had told her that as soon as he got back from the meeting. She had been so relieved, she almost cried. But now his call had been quick and to the point. He had said they were maybe a half hour away, but probably a bit more since they had to carry Tripp, and she should stall as long as possible. Then he had signed off. Now she had to keep this guy interested.

"As I said, I love this new job. It means I'll be coming up here . . . with you . . . every night now. Isn't that nice?"

"You will?" He scratched his chin and cocked his head to one side. "So, little lady, you'll be my passenger from now on, huh?"

"That's right, big guy. Do you think you can handle that?"

"Sure can." He glanced back at the only other couple on the tram. Samantha looked back as well. The man had his arms around the woman, he was kissing her, completely oblivious of anyone else around them. The operator turned back to Samantha. "So where do you live? Do you live alone?"

"Me? Uh . . . yes . . . very much alone. I came to the city looking for work and, well, I finally found it. Isn't that great?" She had no idea how much longer she could keep this going. But she had to try.

"So you'll be coming up every night and going back at about the same time. Midnight. Huh?" he asked, now looking down at his watch. "Hey, it's late. It's twelve fifteen. I gotta get back down. Come on. Get on. If you don't get on now, you'll have to spend the night on the mountain. And I don't think you want to do that."

"Just a little farther. Is he getting too heavy for you?" Joe asked. "Here, I'll take over."

"No, I got him. I think he might be coming around a bit," the team member said.

"That could help," Joe said. "I think it's just around this next bend. I'll go on ahead and see if Samantha's okay." He ran down the path and around a corner and let out a gasp of relief when he saw the tram at the top of the hill. The operator was closing the doors. Joe ran faster and shouted, "Wait. We're coming." He saw Samantha standing off to the side. When she saw him, she rushed to the door and banged on it. The operator put on the brake, ambled over, and opened the door.

"Thought you said you were going to wait it out for your friends," he said. "Course, you'd have to camp out or something overnight. I told you that was a bad idea."

"They're here now. See?" Samantha said, pointing to Joe, who was still running toward them.

"Oh, all right. But tell them to get a move on."

Joe careened up to the tram, pulled out a few bills from the packet in his bag, and thrust them into the startled operator's hand. "That's for waiting. Thanks."

The driver stared at the money and grinned. "Guess this is my lucky night. First I meet a pretty lady, then you come along. Come on now, get on board. We're heading down."

"You get on, Samantha," Joe said. "I'll be right there. I have a few other friends coming down the path."

Then she saw him. His head was hanging forward, his clothes were filthy and torn, his beard made him almost unrecognizable, but she knew it was Tripp. *My God, it's him. They've got him. But is he drugged? Is he sick? What's wrong?*

They got Tripp to the door of the cable car and the operator shouted, "What's the matter with him? Drunk or something?"

"He just had a few too many," Joe said, trying to sound nonchalant. "You know how it is on a weekend."

"Yeah. Had a few of those myself. Not allowed to drink on this job though."

"Appreciate that," Joe said as he helped drag Tripp to a bench along the side. The other couple looked up, surprised by all the activity, and moved farther back in the car. Samantha went over and sat beside Tripp. She put her hand on his cheek. His face was almost gray. "What's the matter? He looks drugged."

"He is," Joe said. "But don't worry, he'll come out of it. I'll explain later."

The cable car lurched and swayed again as it started its descent. Samantha put her arm around Tripp's shoulders and nudged his head so it rested on her shoulder. She looked around at the others.

They were staring out the windows, giving her a moment alone. She didn't know if Tripp could hear her, but she leaned close and whispered, "We've got you back now. You're safe and . . . and . . . I love you."

57

"Samantha? What the hell. Am I dreaming or what?" Tripp said, opening his eyes and looking around the elegant hotel room. He was lying on a king-size bed surrounded by Joe and the team, who were all grinning and slapping each other on the back.

"Welcome back, buddy," Joe said. "Your head okay?"

Tripp tried to sit up but then fell back on the down pillows. "Uh, a little shaky or something. What happened?"

Samantha was perched on the edge of the mattress. She pointed to the men arrayed around the bed and smiled. "Best rescue team in the world, I'd say."

"Last thing I knew I was chained to that god-awful metal bed and two thugs were arguing in the other room. Next thing I know I wake up and see the most beautiful angel in the galaxy."

"Yeah, well, it all worked just as we planned it," Joe said with a note of triumph in his voice.

Tripp gingerly raised himself up to a sitting position. "Got any water around here?"

There was a bottle of water on the bedside table. Samantha screwed off the cap and handed it to him. He raised his head and took a gulp. "God that's good. Had the worst rusty stuff up there. Thanks, honey." He stared at her. "What are you doing here? I can't believe you're here in Venezuela. This doesn't make any sense."

"Relax, I'll explain everything later when we're sure you're okay. Let's just say that I had to do something to get you out of there. The whole government knew about the kidnapping, but you know we can't rely on a bureaucracy in a case like this. So I remembered your work with Greyfield, I got hold of Joe, and well, here we are."

"This is amazing. Positively amazing. When I saw Joe at the meeting, I could hardly believe it. Then I couldn't figure out how he could be involved unless GeoGlobal had pulled some strings and contacted Greyfield. But that didn't make any sense either. You must have been the catalyst." He pulled her down and kissed her cheek. "Uh, sorry, I must smell awful. No shower in that place."

"Don't worry about it," she said with a big smile. "The important thing is that you're here and you're okay. I don't like the looks of that ankle though."

"We've got some salve and bandages and stuff in our rooms," Dick said. "We can take care of that in a jiffy."

"That'd be great," Tripp said. "Damn chain. They never took it off except when we hiked to that meeting."

"Speaking of the meeting," Joe said, "whatever happened to the glasses?"

"The glasses? Well, as soon as you left, Eyeshade smashed them. He was the brains and the accountant of the group, if you could call him that. Said he didn't trust anybody. He figured it was some kind of trick. And, of course, it was. But I got your message loud and clear."

"What message?" Samantha asked.

"When Joe shook hands with me, he palmed a pill into my hand and the last thing he said was that I should 'take care.' I quickly put the pill in my pocket and when we got back to the hideout and I was alone, I looked at it. It was a white pill with the word CARE written in red. Not too hard to figure that one out. So that night, I took it with as much water as I could stand to drink and then I waited. I did hear the helo, but after that, I guess I blacked out. What did you use? The gas?"

"Yeah. We developed a variant of chloroform with a chemical additive. Got it into the place using the usual pneumatic drill."

"Sweet!" Tripp said. "I guess the pill worked."

"Sure did," the helo pilot said. "We circled and saw the images of those other two idiots, but of course, yours was brighter because of iridium-based dye in the pill."

"What kind of pill?" Samantha asked. "You didn't tell me about that."

"It's kind of like the stuff they give you when you have a certain kind of MRI. As it works its way through the veins, it emits a measurable external glow, and we can pick that up with our thermal-imaging equipment," Dick explained.

"Pretty basic stuff," the pilot said. "At first I was worried that there were too many trees up there and we wouldn't be able to see anything, but we lucked out when we found the clearing where you guys met and then we just extended the radius out a ways."

"You guys are amazing," Samantha said. "Now then, how about getting Tripp into a shower or something."

"Do I smell that bad?" Tripp joked.

"Let's just say you'll feel better after you see the bathroom in this hotel," Joe said.

"Where are we anyway?" Tripp asked, easing his legs over the side of the bed and starting to stand up.

"Centro Lido Hotel. We're right in the financial district, not far from the GeoGlobal office. Reserved a special room for your return," Joe explained.

"Pretty cocky that you'd pull it off, right?" Tripp said with his subtle grin.

"Never had a doubt," Joe said. "Hey, you okay on your own here?"

Tripp stood up. "Yeah, I think so. Why don't you guys go get some shut-eye. You deserve it after all of this." He glanced at Samantha and added, "You could stay though. If you want to."

The team started to troop out of the room. "There's shaving cream, razors, all the good stuff in there," Joe said as he headed toward the door. "We'll check in with you later. Maybe have a late breakfast or something. Whatever you want. By the way, on our way back, I called Victor."

"Aguilar? Was he in on this whole rescue thing?" Tripp asked. "I knew those guys had been contacting the company on the Black-Berry."

"Yes. Well, it's kind of complicated. But I'm sure Samantha will fill you in. Anyway, I called him as soon as we got off that cable car, told him we got you out and explained the location. So he'll be working with whatever local law enforcement they think they can trust to go after the kidnappers. Shouldn't be too hard to get them. They're probably still passed out from the gas."

When the door closed, Samantha picked up a menu lying on the coffee table. "You've got to be starved. You look like you could use something decent to eat. They've got everything here. Even T-bones with Texas barbeque sauce," she suggested with a smile. "They've got twenty-four-hour room service here. I can call while you're in the shower." She handed him the menu. "So what would you like?"

He quickly scanned the list, looked up, and said, "A steak, bottle of cabernet, and you!"

An hour and a half later, the room service cart with its gleaming white tablecloth and sterling silver vase containing a single rose stood off to the side of the room. Two empty plates, an empty bottle of wine, and two crystal water goblets sat on top. The wineglasses were sitting on the bedside table as Tripp, freshly shaven with damp hair, pulled Samantha close to him. Her hair was damp as well, since she had joined him in the shower. This was their second foray into warm water and fragrant lather. He had soaped her entire body, and she had done the same for him. They had barely rinsed off before he chased her into the bedroom and they both toppled onto the silky sheets.

She reached over for one of the wineglasses. "Another sip?"

"Why do I need wine when I can taste you?" he said, covering her mouth with his. She left the goblet on the table and put her arms around him as he probed her mouth and deepened the kiss. It was an intoxicating moment. Not because of all the wine, but because he was here with her. Here. Safe. And making love to her. But now, after all he had been through, she wanted to comfort him, hold him, make love to him. She shifted and moved on top of him, leaning down to kiss him again, her hair falling to his chest in a cascade.

"Oh baby, what are you doing? I want . . ."

"Shhhh. Let me," she whispered. Her mouth trailed kisses down his throat, his chest, his waist.

"Wait, you're killing me," he moaned and pulled her to the side. "I've been thinking about you nonstop for days. Ever since they chained me to that damn bed in that spider-infested casita, all I could think about to keep my sanity was you. Always you," he said, framing her face in his hands. "Now that you're here, it seems like a dream, but one I don't want to end. Come here, woman, let me show you how much I've missed you."

He slid one hand into her hair, gently lifting several strands. He let them slide through his fingers. "Beautiful," he whispered. "That's what you are." Her body was trembling as he kissed her ear, her neck, then her breast. She felt his hands begin to roam over her, the curve of her hips, then her thighs. He reached down to her legs and began to stroke them gently at the same time his mouth covered hers once more. His touch was still slow, drifting at a lazy pace back and forth until she moaned and thrust her hips up to meet it.

She pressed her face against his cheek and stroked his back as he continued his maddening pace. He whispered, "I want you too, Samantha, just relax. We'll do this together." But she couldn't wait. Every touch was bombarding her senses. He nudged her legs open and found her core. He touched her again, this time quickening the strokes. Her breath was coming in short gasps, as she once again claimed his mouth and tried to pull him closer. "In a minute, hon . . . in just a minute."

She arched again and felt an erotic wave of sensation begin to wash over her. She cried out as he quickly covered her body and drove home.

. . .

"Here's what I think," Samantha said, clad in the hotel's white terry-cloth robe, standing in the bathroom combing her hair as Tripp stood next to her brushing his teeth.

"What do you think, my dear?"

"Women tend to see things differently after making love. The sunlight is brighter. The coffee tastes stronger. The bubble bath feels warmer. But for a man, the sun just gets in his eyes, the coffee is always too strong, and he never . . ."

"Takes a bubble bath," he said with a laugh "My, my, aren't we just a bit cynical this morning?"

"Oh, I don't know," she said. "I guess it's just that I'm feeling extremely, well, sensitive to everything right now and you're . . . well . . . you're brushing your teeth."

He rinsed out his mouth and grabbed her, knocking the comb out of her hands. "Want to see sensitive in action . . . again?"

She started to giggle. "No, we've got to get dressed, get some breakfast, and meet up with Joe over at GeoGlobal in a little while, remember?"

"I can think of a lot of other things I'd rather do right now. But I guess you're right. Wait a minute. What about your clothes? You just had that skirt and T-shirt from last night."

"We can stop at my hotel on the way and I'll change. No problem."

He went back into the bedroom and surveyed the closet. "Nice of Joe to get me some new slacks and a shirt here. Or maybe it was Victor."

"I think that when Joe called Victor and said he was going to pull off the rescue and had reserved this room for you, Victor had those things sent up. Hope they fit," she said.

Samantha went over to the flat-screen TV and said, "I wonder what's happening back home? I haven't heard any newscasts for a while. Even though the government took over most of the TV stations, it's amazing how many shows they still get down here." She started to surf the channels and then began to laugh.

"What's so funny?" Tripp asked, buttoning his shirt.

"Look at this. It's a morning talk show from Washington and, oh my God, they just said that Greg would be on in the next segment."

"Your boss?"

"One and the same. Can you believe he's on the air on New Year's Eve?"

"What's new about that? I see him on the air all the time."

She sat down on the edge of the bed, turned up the volume, and stared as three commercials rolled through. Finally, the news anchor introduced the Director of White House Homeland Security.

"Mr. Barnes. Welcome. Let's get right to our top story. Can you tell our viewers if you have had any breakthroughs in the pipeline attacks?"

"All of our agencies are working overtime, throughout the holidays, to solve this case of massive sabotage against the energy lifelines to the American people. That's why I'm here on a holiday. To reassure your audience that this administration is doing everything in its power to find these perpetrators and bring them to justice."

"Oh jeez!" Samantha said. "He's laying it on pretty thick today."

"Guess you didn't write those talking points," Tripp chimed in.

"Hardly. Trouble is, I've really got to get back. This whole situation is causing huge problems, price hikes, hearings, and they don't have a clue who's doing it." She looked back at the set. "Well, we'll talk about that with Victor this morning . . . about getting back. But wait, look at Greg."

"Well, Mr. Barnes," the interviewer said, "I'd like to move on to another issue if you don't mind."

"Anything you'd like, but, of course, we are concentrating on national security issues here."

"Yes, I know. However, I have a question for you of a more personal nature."

"Personal?" Samantha said. "They never ask White House people personal questions. I wonder what this is all about." She focused on the screen as Tripp came to sit down next to her.

"And so, Mr. Barnes, our investigative reporter has a story he'd like to share with our viewers. I now turn to Alejandro Rojas with the details. Please watch the screen, sir."

Samantha stared at the split screen where Greg was seated on the set on the left side and the reporter was doing his stand-up on the right. "We have new information about an incident that occurred in Georgetown the Wednesday before Christmas." The camera showed the reporter standing on Thirty-third Street, where several cars were parked along the road. "It was here on that night that an elderly man, a homeless man now identified as Shelby Jones, was walking behind a line of cars, parked just like these. The road was slick and he slipped and fell just as another car skidded on the ice and slammed into him. He was knocked down and he died from internal injuries. What happened to the driver of that car? We have an eyewitness who now says that the driver stopped, saw that Mr. Jones was injured, but he did not summon help. In fact, he left Mr. Jones to die in the gutter and quickly drove away. Who was that driver? The witness claims it was a member of the White House Senior Staff." On the other half of the screen, Gregory Barnes stared dumbfounded at the monitor, his eyes wide with a look of pure horror. "Yes, that individual has been identified as the President's Homeland Security Director, Gregory Barnes."

The news anchor came back on full screen. "We realize it is quite unusual to make a charge of this type on the air, especially with the person involved right here on camera. However, this report just came in and you were here, Mr. Barnes. While we all recognize that any individual is innocent until proven guilty, you have an opportunity now, if you would care to respond."

58

A summer thunderstorm gathered steam outside, but nothing could dampen the spirits of the team gathered inside in GeoGlobal's conference room. They were putting pastries and pieces of fruit on their plates from a buffet set on a sideboard. Tripp poured coffee from a silver carafe and offered a cup to Samantha. "Nice of Victor to put out a spread for us."

"Are you kidding?" Joe remarked. "That's the least he could do. We just saved the company fifteen big ones."

Tripp laughed. "Guess you have a point there. Well, fifteen minus your fee, which I'm sure wasn't cheap. We were never cheap."

"A damn sight cheaper than paying that ransom," Joe said, munching on a chocolate-covered donut.

Samantha filled her plate with fruit and turned to Joe. "I can't thank you enough for putting this great team together."

"And thank you for making the first call," Joe replied.

"By the way, do you ever get up to D.C.?" she asked.

"Sure, from time to time," Joe said. "Why?"

"Next time you're coming up, let me know. There's someone I'd like you to meet. Her name is Angela," Samantha said with a grin. She took her coffee and sat down at the long conference table. Tripp joined her. "Guess Victor will be with us in a few minutes."

"Honey, I was just thinking, in all the confusion and, uh, other activities last night," she said with a mischievous smile, "you never told me what all happened when they had you up in that casita, or whatever it was. What did you do all the time? Did they let you exercise or anything? All you said was that you had that awful chain on. So what went on up there?"

Tripp took a sip of his coffee and finished a bagel. "Well, it was like this. I was in a back room tied to a rickety old metal bed. I tried my damnedest to find a way to get out of there. Tried every single day, but it was really no use. I did take a swipe at one of the guys, thought I could nail him when the other one had gone out. But I was chained, he had the gun, and all I was able to do was really piss him off. It was pretty frustrating."

"I figured with your Navy background, you'd try something like that," Samantha said. "Now that I think about it, I'm glad that you stuck it out till Joe got there. I mean, you could have been killed getting into a fight with those guys."

"I guess. Anyway, they brought a little food once in a while, because they had to keep me alive. And I listened to all their conversations. I could understand them, but I never let on."

"I know you speak Spanish."

"Right. Well, anyway, they played cards, went out every few days for sandwiches and beer, but most of the time they watched games on TV. Well, that and government news programs."

"Could you hear the programs?"

"Oh sure. Place wasn't that big. So I would just sit there, or lie there, and listen to El Presidente give speeches all the time and then hear about how he was making a ton of money because the price of oil and gas was going way up."

"Did they give any reports from America? I mean, did you hear about the other pipeline explosions?"

"Sure. I mean, there I was with absolutely nothing to do but listen to that damn dictator crow about all the good stuff he was doing for the peasants. So I played some mind games trying to keep track of where he was speaking, how many stupid promises he made, and all of that. And I noticed kind of a weird thing. It was sort of a pattern."

"What kind of a pattern?"

"Well, he was making speeches at all these churches."

"Churches? I never thought he was the religious type," Samantha said, taking bites of banana and pineapple on her plate.

"I figure he was trying to appeal to the crowds before the elections, which are next week, you know."

"Yes, I know about that. So what patterns were you talking about?"

"So I'm listening to the speech at Santa Ana's Chapel and then a day or two later, I think it was two days later, they have this newscast about the pipeline that blew up. They said it was the fourth line to explode in the United States and how it meant that the prices would go up again. Then later the President goes to the church of Santa Catarina and a while after that, there are more attacks. There were two on Christmas Day, right?"

"Right. And that's the day I bailed out of the White House and flew down here."

"In the midst of all of that?" Tripp asked.

"I had to. I had talked to Joe and we arranged this whole contract with Greyfield. But wait. Wait. Go back to what you said about that last church."

"Santa Catarina."

"Was he there once or twice?"

"Twice. How did you know?" Tripp asked.

"Oh my God!" she exclaimed, almost knocking over her coffee cup. "This is unbelievable. But it could be. It just could be. . . ."

"What the hell are you talking about?"

"I've got this crazy idea." She tossed her hair back and sat wide-eyed.

"Samantha, what is it?"

"He could have been sending a signal, planning the attacks."

"Who could have?"

"El Presidente."

"What? IIow in the world . . ."

She thought for a moment and then said, "Stick with me on this. The man gives a speech somewhere, a church, wherever, and soon after that, one of our pipelines blows up. Maybe he was giving a time signal or something, and maybe he had agents in those states and they were following orders to blow up the lines."

"But that's crazy."

"Everybody says I'm crazy all the time. Maybe he's crazy, too. But think about it. Who benefits when our lines are sabotaged and the price goes up?"

"OPEC, Mexico, every oil and gas producer all over the place."

"And that includes Venezuela, and he's been bragging about getting more money for his programs, especially before the election."

"But how could we prove it? And how could we find his agents, if that's what they are, before they blow up any other lines?" Tripp asked.

"I don't know . . . yet. But we've got to figure out where he gave other speeches and see if they were right before the first three attacks. And, oh Lord . . ."

"Oh Lord what?"

"There have been six and you said they had seven pigs, so that means one more is coming and we don't know where or when."

"When?" Tripp ran his hand threw his hair and said. "Maybe soon."

"How soon? What do you mean?"

"Well, he made another speech but it wasn't at a church, so that doesn't fit the pattern."

"Okay, so we get a break. But we've got to find out where and when he made other speeches and see if we can tie them to the first three attacks." She looked over at the conference room door and saw Victor Aguilar coming in. "Victor, can you come over here a minute. We need your advice."

"Certainly." He rushed over to shake hands with Tripp. "Sorry I'm a bit late. Good to see you. I can't tell you how relieved we all were when we heard about the rescue. This calls for a big celebration."

"I agree," Samantha said. "But first, we need to check something out. Can we use your computer? We need to double-check some dates."

"Dates?" Victor asked with a puzzled expression.

"Yes. It's really important," Samantha said, getting up from the table. "Can we go use it now?"

"If you need to," Victor said. He waved to Joe and the other members of the team. "Give me a minute, Mr. Campiello. I'll be right back."

Victor sat at his desk and powered up his computer. Samantha told him what she needed. He went to the government's Web site and scrolled through pages of information. Samantha and Tripp leaned over and watched the screen as Victor clicked on various headings. "Here's one. He made a speech at Jane's Diocese. Oh, and here's another one at Santa Ana's Chapel."

"Keep going. Keep going," Samantha said excitedly.

"And, let's see, it looks like the first one was at Santa Catarina's," Victor said.

"That's it," Samantha exclaimed. "Every time he gave a speech at a church of some sort, a day or two later, there was an explosion on one of your pipelines."

Victor swirled his chair around to face her. "You're sure? This is amazing. Unbelievable. The President was tipping off someone to blow up lines in America? How could this be?"

Samantha nudged Tripp, who was still studying the screen. "Wait. Tripp, you said that he made another speech somewhere else. Where was it?"

"Uh, let me think. Oh yeah, it was at Casa Natal," Tripp said.

"That's the birthplace of Venezuela's leader, Simón Bolívar. It's certainly not a church," Victor said.

Samantha put her hand to her mouth and gasped. "Their leader? I wonder what . . . Wait a minute. Let me think."

"What the hell is going on?" Tripp asked, taking hold of her shoulders.

She reached down and grabbed a piece of paper off Victor's desk along with a pen and started to scribble down some names. "Let's put them in order. Victor, you said the first one was a speech at Santa

Catarina, then came Santa Ana's Chapel." She wrote the names furiously and then asked, "And what was the next one?"

"Jane's Diocese," Victor said.

"Right." She turned to Tripp, her pen poised in the air. "And then the ones you saw were, where were they again?"

"Uh, Santa Ana's. Guess he went back there or something. And then the last one was at Santa Catarina."

"And you said he went there twice?" Samantha asked.

"Yeah, twice." Tripp thought for a moment and said, "Come to think of it, he gave a speech and then went back and gave another one. So, yeah, twice. Why?"

Samantha completed the list and held it up. "Number one, Santa Catarina. Catherine of Aragon. Number two, Santa Ana, Anne Boleyn. Number three, Jane's Diocese, Jane Seymour. Number four, Santa Ana, Anne of Cleves. Numbers five and six, Santa Catarina again, Kathryn Howard and Katherine Parr."

The two men stared at her in stunned silence. "The wives of Henry the Eighth!" Tripp exclaimed. "How the hell did you figure that out?"

"And why would the President of Venezuela care about the wives of an English king?" Victor said. "This is completely remarkable." He paused and added, "But come to think of it, we did hear that he likes to read books and see movies about former dictators, kings, all kinds of leaders, so maybe he got this notion . . ."

"And since he's playing some sort of weird game here, the question is, what could be the seventh target?" Tripp asked.

Samantha stared at the list in her hand again, stopped and suddenly waved the page in front of the two men. "I studied English lit at Princeton, and that's how I remembered the names. And Evan, he's on the NSC staff and works on Venezuelan issues, he made some comment about how their President studies the old kings, too. But, wait. You said he spoke at a place commemorating your leader, right?" she asked Victor.

"Yes."

"And the leader of those six women was Henry the Eighth," Samantha said.

"And that means . . . ?" Tripp asked.

"Oh God, no!"

"Samantha, what?"

"Henry Hub!" she exclaimed.

"Henry Hub? In Louisiana? Where they set the price of natural gas?" Tripp said. "You've gotta be kidding. They couldn't blow up Henry Hub. The gas is three hundred feet underground."

"So it's way underground. But tons of pipelines feed into it. So it's different. It's big. It's huge. Gas comes in, gas goes out. It goes out to states all over the place. And if he's planning his last attack somewhere around there, it could be the biggest of all. My God, we've got to do something!"

The National Security Advisor sat huddled with Evan Ovich in his West Wing corner office, going over lists of his contacts working with the opposition forces prior to Venezuela's elections.

"These are the student leaders who have evaded arrest so far," Evan said. "They've divided the city into sections for distribution of pamphlets, cell phones, and all the rest. Then here's a list of operatives in the other major cities and a third list of those working the barrios and countryside."

"So they're text-messaging all day long down there?"

"Just about. They've got to get out the vote and also counter all the promises El Presidente has been making the last week or two. It's going to be close. Really close. Especially if he finds an excuse to arrest any more of those leaders."

"Excuse me, Mr. Cosgrove," Wilma said, opening the door to his office. "I know you said you didn't want any interruptions, but Samantha Reid is calling you from Caracas."

Ken jerked his head up. "Caracas? What in the world is she doing down there?"

"I have no idea, sir, but will you take the call? She's on secure line three."

"Samantha's in Venezuela?" Evan said. "We all know she's been away, but Venezuela?"

Ken got up from the small conference table, walked back to his desk and grabbed the phone. "Samantha? Where exactly are you?"

She quickly told him that Tripp had been rescued by the Greyfield team. She said she would brief him completely when she got back, but right now she needed his help. She explained her theory about El Presidente's speeches and how they might have been a signal to agents in the U.S. Before she could tell him her idea about the next target, he broke in.

"You really believe he was behind those first six attacks?" Ken asked.

"Yes, sir. I know it sounds terribly far-fetched, but the more we analyze it, the more it makes sense. Up to now, nothing else has made any sense at all. Not unless the FBI and CIA and other agencies have found the culprits while I've been away."

"No. Sorry to say they haven't, although they've been combing the states where it's all been happening. We do have one bit of good news though."

"Oh? What's that?"

"We finally got the go-ahead to move forward with Greg Barnes's idea about our domestic satellites."

"Greg's idea?" Samantha exclaimed.

"He's the one who proposed it to me."

"Actually . . . well . . . it's not important now. I hear he's got a big problem."

"Yes. He's under arrest. Awful business. Of course, we don't know if he's guilty. But still, it throws a pall over this White House. And he'll undoubtedly be on a leave of absence until the trial. But let's get back to the pipelines. For now, as I said, we're using the satellites."

"Good. You need to train them on Erath, Louisiana," she said forcefully.

"Louisiana? Why?"

Samantha went through the names of the churches again and their connection to the wives of Henry VIII. She then talked about the speech at Casa Natal and how it could be the final clue to a seventh attack, at Henry Hub.

"This is the most incredible theory I've ever heard."

"I'm sure you've heard a lot of incredible things in your job, Ken," she said. "But when you put all of the pieces together, the puzzle takes shape. You have to admit it does."

"You said he gave a speech at this Casa Natal place day before yesterday?"

"That's right. And that means we may not have much time. In fact, if they follow their previous patterns, we may already be too late."

"I'll get the satellites focused on the whole Henry Hub area, and I'll handle the FBI and local law enforcement. And, Samantha . . ."

"Yes, sir?"

"When are you coming back?"

"As soon as I can get on a plane. There are thunderstorms around here that might delay a takeoff, but GeoGlobal is fueling one of their planes right now so, hopefully, Tripp, uh, Mr. Adams and I will be on our way in a matter of hours. May I call you back while we're en route to see if the satellites have picked up anything?"

"Of course you may. After all, this is your idea. An incredible idea. Call me when you're airborne. I'll be right here as the point of contact all day . . . and all night if need be."

"This is the place," Carlos said, pulling the car up to the fence around the pig insertion station. "Get everything out of the trunk. I'll go cut the chain link."

"There he goes, acting like the boss again," Juan muttered to Simon as he popped the trunk. "Always acting like the big man around us."

Simon hauled the duffel bags out while Juan handled the rest of their tools. "I know what you mean. He thinks he's so important. I'll bet you and I could handle this whole operation by ourselves," Simon said under his breath.

"Sure we could. Well, we're almost finished anyway."

"So what do we do about it?"

Juan scanned the area. "I'd like to get rid of him. Then we split the money two ways."

"I've been thinking the same thing. I never liked that guy. But how do we do it?"

"We can't make any noise," Juan whispered. "There's nobody around, but we can't chance a gunshot or anything like that."

"I may have another idea," Simon murmured.

Up ahead, Carlos cut a hole in the fence and held it open while the others scrambled up and crawled through. Then he followed, and the trio ran up to the section of pipeline that was raised off the ground, making an upside-down U shape. Juan carefully lifted a pig and the two canisters out of one of the bags and removed their outer shells.

"When I first saw those things, I thought they looked like scuba tanks. So what are we doing with scuba tanks?" Simon said.

"They're not scuba tanks," Juan answered.

"What's that writing say?" Carlos asked, peering at the canisters. "What language is that? Arabic or something?"

"It's Farsi and it's none of your business what it says." Juan couldn't read Farsi, and he had no idea what it said. But the Fixer had told him it was a special shipment from Iran, so it had to be in Farsi. It didn't make any difference to him what it said. He had his orders and he had work to do. He reached into his duffel again and pulled out two timers in square boxes and two blasting caps. He twisted the end off of one of the canisters and, as Rossi had promised, saw that there was an inner seal. He fixed the blasting cap to the top of the seal and ran a pair of wires from the cap to a small box containing a timer. He fiddled with the wires and the box. It was taking him quite some time.

"What are you doing?" Carlos asked, holding the flashlight so Juan could work. "That doesn't look like anything we used before."

"Never mind," said Juan. "I have my orders from Rossi, and I know what I'm doing. Just don't get too close and don't mess me up. I have to be careful with this or it'll blow up before we get it inside the pipe."

"Okay, okay," Carlos said, inching back but still focusing the light on Juan's hands.

Juan continued to work, slowly but carefully. At one point, he dropped a tool, tangled the wires, and then had to rearrange them again. It was slow, meticulous work.

"You're going too slow," Carlos said.

"Shut up," Juan responded. "I don't need your advice. These are special. I told you that. Now just keep quiet and hold that flashlight steady."

He finished hooking the wires up to one canister and extended them to the timer. He still had to deal with the second one.

"This is taking too much time," Carlos complained.

Juan stood up. After being hunched over for so long, his back and shoulders hurt. He turned on Carlos. "I said before, I don't need your advice. I know what I'm doing. Turn that light off, I need a break."

"No," Carlos said, waving the flashlight around. "Fix the other one. We've never taken this long to set up an explosion. We've got to do this one and get out of here."

Juan lunged at Carlos, knocking the flashlight to the ground. He took a swing as Simon pulled a knife from his pocket, leaped forward, and plunged it into Carlos's back. Carlos screamed.

"Gotta shut him up!" Juan commanded as Simon twisted the knife and Juan clasped a hand over Carlos's mouth. Carlos struggled, frantically waving his arms until he finally collapsed, smashing his head on the side of the insertion station.

"He almost hit the canisters," Simon said, staring aghast at the body on the ground.

"Can you drag him out of here?"

Simon grunted and reached down to pull Carlos away. "He's not dead yet. But that fall knocked him out. He'll lose blood and, well, who cares?" He reached down and pulled the knife out, swiped it across his jeans, and shoved it back into his pocket.

"Nobody cares. When we're done, we leave him here. Check his clothes. Be sure there's no ID."

Simon leaned down again, fished through Carlos's pockets, and retrieved a wallet.

"Good," Juan said. "Now, I need your help with the flashlight. I've got to get this other canister hooked up. Then we put them end to end into this long pig, set the timers, get everything inside the line, and get outta here."

"I just talked to Ken Cosgrove again," Samantha said, hanging up the satellite phone. "He said the closest FBI agents were surrounding the entire Henry Hub complex and more were on the way, though I did get the sense that there was some bureaucratic argument about who was in charge of the whole operation."

"Nothing new there," Tripp commented from across the cabin. "You want a bottle of water or some coffee?"

"Coffee would be good. I know we'll be landing pretty soon, and I haven't slept a wink. I don't think you did either."

"Nope. Too much at stake right now."

"Ken also told me that they've been getting some satellite images from the surrounding area, and they're racing to superimpose them on maps of southern Louisiana."

"Finally some good news. If they find anything, which of our many bureaus will be going after the bad guys?" Tripp asked, pouring coffee into a pair of mugs from the plane's galley.

"He said the local sheriff and his deputies were arguing that they knew the territory better than the feds, and that they would be fanning out. He gave me the sheriff's number so we can check with them later. I just pray that they find some activity somewhere and get these people, whoever they are. And when they do, I want to be there and find out who really sent them."

"And see if you're right about the whole Venezuela connection?" She nodded her thanks when he handed her the coffee.

"I'm with you on that," Tripp said. "I think we should be landing in Louisiana pretty soon. I'll double-check."

He moved up the aisle to the cockpit. "Did you locate a landing strip close to Erath?" Tripp asked the pilot.

"Roger that. We're coming in to a private FBO. And they've got a helicopter waiting, just like you asked. But aren't there local law enforcement out looking for those attackers? Do you think you can find them any faster in your own helo?"

"I don't know, but I figured an extra chopper roaming around might help. Besides, I brought along night-vision equipment from Greyfield, so we can scan a pretty wide area. So how soon do we land?"

"Should be there in another twenty minutes or so. Better go fasten your seat belts."

"Good. Thanks." Tripp closed the cockpit door just as Samantha was calling out to him.

"Tripp. They've got a lead. Can you believe this? I've got the sheriff's office on the line. They just got word from the feds about activity several miles from Henry Hub. The sheriff and a bunch of deputies are on the way now. The general location came from the satellite. They're not sure if it's the men we're looking for, but who else would be out near a gas line in the middle of the night?"

"It's gotta be them. I just hope they find them before they're able to set off another explosion or whatever they're planning this time. Ask where they're going. Maybe we can get there in the helo."

Samantha talked for a few more minutes, said they were landing shortly, gave the man her cell phone number, and asked the deputy to call her with an update and exact location as soon as the sheriff got there. She hung up, fastened her seat belt, and finally got up the courage to look out the window as they began their descent.

Juan heard it first. A car or truck approaching. "Turn off the light," he whispered. "Somebody's coming." Simon turned it off and crouched down. Juan had just finished his wiring, and he peered down the road.

"What are we gonna do?" Simon asked.

"Stay quiet," Juan said. "Maybe they'll just pass by."

Suddenly, they heard sirens and saw two cars peeling around a corner of the road. The vehicles screeched to a stop by the fence, and four men jumped out with guns drawn. "Stop right where you are!" one shouted as they all ran to the break in the fence.

"Shit," Simon said. He jumped up and started to run across the field. Juan quickly reached over and set both of the timers. Sixty minutes. The Fixer had been very specific about how they had to figure out the distance to the final target. The gas flowed a certain number of miles an hour and they had to gauge it right or their efforts would be wasted. And the hour gave them plenty of time to get completely out of the area and not feel any effects of this final assault. Just as he was about to close the pig and shove it into the insertion station, the sheriff ran up to Juan and ordered, "Hands up. You're under arrest." Juan almost had the pig closed when the sheriff grabbed him and slammed his hands down, leaving the open pig with the canisters and timers lined up inside.

One deputy ran after Simon. Another one started to join him but saw the body and stopped. "Hey, Sheriff, got a body here."

"Somebody dead?" the sheriff called out as he clamped handcuffs on Juan and pushed him down to the ground.

"Looks like he's still breathing, but there's a lot of blood. Looks like a knife wound. I'll go call for backup. We might be able to save him."

"If the scum is worth saving," the sheriff muttered. "Get out there and help Buddy with that other guy. Looks like he's got him cornered, but you better go make sure." He looked down at his prisoner. "Who knifed your buddy over there?"

Juan didn't answer.

"Maybe he doesn't speak English," one of the deputies said.

Simon had stumbled. It was then that the first deputy closed the distance, ran up and aimed his gun at the young man. Simon turned and held his hands up. "Don't shoot," he cried out in Spanish.

63

The plane taxied to a stop. Tripp and Samantha grabbed their bags and ran down the aisle toward the exit. "Thanks for the ride," Tripp said to the pilot as he shoved open the door.

"The helo is over there. Hope you find what you're looking for," the pilot said. "Good luck."

They headed for the helicopter. Samantha fished her cell phone out of her shoulder bag and flicked it on. She saw that she had a new message and recognized the number. "I've got to call the sheriff's office. Maybe they can give us a precise location."

"Okay. Call him. I'm going to tell the helo pilot to get ready for takeoff."

He ran ahead as Samantha dialed the number. She told the deputy they had just landed and were about to board a helicopter, and she asked what had happened. He gave her a quick update, and she listened intently. The deputy explained that they had two men in custody and a third one was on his way to the hospital. Then he went on to tell her exactly what the sheriff had found on the ground.

"C'mon, Samantha," Tripp shouted over the noise of the rotor blades. "Do you have a location? Can't be far from here."

Samantha shut her cell and motioned to Tripp to get off. "Come here. I've got to talk to you," she cried. "We can't go to the site."

Tripp came down the stairs and ran over to her. "What are you talking about? Just tell the pilot where the sheriff is, and we can get there right away. You said you wanted to see who these guys are. It's our chance to question them."

"No, they've got them in custody back at the station. Well, they've got two of them. Another one is hurt or something and is going to the hospital."

"Okay, so we'll head to the sheriff's place."

"Maybe we should. But there's still a huge problem. At least, it sounds like it could be huge."

"What's that?" Tripp asked, glancing back at the helo, holding up his hand as if to say *just a minute* to the pilot.

"The sheriff said the men were messing around with one of the insertion stations."

"But they stopped them before they sabotaged it. Right?"

"They're not sure."

"What do you mean, they're not sure."

"He told me where the site is, and he said that they had sent out a call for a demolition expert, but the nearest one is miles away."

"Demolition expert? But if they stopped the bad guys . . ."

"No, they said they arrested the men but had to leave the area because it looked like there was some sort of timing device there. They didn't have anyone with them who could disarm it, and they wanted to get out of there before anything blew up. Since it's aboveground and not in the pipeline, he figured it wasn't a huge risk. But they've got a man on the way just in case."

"Did they see the timers? See how much time they had?"

"Yes. They said it was counting down to less than an hour." She checked her watch. "It's been a while now, and so that means it's set to go off in, oh my gosh, in something like thirty minutes."

"So we get on the helo, get to the site, and check it out."

"No, Tripp. Are you crazy?"

"So now you're calling me crazy? After all we've been through? Of course we have to check it out. What if their explosives guy doesn't get there in time and the whole thing goes off? It's right next to the insertion station. It could blow that and everything around it if it's big enough."

"But you can't go there."

"Do you see anybody else around here who's had any explosives training?"

Samantha stared at him. Now, just when she had him back, he wanted to go play Jack Bauer. Only they didn't have twenty-four hours, they had half of one. Tripp turned and raced back to the helicopter. Samantha picked up her bag and ran after him.

"You're not coming with me," Tripp shouted as he climbed into the helicopter. "It's too dangerous."

Samantha followed him up the stairs. "Yes, I am. You might need help."

Tripp thought about pushing her back down, but didn't want to manhandle her. Damn woman was frustrating. He didn't want her in the helo. He had no idea what he would find when they got to the insertion site. Whatever was there could blow up. He watched her climb in and heard her shout the location to the pilot, who nodded. Then she slipped into her seat and buckled up.

Tripp checked his watch. So they had about twenty-five or thirty minutes. It couldn't be far. Once he saw the situation, he could order the pilot to take her away. He'd just have to see what was involved and make a decision when they got there. He had experience with explosives, and if these clowns were using basic stuff, he shouldn't have too much trouble disarming their device, whatever it was.

The pilot flew to the site Samantha described and set the chopper down in a field just inside a chain link fence near the insertion station. With the rotors still spinning, Tripp jumped out and ran to the pipeline. The pilot shut down the engine as Samantha hopped out and followed over the uneven ground.

A three-quarter moon cast rays of light over the field so Tripp could see the inverted-U-shaped station. The pilot had also given him a small flashlight. He raced over and stared at the open pig containing the two canisters and two boxes with timers on the top. He switched on the flashlight and saw that the first one read 19:02 and the other 19:03. *Guy must have set these just before the sheriff got to him. Damn!* He studied the timers and saw the wires leading to the ends of both canisters. Then he saw the markings. They were in Farsi.

Tripp had served a stint in Iraq some years ago when they had recovered hoards of weapons shipped in from Iran. Some had markings in Farsi. He and his men had been briefed on some of the more lethal weapons, and he thought he recognized a few of the words on the canisters. Why would there be Iranian weapons in a field in Louisiana if these guys were from Venezuela? Nothing made sense. He trained the flashlight on the markings and shouted, "Oh shit!"

"What is it?" Samantha called out as she ran across the field.

"Get the hell out of here!"

"What? What's there?"

"Unless I'm all wrong, these things are full of radioactive gas! I said get the hell out."

"Let me see," she said, running up and staring at the contraptions in front of him.

"Samantha, you don't understand. These things could blow, and it could be like dirty bombs with radiation everywhere. Don't you get it? Now get back to the helo and tell the pilot to take off."

"I'm not leaving you." She grabbed the light. "I'll hold the flashlight while you disarm those timers. You said you knew how to do it, and you need me now," she said defiantly, tossing her hair back with a shake of her head.

He couldn't let her stay. Sure, he thought he could do it. But what if he couldn't? What if they went off? She could be killed. They could both be killed. But he had been in combat, she hadn't. She had risked her life trying to rescue him. He had to protect her. Save her. He turned to her once more and took her by the shoulders.

"Samantha, look at me. I've only got a short amount of time to work on these things. I can't have you here. I don't know where those goons got this stuff, but if they had been able to get it into the pipeline and release the gas as it's going into one of the salt domes that holds our major supply by Henry Hub, there's a chance it could contaminate the entire source. It looks like these timers were set to go off after these canisters reached the domes, and then the gas would be released."

"And then when it was transported out to all the other lines leading up north and all over the south, it would be radioactive?" Samantha asked, wide-eyed with fear.

"People could die when they turned the gas on. And you could die, too, if I screw this up. You mean too much to me, Samantha." He shoved her toward the helo. "Now, get the hell out!"

Two FBI agents barged into the sheriff's office. "Where are they? The men you arrested? We've come to take custody."

"Now, you wait just a damn minute," Sheriff Bobby Chase replied, jumping up from his desk and confronting the agents. "We've got 'em locked up and my deputy is questioning them right now."

The first agent glanced at the sheriff's badge and said, "Uh, Sheriff Chase, this is a matter of national security. We need to take those men in and do our own interrogation. Lives have been lost. Property has been destroyed. Several states have been affected, to say nothing of the havoc they have caused all across the country. You know that. Now, please take us to the prisoners."

"I told you. They're *my* prisoners. We caught 'em messing with *our* pipelines in *our* state of Louisiana and we're going to bring 'em to justice."

"May I repeat, sir, it appears that they have sabotaged a string of pipelines and caused the deaths of people in a number of states, not just in Louisiana. We need to find out who gave the orders. Who provided their supplies. Who is behind this entire scheme. Surely you understand the gravity of the situation."

"I understand it fine. I've got a call in to the governor. Should be gettin' back to me right pronto. Then we'll see who has jurisdiction over what here in my town."

The agents exchanged a glance. One said, "I understand your concern. And I respect your position, but this is truly a matter of federal, not local, jurisdiction. Now we'd like to see the prisoners. I trust you have them separated."

"Course we have them separated. What do you take me for? They speak Spanish and my deputy, he speaks Spanish. He's in there talking to one of them right now."

"Has he learned anything?"

"Not sure if he's gonna get them to talk right away. Might take a while, but he'll get 'em to spill the beans. You can be sure of that."

"That's another reason we *must* take them into custody. We have our own rules about interrogations."

"That right? Well, I assure you my man will learn more than you feds ever will." He checked his watch. "Should be hearin' back from the governor any time. Now if you two gentlemen want to have a seat. Be my guest."

Samantha trained the flashlight on the first canister. Tripp didn't want her here, but he had no time to wrestle her into the helicopter. Damn woman was impossible. He studied the first canister. He saw a blasting cap attached to a seal on the end. It was small, the color of aluminum, and about half the size of a ballpoint pen. About four inches long, like a bolt with a head on it. He figured it had gunpowder inside, and he had to dismantle the device. He glanced at the first timer. 15:20. He saw two wires leading from the blasting cap back to the box with the timer on top. One red. One black. If he cut the red wire, that might be it. *If this is a standard setup. Big if.*

He pulled a Swiss Army knife that Joe had given him as a keepsake out of his pocket and pried the little scissors out of the edge. He reached down to clip the red wire. As soon as he cut through it, he saw the timer begin to speed up. *Shit! They've got an anti-tampering device on this thing. Bloody hell.* He glanced over his shoulder and saw that Samantha was still standing right behind him.

"This thing's like a booby trap. Get back. Fast. It could blow."

"I'm not leaving you." She steadied the flashlight on the canister.

"Damn it, woman!"

He had no time to argue now. The first timer was down to 1:03 and counting. *What if I cut the last wire? No, I can't take that chance. The blasting cap must be the decoy. Or it's a backup. There must be another charge of some sort in the box. That's it. These guys were smarter than I thought. They used a decoy just in case some-body messed with their handiwork. And damn it, I fell for it. The only other thing here is the timer and that must be it. It's been fastened to the canister. I've got to separate it from the canister somehow.* He frantically looked around. The timer now showed :34. He knew that workers used certain tools around pig insertion stations. *There must be something around here that's strong enough.* :19. He craned his neck, checking the other side of the station. :11. He saw a cheater bar, the kind of metal pipe that could be used to gain leverage on a valve, and also a monkey wrench lying to the side of the station. :06. He grabbed the monkey wrench and smashed the edge of the timer. It flew off to the side. He shouted to Samantha, "Get down."

Samantha hit the ground. Would it blow? She covered her ears, closed her eyes, and said a silent prayer for Tripp. The explosion sent shock waves through her whole body. *Oh my God! Tripp? Was he hit? Was he killed?* She raised her head and saw him on the ground. She got up and ran toward him. She saw his body move. Relief washed over her as he opened his eyes. "I told you to get out of here," he said with a raspy voice.

She looked around and saw a crater in the field about a dozen yards away. "What happened?"

"Had to get the timer disconnected. It had an explosive inside. When I smashed it, it flew off the canister. Now get back. Damn it. I might not be as lucky when I disarm the other one."

"Happy New Year, Samantha. Welcome back!" Ken Cosgrove said when she walked into the Situation Room. "Have you had any rest at all?"

"Not really, sir. We left Louisiana just before dawn and landed at Landmark Aviation out at Dulles, and then we came straight here." She glanced down at her slacks and sweater. "Sorry for the clothes. I haven't had time to change."

"No problem. So you flew back in one of GeoGlobal's planes? And where is the famous Mr. Adams?"

"Tripp . . . uh yes, Mr. Adams dropped me off here and went over to his office to check in with his people."

"I asked Evan to join us so you could give us both a complete briefing on your, shall I say, escapade in Caracas?" he said with a half smile.

"Yes, well, I realize I must have broken every rule this place ever made."

"Just about. The people in your office were searching everywhere. It's the first time we've had a member of the Senior Staff of the White House completely unreachable. And in a time of crisis like what we've been going through, let me just say that it was unprecedented."

"I know, sir, I'm sorry but . . ."

"Never mind that now. I'm sure you'll tell us the full story. Go back and start at the beginning."

Even though she had talked to Ken before, now with Evan in the room Samantha began with the first pipeline explosion and related her suspicion that it wasn't a maintenance issue at GeoGlobal. She talked about her first meeting with Tripp Adams and how they had worked together, exchanging information in an effort to figure out how the lines were being blown up, and how she had speculated that explosives might have been placed in pigs flowing through the line. She didn't explain how her relationship with Tripp had expanded to a great deal more than an exchange of information.

Ken and Evan both took notes as she continued her tale about her frustrations with the CIA, the FBI, and other agencies when Tripp had been kidnapped and how she had contacted Joe Campiello because he had worked with Tripp at Greyfield. She said she had flown to Caracas to meet with GeoGlobal and introduce them to Greyfield.

"Wait a minute," Ken said. "So you're telling us that you arranged for GeoGlobal to pay Greyfield's contract fee to mount a rescue operation? When you went to Caracas, was GeoGlobal under the impression that you were representing the White House with that request?"

"I guess I had to finesse that one," she said with a subdued expression.

"Too cute by half, I'd say," Evan volunteered. "But hey, it worked."

"Highly unusual," Ken said as he made some more notes. "Go on."

Samantha described the meeting between Tripp and Joe, the glasses, the iridium dye in the pill, the trek up the side of El Avila, and the rescue using the chloroform-based gas. She left out the part about flirting with the cable car lech until the team dragged Tripp out of the woods. She also left out how she almost suffered a panic attack going up in the cable car. But then it occurred to her that after she knew Tripp was safe, her fear of heights seemed to abate somewhat on the trip back down.

"Jesus!" Evan exclaimed, jotting down some more notes. "This reads like some spy novel. So what happened then?"

Ken turned to Evan. "She told me some of this when she called from Caracas about the Henry Hub target, but we need all the details."

Evan scribbled furiously when Samantha ticked off the list of speeches El Presidente had made and how they were tied to the six pipeline attacks.

"Yes, our FBI Director called an hour ago with the results of their interrogation of the suspects," Ken said. "More than suspects. The men the local sheriff caught red-handed at the last attack site. He said that the sheriff couldn't get the first two men to talk at all. They completely stonewalled. But there was another one they took to the hospital. Turns out his buddies had attacked him with a knife. Guess they thought they could split their reward money two ways instead of three. So the third man gets stitched up. He survives and can't wait to spill the beans. He asks for immunity in exchange for all the plans. They're working something out on that. So the FBI got this third one to admit they were from Venezuela and had been hired by a government official. And it turns out that the official was none other than Diosdado Rossi, top Deputy to El Presidente himself."

"Rossi?" Evan blurted. "My God, do you realize what this means?"

"Of course I do," Ken said.

"What?" Samantha said, looking from one man to the next.

"The elections this week," Evan said. "Can you imagine the reaction of the Venezuelan people when they learn that their President and his henchman were behind a scheme to attack our energy supplies? And it wasn't just the pipelines, but attacks that actually killed people. Wait until we get this into print, on the streets, in text messages and on the radio broadcasts."

"But there's more," Samantha said.

"Tell us," Evan said.

"The last attack. You won't believe what they were planning."

"You mean at Henry Hub?" Ken asked.

"Yes. They were just getting ready to insert canisters of radioactive gas into the pipeline that feeds into the salt dome where all that natural gas is stored. And they had them rigged with special explosives that wouldn't rip up the line like they did before, but simply let the gas escape and contaminate everything in its path."

"Where in the world did they get the gas?"

"Tripp said it had markings in Farsi."

"Iran," Ken said. "Of course. They've been cozying up to that regime for years now, and Iran did produce uranium hexafluoride at a plant in Isfahan. Rossi must have figured out a way to get hold of a supply and smuggle it into this country."

"And if it got into our domestic reserves, we'd have to shut down all those pipelines, cutting off gas to millions of people, if some of them hadn't already turned it on, that is," Samantha said. "And then it could take months to clean it all out."

"Good God, what a scheme," Evan said. "This is unbelievable." He made more notes and started to get up from the conference table. "I've got to get this story to our contacts in Caracas. We have to hurry if we're going to get all of this out. You know, it's one thing to yell about the devils up north and all that other nonsense he spouts in his speeches. Some of the people really buy that crap. But the fact that he was willing to *kill* innocent Americans, innocent women, children . . . Everybody with a diabolical scheme to raise prices in his own country is absolutely beyond the pale."

"You think they'll really be outraged by all of this?"

Evan headed for the door with his notebook in hand. "Stay tuned."

67

"You idiot! What have you done?" El Presidente bellowed at the Fixer. Shaking with rage, he waved a handful of pamphlets at the man in the tailored blue suit standing in the doorway to the Presidential suite of offices.

"What do you mean? I carried out our plan. To perfection," Rossi said, shooting his cuffs and stepping into the room.

"Our plan was to raise the price of oil and gas by setting a few strategically placed explosives in a half-dozen pipelines."

"And it worked, didn't it?" the Fixer said calmly. "Look at all the money that has been rolling into your treasury. Look at all the programs you have announced that you can now pay for. And with the leftover funds, well, you can imagine what you can do with those." He meandered over to the coffee table in front of a plush couch where a tray was sitting with a pot of espresso and several cups. He poured himself some of the steaming brew and sat down on the couch. "Why are you so upset?"

"Why am I upset?" the President mimicked. "I'll tell you why I'm upset. I told you to send those men up there to set some explosives, not to kill innocent people. And especially not to contaminate their entire southern gas supply. Look at these stories. They're all over town. In every pamphlet, on every cell phone we've confiscated. They're even being broadcast on special frequencies. We can't jam them fast enough."

"I thought it was a rather clever scheme. I told you I'd take care of it. And I did," Rossi said, slowly sipping his coffee.

"Clever? You think it's clever when every student in every city in every part of this country is screaming for my head and telling everyone not to vote for the killer of innocent women and children? Do you think that's clever?"

"Much ado about nothing, I'm sure. Those students have been marching and chanting and raising a ruckus for weeks now and what has happened? Nothing. We've detained some of them in the new jail and the others go to the streets and make a lot of noise. Who cares about noise? All we should care about is election results. And who controls the ballot boxes, now I ask you?"

El Presidente paced in front of his desk. "This time you are wrong. Dead wrong. We have international observers all over the country watching the polling places. You said we should let them in because it was obvious I would win. But now. Now the opposition has all the headlines, all the people, and soon they may have all the power."

"Relax. You are getting yourself overwrought," Rossi said, crossing his legs and leaning back in a relaxed pose.

"No. I will not relax. I never condoned the kind of scheme you put together and yet I may pay the price for your idiocy." He scrutinized the man sitting so comfortably on his couch in the center of his office, and he made a decision. "Diosdado Rossi. I have listened to you for several years now. I have heard your plots, paid off your cronies. I gave you your staff, your villa, your bank account, and put up with your arrogance and backroom dealings. But now you have gone too far."

The President walked to his desk and picked up his private telephone. "Send in my security chief."

Rossi jumped up from the couch with a puzzled expression on his face. "Surely you are overreaching, my President."

"I am no longer *your* President." The door opened and the security chief walked in. El Presidente motioned to him. "Place this man under arrest!"

68

"Madam Speaker, the President of the United States," the sergeant at arms called out as he opened the door to the House Chamber at precisely 9:00 p.m. The President strode in to a standing ovation. Everyone on both sides of the aisle stood and clapped. At this point, they were honoring the office of the President, not his policies. That part would come in a few minutes as he gave his annual State of the Union address.

The President worked his way down the aisle, shaking hands with House and Senate Members along the way. He moved to the front and mounted the platform with the American flag draped behind it. He turned and handed one copy of his speech to Vice President Keller, who was there in his capacity as President of the Senate, and he handed a second copy to the Speaker of the House.

As the applause died down and the audience took their seats, the Speaker banged her gavel and announced into the microphone,

"Members of Congress, I have the high privilege and distinct honor of presenting to you the President of the United States."

Everyone in the chamber once again jumped to their feet and repeated the applause. The one-two punch always amused Samantha. But this was tradition. This was excitement. This was one of the highlights, usually, of a President's tenure, when he could take credit for his accomplishments and also lay out his agenda for the coming year. She was standing in the balcony next to Tripp. On his other side stood the First Lady, clapping and smiling along with all the others. Down below, Samantha could see the backs of the Justices of the Supreme Court, the Joint Chiefs of Staff, and members of the President's Cabinet. All except one, that is. One member always stayed away from this gathering as the symbolic head of a continuity-in-government in case somebody bombed the Capitol during one of these speeches. A few members of Congress were also designated to watch the speech at home on TV or in some other safe location.

The applause gradually died down and the President stood before the podium, glanced at the teleprompters, and began his speech. "Madam Speaker, Vice President Keller, Members of Congress, distinguished guests, and fellow citizens. I begin tonight by saying the state of our union is good." This was followed by applause. He then went on to summarize achievements and challenges his administration had faced the previous year and to outline an extensive policy agenda. After listing a number of domestic priorities, he said, "We all know the havoc that was wreaked on our citizens when foreign agents sabotaged a number of our vital natural gas pipelines. We all saw the trail of death and destruction followed by the disruption of supplies during a fierce winter storm. We all saw the increase in prices, which, thankfully have now been reduced to a more manageable level. And we are all cognizant of the need for a more comprehensive energy policy that will finally lead our nation to a sense of self-sufficiency." The entire audience once again jumped to its feet, clapping wildly.

"My administration will be working with the Congress on a number of initiatives. Many have been tried in the past, but we will devote the time, resources, and talent in a Manhattan-style project to bring these initiatives to fruition. I include in this list the pursuit of more effective clean coal technology that cuts CO_2 emissions. Coal is a plentiful resource, one that we should utilize at home as we also keep exporting it to other countries." There was a smattering of applause from just one side of the hall.

"We will cut the bureaucratic red tape that stands in the way of building additional nuclear power plants. And we will encourage the use of thorium as fuel, not only here but in many other countries planning to expand the use of nuclear power. More work needs to be done but thorium eventually could replace much of the uranium currently being utilized. And, as you all know, thorium cannot be reprocessed into nuclear weapons.

"We will encourage the construction of new refineries along with technologies for solar, wind, and hydroelectric power." At this point, Senator Cassidy Jenkins led the applause. "And we will eliminate the tariffs on imported ethanol as well as price supports for sugar so that we can take in the products we need at affordable prices.

"Energy is not just the responsibility of government and large corporations. It is the responsibility of all Americans to conserve but also to be creative, inventive, and come up with new technologies for use in their own homes and businesses. We will encourage those technologies with new tax incentives and the removal of regulations that might impede their development.

"In addition, and most important for our near-term security, we will work to allow our domestic oil and gas companies to commence drilling in a number of regions formerly off-limits to production." At this announcement, the members on one side sat on their hands but Senator Harvey Walker stood up and cheered.

"And on the subject of our own supplies, I want to take a moment to recognize two individuals who are with us tonight. Two brave young people who not only led us to the culprits who had been sent here to attack our pipelines, but who risked their lives in the process. Now, Presidents do not normally single out members of their own staff at events such as this. We all try to work hard for the benefit of all Americans. But, as you know, we often do invite American heroes so that we may thank them in public. And tonight we have one private citizen and one member of the White House staff to be honored tonight. So at this time, I would like to ask Mr. Hamilton Bainbridge Adams the Third to stand along with Miss Samantha Reid, whom I have just named as my new Director of White House Homeland Security."

He did? Samantha said to herself as she and Tripp stood up and a spotlight focused on the balcony.

"Did he have to use the entire name?" Tripp whispered as they smiled and accepted the applause of the entire chamber.

They quickly sat back down, and the First Lady reached over to shake their hands as the President continued. "Mr. Adams saved an untold number of American lives when he disarmed explosives meant to contaminate our energy supplies with radioactive gas, materials smuggled into this country across our borders, which we are moving to seal in a much more productive fashion. Those materials were sent here by dark elements in a country to our south. Miss Reid was key to their discovery. Her superb analysis led us to the arrest of the saboteurs.

"Also, I am pleased, as I'm sure you all are, to know that the good people of that country, when presented with the facts, went to the polls, exercised their rights, and voted in a new administration—one that already has reached out to us and our companies with the hand of friendship." This time members on both sides of the aisle stood, and the President smiled to accept extended applause.

Tripp turned to Samantha and whispered, "I thought it was pretty wild when you told me the FBI learned it was Diosdado Rossi who orchestrated the last attack and that El Presidente evidently had nothing to do with it. But then he gets the blame for all of it, and now he's history."

Samantha leaned over and murmured, "Yes. I guess we could call that the *final finesse.*"